Midwinter.
C. C. Burns

Claire was born and raised in London. She graduated with a BSc (Hons) in Social Sciences from the OU, and a Creative Writing MA from Royal Holloway. She now lives in Surrey with her family where she is fulfilling her lifelong dream of writing, full-time.
She makes her debut with her series:
Diary of an obstinate, headstrong female.

Copyright

DISCLAIMER: This novel's story and characters are fictitious, with the exception of those details already in the public domain. Certain long standing institutions, agencies, public offices and public figures are mentioned, but the characters involved are wholly imaginary. Any resemblance to persons living or dead is purely coincidental and not intended by the author.

CONTENT WARNING: This book contains some explicit material, suitable only for adult readers, including depictions of violence and scenes of a sexual nature.

C. C. BURNS

Independently published by the author: C. C. Burns (Claire Burns), 2022, England.
www. ccburns.co.uk
Cover artist: @vikncharlie.

Introduction

Midwinter is book 3 in this series.

The series is intended to be read in order for the best reading experience as links and references are made between other books in the series that may not otherwise, be understood.
I hope you enjoy the next instalment!
In this series...

VOL 1: *Vanilla Kisses.* **Vol 2:** *Appetence.*

Prologue.

November 1821. - Annalise.

'What's all this, luv?' Poppy asked, staring at the stacked pile of wares Annalise had brought from the market earlier, which there had been no room to accommodate and now covered the tabletop, protruded from beneath the beds, and the wiry head of a broom stuck out from behind her headboard.

'The greater share of the shopping list we made up earlier. I stopped by the market once I dropped you off and bought as much as I could find. The mattress will be delivered in a week's time, and we shall have to make do with sharing for now until I find another bed for sale. We still have the coverlets and pillows to get, but it's a start.'

'More than a start, luv,' Poppy said, lifting a parcel of tea cloths up to inspect. 'It's all so exciting. Just think, by the end of the week, we'll be sitting over our parlour table taking our dinner at our leisure. No rushing off to serve the upper lot, just ourselves.'

Annalise smiled widely. 'It is hard to believe, isn't it, and yet it is true. Poppy, have you given any thought to the live-in maid?'

'Well, I wondered if you thought Maggie was up to it? She's a hard worker and knows her way around the kitchen well enough. The rest can be shown.'

Annalise threw her arms around Poppy and nodded profusely. 'Yes, yes, certainly she is.'

'Well then, that's another matter settled. Though I can't imagine Cook'll be able to countenance another staff loss. Three all in the same month will certainly raise questions.'

'Well, it serves her so. Perhaps she will learn to have a care about how she treats our replacements hereafter.'

'True. I shan't give Maggie the news just yet, though. I'll give it 'till I've served the rest of my week out here, then I'll put it to her before I go.'

'Well, hopefully, by the time you have, I would have had enough time to get our house into better order, so it will be at least functional once you join me.'

'You got some time off your duties then?'

'You might say that,' Annalise said vaguely. She didn't want to worry Poppy by confessing she no longer had a position to concern herself with.

'She aIn't 'alf good your mistress; I have to give it to her. I never thought for a minute the likes of them would be so generous when even our own upper lot down 'ere are so mean-fisted. But I own, you've had more free time and holidays since you've been in her employ than ever I knew a servant get. You landed on your feet there, girl. No wonder you mean to stick with her for a time.'

Annalise smiled but made no answer. 'Well, I suppose I better get on with the rest of the packing. I shan't have time in the morning. Is there anything you want me to take over with me?'

'No luv, I 'ave time yet to sort through my things. You concentrate on yours. You got enough on your plate with that lot.'

SHE COULD FIND NO RESPITE in sleep that night, even after exhausting herself into the small hours with relentless packing and list checking, until her eyes could no longer follow a line of print. It was as though, if she refused to go to sleep, so morning might refuse to come and with it, both her and Eleanor's departures. She both shrank from the prospect, and willed it to be swiftly over, as she fidgeted and wrestled with the bedclothes and tossed and turned beneath them.

Tomorrow marked an end and a new beginning, and this energy of curdling dread and kindling excitement came like an ebb and flow of crashing waves against her fraught mind. Relentless and dizzying. Circular and protracted. She was simultaneously free, yet shackled by the bind of a broken heart.

By morning, she had but managed a few broken restless hours of sleep and found herself the first up, sitting over a cup of chocolate at the kitchen table and squinting over today's fresh to-do list in the waning twilight gloom. The first task of which was to get as much loaded onto the push wagons as she could, before the house rose and there was anyone about to question her on what she was doing. It was, by now, no secret that she had left Mrs Simpson's employ, but no one knew she was about to depart her mistresses. No one knew she was to move to a place of her own. And that was precisely how she meant to keep it. For now, at least. Of course, in time, it would all come to light, but she hoped that by then, she might have recovered enough of her peace of mind and re-established her new life so as to turn her head away from the fallout of it all. Right now, she knew she was too weak of heart and mind to deal in any other blows to either.

She checked the kitchen wall clock for the hour, noting it was approaching five-o-clock and deciding she had enough time yet, to assemble all her packed-up things ready to push far enough up the driveway to be out of view of the house when the hack came to collect her at seven. She had sufficient time left to get washed and dressed and say her farewell to Eleanor, should she wish to. But she remained undecided on this as she piled up her things outside the kitchen door as quietly as could be managed.

She disturbed only the hall boys from their trundle beds along the corridor as she moved from room to room. And having inadvertently done so, decided to lighten the burden and offer them the chance to earn a few pennies, by employing them to load the wagons and showing them over to the spot where she wanted everything conveyed. She picked a patch beneath the cover of a wide branched Oak which concealed the growing ensemble of luggage from prominent view, but remained close enough to the driveway to load onto the hack.

Whilst they busied themselves with heaving it all over, she got dressed and double-checked the room for anything she might have missed. All this, whilst taking the utmost care to be quiet around Poppy, who was stirring from time to time at the opening and closing of the door, or splash of water into the wash basin.

When she was ready, and all that remained of hers in the room was the folded pile of Cuddington-issued uniform and the box of finer clothes Eleanor had commissioned for her lady's maid attire, she was satisfied she had managed everything as quickly as may be, and returned to check the clock in the kitchen to find it was now a quarter-past-six. She could already hear the stirrings of activity rumbling along the corridors as the servants began to abandon their beds and ready themselves for the day ahead. Soon the basement would be a hive of morning chaos. Whilst she was relieved she need no longer answer to that call, a part of her already winced at the prospect of not being part of it at *all* anymore.

For whatever else, it had been her home for the better part of a year now. The place she had begun to find hope again. Herself again. When she had thought it impossible. She tried to remind herself that just as she had found the prospect of recovering then inconceivable, so her newly fractured heart would mend too. In time. However it felt now. There was nothing to be done but occupy the passage of time until she found herself having crossed that healing bridge without even realising it, until it was done.

So, as a parting gift to her fellow kitchen maids and a mark of finality in her own mind, she put the large kettles to boil for the morning water, removed the fire curfew and stoked the low embers back into life until the flames flickered up and began to roar. *The last time I shall ever,* she thought, as she went about these menial tasks with a marked awareness and particular care. She even began setting out the pans and cookware for the staff breakfast. Then she fetched the bacon from the larder and the basket left upon the back doorstep by one of the farm hands, full to the brim with still-warm feathery eggs. Then, whilst poking about the pantry for mushrooms and bread, a nobbly stem of ginger caught her eye and brought her almost quick to tears.

Eleanor would need her ginger tea today if she was to travel, to ease the sickness on her journey. She thought of her rattling about in the carriage alone, retching into a sack and no one beside her to rub the planes of her shoulders, hand her a handkerchief to dab her mouth with, tell her it should soon pass, and ask if she felt better now. She stared at the ginger, her eyes stinging with the threat of tears. Before she had further time to contemplate, she snatched it up from the vegetable basket and found herself standing over a morning tea tray in the kitchen with the spicy tang of ginger vapours rising beneath her nose.

'Morning luv, well, what's all this?' Poppy asked, coming into the kitchen and noticing the start she had made to the breakfast efforts; the kettle spouts puffing with steam, a loaf sliced upon the breadboard.

'Well, I thought, since it was my last morning here...'

Poppy smiled. 'Thanks, luv. Shall be much easier when we only want breakfast for three, eh? You off to tend your mistress?'

Annalise peered down at the tray she had assembled and nodded. 'Yes, I had better take this up to her.'

'See you at breakfast then.'

Annalise picked up the tray. 'I shan't have time for breakfast. My cab is due upon the hour. I have so much to do today.'

'Aye, which is why you need your strength up, luv. A girls gotta eat if she's to run a hundred and one chores in a day.'

'I shall, later, when I have conveyed everything over to Carshalton. I'd better get on.'

As she climbed the stairs up to Eleanor's room, she thought to change her mind with every step. Had it not been for the passing housemaids she encountered en route who assumed her going ordinarily about her business as they did, she might have taken the tray back downstairs and abandoned the notion. It would be too painful, such a farewell. Too raw were her feelings to scratch them further into shards. And yet where would be the closure if she could not face this final farewell? Where would come her peace of mind when she was eaten up with guilt from denying them both this moment of conclusion? Surely, they owed each other that much?

These arguments kept her treading the boards until she found herself face to face with Eleanor's chamber door, and it was too late to turn back. She tapped lightly at it and, when no answer came, turned the handle and let herself in. She noted the shape of her beneath the coverlet, face turned away and hidden from her view as she trod soundlessly to the table to put the tray down. Then she drew a steadying breath, turned around, walked over to the bedside and peered down at her. 'Eleanor?' she said gently, seeing she was quite sound asleep, her arm draped over the edge of the bed, her eyes, though closed, swollen pink at the lids.

No answer came, and then she considered that perhaps it was better this way. If she was still upset and shedding tears, it would surely prompt more of the same—and her own, too, no doubt. Maybe it would spare them both a fresh ordeal if she was to go away again quietly. Yet as she crouched to better see her face, she could not help but feel drawn to want to rouse her, look into her eyes just one more time, feel a parting embrace to hold onto in her memory.

Despite it all, she had missed her sorely these days past. As the anger dulled a fraction with the hours turning, her yearnings grew stauncher and gave way to such deep longing it frightened her to face the want in her own being. Understanding, as she lifted a curl from Eleanor's cheek, the power this woman still had to render her resolve so easily broken; to draw her back into her arms again when she so much wanted to be there, despite herself. She lowered her lips to her face and placed a soft kiss upon her cheek, uttering a silent farewell as she rose again and padded lightly back out of the room; the salty taste of her upon her lips as she closed the door behind her. Tears clouding her vision as she stepped away.

Even as she journeyed over to Carshalton, she could not shake the image from her mind, however much she tried to divert her thoughts away from it. She felt haunted at every turn. Bereft. Like she was being offered a glimpse of what was to come, now they had finally parted. She would still be with her in thought, heart and memory, but it was the yearning deep within, beneath skin and bone she could not make peace with. The crying out of her flesh to be reunited with her love, as if some vital organ was missing and whilst she could not account for its function or purpose, she knew that without it, she could not function nor find a moment's peace.

Even as she unloaded the cab of her things and carried them into the kitchen, this premonition did not diminish, and before she was finished unpacking the first basket of her market wares, she knew she couldn't do it. Let her leave. Sever their connection with such finality. She gave way to a burst of tears, abandoned her tasks, locked up the shop, and ran as fast as she could over to the *Greyhound* to find a cab. Hoping there was still time to catch her and praying for the fortitude to accept whatever outcome lay in store, as she darted into the basement and found Will on his way back down the stairs.

'Will, has my mistress left yet?'

'No. We have just had orders to load the coach up. You want to see the amount of stuff we've got to cram into it. We need twice as many pairs of hands if she wants to set off by half-past.'

'Half-past, you say?'

'Yes, why? What's the matter?'

'Nothing. Only, there has been a change of plan. I am to go with her, after all.'

He frowned and said more seriously. 'I see. How long will you be gone for?'

'I'm not sure. But for a time.'

He nodded. 'Well, I hope you've packed a warm cloak and stockings; them Scottish winters are not like ours.'

Scotland, so that is where they were to go. She shrunk at the prospect of such a journey, such a distance. But it was not enough to deter her from this course. She went directly to the kitchen and pulled Poppy away from her duties.

'What you doing back? You forgot somein?' she said, following her into the bedroom with a puzzle about her expression.

Annalise nodded. 'Poppy, there has been a very sudden change of plan. My lady is to travel to Scotland today, and I am to go with her.'

'What?'

'Will you manage without me?'

'How long will you be gone for?'

'Months, I believe, although I'm not altogether certain.'

'But what about the shop?'

'Well, I was hoping you and Maggie could get started without me. Perhaps you could bring on some additional staff. If my room is to be vacant now, you shall have more space for their board. I can send back my wages so you can tend to theirs.'

'I see.'

'Poppy, I'm sorry. I know I spring this on you, and this was not how it was supposed to be. Not what we planned. But I have every confidence that you can get things fired off without me, or I should never ask it. But, it's important that I go...'

'Oh luv, I know it is. It's your duty... and without my wages to count on, we shall certainly need some to keep us afloat whilst we're starting out. I just hoped we'd be doing it together, that's all. But it can't be helped. I shall do me best, luv, to hold the fort 'till you get home again.'

Annalise gathered her up in a squeeze. 'Thank you, Poppy; you muster up as much help as you need to, alright? Do not struggle; I shall have enough to pay a fair wage. I shall send it to you in the post and a letter which you may take to Miss Lockheart to read for you. I'm certain she will be happy to pen a reply, let me know how you are getting on.'

She left Poppy with a quickly scribbled note for Miss Lockheart, prevailing upon her the favour of enlisting the Old Mill Street volunteers on Saturday morning to collect the outstanding furniture, and counting out the money to pay for it. Then she tucked the remainder of her purse into Poppy's hand, squeezed her into another hug, and wished her luck and a reluctant farewell. For she privately knew they must away for at least seven months, and if they were to be as far abroad as Scotland, the opportunity to nip back for even a brief holiday would be implausible. It would be the longest they had ever been separated from one another. Ever. And yet, even as the prospect pained her, she knew it the less of evils to the pain that was already starting to diminish at this change of course. And so she went swiftly about her business, having her box of Abigail's clothes loaded onto the coach, pressing her friends into hugs and settling into the carriage, just ahead of Eleanor's appearance on the vestibule.

DESPITE ALL HER ANXIETIES and the panic of it all, she felt certain, as she sat beside her in the coach, barely relenting in their embrace for the first leg of the journey, that she had made the right decision. However much they each had to resolve and learn from their recent troubles, it was better to make a try at salvaging things than walk away without ever knowing if they could. Realising that they had only to journey to Cambridgeshire, too, was welcome news.

She still did not know how things would turn out, even as she fell into step with the leisurely pace of life in their new Cambridgeshire retreat. Living, she supposed, much as man and wife might live out their days in private romance and comfort. But with the exception of their intimate lovemaking, which she had shied away from, as she found herself haunted by the images cast upon her mind of all that had passed between Eleanor and Mr Richards. Until they faded from her memory, she knew she could not move beyond her kisses. But for now, it was enough to be back on terms again, to be in each other's presence again, to cull the deep pain of separation. To know that however uncertain the future remained, she would not live out her days, never knowing what might have been. And Cambridge was not so far as Scotland. Should it all turn out ill, she had not so far to journey to number sixteen at Carshalton from here; a day would suffice.

AS THEIR FIRST WEEK in Cambridgeshire passed and the home-sickness set in, the thought that Poppy and Maggie would have moved into the house by now, warmed her. Imaginings of them settling in and making a home of it, bringing life into the walls. The inky and paint-pungent air fading, and the smell of Poppy's cooking filling it instead. Warm and fragrant. A good fire stoked in the back parlour for them to sit about in the evenings, and: peace. No demands from Cook or the bell ringing. None of Fanny's amateur dramatics to pay mind to. No sixteen-hour days or early winter risings. They may be at ease. Possibly for the first time in their lives, since infancy. This heartened her as she snuggled against Eleanor's bosom, toes pressed out towards the fire's warmth. They, too, were in comfort. They, too, would know peace.

This was the sentiment conveyed by Poppy's letter she received the next morning, having sent word of her safe arrival almost a week since.

Dear Annalise,

Thank you for your letter and the draft to settle Mr Benson's bill, which I passed on to him the very same day. – He confirms he is happy to bill you separately for the extension and groundworks at monthly intervals as the work progresses. I will forward them to you accordingly.

Presently, the yard looks like a trench has been dug out of it. But he assures me this is how the foundations are to be laid, so I ask no further questions now and leave him to it, however loud the din and thick the dust out there.

Maggie is in the habit of going out to the pump for the days' water before Mr Benson arrives to avoid walking through all the mess, and that has worked out all the better now we have a routine. She says hello, by the way, and sends a million thanks for this chance to be a part of Poppy's Pies & Puddings. She is getting along famously, just as we thought she would. We had the whole kitchen scrubbed, polished, and reorganised, within our first two days here, so I'd say we are making a fine enough team so far, even if it is just the two of us. It was a good job you thought to buy a bathing tub! We were in much need of it by the time we were done with all the cleaning. I've never seen such filth as we scrubbed from that kitchen! There's not much in kind words I have to offer on Mrs Simpsons' behalf, especially with how wicked cruel she was to Maggie when she gave her the news of her going, but I will credit her with knowing how to keep a clean and orderly kitchen, now I've seen the likes of this one.

Anyway, now that's behind us, we've set to our real work. We've got ourselves a flour supplier and made an agreement with a dairy farmer in Wallington, to supply us with regular butter and eggs at a handsome discount, if we can keep to the quota. We've been busy testing out my pie receipts on the Bensons and ourselves, and so far, the results have been very happy! I wish I could send you one through the post like this letter, to have your opinion on it. Anyway, hopefully, it shan't be too long before you're sitting at the table with us supping. – Do you know yet, when you will return?

Anyhow, I have to leave Miss Lockheart in peace now as she's to go and teach her lessons, and I'm to stop by at the drapers' and pick up the new bed coverlets and pillows on my way home.

Write to me soon and tell me how you do. I miss you love.

Poppy x.

P.S. The rest of the furniture is set out finely now and looks so handsome in our freshly painted rooms. I can't wait for you to see it for yourself. When it was collected on Saturday, we had trouble getting some of it to fit up the staircase, so we had to leave it in the parlour until Mr Benson could dismantle it enough to convey it to the bedrooms for us. All is now well, and Maggie and I had the best sleep in our new bed with the plump mattress and feather coverlets. We wonder how we shall ever force ourselves out of it on these frosty mornings, now we are at liberty. But the excitement and tasks of each new day compel us from it, and we settle on early bedtimes instead, now the nights are drawing in so dreadful dark and gloomy. How is the weather where you are? Are the winters full of frost and snow up that way? We have been fortunate so far and have avoided snow. Mr Benson has been rained off these past days and will resume when the drier weather returns. It currently looks like we have some oddly shaped ponds in the yard.

P.P.S Dear Annalise, Miss Lockheart here. I hope all is well with you. –Just a quick note in response to your letter to say you are very welcome, and it has been my pleasure to help you in these endeavours. How lovely the place comes about now, looking more and more like a cosy home each time, I visit. How hard and diligently these ladies have worked to bring it about. I know you would be very proud of them. I have even been converted to an appreciation of pies since Poppy was kind enough to bring one with her today to collect her letter. I passed on your regards to the Bartlett's (who say they miss you already), and your thanks to Saturday's volunteers. Mr Harrison is well and tells me he has already sent his reply to your last letter, which may have already reached you by now. Best regards to you and Mrs Craythorne, Faithfully, Miss Lockheart.

She could tell from the eloquence of the writing that Miss Lockheart had paraphrased Poppy's directions, and though she was grateful for her having taken the trouble to write at such length, she missed the tone of Poppy's voice in the words, even if the sentiment remained unaltered. How she wished Poppy could pen her own reply so that she may recognise her character in the pages. It would be such an age until she heard her voice again, but she could not tell her so. Not yet. Once they had both grown used to their separation, it might prove easier to mention that it would likely not be until after June, if Eleanor's confinement was to run to course.

Summer seemed a world away from the crisp winter mornings and frost-glazed windowpanes that greeted them now upon rising. The weather was colder and more drab in Cambridgeshire, she was certain, although better than she imagined Scotland would have proved, and still without the threat of a snowstorm at least. But the chilly days did not keep them in, and they still took to the park to exercise each day. Eleanor having now ceased her riding routine for fear of causing some injury to the child, but fearing idleness in equal measure. On finer days, they ventured out along the river Cam if they had dressed warm enough for the adventure. But it was even quieter and slower here than in Cuddington. Little more than endless plains of countryside and farmland at every turn. They were but less than ten mile from the city of Cambridge; Eleanor had told her, and given her a promise that they would venture there for a trip before Christmastide so they might find gifts for each other and the staff. But it was cosy, if obsolete, and for the first few days of their arrival, they had barely moved from each other's embrace. The necessary healing of the rift between them, seemed to call for such close connection, as if the tether between their hearts needed them to hold close enough whilst it recovered its strength and re-knitted itself anew.

Stapleford Hall.

December 1821.- Eleanor.

Our first days at Stapleford had quickly fallen into an easy pattern of almost nothingness. A simplistic routine that suited us both well after the rattling journey on the stagecoach and the fractious, sorrowful days that preceded our leaving. But much had been restored since then, in the luxury of this newly afforded privacy we now enjoyed. The house practically empty above stairs unless we summoned someone. The place so out of the way that there was not so much as a passerby to take note of. Breakfast delivered on trays we took on our laps, sat up in bed, between tangling and tumbling in the sheets 'till midday. Gentle walks in the afternoon before the progressively earlier winter darkness set in. Evenings with our feet and palms stretched towards the heat of the fire as we read and conversed in increasingly deeper confidence. And nights of intimacy burning as fiercely as the flames in the grate. It had been weeks in the building up to such passions. Annalise slow to come about to my advances after all the bad business with Richards. But it had not lasted out the month with so much newfound understanding growing ever brighter between us.

It had not all been roses in bloom. There had been difficult conversations, frozen silences and sulks, raw truths exposed and fresh injuries arising from them. But the more we dared to venture into these shadowy parts of ourselves and each other, the deeper we grew to know one another, the stronger the connection bound us.

The keeping of so many secrets rendered us both keen to excavate our pasts and bring our histories into each other's knowing after the uncomfortable revelations of the past weeks, and how dangerously close it had come to devastating us. She had had the whole now on everything about Richards, Sheldon, and a sprinkling of details about Mariella and Giles, though not all the finer aspects. It seemed too much to revisit now, too much to ask of her forbearance to endure such a twisted tale that sounded too fantastical for even me to believe in at times. But I would give up the rest, eventually, until there was nothing else left to disturb our peace and threaten our happiness again.

She had confided in me, too: the mystery of her father and her unexpected inheritance. The shop in Carshalton she recently took ownership of, and I was astonished and proud in equal measure to understand her to be a woman of property and independent means. However humble the dwelling might be, what a triumph for a kitchen maid, for a woman...

Even I could claim nothing of my own, no independence to ensure my future, and here she was, her prospects secure without the bind of being leg shackled or widowed to account for it. It gave me faith to see the future I dreamt of with her was now possible. Between the box of treasures and trinkets I had procured, and her having a home of her own we could settle to if need be, it all seemed attainable now. She, of course, would hear none of it. A baron's daughter living out her days in a pie shop! Did she not understand I would have settled to Old Mill Street so long as I could curl up close to her each night, awake to the sight of her perfect sleeping face each morning? Granted, it would not be ideal sharing a home with others who might find us out, or being so close to Beddington. For those reasons, I meant to try to raise enough for our own little hideaway, but to know that one way or another, we could plot our future together, warmed me in the midst of so much insecurity. There was much yet to settle, to endure. I still had no notion of what I was to do about my impending arrival. I supposed I was quietly resigned to my mama's suggestion of placing the child with Harri and tried to think no more of it. There had been enough to resolve of late that I needed a reprieve from such muddling thoughts, and for now, I still had a six-month to work it all out.

MIDWINTER.

FEELING A REASSURING sense of anonymity now we had settled into Stapleford, and growing familiar and trusting in the staff, we decided to venture beyond our retreat today and take a journey into the town to familiarise ourselves with it. Mrs Duckworth, the Housekeeper, was going anyway to place orders with the merchants for the Christmastide feast. So we took advantage of joining her on the journey, squeezing up on the trap, dressed plain and demure so as to not warrant any particular interest or curiosity. If we looked and travelled like simple folk, I was hopeful we would fade easily into the place and maintain such anonymity. I borrowed one of Annalise's old plain dresses, and she adopted a similar style so that there would be no distinction in our rank to mark me out.

Beyond the knowing of Mrs Duckworth and the Butler here, to everyone else, we were simply the Ashlyn's' tenants, taking up a lease for the year. I had assumed the pseudonym of Miss Andrewes, a gentleman's daughter of no great consequence and sent to the country here for my health. It was not entirely untrue, my enduring sickness indeed lent credence to the story, and since my condition was still not showing any sign of declaring itself, no one seemed in the least suspicious...yet. Of course, there would be a time when it would give me away, a time when we would not be able to venture out like today, and so I knew we must make the most of the opportunity to do so, before I was forced to hide away behind closed doors.

The village of Royston was quaint and pleasant, with all the offerings one could expect of an old rural market town. The bustle of the streets were both daunting and reassuring after almost a month of isolation from other people. Still, I felt a little comfort in our humble disguise, quickly noticing the disinterest of passersby. Had I realised the anonymity such plain and simple dress afforded, I might have tried it back in Cuddington or London when my troubles first began to show themselves. It rendered us perfectly invisible amongst the townspeople, and I quickly ceased looking for familiar faces in everyone I passed and relaxed into the distraction of it all. Market stalls adorned with Christmastide candelabra's, velvet bows and potted evergreens. Above us was heavily festooned with reefs of glossy green ivy, holly and mistletoe. The gardener at Stapleford had begun to set aside cuttings of the very same from the estate, but Mrs Duckworth was adamant we were not bringing it into the house for decorating until Christmas eve. Given my luck this year and the recent better turn of my fortune, I thought it best not to tempt fate and invite any omens of bad luck upon us.

I was happy at last. We were happy together, I thought, as we found ourselves inadvertently standing beneath a kissing bough, berries hanging translucent-white above our heads. I resisted the urge to lean forward and act upon it. Instead, we exchanged a knowing glance, stepped out from beneath it, and headed towards the post office. Even the sound of so many feet and wheels against the cobbles seemed odd, having only trod the muddy tracks of countryside and river path, and heard only the occasional creak of Mrs Duckworth's trap.

'Well, shall we see about taking a little refreshment?' I asked, when Annalise had finished despatching her parcels with the postmaster. We still had a half hour before we were due to muster at the trap and meet Mrs Duckworth for our journey home.

Annalise tucked her purse away, stepped away from the post office counter and frowned thoughtfully.

'There was a pretty looking place to take tea we passed on our way through, near the green opposite the inn Mrs Duckworth set us down by,' I offered.

'I daresay it was, but we shan't be admitted to it looking like this,' she said wisely. It was only then that I realised the downside to our disguise, remembering the tearoom full of people dressed in fine winter coats and hats, sitting over tables of equally fine china. I looked down at my scuffed boots and thinning cambric skirt hems and shrugged. 'Well, what should you like to do for our last half hour then?'

'Well,' she said, passing her arm through the crook of my elbow and urging me back out onto the street, 'there are other places we are dressed perfectly well for,' she grinned. 'If you have the stomach for it?'

'Well, I am game for the finding out,' I replied, meeting the challenge in her eyes, which sparkled a flicker at my acceptance, and she led me off in the direction of a large marquee with a banner proclaiming: *Royston Frost Fair* draped across the entrance.

MIDWINTER.

Although there was neither frost nor a frozen waterway to skate upon, the spirit of the place seemed well set for festive merriment. And it seemed we were suitably rigged out for such a casual gathering as we entered a den of loud music and chatter where the patrons were sitting about on barrels and hay bales, drinking from tankards or dancing merrily about a folk band that I could hear but not see, amongst the jostling floor. Around the periphery, there were skittle alleys and other gaming trifles, as well as stalls set up offering ale and festive foods for prices I did not think viable, let alone likely to render anything edible. But I was pleasantly surprised when Annalise procured us both a cup of mulled cider and a mince pie from one of them, and we eventually found an empty bale to occupy whilst we ate.

'Well?' Annalise said, watching me as I inspected the offerings for a sign of some trapping.

'Rather good, actually,' I replied, brushing crumbs from my heavy woollen cloak, which was suitably warm, but scratched harshly against the bare skin at the nape of my neck and décolleté.

'They're not bad. Although I'm certain Poppy's shall be far better,' she said thoughtfully, staring into the crowd of dancers.

I knew she missed her friends sorely and was desperate to see how they were getting along at Carshalton. It pained me to be the cause of such separation. Yet I knew neither of us could bear the torture of our own parting any better. We had tried and failed in that quarter, and both seemed more cautious for the trials of it. I had, however, offered to arrange for her to be conveyed back to Surrey for a week over Christmastide should she like to pay them a visit, but was relieved when she declined, that the prospect was as daunting to her as it was to me. She said she wanted to spend Christmas with me, but would go in the new year; a week would suffice. I wondered how long it could last: her preference of my company over that of all other company, and at such length and in such a remote and idle situation as ours. If I found it dull here, I knew that she, used to being so busy and industrious, must find it thrice as challenging. But she kept herself occupied in the gaps between our lazing, petting and lovemaking. Sewing Christmas gifts of embroidered handkerchiefs for her friends, the last of which, she had just sent off at the post office today. I wondered what might take the place of that past time now. Of course, we had our reading and might still manage a little walk in the best part of the daylight hours whilst the snow held off, but it was difficult to imagine anything much beyond that. I watched her as she followed the dancers about the straw-laden floor with the shine of their merriment dancing in her eyes. Then I remembered; she liked music and was fit to play the pianoforte now her hand had regained its full vigour, and yet I had not seen one at Stapleford, I was sure. I made a mental note to enquire with Mrs Duckworth on our return.

Annalise drained her cup, stood up and held her arm out to me.

I swallowed my last mouthful down and rose. 'Are you ready to go?'

'We've only just got here,' she frowned. 'Do you find it terribly shabby?' she asked.

'No. I find it very merry, in fact.' It was true. I did not know if it was owing to the festive season or lively music, which was unfamiliar to me but no less pleasant for it, but there was a relaxed yet cheerful spirit amongst the people, who seemed to be making the most of it. It reminded me of a scene from a village fair or servants' ball, but free of all heirs and formalities since it seemed only the commonfolk were frequenting it, and there were no masters present to curtail all the fun.

'Good, then you will not object to dancing with me then,' Annalise said, straightening up her shawl and tying the ends together before pulling me towards the hubbub.

We linked arms and pranced about in poorly coordinated steps for a moment before picking up the rhythm. – This was to be our only guide, I realised as I looked to the other dancers to glean the steps, only to find that there appeared to be no particular sequence, and each dancer made up their own to suit them. And so we did the same, and as I found myself inadvertently resorting to dance steps I knew from country sets, I noticed that Annalise had an ear for the rhythm and seemed to flow beautifully with it at every turn and stride. A levity and cadence in her limbs which was pleasant to watch. I soon realised, as I brushed back to back with other prancers and dancers, that I was spending more time privately amused by the sight of her than concentrating on my own. It was at that moment, wishing I could somehow capture the image of her carefree laughing face, chin turned up skyward, that an idea struck me. I had been struggling for a better gift ever since St. Nicholas' day, having given her a Palais Royal workbox for her present. It was a lovely piece of craftsmanship, and she had been happy with it, reorganising her sewing tools into neat order and making good use of it since. But it was merely a practical gift. I wanted something more personal, of sentimental value, and I was surprised I had not thought of it before. I would book a sitting with an artist to have our miniatures taken, just an eye miniature perhaps, thinking that less likely to disclose our sex. We were forbidden many of the rites of passage of ordinary lovers, but this one, we could secretly partake in.

And so on our return to Stapleford, having ascertained that there was no pianoforte, I wrote off, first, to a piano shop in Cambridge to arrange the hire of one on Mrs Duckworth's direction of the place, and also had her make enquiries after a local portrait artist. The latter was also to be found in the City of Cambridge, and so I supposed I could no longer put off our visiting the place. I had succeeded, at length, for fear that since half the sons of the ton could be found at the university here, my chances of bumping into someone who might recognise me was all the more risky. But it was four days until Christmas, and I concluded that such sons would have likely returned home for the yuletide season now and hoped to pass without encountering anyone. Still, we took the precaution of plain demure dress as our disguise and hired a cab to make the journey. And "Miss Andrewes" and her companion "Miss Brown" went about the City like any other insignificant tourist, perfectly unhindered, seeking out the sights by strangers' maps.

It proved worth the risk just to see Annalise's eyes light up at the splendour of all the old buildings. We took tours of the chapels that were open to the public for advent prayers and skirted around the periphery of the grand stone buildings of the colleges in all their vastness and magnificence. It was a beautiful city, a hybrid of town and country overlapping. At one turn, we were met with rugged stone walls and ornate gothic steeples rising out from beyond them. At another, beautifully kept lush pleasure grounds and views to the river. We spent a while watching the boats passing along it, still benefiting from a lack of frost and making the most of it before it froze over. It certainly seemed as though it was cold enough today as the tip of our noses coloured red and our breath misted like smoke from chimneys as we conversed. But we kept on the move, which spared us the worst of the chill, and by the time the hour of twelve-o-clock chimed on the clock of St. Mary's, we had spent a happy couple of hours meandering the streets and arrived promptly at Mr Darracott's studio, which was situated above a row of shops on Bird Bolt Lane.

'Miss Andrewes, I trust?' he said when his manservant took us up a narrow staircase and deposited us into a small but handsome anteroom, furnished with a long sofa and well-stoked fire.

'Yes, Mr Darracott, pleased to meet you, and this is my companion, Miss Brown.'

'How do you do?' he said, looking us over with what I made out to be a curious air of distrust. I supposed we did not appear to be the type of persons who had purses for the commissioning of portraits. Whilst it had served us well in maintaining our public anonymity, I realised that, in this circumstance, it had rendered us suspicious to him. He seemed curious to me too, though. Not at all what I expected an artist of his tender years to look like. Something more reminiscent of a libertine had captured my imagination, yet he seemed more fitting to a young rector or the like, neat and prim beyond his years.

'I hope your journey here went well?'

'Very well, sir, I thank you,' replied Annalise, and he waved an arm to offer us a seat on the sofa, taking up a chair of his own once we had settled to it.

'So, I understand you mean to have eye miniatures painted?'

'Yes, sir, we would have one each to send as Christmas gifts to our betrothed. – They are serving abroad in the military, you see, so we thought it would make a fine present until their return,' I offered in my most convincing style.

He nodded. 'And where are they posted to?'

'Malta,' I said, thinking quickly back to Sheldon and searching my memory for the regiment's name should he question us further.

'Well, it shan't take long, but I think you have left it a little late to send them away as Christmas gifts,' he said a little more wisely than I liked.

'Indeed. It shall, of course, have to be belated now. Anyway, do you think both can be completed today?'

'I should think so if it is only the eye miniature, although if you are engaged, would it not be more appropriate to have a full miniature taken?'

'Well, we had considered it, but our stay here is brief, and we thought expedience more pressing.'

'Very well,' he nodded to his manservant, who took a roll of stiff black velvet from a locked cabinet and rolled it out before us upon the table, revealing a selection of blank tablets in various shapes and sizes.

'Watercolour on ivory is usual. I shall leave the size and style to your judgement, though the prices increase with the more elaborate choices. Each shall be enclosed in a simple glass-fronted locket, but we have a connection with a jeweller along Petty Cury who can arrange suitable adornment of the tablets to your choosing. Pearls or precious stones set about them, or inserted into a brooch, a ring, a pendant or the like—'

Even I was not bold enough to consider we might get away with wearing them upon our person with such flamboyance. They would be for our private amusement and cherishing, not for decorating ourselves and inviting unwanted questions. 'Thank you, sir, that does indeed sound pretty, although, as I said, our time here is brief, and we should like to take them away with us today and make the final post before Christmas.'

'Indeed. I shall leave you with Barnabas, who can advise you of the pricing, whilst I set up. Now, who shall sit first?'

'I shall,' I said, having had enough practice sitting for full-size portraits that I hoped it might put Annalise at greater ease to watch me go first.

He stooped to examine my eyes and said: 'Very well. The right eye, I think. Now, will you take some refreshment while choosing your tablets?'

'Tea would be very welcome, sir, I thank you,' I answered, wondering vaguely what was superior about my right eye over my left, having never noticed any particular difference.

He rang the bell. 'Mrs Wallace, my Housekeeper, will wait upon you. I shall prepare my palette and leave you with Barnabas to settle the matter of payment.'

'Yes, of course.' I said, pulling my reticule into my lap, which was thick with coins and seemed to satisfy him of our ability to pay. Although I suspected he must already be satisfied of as much, for there were things that even costume could not disguise, and I knew he could tell from my manner and speech that I was not what I purported to be, despite my best attempts to gull him.

After a passable cup of tea, enjoyed more for its scalding heat than flavour, and a rather humble offering of fancies, we were taken through to the studio where we each sat in turn for over an hour each, in relative silence. Mr Darracott working frantic against the constraint of waning winter daylight at the windows. Our bottoms growing heavy and near-fossilised at the prolonged stillness of posture as we posed or sat watching the other. These pursuits were always so dreadful tiresome, and difficult to suffer. Still, for once, I knew it worth the end result as I watched Mr Darracott's clever hands capture such a perfect and lifelike likeness of Annalise's beautiful, golden-flecked hazel eye. I should so desire to possess such talents as this, so deft and effortless seemed his working. Quick, accurate, and yet so very detailed as he added more and more layers of colour to the ivory, which seemed to coax the image of her eye into increasing life. We had both picked tablets of moderate size with a slightly domed rise. Which I noted now, helped the image rise at just the correct peak to mimic the eye; the brow set upon the flatter plane and a wisp of blonde curls we had set with the irons this morning, just framing the left edge of the tablet. The subtlest hint of a blush at her cheekbone, owing to the heat of the fire, which was kept burning lively throughout. Any flame in my own cheeks, I attributed to the inflammatory thoughts I could not prevent from rising in my mind as I imagined, what I should like to do, if I had such a talented hand. As he dipped his brush and trailed the almond-Esque curve of her eyelid, I imagined the brush poised in my own hand, capturing the curve of Annalise's bare breast, the peak of her nipple as she lay out-sprawled upon a chaise before me. I was certain we could pass the winter season quite perfectly here with such preoccupation as capturing a catalogue of portraits of each other that were unfit to be hung on any wall.

Instead, we must try to make do with a little music and reading. Which seemed all the staler a prospect having entertained better imaginings for such a time. Until finally, Mr Darracott declared the pieces finished and bid us to take another cup whilst the latter tablet benefitted from a little more drying time before he could encapsulate them into their glass lockets. The room seemed to me so hot that it must have dried instantly, and I asked Mr Darracott if we could prevail upon him to open the window and permit us a little air, and he showed us back into the anteroom and obliged us.

Having already settled the bill with his manservant, we were left to the care of the Housekeeper, who furnished our request for a tumbler of barley water as we waited for the miniatures to dry out. 'Well, what did you think of it?' I asked Annalise when we were left alone again.

'Quite marvellous how well he captured us in such small images, and so quickly, too,' she said between sips from her glass. 'But I am grateful he was timely, for I could not have sat another moment in that chair and in such stuffy heat. It reminded me of working back in the kitchens.'

'Yes, it was certainly unpleasant, but the duration at least was manageable. I sat for the better part of a week for my last portrait, and that proved quite the trial indeed.'

'I own, I don't know how you managed it.'

'Nor I, you managing to work in a kitchen in such stifling heat.'

'Me neither; now I am free of it. Although, I thought it might be nice to offer my help to the kitchen for the Christmas feast since there are so few staff here. If you have no objection, I will speak to Mrs Duckworth on our journey back?'

'I have no objection. They seem to me like very good people, and I should like to ease their burden so they might make merry of the day. Perhaps there will be something I can help with. I mean, I know nothing of kitchen duties, but I do know how the table is to be set, and I could help with the decorations too.'

Annalise beamed back at me. There was an air of pride in her eyes, like I had pleasantly surprised her with my response, and it warmed me. 'Perfect, if we all muck in a little, then we might all make merry. —What was that?' she said, sitting upright at the notice of a terrible din that came up through the window and captured our attention. We both stood, put down our glasses simultaneously, and rushed to the window to discover the cause.

'Whatever is going on?' Annalise exclaimed at the sight of two fellows dragging a screeching female along the street by each of her elbows as she struggled and screamed at them to release her.

'Unhand her at once, you villains!' I shouted down from the window in a tone quite unlike myself. It was a harrowing scene. She was small. Young from what I could make out. Our view was unobstructed, them being directly below us, but they had her in such a grip it was difficult to make her face out beyond a glimpse. 'Unhand her, I say!' I bellowed again, and a gentleman, who appeared to be dressed in a don's robing, stood only slightly apart from them, looked up in our direction. I was utterly astounded by his indifference. 'You sir, I say you, sir, stop these villains at once, upon your honour! Send for the Constable!'

I had not noticed Mrs Wallace rush back into the room at all the noise. 'Ma'am,' she said, sliding in beside us, beckoning us away from the window, 'Please come away and stop bellowing.'

I ignored the petition, thinking her insensible of the scene outside the window. Instead, I reached for my half-finished cup and threw the contents out of the window in the direction of the don, missing only very slightly as the spray of water barely hit the heel of his boots.

'Milady, please, be civilised!' said Mrs Wallace, leaning over us to close the window and preventing us from hearing the man's retort.

'Be civilised? Those men are attacking that young girl in broad daylight, and no one is intervening! I bid you summons the Constable at once, Mrs Wallace; that girl is in danger.'

'Perhaps we should go down there and tell them we have sent for the Constable and will bear witness to the scene,' Annalise added, still watching through the closed window.

'Fat lot of good that'll do,' Mrs Wallace said, 'they 'ave more say than the Constables, round here.'

I was about to ask her to explain when Mr Darracott burst in looking flustered. 'What is going on in here?' he demanded. 'Bellowing from my windows!'

'Sir, you are a man of reason,' I said, turning to him and pulling him on towards the door out to the staircase. 'Do your duty, sir, and intervene, will you. There are rogues on the street below trying to spirit off a young girl against her will.'

He shook off my hand. 'Control yourself, madam!' he said to me in irritated accents and stepped back into the room.

Annalise and I shared a puzzled glance at this apathetic attitude.

'They are not rogues,' he said, 'it is the Proctor you attempted to throw something at, and they are the Proctor's men executing their duties. That is no innocent, but a woman of lewd employ being duly taken to the *Spinning House*.'

'The what?' We chorused.

'To the Bridewell, just about the corner here.'

'It did not seem like the work of officials, sir. I think you quite mistaken...'

'You are not from about these parts, Miss Andrewes. I assure you this is nothing above the ordinary here. We are under the corporation's jurisdiction in Cambridge, and the University Proctors have a duty to keep these harlots from beguiling the students in their care.'

I did not know whether to laugh or cry at the absurdity of his attitude and speech. 'Beguiling?' it came out more in the tone of an incredulous laugh. 'Sir, she looks not a day above fourteen. You cannot be serious in suggesting her capable of "beguiling" educated gentlemen above her own years, can you?'

'Quite serious, Miss Andrewes. It is an epidemic problem in these parts. Perhaps you are more fortunate where you live?'

I did not like the insinuation in his eyes which confirmed he knew me to be beyond the class I posed as and no doubt suspected me of some scheme. 'Well, I hardly know what to say of such a crackbrained mode of thought in a city I thought to be famous for its advanced intellect, not its narrow-mindedness. She is but little above a child, sir!'

'And I, ma'am, thought you more ladylike a creature than to bellow from my windows and insult the Proctor!'

'Well, it seems us both mistaken!'

'Miss Andrewes, I shall fetch your paintings and bid you on your way, I think.'

'I beg you do. I could not bear to stay here another moment.'

31

'Mrs Wallace?' he nodded, and she opened up a cupboard where she had hung our cloaks, and he disappeared back into his studio.

'Imbecile!' I said of him to Annalise whilst Mrs Wallace assisted us with our cloaks. 'I should never have come here had I known what sort of man he was,' I assured her.

'You will find him of a like mind as most the University folk of the city, ma'am,' Mrs Wallace cut in. 'He is not a bad man or master—'

'So you too, advocate the rough snatching up of girls of an age barely out of the school room?'

'Of course I don't, miss. But it's the way o' things around here. Lamentable as may be.'

'Where is this Bridewell, Mrs Wallace? I mean to find it out and give the magistrates a piece of my mind when I do.'

'Ain't no magistrates involved, miss. It's all the university masters that have authority over this place.'

'No magistrates? Whatever can you mean, Mrs Wallace? Have you no constables or magistrates in these parts?'

'Aye, we do. But they 'ave no say on university matters, ma'am. They set the laws of their own making on this side of the city.'

I could hardly believe her serious, and yet I could see from her plain and frank expression that she was convinced it was the way of things. I had learnt a lot from my time at Old Mill Street and since growing in fonder acquaintance and intimacy with our small staff at Stapleford. It seemed that ordinary folk were much more reliable to fathom since they were inclined to plain speaking, which made for simple understanding. I had enjoyed this discovery. The simplicity of frank and open speech when I had learnt to converse in these Banbury styles the ton favoured, which I realised now, was a language all of its own, however much it proclaimed to be English. It was the language of the snide and subtle, the cunning and the ambiguous. Not so much in the matter of words, but the style in which they were employed, to say one thing and mean quite another. 'What can you tell me about this place, Mrs Wallace?'

'Not a lot, ma'am. My master shall be back any moment with your portraits.'

'Then you will at least tell me its direction?'

'St. Andrew's Street, just around the corner. After the Castle Inn but before you reach the Fountain Inn.'

At this precise moment, Mr Darracott returned to the room bearing our miniatures in their enclosures. We bid each other the stiffest of farewells before Mrs Wallace insisted on escorting us down the staircase and to the front door. When we got there, she whispered: 'Don't go there though, will you miss? They don't need any grounds to lock you away, you know, and you'll have no trial.'

'Thank you, Mrs Wallace,' I said with a gentle smile as the cold air swept through the place and we stepped out onto the street. The young girl and the brutes accosting her were nowhere to be seen now. Though I wanted to go and find her out and discover this so-called Bridewell, which appeared to me to have no semblance of merit in what I had studied of English law. But I thought better of getting us into such a fix before making further enquiries to ascertain exactly what it was. So we walked our way back in the direction we had come, and hailed the first hackney that crossed our path.

Bulldogs.

December 1821.- Eleanor.

At dinner this evening, as Mrs Duckworth and the Butler laid the soup tureens upon the table, I bid them both take a seat with us a moment.

'It wouldn't be right, ma'am,' Mrs Duckworth protested at this invitation.

'Well, if you shan't mind it, I won't, and who else is here to know?'

She and the Butler exchanged a perplexed glance, and each pulled out a chair.

'I shan't keep you long, only there are a couple of things I wish to ask you about. Firstly, Miss Brown and I wanted to offer our services for the Christmas feast preparations, if you would be so good as to give us directions on what we might help in. Miss Brown knows her way well about the kitchen, I the dining table...and before you protest on account of impropriety, I assure you, we mean it in good faith and know that you are quite capable, only, we hoped that since our party shall be so small, that perhaps we might all dine and make merry together. It is Christmas, after all.'

'Ma'am, you are very good, but it isn't proper, and we are not the sort of folk to take liberties.'

'Which is precisely why we wish to share our table with you all and make lighter the load, so you may come and join us and enjoy something of a holiday, for at least the afternoon. And really, it will be you doing us the service. How can we get up any jolly parlour games, singing, or dancing with only us two? We shan't have the benefit of family for the festive season, but could we not all join forces to become a happy substitute for the day?'

'Oh miss, you are a smooth talker. How can I deny you when you make such petitions?' said Mrs Duckworth, blushing a fraction and showing a hint of her delight at the scheme.'

'Then it is settled!' I declared, smiling. 'We shall all pitch in on Christmas morning and enjoy a happy Christmas feast and holiday for the remainder.'

'Well, I say, what generosity.'

'Is it not the season of precisely that?'

'Indeed, it is,' Annalise concurred.

'Well, you are very good, and I'm sure we shall all be very grateful for it,' Mrs Duckworth said pointedly, casting a glance in the direction of Mr Fulton, the Butler, who remained silent. I wondered if he was much aghast at the oddity of these arrangements. He was a kindly-natured fellow but well-schooled in the old-fashioned ways of his office and seemingly quite set in them. I hoped he would come about to the idea by Christmas day.

'Well, we shall await your directions on what is to be done. Anyway, there was another matter I wondered if you could enlighten me on. When we were in Cambridge today, a most curious scene occurred before us, which caused great alarm.

'Oh?' said Mrs Duckworth frowning, and Mr Fulton sat forward in his seat.

'There were a couple of men dragging—in a most unconscionable manner—a young girl by her arms, quite against her will. Another gentleman, I did not at first associate with them—for he was dressed finely in the like of one of the university dons—I was told was the Proctor, and that the girl was being taken to some Bridewell under his authority.'

'The *Spinning House*?'

'Yes! That was the name given to me, and I could not understand what kind of establishment it was. When I mentioned I wished to complain to the local Magistrate about this harsh treatment of the girl, I was told it was not within his power but the university's. And whilst I thought it sounded like some sort of Banbury tale, I was assured it was the case.'

'I believe it is the case, ma'am, for the little I know of it. When I grew up in Barnwell as a girl, we all knew not to be found about the city streets alone or in close range of the gowns, for fear of the Proctor.'

MIDWINTER.

'So, it is true?'

She nodded. 'Last I knew of it, anyway.'

'I see.' I was perfectly astounded to think such power was granted to a bunch of schoolmasters. It seemed quite contrary to anything I understood of such matters. I knew from my brothers' dealings at Oxford that the students could be in for quite a stern admonishment when at mischief, but that was an entirely different matter than girls' beings plucked from the street. 'The Housekeeper in Cambridge mentioned they can be accosted without grounds or trial, surely in that she was mistaken?'

'Well, she's likely better informed than I am in such matters since I've not lived in that district for nigh on twenty years. But I do recall a story that went about in my youth of Mary Saddler, who swore she got locked up for a week for doing little more than walking home along Trinity Street by herself at half-past- six one day. Said she'd spent a week in the damp mean place at the vice chancellor's pleasure.'

I was baffled at this. A week's detainment for walking down the street alone? By all means, a sadly stupid thing to do, one I myself was guilty of, but a crime? Only of a social nature, and certainly not by law. 'And did she have the opportunity to be heard at trial?'

Mrs Duckworth shrugged. 'I don't rightly remember if she told me, it was so long ago now, and I weren't allowed to speak with her after it got about, for it ruined her and my pa was not to have us mixing with the unfortunate kind.'

'And is it a bridewell or a gaolhouse?'

'I'm not certain of the difference, ma'am. I only know that it used to be Hobsons Workhouse, then the university masters made it a place for detaining unfortunates and vagrants. —Daisy might know, she's from around those parts. Used to be a bed-maker at the university.'

'Excellent. Who is she?'

'The day maid that comes in from time to time to help us out with the bigger jobs, like the laundry days or carpet beating. Her son Jack is the hall boy here.'

'Oh yes, I would very much like to speak with her if she would be willing to.'

'I shall find it out, ma'am. Will that be all? I fear your soup will be turning cold.'

I had quite forgotten we were sitting for dinner. 'Yes, thank you, Mrs Duckworth, Mr Fulton. Sorry for detaining you.'

IT TURNED OUT THAT Daisy was next due in on Christmas Eve to help with the preparations, so I waited until she had finished for the day before inviting her to take tea with Annalise and me in the small parlour. It was one of our favourite rooms at Stapleford. Cosy and a little shabby in the most delightful manner, with its slightly sagging sofas draped in mismatched blankets and an over-embellishment of assorted cushions. It also served as a breakfast room with a round rosewood table to seat six, ensconced in a bay window that overlooked the cottage gardens. We sat around it to take our tea, the night set black against the window glass and the reflection of the fire shimmering in it.

'Thank you for agreeing to speak with us, Mrs Dyer. I understand you have already been briefed upon the subject I seek your intelligence on?'

'Yes, ma'am. Mrs Duckworth said you wanted to know what I could tell you about the Proctor's involvement in the Spinning House girls.'

'Please, if you would. You see, this is the first time I have heard of such a scheme, and I am at a loss of where to direct my complaints on the mishandling of a girl we witnessed just the other day.'

'Well, I will tell you as much as I can ma'am. What precisely do you want to know?'

'Well, is it true that they apprehend girls for simply walking along the street alone?'

'They do, ma'am, and for a whole lot more too.'

'I see, and you mean for being found out in a compromising situation with the undergraduates?'

She nodded. 'Yes, but it rarely happens. Unless they are up to no good round the backs, of an evening.'

'The backs?'

'The parkland behind the colleges that backs onto the river. It's where they often go to ply their trades, and the gowns all know it and will attempt to find mischief there if they are so minded. The thing is, the Proctor and his bulldogs know it well enough and patrol it often, so a great many will find themselves caught out there and taken off to Hobsons if they are in its vicinity.'

'I see. So they use bulldogs to patrol the area?'

'No, I don't mean hounds. Forgive me, ma'am, I meant no disrespect, only it's what all the townspeople call 'em: the proctors' brutes who do the dirty work for them.'

'It seems a perfectly fitting description from the example I saw of them. —And when they are taken to this place, do you know what happens there?'

'Only from bits and pieces I've heard spoken of. It's not a place you'd like to go by any account. Damp beds and filthy as an alley cats slum, I am told.'

'And what about their trial? What courthouse is it held at?'

'Ain't no court trials. They're presented to the vice chancellor the next morning to hear their punishment, and once they've served it, they're released.'

'Impossible,' I declared. Trial by jury was the right of everyone in England, that much I had read up on and knew for a fact. I thought back to the *Magna Carta* manuscript I examined at the *British Museum* last summer. If the Magistrates were bound by it, surely a University Principal would be bound by at least as much.

'It's the truth as I know it, ma'am.'

'Who is the vice chancellor, Mrs Dyer?'

'I'm not sure I've heard mention of the latest, for they usually elect a new one each winter. I daresay it was mentioned in the *Cambridge Chronicle*, that's usually how town folks find it out.'

'I shall make enquiries.'

'I might be able to find it out for you, ma'am. I still have friends who work as bed-makers there, though I rarely see them, and it wouldn't be 'till after Christmas now.'

'Thank you, Mrs Dyer. I would be grateful for anything you may find out for me, or if indeed any of them would be willing to take an interview with me themselves. Strictly in confidence, of course. I would take no risks with jeopardising their positions with the University.'

'I'll see what I can do, ma'am.'

By the end of our interview, I had decided I must return to the city after our Christmas holiday tomorrow and get to the bottom of this mystery. It sounded out of all reason impossible that these actions were lawful, and yet I had been consistently given the same account. Girls apprehended and taken to this hovel without grounds or trial, and school masters playing judge and jury, obstructing the lawful right of an English inhabitant. I was tempted to write to Edmund to see if he had heard of this irregular scheme: he had been an Oxford man himself, but I wondered if the same practices were in place there too. Certainly, he could confirm my position on the right of trial by jury and the need for reasonable grounds for detainment. But my prior petitions to him had caused relations to grow ill between us, and I considered that perhaps it was time I learnt to stand on my own two feet, since this was to be the way forward in my future now; to rely on my own wits and resourcefulness to establish my future with Annalise. The problem was, I had not brought the law books I'd been studying with me, and the library at Stapleford was barely above the size of a dressing parlour and sadly diminished. Little had been done to restore the place since my father's purchase of it, and though, on the whole, it was in remarkably good condition for sitting vacant for so long, it was lacking in certain areas of furnishing and personalisation. Whatever the previous occupants had left behind in the place and little beyond the necessary remained. So, I put the scheme to Annalise, that we must go back to Cambridge after our Christmas holiday and learn what we could by covert observation and talking to such folk as might prove willing to enlighten us.

'Do you not think that a rather risky pursuit, given you are lying low here?' Annalise said as she helped me undress for bed.

'Not if we are careful to maintain our disguise. —What?' I asked in response to her snigger.

'Look at this face,' she said, turning me to meet my reflection in the looking glass with her palms pressed to my cheeks.

I peered into it and saw nothing out of the ordinary, except I was a shade paler than usual, owing partially to the recent loss of the strong tan I had carried through the summer. I supposed the rest may be attributed to the pregnancy. I certainly felt fatigued enough to account for it. Although both this lethargy and the dreadful sickness had of late, seemed to be in decline. 'So I am a little peaky.'

'Not that silly.'

'Then what am I looking for?'

'For a face that carries features of uncommon beauty and distinction. Which means that whether you are dressed in your finest silk evening gown or my sad old threads, you are not much disguised into the common look.'

'Flatterer,' I accused, pulling her into my lap and wrapping my arms about her waist.

She draped her arms about my shoulders. 'If I wanted to flatter you, I could think of more preferable means, I assure you,' she teased with a peck at my mouth before withdrawing back to look at me better. 'I mean it, though. That disguise didn't fool the artist did it, and he does not know you in the least. I think someone who knew your face would not be hoodwinked by your drab dress.'

'Well, then, what do you suggest? I can't change my face. Perhaps my hair would suffice. I could see about a dye for it. That might help.'

'I suggest you have a care and keep out of the way of any such schemes that might land you into bother.'

'What, and forget about that poor young girl being brutishly dragged along the streets without batting an eyelid?'

'No. I feel as distressed as you do at the circumstances, but I do not forget that my first thought is for your safety. Let me go in your place instead.'

'Ah, but since you suffer the same charge of uncommon beauty, I see no improvement upon the scheme.'

'Ha! Well, it is of no consequence since no one knows who I am, or that I am with you. Let me undertake these interviews and enquiries in your place.'

'No. It might be dangerous. You could be apprehended by the Proctor and his "bulldogs" for lurking about the area on your own like the girl Mrs

Duckworth told us about. At least if we go together, we can vouch for each other.'

'I'd imagine a proctor insensible of following the laws of this country shall have no qualms about carting the pair of us off to the bridewell should we come to his notice.'

'Hmmm. Then we must improve upon our disguise so that we *don't* come to his notice.'

'And how will we do that?'

'Well, at the theatre houses, they do all kinds of tricks with face painting that are most convincing. I once saw Maria Davison performing as *Medusa* in very credible style. I was shocked to the utmost to see her perform in *Rivals* last summer, where she looked unrecognisable from her part in *Athena*. Maybe we could employ a theatre dresser to teach us how to transform our looks.

'That's all very well, but we are not in London now, nor can we go back there whilst you are still in hiding.'

'No, but there must be a theatre somewhere else we might go to. Or I could write to enquire or advertise for one.'

'Well, let us enjoy tomorrow, and then we can set about the task, hmm? Come on, it is late, and we are to be up with the servants tomorrow. Let us get to bed.'

Christmastide Feast.

December 1821. - Eleanor.

'Happy Christmas!' Annalise was up first, dressed in apron and cap, ready to offer her services to the kitchens.

The image of her struck me as one plucked directly from my early memories of her at Cuddington, and it made me smile to think of it now, how far we had come since those days of awkward formality. 'Happy Christmas,' I muttered into my pillow. I felt too tired to rise at such an hour, the room still misted in the early winter morning gloom, even though the drapes had been drawn back. But I forced myself up to receive Annalise's help with dressing and furnished myself with one of her aprons. 'Well, it seems we shan't have a white Christmas, but what a howler that wind is whipping up,' I said, casting a bleary-eyed gaze out of the window as she tied my apron strings for me. The grass was frost-tipped but not a sign of snow or the pallid skies that oft preceded it. Instead, the shrubs and trees had their branches thrown about violently in the wind, and the sky threatened rain with heavy plumes of grey thickening above us.

'Well, we shall have a merry Christmastide in spite of it!' said Annalise with a note of defiance, leaning forward to kiss the side of my face.

'Yes, we shall. To spend it with you is all the ingredients required to make for the best Christmas I could ever ask for.' I kissed her back, and we headed down to the basement.

Mrs Duckworth and Mrs Dyer—who had been drafted in today not only to help in the preparations but to join us in our Christmas feast—were already at the kitchen table peeling and chopping away with a speed and absentmindedness that made me fear for their fingertips.

'Merry Christmas,' Annalise and I chorused.

'Merry Christmas to you too. How are you this morning? Did you sleep well?'

'Yes, thank you,' I replied. She always asked us this, and I had wondered if the noises from my chamber at night had given her the false impression I was a nervous or restless sleeper. Moving the bed frame but a fraction from the wall had improved the problem somewhat, but it was a rickety old piece of furniture, and I doubted it had entirely ameliorated the creaking in our more passionate moments. We had also tried out Annalise's bed, hoping to find some improvement, but to no avail. So now we swapped between rooms to suit our fancy and ensure that Annalise's bed linens were convincingly worn in enough on laundry days.

'Now, will I fix you both a small breakfast?'

'No, thank you, Mrs Duckworth. We are not used to breakfasting so early, and we come prepared for our duties if you will be so good as to direct us in what they shall be.'

Annalise took over the peeling, and Mrs Duckworth—reluctant in this scheme but relenting in her protests—showed me to the cabinet in the Butler's pantry where the best chinaware was kept locked away. Then to another where the table linens were piled neatly pressed and folded, and left me to it. I used the dumb waiter to convey much of it up to the dining room, frightened at the prospect of cracking a glass or plate if I attempted to carry them up the stairs. These were of a fine and antique variety that I did not want to risk: A family heirloom, perhaps, from my mama's line. I stacked them carefully, and the linens I used to pad around them for extra protection. The fancy candelabras, I trusted to my arms, treading carefully with them. I wondered how the footmen managed it with such seeming ease and grace. Whenever they cleared the tables after the removes, they piled numerous trays and plates upon their forearms and swept them away as if they were as light as a paper bird. I was sure I had never seen them drop one.

Like everything at Stapleford, the dining room was small compared to the grand table that would be laid in all its glory at Cuddington today, complete with fancy sugar craft sculptures and festive gingerbread scenes. But it was full of old Georgian charm from my parent's era, and the picture rails still held numerous gilded portraits of my mother's ancestry, including one of her and her siblings in their youth. I paused to examine them a moment and wondered how my mama was coping with my latest travesty. Today at least, I knew they would have the company of my siblings to cheer them and fill my empty space at the table, except for Caitlyn, who never made the journey from Scotland at this season, but would often come down for Easter when the improvement in weather lent to more favourable travelling conditions.

Carefully, I emptied the contents of the dumbwaiter onto the side table that sat below it and tried to work out which tablecloth would best suit which of the tables. It had been necessary to borrow the breakfast room table since the dining table here would only host a party of eight place settings comfortably and were to be a party of fourteen by the time the gardener and groom's families joined us later. It made for an oddly shaped arrangement: the traditional oval-shaped dining table running the greater length of the room and the round breakfast room table butting up against the end of it, wide and mismatched. But once I had found the right arrangement of the table covers to dress them in, they looked a little less odd. And as I proceeded to decorate the centre of the tables with evergreen wreaths threaded with pinecones, candles tied with red ribbon, cinnamon sticks and glazed orange peel slices, the eye was less drawn to the irregularity.

When Mr Fulton came into the room with his footman carrying the silver plate, I was halfway through laying the glasses.

'Well, what a spectacular scene, is it not John?' said he to the footman. 'We have not had cause for such a grand arrangement since the nineties.'

I smiled brightly, noting his approval. 'Well, thank you, Mr Fulton. I am glad my efforts meet with your approval.' He had been the Butler here during mama's childhood and no doubt lamented the sad decline of its use from the days of such a full and vibrant household.

'Certainly, ma'am, a handsome job you have done, but you need not exert yourself further. You've done quite enough. John and I can see to the rest.'

I took this as my cue to exit gracefully. I knew this mode of doing things was a violation of the Butler's stiff schooling in his trade, and I did not want to make him uncomfortable with my presence, and I had only a few more glasses left to set about. So I took my leave of them and found the ladies in the kitchen, hard at work over steamy pots and floury tables. The air was thick with a curious mix of spices and cooking odours. Cinnamon and brandy I could make out, but they were diluted with other fragrances I couldn't quite place. With Annalise's guidance, I joined in the rolling out of pastry – something I had never before seen its raw and rudimentary form, and found it quite fascinating to flatten it out and cut it into the shape of little leaves to decorate the Christmas pie with. It was quite a pie indeed, containing every kind of wild fowl Mrs Duckworth could procure, wrapped in layers of each other and stuffed to the brim, leaving the pie top Annalise was trimming to size in a rising dome once she layered it on and pressed it into place.

At Cuddington, we were used to having roasted goose and venison as the mainstay of the Christmas feast, with a variety of less elaborate mince pies to accompany them. But nothing in the style of this grand Yorkshire Christmas Pie Mrs Duckworth had settled upon. There too, were all the regular trimmings of buttered vegetables, soups and a rich plum pudding, cheeses and a ham that was still boiling in the pot, its salty scent causing my stomach to rumble now we had surpassed our usual breakfasting hour. There was no time to tend to that now, though. We had barely finished egg washing the pie in time to change out of our working clothes and leave for morning mass at the village church. Mrs Dyer took the office of staying behind to watch over the baking and the house in our absence. Mrs Duckworth told me not to feel bad about it, that Mrs Dyer had long lost her faith in the almighty when she was made a young widow and had already been parted by the grave from nine of her ten children. Jack—the hall boy—being the last to remain to her and all that was left for her to live for in the world. 'She 'as no prayers or kind words to say at the pew, my love, I assure you. So, believe me when I tell yer she's more than happy to stay behind. Jack shall come with us, though. That she'll permit.'

I thought about this as we sat listening to the sermon. No wonder she was faithless, having endured so much loss and sadness, and suffering so many unanswered prayers. A life as hard as hers would make one more inclined to believe that we were already living in hell, so what was left to fear in damnation? I had little care for the sermons or prayers myself, but the spirit was festive and merry, and I enjoyed the carolling outside as we arrived there and the festive hymns we sang, breaking up the monotony of the rector's lectures, which were in large measure drowned out by the sound of the fierce rains that pelted the church roof and windows about halfway through the service.

We returned weather-beaten and drenched. A wicked wind had spiralled out of control, felling trees along the journey we made in the open-top trap, which had no provision for keeping us dry as the rain broke out again with a vengeance. But it was the manservants I felt pity for, as there were only four spaces in the trap, and they had given them over to us females and took the journey by foot. Had I foreseen how ill the weather would turn on setting out, I might have had a thought to find out if there was a cab we might hire, or at least bid us all be conveyed in turns. Now there was only me and Mrs Duckworth who were capable of driving it back to them, and it seemed a wanton thing to send her back out there alone, especially when she had the dinner left to complete. So I waited for the others to disembark, and before there was any time for an argument over the proposition, I took up the reigns and told them I was going back for the others. Their protests carried off in the bluster of the wind, and me already turning the trap about and setting off along the driveway. I knew it a foolish thing to do, and so there was no use in arguing upon a point I could not defend. But I knew I could not leave them to the fate of being struck by a tree dropping over them, or Mr Fulton, in his senior years, catching a terrific chill from being so long out in the wet. So I kept this in mind as I drove the horses hard along the lanes, which had begun to pool with water, the carriage wheels sliding in the mud when I failed to notice them in time and was forced to slow the horses for fear of turning us over. But the journey to Orwell was short, even if seeming suddenly treacherous, and it was not long before I caught sight of them at the roadside, coats pulled out above their heads like canopies. There were four of them to fit into the trap but space for only three, so I bid Travers take the reins and had Jack, the hall boy, take my lap for his seat. It was a most unseemly thing to do, yet there was nothing else for it. And whilst Mr Fulton was too weather-worn and relieved at my conveyance to say anything upon the matter, I saw the disapproval in his eyes as he drew his coat tight about him and looked fixedly in the direction of the horses ahead. But no amount of disapproval or propriety was enough to convince me to leave any one of them behind—least of all Mrs Dyer's only remaining child—in the hope they would manage until the trap could be brought back again. And when a heavy old elm tree a little way behind us, creaked so loud we all turned to hear it through the howling wind, as it toppled over less than fifty yards behind us, I knew it had been the right thing to do. That they might have been walking beneath that very tree by now if we were not already making down the lane at horse speed. I did not like to think of the scene that might have played out had I failed to come or was a moment later, and I knew now this was understood by everyone, given the sobering silence amongst us for the remainder of the journey.

It had taken me little above ten minutes or so to reach them, but the journey back took double. The lanes I had driven along to get here now being tree-strewn and impassable, Travers having to make lengthy diversions as the need arose. I was only grateful that this had not happened on my journey here, for I would not have had the knowledge of how to navigate away from the main lanes if I had been forced to, and who knows where I would have ended up.

But despite the odds stacked against us, we arrived back at Stapleford in one piece, a little shaken and soaked through, but no real harm had been endured beyond our nerves.

Annalise snatched me up in a frightful hug as I stepped off the footplate. It was neither quite a tender embrace nor a reproachful squeeze, but something between the two.

'What the deuce were you thinking!' she whispered to me as we went into the house, but it was not a question, and I made no answer.

I was grateful to see she had not simply fretted in my absence but had kept a practical head and set to work at seeing all the kettles on to boil, the tub put before the fire in one of the spare bedrooms, bathing cloths and sheets piled high on the unmade bed and a ready pile waiting at the door for us to tend the worst of it.

There was no specific water closet or bathing tub at Stapleford. Only an old-fashioned copper, just about big enough to sit in. And it was the only one we had, so it was to be shared among us. So we made quick work of it, spending not above five minutes in the water submerging our cold-numbed limbs and washing the mud and grime from our skin and hair before topping it up with more hot water, ready for the next in line. It was only Mr Fulton that refused his place in the ritual, and being used to his way, Mrs Duckworth settled for shrouding him in bath sheets and blankets by the fire and forcing tumblers of brandy down him instead.

It had hardly proved the Christmas holiday we had all looked to insofar, but by afternoon, the bad business was all behind us, and we were all dry and well, and sat at the table with ready appetites to devour the feast laid out before us. The groom's family soon joining us as well as the gardener and his wife, all of which had their own cottages but had a fancy to take up our invitation and enjoy the festivities in greater company.

And it was indeed the merrier for it. The fractious events of the morning seemed to render us more eager to forget our troubles and determined to enjoy the luxuries of good food, a well-stacked fire and cheery company to enjoy it in. Even Mr Fulton seemed at greater ease now, owing no doubt, to the brandy, which had not only worked to warm him up and spare him a chill, but ease his stiffness of mind just enough to throw caution to propriety awhile and make merry with us all. 'Well, this is as fine a spread as I've ever laid eyes on Mrs Duckworth,' said Jeb, the gardener. 'You've quite exceeded yourself.'

'Here, here,' added Mr Fulton as he carved open the splendid Yorkshire pie, revealing colourful layers of meats, steam rising from beneath the golden crust and a smell so divine, my mouth watered.

'A toast,' I said, raising a glass with the slightest splash of wine in it. 'To Mrs Duckworth and Mrs Dyer, with thanks for this delightful Christmas feast.' This was met with cheers to the same and nods of agreement which soon fell into silence as the pie platter was passed about the table in generously cut wedges.

We all ate heartily for the better part of two hours before we were defeated, leaving a great many leftovers for tomorrow. It was just as well since it was *St. Stephen's Day,* and the staff were to have their formal holiday. We would all manage well enough off these remnants awhile without a pot needing to be put to the stove plate.

We made a concerted effort to clear the table and convey the leftovers to the cooling cupboards in the larder, then withdrew into the drawing room to sit more comfortably on padded sofas and easy chairs, a number of which we had to borrow from other parts of the house to ensure everyone had a leisurely seat in which to digest their food.

The conversation flowed readily; talk of the ill weather and fears over the rivers rising and flooding the fens if it was to continue so. Talk of what all the staff planned to do with their holiday tomorrow. Most had prior engagements with their extended families that they hoped would not be put off by the winds. Mrs Dyer meant to take Jack to Cambridge for a new coat. Mrs Duckworth was to go to her sisters in Barnwell and Mr Fulton was, by this time, snoozing in his chair with his head cocked at an angle and his mouth hung at a gape.

We played at charades and forfeits, and when our repose had worked its restoration, Annalise and I took turns on the hired pianoforte whilst the others rolled back the carpets and jigged about the drawing room. And when we were spent of our more lively pastimes, we passed a little while reading Christmastide passages from the bible and singing carols. It was nothing like the Christmases I was used to at Cuddington, and yet I felt certain it was amongst the best I had ever known. And as the gardener and groom's family left and the others retired, leaving Annalise and I sprawled out upon the carpet in front of the Yule log burning in the grate, I felt nothing but deep gratitude in my heart.

WE WOKE UP IN THE TWILIGHT hours, having both fallen into a doze upon the rug without meaning to. My left arm was numb from having slept on it against the hardness of the floorboards running beneath the pile, and I shook out the tingles and waited for the blood to start flowing into it again before lifting myself up to my feet with Annalise's help.

'Come on, let's get on up to bed,' she said, yawning between words.

'The staff Christmas boxes!' I cried, as a mental reminder to see to it bloomed into my stirring consciousness. 'We must lay them out before we go to bed, or they shan't have them in time for rising.'

'Oh yes, are they still in the dressing parlour?' she asked, wiping her eyes and picking up a few of the scattered cushions that lay about our feet.

I nodded and stepped into a convulsive stretch before helping her with the remaining cushions, and we set off upstairs to collect them. The house was almost soundless, still thick with the scent of fresh pine and evergreens and waning aromas from our feast earlier. We trod about the place as quietly as could be managed and laid out the boxes upon the servants' parlour table in each of their place settings.

'What a lovely sight they shall wake to,' said Annalise, arranging a curl of ribbon about the writing board she perched in the middle of the table amongst a scattering of pinecones. We had found it in the old school room last week and had chalked the words: "Thank you all, and happy St. Stephens Day!"

My parents were in the habit of simply distributing monetary gifts to their staff, and this year, I had been charged with drawing the draft on their account and dispersing the veils between them in accordance with mama's instructions. But Annalise and I had a mind to add a few little personal touches to convey our gratitude for their unwavering kindness and service since our coming. Nothing was ever too much trouble, and their small number meant that despite the modest size of the place and having only the two of us to wait on, they were often hard at work, multi-tasking to keep everything in good order. Annalise was of the opinion that it seemed to them a pleasure to tend to us, like the many years on board wages, instead of inducing them into habits of idleness and advantage-taking, had produced quite the opposite effect. They took pride in their work and in Stapleford, keeping it in pristine order and trifling over our every comfort. The difference, she noted, from her observations, was that they were happy here. She suspected their (usually) lighter load and not suffering from being overworked accounted for it, and insisted that she meant to take the example into her own staffing arrangements in Carshalton when we returned. 'Happy staff are hardworking staff. Their commitment and loyalty are borne of pride and a balance of work and rest,' and this she believed to be the way things must evolve; out of the outmoded ways of thinking that the answer lay in harsh discipline and continuous exhaustion. It certainly stood to reason. Although I doubted most of the ton gave the slightest thought to the needs of their servants beyond the obligatory necessities. But like most things I had learnt of late, I was finding my own sensibilities less and less in sympathy with the ways of the ton, and I had no intention of being led by their example.

We added a few further decorations to the table and padded quietly out of the parlour with one last glance back at the pretty scene we had left behind us. I imagined the joy in their faces when they rose to see the spectacle of it: pretty boxes for each we had decorated ourselves, containing not only the standard package of coins and a letter from my parents stating: *"Lord and Lady Ashlyn would like to thank you for another year of service and wish you merry tidings for the season and good health for the year ahead..",* but in addition, we had placed within each: some wax candles, a bar of fragranced soap, flavoured taffy and a portion of pomfret cakes. Then to each a more personal gift: Mrs Duckworth had a charming hat pin, Mr Fulton, a quarter of good snuff, to John the footman, a penknife, to Gilly the housemaid-come-laundress, a tin of nourishing hand salve, to Jack a fishing reel and net, and to his mama, a cashmere shawl. To the cottaging staff, we had a pound of good tea and sugar sent for each of them.

I hoped we had judged correctly with our selections. It was difficult to think of what to give to people you did not know well, and yet there was an odd sense, despite the brevity of our acquaintance, that we had all become quite intimate in the confines of this isolated little house.

We slipped into the cold sheets and fell swiftly back to sleep, waking little before noon and realising we had slept more than half the daylight hours away, the dusk setting in before four o'clock now, rendering any outdoor plans brief and fleeting.

I had wanted to venture into Cambridge and begin on our enquiries of the *Spinning House* but realised that a servant's holiday was not the best day to set out on such a scheme. Tomorrow would suffice, I considered, lifting the curtain to look out upon the grounds. The violent winds of yesterday had settled at last, but now the rain pelted unrelentingly against the panes and dulled everything in sight in its greying gloom. Hopefully, it would get it all out of the way today, and we might travel in calm and dry conditions tomorrow.

MIDWINTER.

But it did not let up, not the next day or for the next two weeks, and we were held captive by its dismal persistence. The servants had returned late from their *St. Stephens Day* holiday with tales of the Cam rising, the fens flooding, and many roads proving impassable on their journeys back to Stapleford. It was not an uncommon occurrence in these parts, they said, although it had been a great many years since they had dealt with it so violent and enduring. So, we stayed put where it was dry and safe, despite being desperate to venture out and initiate our enquiries. Mrs Dyer had at least given us the direction of one of her bed-maker acquaintances who was willing to speak with us, provided we could maintain her confidence. But every day I hoped would be the day we might set out on a visit to her, we were met with the news of some new area flooding or difficulty arising out of it. So far, we had been spared the worst here. Although the lands were sodden and marshy now, and the sandbags had been set against the lowlands of the estate, Stapleford enjoyed a slightly raised prospect and reasonable enough proximity from the Cam to not prove an immediate risk. Although the reports of other localities suggested they crept nearer by the day, and if the rain did not soon cease, it might only be a matter of time.

So we did our utmost to pass the days of confinement as best as we could. It had been easy on St Stephen's Day with the house empty. We had made love in at least half of the rooms in the house, walked about in little more than a bed jacket and slippers most of the day, and then having to tend to our own meals and care, kept us occupied in the gaps. Annalise had taught me how to make scrambled eggs and toast bread over the fire. I had never so much as stepped into the kitchen for any purpose of food preparation before we came here: pouring tea and buttering bread had been the extent of my experience, and as humble as it must have seemed to one so capable as she, it filled me with delight to manage this small accomplishment. To prepare my own breakfast from scratch. It was quite the novelty to take a feathery egg in its rudimentary form and create something edible from it. To understand what equipment from the kitchen to select for its purpose. To learn the methods of preparation and signs that showed it ready, and to finally sit down and taste its delicious salty warmth from my own endeavours. I knew my astonished delight in this small fancy perturbed Annalise somewhat. As had my recent inclination of

53

sitting in the kitchen and watching Mrs Duckworth at work and asking to help in any tasks that looked manageable, from kneading dough to peeling vegetables and my latest fancy of trying at plucking the wildfowl. This was a messy and unpleasant business, and yet despite that, I enjoyed an odd sense of industry in its challenge.

I wondered if it was some effect of the pregnancy, the impending preparation to give care to another life. Some primal instinct drawing me to better understand how to undertake these practical things that I had never before had a need or desire to. Or whether it was owing to the recent diversion of my future, which was headed in an utterly different direction from the one I had expected or been prepared for. Living out a humble independent life was not within my knowing or learning, and yet whichever way it was to be realised, it would not be in any pattern reminiscent of the privileged life I had insofar led. So it seemed wise to take the opportunity to expand my remit of accomplishments whilst I could, however rudimentary they might be. Besides, I was beginning to feel an upturn in my energy. Where the past months had plagued me with excessive lethargy and nausea, I had now counted down at least a week without feeling either to be the case. Quite the reverse, in fact. I did not know what accounted for it, but I was grateful all the same and eager to capitalise on this new buoyancy. It felt something like the effect of spring-time renewal I felt every year after a long winter, except the season was surely not to account for it in this instance.

Dangerous Beauty.

January 1822. - Eleanor.

The twelfth night celebrations had come and gone, the wassail bowl emptied by all but me, and we had burnt all the evergreens in the fire before the rains eased off and the roads were cleared and finally declared passable for travel again. We needed no further encouragement and set off in the trap for Cambridge directly that morning once the light was up. Blankets tucked tight about our laps against the chill, my thickest fur lined leather gloves to protect my hands as I steered the reigns, and Annalise's wriggled tight into her muffler.

We were first to head to Petersfield to call on Mrs Humphries, the University bed-maker, to see what she could tell us before taking the toll gate into the city and locating the Spinning House. Then, finally, onto the *Theatre Royal Barnwell*, which, contrary to our thinking that there was no theatre here, sat just outside the city bounds on the Newmarket Road. Apparently, the prohibition of theatre houses in Cambridge City was also a result of the University's diktats, and they could not be situated within a five-mile radius of it. As if, I thought, a five mile would be enough to prevent the undergraduates from venturing out to it. I had once known Henry threatened with expulsion from Oxford on account of he and his coterie taking hired horses into London one night to visit the Drury Lane, and no doubt, not only for its theatrical offerings.

Still, I was grateful not to have to venture as far as London to find a dresser, so a five-mile diversion on the way home was nothing to answer, so long as the daylight held out long enough to make the round trip. With the pressing time much at mind, we sat at Mrs Humphries small parlour table, declining her offer of coffee and moved directly to the purpose of our visit.

'Mrs Humphries, I want to assure you, you may speak openly with us. We shall keep your confidence at all costs. You have our word,' I began, noting her slightly nervous air as she tossed another scuttle of coals onto the fire and sat down with us. She was a softly spoken lady of middling years, dressed demurely and giving the impression of a kindly and mild-natured creature. This ran contrary to the hard features of her face and the stout comportment of her figure. She had the look of someone who wore the burdens of her life upon her face, tiredness etched into its creases and folds. I supposed it must have taken a lot of hard work to meet the cost of a small cottage such as this. It was better sized than the cottages on the Stapleford estate, with two well-appointed rooms on the ground floor and a winding staircase creeping around the rear corner of the one we were sitting in. It was well furnished and neatly kept, and I supposed it took a lot of upkeep to maintain it so well and manage rents on a property of its bearing.

'Mrs Humphries, I know it takes courage to speak out against the wrongs you must witness every day being in the University's employ, but I would do nothing to jeopardise your position, so I hope you will be at ease to speak freely.'

Annalise, too, offered a reassuring nod of allegiance to this effect, and Mrs Humphries cleared her throat.

'I thank you. Can't be too careful, you understand. They have it in their power to finish folk like us,' she said in whispering tones as if we were at risk of being overheard. Although it seemed to me we would not be, the youngest of her children, a boy of five, being sent across the street to sit with a neighbour upon our arrival. The rest of her family, which comprised of two more sons, out to work in the brickyard in Barnwell, two daughters, one of which worked as she, for a university lodging house, the other thought too fair of looks to be employed in the same, had recently found a place in a respectable house by Parkers Piece. Her husband, she explained, was away to sea and not due back till Lent.

'I do understand Mrs Humphries,' Annalise said with an encouraging smile, 'I myself was brought up in service until my recent inheritance. I am an orphan now, you see, but my mama was a Housekeeper all my childhood years, and I followed her into the trade. But she had a difficult time of it, sacrificed much to keep a roof over our heads and look after my interests.'

This seemed to have the mollifying effect required to loosen her tongue. 'Well, that's why I'm doing it, talking to you. I'm scared for my daughters, you see. For their futures now they're of age. – They're good girls, you know, respectable and innocent, but even that won't save you from the proctors about here. And it's getting worse. I hear about it, you see, the gowns don't think to hold their tongues around the likes of us. —It's like they don't think we have ears and tongues in our heads.'

'Worse than that,' I interjected, 'they are so sure of themselves—of their superior standing—that they do not care what you hear. For they think you never likely to repeat it, and even if you did, that their own voice would easily counter yours. And that is why Mrs Humphries, you are doing the right thing in speaking up. We shall not fear to be a stalwart voice for you and your daughters. To challenge these men and their practices, as we have nothing to lose by them. We are not from Cambridge, you see. We are but here for only a holiday.'

'What do you mean to do about it, ma'am?'

'Well, that's what I am here to figure out. In usual circumstances, I would intend to use my connections to apply pressure to the borough magistrates, but from what I gather, it is not they who hold authority in this case. A peculiarity I have never come across before. Which is why I need to better understand how things stand here and consider the best way to deal in it.'

'Be easy, Mrs Humphries, my friend has experience and connections adequate to mount a challenge to the University, but you understand these things must be carefully considered and managed,' Annalise put in, and Mrs Humphries looked mildly puzzled at what must seem very grand claims from persons who looked only slightly better positioned than she.

'It would be helpful, Mrs Humphries, if you could explain exactly how things work here. I mean, the young girl we witnessed being apprehended just before Christmastide, how would it come about? What would be the process undertaken by these proctors?'

She leaned forward and reverted to her whispering tone again. 'Well, with the undergraduates, the proctors take a stiff stance to their mis-behavings, it is true, but an even stiffer one to townsfolk, mainly the pretty young girls who they think are all of the same mind, to set upon mischief with the young men. It used to be more orderly and more justified. They'd stake out the unfortunate lasses round the backs who *were* up to no good. But every now and then, a new Proctor takes up office who's out to get any lass fair of face and haul her off to the Spinning House and ruin her good name. – It seems we might have such a wave upon us again.'

'But even prostitution is not illegal, Mrs Humphries, reprehensible as it may be, it is not against the laws of this country. I know this for a matter of fact, and so you see, I fail to understand how the Proctors can lay such charges at anyone, innocent or otherwise, when the law does not allow for it.'

'Ah, but they do 'ere, some Royal Charter granted by Queen Elizabeth herself, so it is said.'

I took out my notepad and scribbled this down for later investigation. 'Thank you, that is very helpful. Now, these innocents they apprehend, what cause do they have? I mean, there is always a threshold of evidence to be met in such matters. Do you know what is considered enough evidence to make an arrest?'

'Whatever the proctors see fit, ma'am. There's no rhyme or reason to it that us town folk can make out anyway. Some of them might be caught red-handed in compromising situations. Indeed, I myself have found evidence of ladies' belongings in the undergraduates' lodgings, forgotten hairpins, the occasional reticule or discarded stocking.'

I was astonished they would manage such a feat, given the strictness my brothers had always reported of their university days.

'But no one minds when it's a case of justice, ma'am. Us townsfolk don't want unseemly characters about tempting our own sons any more than the proctors want the gowns beguiled. The trouble comes when they take to whisking a respectable girl up for no more than walking along the street alone or being seen to utter even the most innocent of how-do-you-do's to a fellow. There was a girl last year who got locked up for a week for giving a new undergraduate directions to the College Library. Respectable family and a girl of untarnished character, all turned over in a heartbeat.'

'So it is entirely arbitrary then, a matter solely for the proctors' judgement, it would seem?'

She nodded vehemently. 'The prettier they are, the harsher it seems. Like a girl can choose her face any more than they!'

'Indeed, a ridiculous notion.'

'I mean, it's not as though they are rouged and wearing feathers in their hair. Just plainly dressed young maidens with a certain natural bloom of fairness in their cheek is enough to set the bulldogs on their heels of late. Most of 'em know to travel in packs and not walk out alone in the town. But sometimes it can't be helped; if, like my dear Faith, her misses sends her out on an errand in town as she sometimes does,. And it doesn't half worry me, ma'am. It's her I fear for the most.'

'Yes, I see that it would be worrying for you. But surely your daughter is in service to a respectable household, who could vouch for her character Mrs Humphries.'

'Aye, she does, but even that isn't enough to be sure of her safety. The damage is already done to a girl's reputation by the time she is released from that place.'

'Surely a character can be given at trial to prevent this? Or are they kept incarcerated in wait of the trial?' I thought of Tilly then, months spent sleeping on that putrid stone floor, only to be declared innocent of the charges laid against her.

'Ain't no opportunity for none of that, ma'am. Unless the arrest is a matter of public spectacle and talk, the first a family usually knows of it is when the girl's spent her term and released from the place. The number of poor mamas who must 'ave sat up at night worrying as to why their daughters ain't come home, fearing some wicked accident befallen them.' She wrung her hands which had been resting on the tabletop.

'Shame upon these proctors,' Annalise said, her mouth hollowed into the shape of the gasp she ended on. I wondered if she was thinking of the kind of worry her own mama might have suffered if such a fate had ever befallen her.

'So, Mrs Humphries, let me get this straight: the families and the public are not informed at all – and the public, may they attend the trial?'

'Oh no, ma'am, it's all done quietly, no public galleries, if that's what you mean, not like up at the Castle.'

'The Castle?'

'The county gaol up on the hill.'

I had noticed the rugged walls of a stone fortress rising beyond the steeples of the college chapels but had not realised it was a gaol house cut against the gloom of the dull winter skyline. An old historical relic, I had assumed it. This was worthy of a trip to try to understand why townspeople were being held in a bridewell that did not seem of a proper order when there was such a nearby facility as a county gaol.

'What do you know of the processing of the prisoners, Mrs Humphries? Can you give me an account of how it works from start to finish?'

'Well, only from what is heard, ma'am, not first-hand. From what I gather, if a girl is taken in by the proctors, she is handed over to the matron and given a bed in one of the cells. They are famed for being dreadful damp, and filthy. No fire, even in this season. The following day she is to face the Vice-Chancellor, who declares the sentence, and she is either duly committed or released. That's about all I know.'

'So it is the Vice-Chancellor who delivers the sentence and decides the verdict?'

She nodded.

'Astonishing,' I declared. An educator playing the role of judge and jury, set against all I understood of our constitution and what Blackwell had made abundantly clear in his volumes. 'Do you happen to know the name of the Vice-Chancellor?'

'Yes, ma'am, the newly appointed Rev. William French.'

I scribbled down the name. 'Thank you. And typically, how long are these ladies usually imprisoned for?'

She shrugged. 'Seems to be anything from overnight to a few weeks. The new ones usually get a shorter spell, but the ones well known and who've been taken in before, often end up longer.'

'Thank you, Mrs Humphries, this has all been very helpful. You have given me much to consider, and I shall set right to it. Of course, your name shall never be in the mention, rest assured.'

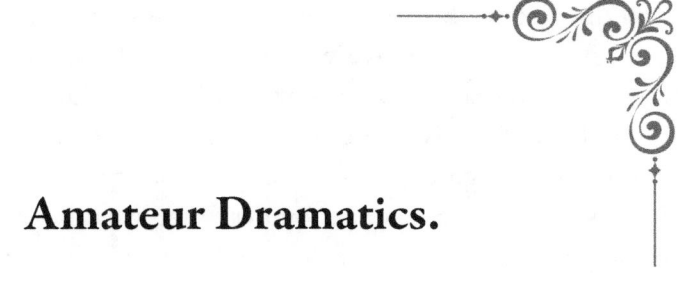

Amateur Dramatics.

January 1822. - Eleanor.

'What will you do now?' Annalise asked when we were back in the trap and headed for Parker's Piece, from where it would be easy to navigate our way to the *Spinning House*, according to Mrs Humphries's directions. Annalise was turning the strangers' guidebook in her hands to make sense of them, but the featureless plains of grassland surrounding us did little to distinguish our whereabouts.

I slowed the horses to allow a moving herd of cattle to cross the lane into the adjacent field. 'I need to find out more about this royal power she mentioned, firstly. But honestly, Annalise, this runs contrary to everything I have read in the law books. I am utterly perplexed by the arrangements here, and if I have any hope of intervening, I must first understand precisely what jurisdiction they are operating under. I mean, gosh, we both know the judicial system is sorely lacking, even when in the hands of the proper officials, but all of the prisoners we've seen have their say at trial and a jury to sit before if nothing else.'

'What about the Society? Could you write to them for guidance? They may be familiar with the arrangements here.'

'Better still,' I said, an idea ripening in my mind as I spoke, 'I shall visit them, or Lady W. at least, once I have found out all I can at this end.'

'You can't go back to London now. You know that. You said so yourself. It is too dangerous—'

'Yes, well, that was before I understood just how well a simple disguise could fare.'

'Len, do not be so rash. Write or send me if you must, but please, don't take such reckless risks.'

I directed the horses on and made no answer. I did not intend to take a risk but eliminate it. We were headed to the theatre after this to find ourselves a dresser, and our interview with Mrs Humphries had confirmed to me the perfect disguise to take up, not only to allow me to travel back to London incognito but to ensure our safety from the proctors about the town when making our enquiries. From what I could gather, our faces would put us quite at risk of alerting the proctor's attention, particularly if we were seen to be poking about in places they were likely to frequent. The object of our engagement of a theatre dresser was to eradicate any trace of our youth or beauty from our person so that we might go about perfectly unhindered.

'Turn right at the end of this lane,' Annalise said, battling a flyaway strand of hair in the breeze, her cheeks and tip of her nose rosy with cold. We had left the pasture fields behind us now and were travelling beside a more level and orderly field, which I assumed was Parker's Piece, the famous cricket and footballing pitch much talked about by the young fellows of the ton. It was vacant now, a hazy mist hovering above it, its tree-lined edges baring their woody leafless branches save the occasional evergreen standing brilliant-bright against the colourless hue of daylight. 'St. Andrew's Street should continue directly on from this one. – Oh look, *The Castle Pub*, was that not the one the artist's housekeeper mentioned?'

'Yes, I think it was,' I said, slowing the horses again, and it was not long before we came upon the sight of a plain-faced, drab brick building that looked far less foreboding than I was expecting. Indeed, I might have driven right past it without the slightest notion of its purpose, for it was neither tall and imposing like the prisons I had seen—scaffolds perched upon the rooftop—nor surrounded by vast walls and iron bars at the windows. There didn't even appear to be a gatehouse, just an unextraordinary two-storey windowed facade with an iron-barred doorway at its centre, fronting directly onto the roadside. 'Well, there is not much to see,' I said to Annalise, parking up alongside it and lowering the reins. I wondered if that young girl was still contained behind its walls or whether she had been more fortunate and spent a lesser sentence. The thought gave me chills as I retraced the memory of her being dragged along the street by those "bulldogs". But today, there was no sign of any such activity. The roads were quiet, with only a few wagons rolling along the lane every now and then, the odd ushering of cattle, street vendors, hawkers or passersby. After ten minutes of sitting outside watching for any sign of movement, I realised that the only way we were likely to get a clear idea of the place was to find a way to get into it. But I doubted our chances of succeeding by any legitimate means, and despite my curiosity encouraging me to consider *less* legitimate ways to get inside, I knew that damp rooms and infested beds were not fit for a woman with child. So I decided against concocting such mischief.

After a quarter-hour watching the street trundle by in its mundane rhythms of daily motion and the chill creeping beneath our blanket and into our limbs, we set back off in the direction we had come to embark on our final stop of the day.

We ventured further out of the city this time and journeyed through several fields laid to pasture, the occasional windmill or farmhouse, before finally arriving in what fast became clear to be a ramshackle slum of a village. The windmill and fields of grazing cattle seeming a world behind us, not merely a few hundred yards. We crept along a busy lane which threaded its way through crowded buildings: shops, public houses, and tenements pressed closely together.

Then pulled up at the *Sun Inn*, where Mrs Humphries suggested we could stable the horses and trap for a trifle whilst going about our business. Unlike the quiet little row of Petersfield cottages we had just left, Barnwell, said Mrs Humphries, was not a place to leave anything lying about unattended if you wanted to see it again. Her meaning required no elaboration as we trotted through the mean streets and its dilapidated rows of overcrowded dwelling houses and plain terraced cottages. It was more consistent with a London poor district, thick with dubious-looking taverns and poorly maintained blackened brick facades, which I assumed had resulted from the by-products of industry that seemed to predominate the area. Industrial yards and their oversized pluming chimneys and oddly shaped structures rising beyond the rooftops or offering an unwelcome interruption to a plane of open field or pasture.

We stabled the horses without difficulty and asked the groom's directions to the theatre house, which he pointed a little further up on the opposite side of the street. It seemed a very odd district to house a Royal Theatre. I struggled to imagine high society disembarking their teakwood coaches in their finest dress upon the neglected manure-littered cobbles.

It was a small, odd-looking theatre, reached by an obscure alley between two houses. The entrance was humble, a low-rise porch with the name; *Theatre Royal Barnwell* tacked above its doors. I stepped up to them and peered through into the dimness, thinking it not very royal at all and more like a miniature copy of the humbler circus halls of London. I stepped back and caught sight of a poster hanging in the window advertising: *Lovers' Vows,* a comedy, 1st November. I wished we had known of it upon our arrival. It might have given us some amusement to visit the theatre of an evening. Another poster hung beside it on the other pair of doors announcing a three-week season of plays in the summer season next, including a performance of *Virginius*. I hoped there was something due to be performed before that, or I feared our journey might be wasted if the place was shut up for the winter season. I gave the door a gentle nudge and found it locked.

'Perhaps it's too early. It is only just past midday,' Annalise said.

'I fear we may be six months too early from the look of the playbills,' I sighed, stepping back from the building a fraction to work out if there were any other ways into it. I noted a narrow walkway snaking around the right-hand side of the building and beckoned Annalise to follow me down it.

We soon found a pair of plain black windowless doors which were battened down. I let out a sigh, thinking it hopeless. Then in a bold surge of desperation, headed up an exterior stairwell that ran nearly the height of the building. The door at the top of these was ajar, and suddenly the rumble of voices could be heard rising out from it.

'Len, we can't just let ourselves in,' Annalise protested, tugging at my sleeve.

'Why not? We mean no harm, and I can hear people in there. Come on.'

'About time,' said a voice from out of nowhere as we edged into the dim corridor and pulled the door behind us. I turned around to see a young boy of about ten standing behind us at the other end of the hall, a chair perched behind him he seemed to have risen from.

'Hello,' I said, 'I tried the other door but—'

'Well, of course it was locked. I can't be everywhere at once, can I? I've had to work the pulleys and trim the candles since you two are so late, and the pulley boys have had to take your parts for the rehearsals.'

'Our parts?' I frowned at him.

'Come on, no time for all this, you're nearly an hour late, and Fortescue's in a right foul attitude,' he said, ushering us forwards along the narrow hall with such conviction we both edged along it, slightly bewildered.

'Well, alright,' I said, looking back over my shoulder at him, 'we shall come with you, but you are mistaken. We have no appointment here, we—'

'Oh, thank goodness!' came another voice, this time a young woman dashing up just ahead of us.

This time I stopped. 'Look, I'm sorry, I'm not sure who it is you think we are, but you are mistaken—'

'Olivia and Pen, the new London actresses?' the pair chorused.

We both shook our heads, and they both frowned and looked dismayed. 'Well, who are yer then?'

'Nobody. I mean, we have come to make enquiries.'

'Jesus be wept,' cried the girl in accents of despair that made Annalise frown with concern, ''e's gonna go spare when I tell him they've not come.'

'Rather you than me,' said the young lad with a look of sympathy in his eyes as he widened them.

'What are we gonna do?' said the girl.

He shrugged his narrow shoulders and looked between Annalise and I curiously. 'Can you act?' he asked us after a thoughtful pause.

Annalise's frown grew deeper, and I let out a note of a sardonic laugh. 'We are not actors, like I said, and I have not play-acted since I was a girl, making fun with my sisters.' Then suddenly, a contradictory image bloomed into my memory, of Mariella and I pretending at Romeo and Juliet at Betsy's fundraiser last year. I shook the image.

'So, you have a little experience?' The girl asked now, seeming to turn her mind to the proposition the boy had levelled at us.

'Hardly,' I protested.

'Can you read your letters?' asked the boy, and the more he spoke, the more inclined I was to think him quite the little man inside a child's body, confident and enterprising.

'Yes, but I suspect there is a little more to acting than being able to read out lines from what I can gather of the theatricals I have seen.'

'Well, you can't be any worse than the pulley boys: they can't read their letters or act. Besides, you're much prettier. I reckon you'd make a good Queen with that posh voice of yours, and you, Miss, you've not said a word. How are your pipes? Can you sing?'

Annalise broke into a spell of wry laughter at his cheek, but both he and the girl were in earnest.

'You'll be paid and given lodgings if you can pull it off,' he said as if this might seal our agreement.

'Listen,' I said to the pair, 'We have come only to enquire about the hire of a dresser, a good dresser who is handy with paints and clever effects. That is the business on which we have come, nothing more.'

'Well, I might know of just the person,' said the young lad, 'How 'bout a favour for a favour?'

'What do you have in mind?' I asked.

'Well, if I give you the direction of the costume artist you are seeking, and you agree to stand in for today's rehearsals – I'd say we have a bargain.'

I bit down on my lower lip in an effort to hide the smile that was forming at these ridiculous negotiations. 'You cannot be serious?'

'Listen, Miss, if we don't get these rehearsals approved for the circuit tonight, we'll all be out of a job in the mood Fortescue's in, so I am deadly serious.'

'Out of a job because someone didn't turn up?' Annalise said in disbelief.

Both he and the girl nodded, pleading in their eyes.

'This deal is to be the making of this circuit, and if Mr Smith approves of the production this evening, we'll be on tour all over the gaff for the better part of the year. But if he don't, we're all in the suds, so...'

'Alright, I get the measure. But even if we can pull it off—and I am not saying we can—what about after today?'

'Don't matter after today if all the contracts get agreed. We got weeks to find replacements. If it keeps Fortescue sweet today and gets this tour on the road, he'll not be bothered by having to audition a few more girls.'

'And in return for our services today, you can be certain this costume artist will see us, help us?'

'Well, he's one of the best, so I can't promise he'll help. He's quite particular about the work he'll undertake, but I can promise you will find him where I tell you, and if you say Madame Bijoux sent you, he'll certainly hear you out.'

'Who is Madame Bijoux?'

'I'll explain all that later, now; what's your answer?'

I peered across to Annalise, 'Well, give us a moment in private to confer, will you?' I told the pair, and they pulled back a heavy drape and ushered us toward it. We found ourselves on the third tier of the theatre in what I assumed to be someone's private box. I had never seen an empty theatre house before, rows of empty velvet chairs peered back at me as I swept a glance over its panorama, then stared through the dimness to see the shapes of people on the stage, too small and dim to make out well from this height, but we could hear the recital of their lines rising up towards us. 'Shakespeare, it seems. Well?' I said, looking back at Annalise now, who was also taking in the peculiarity of the view.

'You cannot be serious; I have never play-acted and wouldn't know where to begin, even if I wanted to!'

'Well, what have we to lose in the trying? We don't know these people, and they know nothing of us—'

'My nerve, for a start,' she said, already showing a nervous tremor in the brittleness of her tone.

'Very well, I shall do it, and you can watch and tell me how terrible I was afterwards.'

She threw me a bewildered glare, 'You are not nervous?'

'A little, but it looks as though it may be fun to try it, and when else would we be offered such a chance to step onto a real stage? And, to help these people keep their jobs, perhaps, anyway.'

'You two made your mind up?' came a voice and a swish of the velvet curtain, two pairs of anxious eyes staring back at us.

'I am willing to do it, but my friend has decided against.'

'We need both of yer or no deal,' he said flatly.

'Fine, good luck with your tour,' I said, stepping out from the theatre box and into the narrow corridor which led to the exit doors and fire steps.

'What exactly would I have to do?' I turned back to see Annalise talking to the pair.

'Miss Brown, there is no need to alter your decision. We shall seek out another dresser in London if need be.'

'I could get Florence to swap out with you so she can play the Duchess, and you can play her part: one of the Queen's ladies. They don't have much to say at all if that better suits you?'

'Very well, you have your bargain, Master?'

'Puck,' he said, taking up her outstretched hand and shaking it before offering it out to me.

'Miss Andrewes,' I said, and before we had a chance to ask any further questions, the young girl who named herself as Lily, shoved a booklet of scripts into our hands and spirited us off down endless corridors and stairways until we reached a dimly lit hall of doors, one of which she opened and led us into.

'You'll 'ave to share this dressing room with the other girls, but there won't be any costume changes until the Smith gentleman comes this evening. You can leave your things here,' she said, pointing to a wardrobe. 'Now, I'll go and smooth everything over with Fortescue and give him the excuse that you were late in coming due to a broken carriage wheel, alright? I doubt he'll ask anyway,' she scanned through a bundle of papers she'd been clutching to her waist. 'You are Miss Olivia Cartwright,' she said to me, then peered up at Annalise. You are Miss Penelope Yates, should anyone ask.'

'So many aliases,' I smiled at Annalise, 'this is turning out to be quite fun.'

'Well, you've about twenty minutes to learn your lines. That's the best I can do. You'll be wanted on stage for act two. You shall play Queen, and you, Queen's lady two.' And with that, she vanished out of the door in a fluster, and we were left alone in this peculiar dressing room.

I turned about to look at it; a row of dressing tables were set against a large wall-mounted strip of mirror running horizontally across its length. A giant spherical oil lamp poised on each table. A scattering of portraits and a few signed playbills tacked to the walls. Untidy hat stands, hanging rails, and a clutter of travelling trunks beneath them. It all seemed so fascinating to me, having often wondered at the backstage realms of such places when sitting at Drury Lane.

'Well, Miss Penelope Yates,' I said to Annalise, pulling out one of the dressing table chairs for her to sit at, 'It's a pleasure to meet you.' I planted a kiss at her temple as she took her seat. 'Thank you for doing this,' I said more earnestly.

'The scrapes you get me into,' she said mildly and began turning the pages of her script book.

'Well, I think this one could be quite the adventure.'

IN WHAT I WAS SURE was no more than a quarter hour later, Lily was back in the room, ushering us to hurry along, for we were due on stage. If there was any point I was to find myself as nervous as Annalise, it was the moment I stood in the wings, beholding the vast look of the wooden stage from this odd perspective. Its footprint trampled floor, showing up all its marks and imperfections in the glow of amber orbs of candlelight pooling onto it.

'Right, Dickie over there will call out Act two, scene one, any minute, then Teddy will come on, and once he's finished his line, that's your cue, alright?'

I nodded, tracing her fingerprint across the line of script she pointed to. 'Lily,' I said, wondering why she was not on the stage filling in if she was so familiar with the script, 'What is your position here?'

'Senior Runner. Now, clear loud voices or the soundboards won't pick you up,' and with that Dickie called out the act, and she shoved me forward into the glare of light, and I found myself faced with the blackness of the empty theatre, the silhouettes of a few faceless people sat in the pit and a scattering of actors about the stage. The stage was not dressed with scene boards or props, only a black drape at its rear. I heard the click of my steps against the floor and cleared my throat. 'How fares our noble uncle, Lancaster?'

'Cut,' came a voice rising out of the pit, which required no introduction. I could tell from his impatient and obnoxious tone he must be Fortescue, the peevish theatre director who held their jobs by a thread. 'Speak up, damn it girl, if I can't hear you in the pits, how will they hear you in the balcony?'

'Apologies, sir, the soundboards must be better fitted at Drury Lane,' I said with greater volume, and this was met by stifled chuckling from my audience, and I realised that perhaps, the response was neither welcome nor expected. In any case, he seemed to know not what to say to this and, in an even more agitated tone, commanded: 'from the top.'

I stepped back into the wing, and this time, when I came out on cue, I was not so dazzled by my surroundings and took a deep breath and bellowed out my lines with my best conviction. I assumed this to be of satisfactory volume since, this time, the script continued on for the duration of the scene, only interrupted by the occasional elaboration of a stage direction given to someone else.

By the time we had completed Act two, the nerves had dissipated, and I was comfortable again. No, more than that, I was beginning to enjoy this impromptu challenge. One I could have never dreamt up. A possibility as outrageous as unrealistic to a lady of my rank, and yet here I was, playing Queen on a real stage. I even noted that Annalise was more at ease now, having been spared any lines insofar and having only to follow stage directions or chorus in a little laugh or flutter of her fan.

It was then announced we would break for ten minutes whilst the scene boards were set, and I was relieved, for whilst I had managed my lines so far, I had not had ample time to practice the rest. So I went immediately back to my script book and mentally recited them. I was grateful my lines were few, and I knew from the previous act if I was unsure of my cue to speak, a side glance at Lily gesturing to me would prompt it.

MIDWINTER.

BY THE TIME WE COMPLETED the final act, I had begun to see the monotony of this task, the initial thrill of it having burned out after repeating the same line seven times before King Richard got his lines correct and was dealt several harsh admonishments from Fortescue. But unlike those on the stage with me, I would not have to repeat the task day in and day out, and for that, I was grateful now I had a taste of the tedium of repeating the same words in such quick succession.—I had often wondered at how actors committed so many lines to memory as to manage an entire show without prompting, and yet I could see now how it was possible, relentless repetition etched into memory and mime. I even knew half of King Richard's lines by heart at the end of the final rehearsal and could not prevent myself from mentally reciting them too.

When Fortescue called out our supper break with strict instructions not to overindulge and return sluggish and to be back on set by six-o-clock, or else, I had wondered at whether I could face going back for the actual performance, feeling utterly bored by it now. Not that it was a public performance, at least. Just enough to impress this new patron, I was told. But a bargain was a bargain, I reminded myself as we crammed into the dressing room to fetch our cloaks, hats and gloves. Whereas Annalise and I could return to the comfy confines of Stapleford this evening, putting this odd day down to experience, these people could be out of a job—their very livelihoods—by the end of the day if things went ill. So with this in mind, I pushed through my growing mood of ennui and followed the ladies out of the dressing room, through the proper theatre entrance and down the Newmarket Road to a nearby inn where they were boarding and had a supper room set up in wait of their timely arrival.

'I don't believe we've met before,' said an actress who had been playing Duchess of Gloucester, as we filtered into the dining parlour to find a seat. 'Theodora Bradley, but everyone calls me Theo,' she said, pulling up a chair beside Annalise and I.

'Olivia, and this is Pen,' I said, carefully checking my memory for our newly acquired names. It had taken me months to adjust to being referred to as "Miss Andrewes" at Stapleford, so I was glad inhabiting this new alias would be but a brief and fleeting spell. 'Pleased to meet you.'

'So, you're from the London theatre circuits then?' she said, and I suddenly knew I was to get no relief from play-acting, even in this much-needed break before our return to the theatre house.

'Yes,' I said briefly, busying with my napkin and filling my glass with what I hoped was only barley water or cordial.

'So what brings you to the Norwich Circuits?'

'Unforeseen circumstances,' I said, hoping my guarded accent would stifle any further questions on that head.

She nodded and took a sip from her glass before saying, 'Well, let's 'ave your top ten then?'

'My top ten?'

'Yeah, it's a newcomer's tradition. You have to regale us all with your top ten roles. Five of the best and five of the worst,'

'Ah, I see,' I smiled, trying not to meet Annalise's terrified glare in my peripheral view as I searched my memory for some of the plays I had seen in London recently, as all eyes fixed upon me around the table. 'Well, I don't have that many to offer you. I've only been acting this past year.' I took another long sip from my glass. 'But the best, I would say, was Countess de Morvill in *Therese*, and the worst: Phoebe in *Rosina*. Ah, what's the soup, please, footman?' I asked as he placed a steaming tureen pot down on the table.

'Ah, fresh talent,' said Theo, and I nodded and swiftly moved on to permit no further questioning.

'White soup, ma'am,' he said, and I offered out my bowl rather quickly, hoping to fill my mouth with food and render conversation impossible. 'It's my favourite,' I said to the rest of my company and decided, whilst sipping slowly from my spoon to draw it out, that the best way to avoid unwanted conversation was to answer a question with another question. So when my bowl was cleared for the next course, I made an active effort to direct the flow of conversation and level all manner of questions at our company, leaving them little room to pose any further at Annalise or me. And since people seemed fond of talking about themselves, it was not too difficult to draw them out with a display of keen interest and understanding. It was during their own speeches, which had proved more interesting than I had supposed as they spoke of their backgrounds, accomplishments and mixed experiences, that I realised what an opportunity this posed for us to make connections with the town folk. Maisy (or Queen's lady one), was a local girl and had the street-wise airs of someone who had been about the town in her time. The others were from all over the place, but undoubtedly familiar enough with the area as they discussed which taverns they would frequent later on, to either celebrate their new contract or drown their sorrows, depending on which way their luck fell.

By the time we were crammed into the dressing room at half past five, all fighting for a space to put our costumes on, we had become friendly and comfortable amongst each other. The awkwardness of our introduction seemed fast forgotten as we offered each other our backs for assistance. It struck me that I had never before been amongst so many unclothed ladies, and ones who seemed little conscious of it as they lifted off their winter layers and exchanged them for over-embellished medieval dresses. It was me who felt conscious for a change, wondering whether the modest, but certainly more rounded, shape of my waist could be noticed beneath my shimmy. I clung close to Annalise in the hope of being better shielded from view.

We were waiting in the wings by ten minutes to the hour when Lily huddled us together in a whisper, to convey Fortescue's message that Smith and his men were now arrived. This was make or break, and no time for low voices or forgotten lines. Then, without further ado, Dickie announced the play and Teddy stepped out onto the stage to deliver the opening lines whilst the rest of us watched on in trepidation.

Bedbugs.

January 1822. - Eleanor.

'Thank the lord that's over with. For better or worse, it's done, and I need a stiff drink,' said Theo, as we changed back out of our costumes.

'How d'you think it went, Theo?' asked Maisy as she lifted her foot to the chair and unlaced her boots, flashing a pale leg up to the knee.

'I think it went well, our best yet anyway,' she said hopeful, and this was met with sighs of relief which told me her opinion was well regarded and she was perhaps the most experienced amongst the troupe. I made a mental note to take better care to avoid such direct conversation with her and risk being found out, now I had ascertained this.

'If only Teddy hadn't bungled his lines in scene three,' Florence added, 'I'd say we otherwise must have impressed Smith. Forty really needs to warn him off the ale so early in the day—small beer only for him until after the show.'

This was met with general agreement as fabric shifted and rustled, and boots dropped onto the dressing room floor with a thud.

Annalise and I changed quickly, relieved to be at the end of our day's work and eager to seek out Puck to receive our part in the bargain, and the direction of this dresser that had been half-forgotten throughout the course of the day, amid so much pressure to remember our parts, and not only in the play. But our exit was not to be swift as Lily announced we were to go directly to the stage to hear Fortescue's announcement once dressed. I wasn't sure I wanted to stay to hear it. If it was ill news, I would feel responsible for it. And as we single-filed our way back onto the stage through narrow corridors, I felt the faintest stir of nausea starting up.

'Well, he said, stepping up onto the stage and looking at us each in turn, 'It's been a tough day and not your best. But. You shall have a chance to improve on it since we've just been signed for a preliminary three-month tour on the Norwich circuit!'

'Yes!' shouted Puck, punching the air, and Letty flung her arms about Theo's shoulders and pulled her into a squeeze.

'Go out and celebrate because you've got two days' holiday before we set off for Bury, which has been allocated as our home for the rest of the rehearsals and will be home to our first performance on the circuit before Lent, starting as a subsidiary act before the usual player's feature. If that's well received, we'll get a prime spot at Norwich. So let your hair down now because once we leave, there'll be no holidays until we've nabbed that prime-time spot. Do you understand me? Lily will have all the details of our onward journey by tomorrow. Now get out of here. —Not you, Miss Cartwright. I want a word.'

I baulked at this when I registered he was talking to me, and I looked up to see the faces of the other girls' disapproval, although I wasn't sure what it meant.

'Go on, clear off the rest of you,' he waved a hand in their direction and they filtered out towards the wings accordingly.

'Don't be long Liv. We'll wait for you, alright?' Called Theo, as they vanished beyond my view.

I nodded vaguely, wondering what on earth that meant, as Mr Fortescue stepped forward and ushered me along with an open arm. 'Miss Cartwright, may I call you Olivia?'

I smiled thinly whilst mentally declaring him an impertinent bigot. 'What is it, sir? I don't mean to keep the ladies waiting,'

'Have a seat with me, will you, Olivia,' he said, directing me down the stage steps towards the pit benches where he had been sat barking orders and reprimands for most of the day. I was careful to maintain my distance as I lowered myself onto the nearest, expecting some admonishment for our "late" arrival today, reminding myself to accept whatever reprimand was coming with good grace since I would never have to see this irritating man again, and I did not mean to spoil things for the others.

'Well, sir, what do you wish to say to me?'

He seemed a little taken aback at my address but made no remark upon it, 'Well, firstly, Olivia, I should like to offer you my personal congratulations for such a stellar performance, you were the star of our show tonight, and it did not go unnoticed by Mr Smith...'

It was not what I had expected him to say, but I accepted it with a meek smile and thanked him for his compliments.

'In fact, Mr Smith has expressed a particular wish to pay his compliments to you himself over a dinner at his house tonight.'

'How very considerate of him. But as you said, sir, we shall not have another opportunity for a holiday after this, and my friends are waiting for me,' I added, rising from my seat.'

He put an arm out to obstruct my leaving but fell short of touching me. 'Olivia, you understand how *important* it is we maintain a favourable relationship with Mr Smith, don't you?'

I stepped back in the opposite direction. 'Hmm, perhaps you should go to dinner with him then, sir, since I cannot.'

'Don't be such a fool, girl. You pass up an opportunity like this when a gentleman like him can make a sensation out of someone like you. Think of your career. Of what it could do for you—'

'Liv,' came Annalise's voice as she stepped out onto the stage, '...everyone's waiting for you.'

'I'm coming directly', I called back. 'Goodnight, Mr Fortescue.'

A HALF-HOUR LATER, we were sat around a large oval table with our new colleagues in a shabby tavern, packed to the brim with merry drinkers, of both sexes. I had never been anywhere like it in my life, and though my first instinct was to turn around and walk straight out of the place in abject disgust, I had started to thaw and find it not altogether too bad in our happy company. For everyone was happy, now they had secured their jobs, and laughter and generosity flowed as freely as the ale—which I had tried to decline politely—only to find one actor or another had bought a tankard for me anyway. I pretended to sip from one of them whilst pushing the others in front of someone whose cup was nearly empty.

It seemed that Annalise lacked the conviction to decline their insistent invitation to celebrate during my short absence, and the minute we stepped into the theatre corridor, our arms were scooped up into theirs. We were shuffled down the Newmarket Road to this tavern without a hope of getting a word in to the contrary. We had at least managed to get the direction of our costume dresser from Puck; someone named Jasper who was currently found at the *New Theatre,* Bury St. Edmunds, until he moved onto Ipswich next week with the rest of his troupe. He was in the employ of the *Norwich Players* circuit and toured everywhere with them, whereas they were new to this circuit, having toured in several provinces about the country and been long since trying to settle to a more regular routine. That was Fortescue's trouble retaining their actors, they explained, the constant shuffling up from one place or another and from inn to inn. Dickie, Letty and Theo were the only surviving originals since the troupe started up five years ago. Now they could settle if it all worked out. Fortescue had promised to secure them proper apartments somewhere central to the circuit so they could have rooms of their own and a sense of belonging to a place—something most of them had long left behind them. From what I could gather, it sounded an exciting but exhausting way to live, but I supposed that was why they were so tight-knit. They were each other's family, and home, all rolled into one whilst their feet barely touched the ground.

It felt wicked to go along with the charade of us travelling on to Bury with them when they had been so open and welcoming to us, even if a little over-familiar. But Puck and Lily were adamant they would deliver the news themselves tomorrow and not spoil the merry mood this evening which had been hard-won, and much looked to. So, we agreed to keep our silence, and since we had no choice but to return to the inn with them that night, the roads no longer drivable in the dark, we thought it best to slip out early in the morning and leave the task to them. I was grateful Annalise had the foresight to have the innkeeper dispatch a courier to Stapleford at dinner earlier, to let them know not to expect us back on time. Now, as we sat in the tap room whilst the innkeeper's wife fetched the keys to Miss Cartwright and Miss Penn's room, we were obliged to pay double the fee to dispatch another message to them at such an uncivil hour to say we would not return until tomorrow. I wondered what had become of the real Olivia and Pen, why they had not turned up and whether or not they would. Hopefully not tonight, in any case, to discover us occupying their room.

With reflections of this odd day circling my thoughts, I snuggled into the hard bed. The mattress seeming to have long lost the plumpness of its stuffing and the blankets stiff and scratchy against the bare skin of my arms, I felt myself floating into the in-between veil of sleep.

I don't know how long had passed when I woke to thunderous rapping on the door, which startled me quickly to consciousness. Annalise was already up, calling out: 'Who's there?'

'It's me, Theo,' came the reply, and I let out a sigh of relief, grateful it was neither the London actresses nor some rough fellow chancing his luck. It certainly was not the respectable kind of inn I had occasionally stayed in when breaking a long journey to relatives. With all the late-night ramblings and hullaballoo coming up from the street below as the many taverns continued to empty, I was half afraid of meeting with some catastrophe in such a low place.

As it happened, the only calamity had been that Letty, having overindulged on the gin tonight, had vomited all over the bed Theo had been sharing with her. The place was now uninhabitable, Theo explained when Annalise let her into the room.

'Could I bunk up with you two? Letty's gone in with Maisy, so they're full, and there's no answer at Flo's door.'

It seemed impossible to decline her at such an hour, and whilst I did not feel entirely comfortable with sharing a bed with a stranger, she at least was not out of her wits cropsick like the others. However many she had sunk, she was obviously better at holding her cups than they were.

We offered her the middle of the bed and settled back into it once she had stripped down to her night dress, the uncomfortable mattress crammed up with the three of us, making it impossible to avoid pressing in close to one another. It was for this very reason I preferred her to go in between, in case, through some force of habit, we forgot her presence through the night and snuggled up a little too intimately together as we often did at Stapleford.

I looked forward to returning to our generous plush bed tomorrow, feeling quite out of comfort with our surroundings just now. Perhaps it *had* been a crackbrained idea to enter such an irregular bargain. Yet, despite it all, I knew I had enjoyed the thrill of such a spontaneous adventure into this unfamiliar realm of life.

I was staring into the darkness at length, listening to the deep familiar hum of Annalise's breath, which told me she'd got back to sleep. I, however, could not settle, and every time I felt the relief of it within my grasp, I'd feel a brush of Theo's icy toes against one of my own as she wrestled to get comfortable in the space between us.

In the end, I got up, tired of the restless spinning of mind competing with the bodily fatigue of a long and eventful day. I moved to the window and peered down onto the street that had quietened slightly from its earlier raucous.

'Can't sleep?' came Theo's voice causing me to start and turn at the sound of it.

'No,' I said quietly and turned back to the window.

'Me neither,' she replied, getting up from the bed and coming up behind me to discover what I was looking at. 'D'you mind if I go out for a smoke?'

'No,' I shrugged, wondering why she would want to go out there with all the ruffians that seemed to be loitering about the place at such an hour. But when she pulled her bed jacket and shawl back on, lit her cigarello from the waning fire embers and opened the window to its fullest extent before stepping out onto its ledge, I realised she did not mean to go down.

'You coming?' she asked, exhaling a curl of smoke and offering out a hand to me through the sash opening.

I moved in closer and peered at the ledge. 'Is it safe?'

'Sturdy as an Ox's back,' she declared and helped me onto it, the January night air throwing up a cold damp breeze as I cleared the window and stepped furtively along the path of flat rooftop, a shiver creeping up the length of my arms.

I followed Theo around the ledge until she sat down, slumped against a pitched rise of roof, and puffed a silvery plume of smoke up towards the night sky. I sat beside her, the slate cold against my back and stared up to see the sky thick with stars, glittering like scattered shards of glass about to reign down on us.

'It's great up here, isn't it?' she said, her chin turned up, staring into the depths above.

'Yes, but arctic!' I complained, clutching my knees into my elbows and tucking the hem of my shimmy snug about my ankles to hold tight against the cold.

'Here,' she offered, out sprawling her cloak and offering me a length of it to crawl beneath.

'Thank you.'

'How'd it go with Fortescue?'

'Brief.'

'I thought he'd be out to try his luck with you pretty new recruits.'

'Well, his luck was in short supply tonight. '

She laughed, 'Gave him the brush off, did yer?'

'Yup.'

'Good for you. Not your type then?'

'Couldn't be further from it. Obnoxious git.'

'Ain't they all?'

'What, theatre directors?'

'Men.'

This time I laughed, took the offered cigarillo, and put it to my lips, taking her example. 'Not all of them. But I daresay a great many.'

'In my experience, it's the lot of 'em. Oh—steady on,' she said, slapping my back as I coughed and spluttered, the smoke burning my throat. 'You're not s'posed to inhale it, yer know.'

I handed the cigarillo back to her.

'More of a snuff girl, are you?'

'Neither, actually.'

'Probably for the best,' she said, still laughing at my recovering splutters whilst drawing expertly upon the thing without a hint of irritation. 'So, why'd you turn him down anyway? You already have a sweetheart?'

I avoided the last part of her question. 'Why shouldn't I? I've no interest, like I said.'

'Not many turn him down...especially the new ones.'

'Well, I'm thankful not to count myself amongst them then, for he had all the charm of a hyena and the manners of a wild boar.'

'Can't argue with that.'

'Anyway, it wasn't himself he was trying for, but Smith—encouraged me to accept his invitation to dine this evening and receive his "personal compliments."'

'Don't tell me: you were the star of the show and you're going places, or at least you *could* be...just so long as you went to dinner?'

I laughed again, 'Almost word perfect.'

'Well, unlike you fresh-faced innocents, I've been in this line for over a decade, seen it all, met a million of Fortescue's cut, and a fair lot worse too.'

'How have you managed it all the years?'

'Goes with the territory I suppose, you get used to it, and Fortescue knows the score with me and doesn't give me any trouble.'

'Oh, how's that then?'

'Well, let's just say he's fully aware he is not to my taste and if he does think of directing anyone else my way, then it had better be in the petticoat line, or they'll be met with my best right hook and maybe worst still if I've had a good spell in the tavern.'

I was quite taken aback by her frank and candid answer. Was she saying what I thought she was?

'Don't look so stunned, Queenie. I know you know what I mean. I reckon you understand my taste better than you like to let on.'

'I don't know what gives you that impression,' I said far too defensively to weigh it with any real conviction. 'Anyway, my name's not Queenie.'

'Not Olivia either, is it? But Queenie suits you better anyway. You talk like a Queen, have the right airs, and you certainly have the fine looks of one,' she grinned teasingly and winked at me.

I stiffened and sat upright. 'I think I'm going to go back to bed,' I said.

'Ah, don't be like that. I'm only funning with yer. I don't care what your name is or who you like to fuck. Believe me; I'm the last person who'd take strife with yer on either account. I'm just glad you and Blondie managed to save the day, or we'd all be in a fix tonight.'

I relaxed back into my position. 'What gave me away?' I asked instead, perplexed by this superior wisdom she seemed to possess, despite how careful we'd been to conceal ourselves.

'Well, for a start, I know Liv and Pen from my early runner days at the Haymarket, so that was no great mystery to solve since neither of you look anything like 'em.'

'I didn't mean that. I meant—'

'That you're a girl after me own heart?'

I nodded, and she shrugged and tossed her cigarillo end over the rooftop, a fleeting shimmer of amber sparks flashing across the sky. 'Dunno, really. I suppose you can just tell after a while. Call it instinct if you like.'

'Well, that's some instinct. I hadn't a clue you were...' I couldn't find the right word.

'A Tom? Well, according to the rest of the world, it's as clear as day, so you really do need to sharpen your wits if you've a hope of recognising your own sort.'

'A Tom?'

'Dash it, Queenie, you really 'ave been living in a castle fortress, haven't yer. A Tom. A Sapphist. A Tribade, call it what you like. I prefer *Fricatrice* myself.' She laughed at her own joke, but to me, it was not funny. It was a revelation. There were actually words to describe people like me. Like *us*. And there were others. We were not an isolated anomaly...

'And these names, they are well known, to describe lady loves?'

'Lady loves,' she repeated, bursting into a gut-rumbling fit of laughter and slapping her knee. 'That's a gooden, lady loves.'

'If you are just going to make fun of everything I say, then I may as well go back to bed.'

She curtailed her laughter. 'Alright, alright. I'm still a bit on the squiffy side, and I'm not used to talking to such a square.'

I frowned and blew into my cupped palms to warm my hands.

'Let's start again, shall we? What would you like to know?'

'Everything, I suppose. I didn't know it was an acknowledged thing.'

'Well, it is, and it ain't. – That is, most folks prefer not to acknowledge it, but even they know about folk like us.'

'They do?'

'Well, maybe not in your circles Queenie, but in the world, as I know it, everyone knows about Toms and Molly's, even the ones who prefer to turn a blind eye.'

'Molly's?'

She rolled her eyes and then said more patiently: 'Men who like men, the effeminates. It's where the name "Molly House" comes from. —You've really never heard of this before, have you?'

'No,' I said, shaking my head in earnest. But I meant to find out as much as I could whilst in the company of one who not only did, but seemed perfectly well versed in such matters. 'So why do they call their houses Molly houses? I mean, it is a rather brazen advert for something I'd imagine they'd prefer to keep quiet. I saw a fellow sentenced to death for... relations with a man.'

'Yes, bad luck for them if they get found out, poor buggers. But a Molly house isn't a name for where they live. It's where they work, although I suppose there are some that board too.'

I frowned at this.

'You know, selling their wares. Their *services.*'

'To other men?' I said, astonished, the penny dropping.

She nodded. 'Big business. Never short of a customer in that line. Shame it's not the same for our sex, or I could happily make a career change and tell Fortescue where to shove his script.'

'Is it really?' I had never thought there was such a thing as male prostitutes, less still for it to be a busy trade.

'Seriously. My old bud Franco made his fortune by the age of nine and twenty. Set himself up nicely in his own place in Paris and now lives the high life like one of the toffs. He was particularly fortunate, though, very well suited. A right pretty femme type he was, attracted punters like flies on horseshit.'

I tried not to baulk at her vulgar language and was temporarily distracted by the hissing screams of fighting alley cats in the streets below.

'Ah, I miss him, though. Those were the good old days, at the Haymarket in London when work flowed easily and I had a bed to call my own.'

'Does he ever come back here to visit?'

'Nope, and you can't blame him. He'd be hanged if he ever returned. The peelers spent years on his tail. In the end, he was infamous in his trade and had no choice but to hop across the channel.'

'Why France?'

'It's a safe haven for Molly's now. Napoleon changed the laws there, didn't he, and now it's every Molly's dream to ship off over there where they can live in peace without fear of the gallows.'

'And are Toms left alone there too?'

'We're left alone everywhere, even here. Ain't no laws against the game of flats,' she winked, and I sighed in relief, having long sought an answer to this question. I couldn't wait to tell Annalise in the morning. 'So, you say there are no women in the same profession, I mean, not for the purpose of serving men.'

'Not many, though it's not unheard of. A few listed in *Harrisons* cater to such tastes, but rarely exclusively. The demand from men is far more lucrative, and if you want to keep your belly full, I suppose you have to go where the coin is offered. You couldn't pay me to switch sides, though. That's why I'm stuck with Fortescue and his troupe.'

It startled me how matter-of-factly she spoke of this. Like the consideration of prostitution was like any other kind of trade. Like switching your theatre costume for an apron. Then I thought back to Tilly, our declined offer to help her out of that line and her eagerness to return to Madame. Was such an intimate task really a matter of calculated pragmatism to those who relied on the money? A matter of indifference so long as they could pay their way. I found it hard to believe, given my limited but ghastly experience of bedroom duties with Giles. No amount of gold upon the earth could compensate me for being at his disposal each night.

'What's on your mind? You thinking of a career change?'

I nudged her shoulder with mine playfully. This time I knew she meant to tease me and was learning this was her style. 'What do you know about the Spinning House?'

'That I'm not any good at spinning wool, so I think I'll stick with Fortescue for now.'

'It's the name of a gaol of sorts, for fallen women, in Cambridge.'

'Fallen women, gosh Queenie, you do live up to your namesakes, don't yer?'

'I didn't mean it as an insult. I just meant women who have found themselves in difficult circumstances and have to resort to—'

'The oldest profession. Tell me a girl who ain't found herself in difficult circumstances at some point?'

I shrugged. I had no answer to give, for I had never known anyone who had, beyond Tilly.

'Well, Queenie, I'm starting to think you haven't even been in the theatre line for a year with how green you are. What are you really doing here with us lot? I mean, *really*.'

'Promise you shan't breathe a word.'

She nodded.

'You will learn it anyway in the morning, so a few hours shall hardly make a difference. It was a mistake. We came this morning to make enquiries after a costume dresser and Puck mistook us for Olivia and Pen. Struck a bargain with us that if we agreed to take their place for the day, he would give me the direction of an excellent man who could help us.'

'He's a wily little scamp, that one. I told Fortescue he'd be worth taking a chance on. He'll be going places with wits like that. Only twelve, and able to gammon a couple of fine ladies into such a bargain. So, are you even actresses?'

I shook my head.

'Be Jesus, girl. You're full of surprises, aren't you? Well, you must be a natural then, for you had us all fooled. I mean, I could tell Blondie suffered the stage fright, but you, you walked on up there like you'd done it a thousand times before.'

I supposed I had really, every day since my childhood. Society acting. Was that a thing? I was sure it was not so different, really.

She frowned thoughtfully a moment, 'What d'you want with a dresser then if you ain't actresses?'

'It's a long story.'

'The night is young sweet cheeks...'

'I need a disguise.'

'Ooh, now you've piqued my interest.'

'The University proctors are locking girls up in that excuse for a gaol upon no lawful charge and conducting private trials and distributing sentences without a jury.'

'Bad business, to be sure. But what's it gotta do with you?'

'Come, Theo, you must see that if these men can go about plucking our sex from the streets for little more than suspicion, it is a very bad tone indeed. Surely it's the responsibility of all of our sex to be naturally outraged at such a treacherous scheme. Such unfettered power is always dangerous to us all.'

'Aye, I do see. But no one listens to the likes of us, especially against that sort. So what's to be done?'

'Well, if I could just get into the place and work out what precisely goes on in there, I have some friends in London who are well connected and can get their voices across the line, use their influence to improve things. They form a society that helps women in such circumstances.'

'Fallen women?' she smirked. 'So how do folk like you come to have such grand connections? Hmm, tell me that...'

'Does it matter?'

'It does if you want our help to get you into that place.'

'You would help us?'

She nodded. 'It's a worthy enough cause. I daresay if you've got the brains and connections, I could rally up a professional troupe of actors into your service. Besides, it seems we are in your debt.'

I squeezed her into a reckless hug. 'Thank you, Theo. Yes! That's it. We could conjure a scheme to get in there, surely. Although I'm not sure what,' I said thoughtfully, peering blindly across the horizon of rooftops, clouds of warm air curling from the chimneys as our breath fogged with our words.

'I'm sure we can think of something. Maisy's the one to ask for pointers. She's a local. Only been with us a couple of weeks since we started rehearsals here and Sal did a bunk with that circus ringmaster. We've not got long, though, if we are back on the road up to Bury in a couple of days. I take it you won't be coming with us then, after all? '

I shook my head. Lily was going to tell you all in the morning. She didn't want to spoil the celebratory mood this evening. She said you have time to find replacements now you've secured the contract.'

'So were you just gonna creep out at first light without saying goodbye then?'

I turned away guiltily. 'It seemed for the best.'

'Shame. You and Blondie could have made a happy addition to our troupe. Especially with how you handle Fortescue. I've never seen him so tight-lipped since you gave him that cutting reply. – Oh, that did make us laugh. Won us all over, you know.'

'Did it?' I asked, searching for a recollection of what she referred to.

'He'll be sorry to lose you, though, I daresay. Not many can pull off a Queenie like you did today. Where'd you learn to talk like that anyway? You from one of them gentlefolk families, I bet.'

I nodded.

'So what happened? Why are you—'

'In reduced circumstances?'

'That's one way of putting it.'

'I ran away.'

'Any particular reason?'

'I didn't want to marry the man I was intended for.' It was only a half-lie, I considered, thinking it for the best to keep it simple.

'Fair enough. So, what's the score, you and Blondie together?'

'No. What about you, are you and Letty a pair?'

'Nah. Not really. She dabbles. Anyone's after a few gin's ...'

'Dabbles?'

'Yeah, you know. Will have a night's pleasure and flirtation with a girl, but nothing serious, because the next night she'll be off with a bloke from the audience.'

'So she likes men and women?'

She nodded. 'Plenty do. In this line, anyway. That's what makes it so hard for girls like us to find a real sweetheart.'

'It's common then?' I asked, an irritating flashback to Richards rousing the question: was I one of *those* types of girls?

'Seems to be if my luck is anything to go by...'

'There must be others of the same mind as you?'

'There are. It's finding 'em that's the trouble. In London, it wasn't so difficult if you knew the right haunts. But out in these provinces we've been touring for the past five years, it's harder to find such places.'

'There are places where like-minded females...frequent?'

'Uh-huh. I mean, it's not as clear cut as it is for Molly's, they need only look for the nearest pillory for a flagpost, without the speciality houses, taverns and well-known haunts. But a few taverns and coffee houses around the London theatres attract a more particular crowd of lady folk. And if you're lucky, you might get invited to the private parties that are completely off the radar.'

This was all such a startling revelation to me I could hardly take it all in. There was a whole community lurking in London's underbelly, and I had likely been but yards from such places without ever knowing it. If only I could take Annalise to such a place, show her we were not alone. Show her there were places we might be at ease. 'Do you remember the direction of any of these places in London?'

She sat a moment thoughtfully before answering. A few, but they'll eat you alive. Such a green pretty thing. I could take you, though, look out for you. We got us a couple of days' leave now, so we could take a cab into London tomorrow afternoon. I'll take you about the town in the evening. I've still some old friends there who'd put us up for a night.'

'Oh no, I'm sorry, Theo, you are very kind, and it is a very generous offer, but—'

'I'm not your type...'

'No. No, it's not that, you see, I can't go to London. I'm in hiding, remember, and London is dangerous territory for me.'

'Well, it's better than the usual line of brush offs.' She winked.

'I'm hoping the dresser in Bury can give me a fitting disguise that would permit me to move about freely again, wherever I am. That's when I shall go to London again.'

'So, who is this dresser?'

'Jasper Finley, at Bury.'

She laughed out loud. 'Well, if anyone can sort you out, it's him. And you'll meet your first real Molly. –Though he's more of a Queen than even you.'

'You know him then?'

'Everyone knows of Jasper in the theatre world. He used to be the most sought-after name in London before he got outshone by the Gaynesford brothers and disappeared. I didn't even know he was up this way now.'

It was reassuring to hear that Puck had lived up to his part in the bargain and this fellow was both a known entity and renowned in his trade.

'So I'll guess we'll be seeing you in Bury at some point then, if you're planning to seek him out?'

'Yes, to be sure, the sooner, the better, before he moves on.'

'Well, we better get some kip. You'll be growing icicles off them rosy cheeks if we stay out a moment longer.'

The Mermaid.

January 1822. - Eleanor.

'**Y**ou told her about us?' Annalise barked at me in accents of accusation.

We were journeying back to Stapleford in the trap in the first morning light, cutting our way through swathes of grey fog lying low over the lands, and doing our best to keep warm as the icy wind threatened temperatures conducive to snow. 'No. Not about *us*. I confessed only on my own account. And she had guessed as much anyway, so there was no point in denying it.'

She relaxed back into her seat a little now, quietly contemplative.

I had hoped she would be pleased with the news I gave her this morning. News of our safety from the wrath of the law, news that we were not alone, that there were names for us, places we could congregate. But it had not seemed to produce any happy effect on her. She seemed more concerned with me giving away clues about us than what wisdom Theo had bestowed upon my understanding.

It was a marvel to me. It had kept me up long into the night, reflecting on it all. Theo snoring into the pillow beside me, and Annalise sound asleep, perfectly oblivious to the revelations fizzing through my head. It all seemed now a matter not perchance, our walking into the theatre at such a precise moment, but a matter of some higher alignment. Our paths intentionally crossing. A happy kind of fate, where we got to spare them their jobs, and in exchange, we got answers to long-held questions; to learn about our place in the world. That there *was* a place in the world for women like us, however obscure. We were not the first or only, but part of a lesser-known populace. Operating beneath the radar of ordinary society and yet in plain sight. I had started to look at people differently now, looking out for any clue that they could be of the same persuasion, seeing if that sign Theo was able to detect my inclinations from could be fathomed out.

I wondered what it would feel like to be amongst such liberating company. To be able to embrace Annalise tenderly without concern for our whereabouts or other eyes upon us. I had had to be so guarded and aloof when we were not alone, frightened of forgetting myself and offering some hint of our real affections with some unguarded faux pas. I had not even been able to kiss her for the better part of twenty-four hours now. It was the thought of returning to that privacy which kept me warm as we weaved our way through open windy lanes, our lips chapped and noses red-tipped. The comforting thought of locking ourselves away in our quarters when we returned home and lavishing each other in all the stifled affections that had built up this past day. A large clean bed and generous fire to bask in the glow of as we stripped down to nothing.

We had woken up with what Annalise was certain were bedbug bites upon our legs from our night at the inn. It gave me a renewed sense of appreciation as we sunk upon our plump, clean mattress at Stapleford, having had a spell in such an unpleasant chamber.

And so that's how we spent our brief interval back at Stapleford, from the moment we pulled our gloves from our rigid fingers stiff with cold, to the moment we set out for Bury St. Edmund's by way of the stagecoach four days later.

It seemed inevitable we would meet up with the theatre troupe since they would now be in situ in the very place we were to seek out the famed Jasper. I meant to call on them whilst there. I had not forgotten Theo's pledge to help us with the *Spinning House* coup. – Although I still hadn't figured it out entirely, I had a vague notion that we might create some fitting charade between us. Pretend to be tradespersons arrived to undertake some task or the other, or be enquiring after a prisoner or some such thing. We could all go in disguise if Jasper was willing to help. That way, we would all remain anon should anything go ill.

We arrived at the *Angel Hotel* with Annalise dressed in her maid's clothes and me in a black veil and dress, bearing my wedding band and a Banbury tale to offer the hotelier about attending a funeral in the district and being forced to travel alone since my husband was away to sea—a Captain in the Royal Navy—I told him for good effect. He accepted us into the place without any trouble. Perhaps I *was* a natural at this acting game after all, for I was expecting to be turned away and forced to find another place. After our stay at the Barnwell Inn, I had no intention of putting up at another low establishment after that uncomfortable chilly night beneath scratchy blankets. Besides, I did not want to risk booking into the same one as the theatre troupe either, by way of accident. For as much as I liked them, I did not fancy another night of being squashed into a bed with Theo because Letty'd had too much gin again, or to have to hear Teddy singing vulgar ditties through the wall when he finally came in from the tavern. Besides, I knew it would make Annalise feel better about reuniting with them if we were beneath different roofs.

It had taken me a time to get to the bottom of her poor initial reaction to my conversation with Theo that night. It transpired that she was suspiciously jealous of me after finding out Theo was similarly inclined and that I had spent a while up on the roof talking intimately with her, then the remainder of the night pressed back-to-back with her in the bed. I supposed it was to be expected after Richards. Trust took time to rebuild, and I knew not enough had elapsed yet to put her at complete ease, however far we had come since the fall out of it all. But it did not take long for her to see I was in earnest, realise that it had all been perfectly above board and that nothing untoward had passed between us. Nor did I wish it to.

It was true that I liked Theo. She was interesting company full of fascinating anecdotes and not afraid to speak openly on matters most would not even countenance the mention of. She was certainly brasher than the company I was used to keeping, but I liked her, in a perfectly platonic tone of affection, nothing more. Yes, she did exude a certain kind of easy confidence I could not deny I found enchanting, but there was not an ounce of intention on my part in that direction. I was reminded every day upon waking next to Annalise how lucky I was to still have her beside me. How close I had come to risking my true heart's desire for such fickle diversions. When I looked at her, I saw my future. Everything I wanted and needed to be happy. My only wish was that we need not hide away to live as we desired. To be able to hold her hand as we walked the streets together, kiss her good morning whether there was a servant about the room or not. I knew that the world at large would always bind us to secrecy, but knowing there were parts of it, however rare and obscure, where we could be at ease in the company of other like-minded ladies, might just be enough to make it all the more bearable.

It was for this very reason I had insisted we lodge overnight in Bury, even though the journey was fairly short, and the matter might have been dealt with in the space of a day. I wanted Annalise to have a chance to talk to Theo and hear what she had to say for herself, not just my overexcited paraphrasing. I wished she had been awake that night to sit up with us and share in the revelation of such a conversation. Had I known beforehand how it was to turn out, I would have woken her expressly for it. But it was the last topic I had expected to flourish, and with a stranger at that.

So once we had set our things into our room at the *Angel Hotel*, we wasted no time in heading for the address Puck had furnished us with. It was a little walk from our lodgings but turned out to be a fine terraced house set in a pleasant row but a stone's throw from the theatre on Westgate Street. It certainly seemed like his line of work paid far better than the acting troupes by the look of the middle-class dwelling and the finely dressed manservant who answered the front door, only to turn us away almost as abruptly when we explained our business.

'You were supposed to say Madame Bijoux sent us, remember,' Annalise reminded me when the door was closed upon us. I turned about and knocked again.

'Yes?' said the manservant in exasperated accents.

'Sir, forgive me, but I forgot an important part of the message; please tell your master that Madame Bijoux sent us.'

'I see,' he said, to my astonishment, stepping aside and admitting us into the house. Annalise and I shared a glance of bewilderment as we were led into a pleasantly decorated anteroom whilst the manservant disappeared.

'It was a code word, wasn't it? Madame Bijoux does not exist,' Annalise whispered to me as we took a seat on the Chinese silk sofa.

'Well, whatever it means, we are in at least. I had started to fear we had made a wasted trip.'

Annalise nodded, then sat upright as steps returned along the corridor.

'Come with me,' said the manservant, and we both rose the very instant and followed him the journey up to an exuberantly dressed drawing room, draped in flouncy linens and decorated in bold oriental style wallpaper and a gallery of nude portraits upon every patch of wall space they could be hung.

'Make yourself comfortable. My master will join you directly.'

But we did not sit. Without saying a word to each other, we both began an impromptu perusal of the picture frames. We had barely surveyed half of them when a tall, thin man dressed in a garish silk bed jacket came into the room, wiping sleep from his eyes.

'Who on earth are you? He said with a heavy frown across his unusually high arched brows, which seemed to form the shape of an 'M' as he looked up through thick black lashes, examining us with a studious eye.

'Good afternoon, sir. I thank you for seeing us. This is Miss Brown, and I am Miss Andrewes.'

He peered blankly between us. 'Who?'

'We haven't had the pleasure of meeting yet, and I hope you will forgive our lack of introduction, but I was seeking a skilled costume dresser and you were given to me by way of recommendation.'

'Who's recommendation?' He pushed a thick mop of shoulder-length black hair over to the opposite shoulder.

'Puck.'

'Never heard of him, and I am not taking on any new projects now. I shall be out of town as of Tuesday anyway.'

'To Norwich, yes I know, sir, which is why I hoped to catch you before you left—'

'Who did you say sent you?—Actually, it matters not. I have a busy day, and as I said, I am closed for business. I bid you adieu, ladies.'

'Please, sir, we can pay well, whatever you ask. And it is more of a one-off type of commission. I expect it would not take too long for someone of your skill...'

'Does it look like I am in need of money?' he said, waving a flamboyant arm about the room. 'No, what I am in need of is a few days' holiday before

I travel, and right now, I need to get back to bed. What the devil did you come so early for anyway?'

'It is two-o-clock,' I said, confused.

He waved a dismissive hand then called out for his manservant. 'Show these two out, Sandro, and get Piku a fresh bowl of milk, will you,' he said, peering down at a snowy white cat that brushed in and out of his legs meowing.

We left the flamboyantly decorated house on Westgate Street in high dudgeon, wondering what to do now. All hopes and plans had been pinned on gaining Jasper's assistance, and it seemed all would now be lost in our schemes to investigate the activities of the Spinning House and for me to accompany Annalise back to London in disguise at the end of the month.

'We shall have to seek out someone else. Fortescue's troupe will surely have their own costume dressers if they are to perform, and so we must find out their direction instead. Hopefully, they won't be as haughty as that fellow,' I said to Annalise as we re-traced our steps and stood outside the theatre doors, which were locked up shut. I studied a poster in the window explaining that tickets could be obtained from Mr Hunt between the hours of eleven and two. 'Well, that was ill-timed,' I said, looking about the facade for a sign of another door to try. I needn't have bothered. As I spun about, I caught sight of Theo and another pair of women heading directly towards us. 'Theo,' I called out, waving an arm to be met with a puzzled frown.

'My, you don't 'alf scrub up well,' she said when she levelled with us, 'If it isn't Queenie looking more fitting to her station! Well, I almost didn't recognise yer!' she declared with her customary wink, lifting my veil a fraction. 'And Blondie, what's happened to you? You gone into service?' she turned and said to Annalise, who was puzzled by the reference. I had never thought to tell her of the nickname Theo had bestowed upon her.

'No,' I said quickly, 'We are in disguise.'

'Oh yeah, well, it works, from afar at least. Not easy to mistake these handsome pair of faces close up, though. I think you're gonna have to improve upon it some, yet. I'm surprised at Jasper, a widow and her maid seems like a bit of a morbid style for him. He must 'ave lost his touch.'

'This is not Jasper's work. He will not help us,' I sighed. 'We have just come from him now, and he refused us flatly.'

'Jasper, is he here?' said one of the ladies at Theo's side, a redhead with a spattering of prominent freckles about her nose and striking green eyes that seemed to be taking in every detail of me with a disapproving slant.

'Yes, forgive me, my manners, ladies. Liv, Pen, this is Queenie and Blondie—'

Annalise looked ready to correct her but was equally stunned at this revelation as I was. 'Oh,' I said uncomfortably. 'Pleased to meet you both,' I lied. Did they know it was we that impersonated them yet?

Pen, a mousey-haired woman with a complexion so pale she looked in the shade of a powdered medieval monarch, smiled and put out her hand to us both. Liv, the redheaded woman, nodded studiously and said nothing.

'These are the ladies that came to your rescue,' Theo added pointedly, and they chimed in with appreciative smiles of recognition, although whilst Pen's seemed borne of gratitude, Liv's seemed not a groat beyond obligatory.

Since they did not seem annoyed by our impersonating them, I wasn't sure what this poorly veiled hostility was owing to until much later in the day, when it transpired that Theo and Liv appeared to be an item as we watched them flirting unrestrained in the theatre dressing room.

We had taken up Theo's invitation to sit out the afternoon watching their rehearsals, with a promise at the end of it, that she would take us to a rather interesting place she had found off The Buttermarket, and pressed Liv to a promise that she would use her influence with Jasper to try convincing him to help us. It transpired the pair had been well acquainted in London, having worked in the same theatres and that her persuasion might bring him about.

Since the troupe were not to be joined by any costume dressers for at least a month, it seemed our only hope lay in the efforts of this hostile-mannered redhead who had taken a strong dislike to me. And yet we had nothing to lose in the trying, since our only alternative was to seek out a London one. An impossible prospect without a disguise to get there under.

Bury itself seemed a civilised place, with its own assembly rooms, clean paved roads, and many of them well-lit with gas lamps. A malty scent from the breweries lingered in the early evening air as we followed Theo to this mystery place she had kept referring to as "a happy surprise".

It was hard to see it as such when we arrived at a curiously named tearoom called *The Mermaid*, which we reached via a narrow alley that trailed away from the main market square and into a small ramshackle square of its own. A former yard of some kind, I considered, looking about at the oddly shaped buildings around the periphery.

When we entered through the low-eaved door, bell ringing above our heads, it seemed little more than an unremarkable cramped tea parlour with a few mismatched tables and chairs crammed into it, creating pinched walkways between them, and a serving counter that housed the most paltry offering of pastries I had ever seen. I was hardly surprised to find it empty. Annalise and I shared a glance of confusion as Theo stepped gleefully up to the counter and spoke to the middle-aged woman sitting behind it, sewing an oddly shaped object I couldn't quite make out.

'Will it be tea for four?' she asked, dropping her sewing into her basket and rising from her seat.

'No. We've a fancy for an Oyster supper,' Theo said with her customary wink, and the lady nodded and said, 'That'll be one and six a head.'

'Theo, we are not hungry. We are to dine at the hotel this evening—' I intervened, thinking nothing might induce me to eat in this odd and derelict place.

'Ah, but it's Oyster soup on the menu tonight, Queenie,' she winked and pulled me up to the counter with a squeeze of my arm and whispered: 'trust me.'

I smiled at the hard-faced lady and felt instantly obliged to fetch my purse and count out the coins for this Oyster supper I neither wanted nor bargained for. Besides, my tastes had been ever fragile and changing since my condition and whilst I had once enjoyed Oysters, presently, the very idea of them caused me to swallow down a retch.

'Follow me,' said the woman when she had finished counting out all of our coins and tucking them into her apron pocket. She pulled out a key and led us to a door I had not noticed, to the rear of the place. I was the last to filter through it, hanging back to find an opportunity to signal to Annalise we would be leaving shortly, to no avail. I heard the chink of glasses and the hum of busy chatter before I could make sense of its direction. 'What the—'

'Thank yer, milady,' said Theo, doffing the sailors' cap she was wearing—a prop she had taken from the theatre dressing room earlier—and the lady bowed and left us, locking the door back up behind her. It was then I took in the view of what transpired to be no shabby chop house or the like, but something I had no words for, no concept for defining. Part tavern, part saloon, part theatre, perhaps? But the layout of the place was the least astonishing of my realisations at that moment as I scanned the velvet sofas and leather easy chairs that reminded me of a gentleman's club. Firstly, it was filled to the brim with women, and secondly, these women were being openly tactile with each other.

'Well?' Theo said to me expectant. 'I said I had a surprise for you, didn't I?'

I nodded, too stunned to find words of reply. I caught sight of Annalise as I took in the full panorama of the room, jaw dropped as if finally realising that what I had been telling her for days, was actually true. I could barely believe it myself. I watched as the realisation unfolded in her face, her features shifting from paralysed bewilderment to a softer shape of curious intrigue. Now it made sense why none of the others were joining us tonight, such a place would not be...appropriate, I supposed. I wondered if they knew about it. If they knew about Theo. After this afternoon, it would be difficult to imagine they didn't. Liv looking for every opportunity to detain Theo's full attention and not missing one to linger a little too long over helping her to change in and out of her theatre clothes, remarking at her handsomeness and talking in playful teasing tones to her and only her.

'Well, shall I get in the drinks whilst you find us a spot?' Theo said to Liv and then gathered me up by the arm, 'You can 'elp me.'

'Yes, of course,' I said distractedly as Annalise followed Liv and weaved her way through the room behind her, no doubt insensible of all the eyes that followed her as she went.

'It's alright, Liv'll look out for her. Now, what you having?'

I looked over to the bar counter and shrugged, not knowing what was on offer or the likelihood of it being something I could drink anyway. My Christmas gift from Harri had been a manual for new mothers, and

I had read in it that: "No alcoholic libations should be consumed during pregnancy..." 'Tea?'

Theo laughed. 'You do know it's not really a tearoom, don't yer?'

Of course, I realised this was neither a tearoom or an eating house for suppers, but I had heard the lady upstairs offer us tea. 'I thought tea for four was on offer before?'

'Oh, Queenie, you never cease to beguile me with that innocent teasing. The old maid up there ain't in the business of brewing tea leaves, love. She was busy to work before your very eyes.'

'Oh, you mean sewing.'

She nodded. 'Of a sort, I suppose. But hers is a particular specialism of craft...'

'What does she sew?'

'The best silk dildos for miles about, so I'm told, anyway. Haven't had a chance to place an order meself yet. Fancy going halves with me?' she grinned.

'Dildos?'

Before she could answer me, the barmaid leaned across the counter and asked what she could get for us. Two Gins and—don't shoot the messenger here—but any chance of two teas?'

The barmaid let out a rip-roaring peel of laughter before realising her in earnest and saying, 'best I can do yer is a couple of small beers?'

'Perfect,' I said to her, noticing after a time that this was not a maid at all but a man dressed in the like of one. I tried hard not to stare as the glasses were filled and pushed across the countertop towards us. Were we in one of those Molly Houses she had told me about on our last encounter? 'Are they all men dressed in lady's clothes?' I whispered to Theo as we collected our glasses and the barmaid moved on to the next in line.

'No, it's a mixed bag in here from what I can gather, but it seems the lady folk keep earlier hours and the men start filtering in around seven.'

'So, men are welcome here too?'

'Only of the Molly persuasion, relax. With a bit of luck, Jasper will be down later. I got Liv to send a message to him earlier to ask to meet up here; a little reunion. Hopefully, he'll be in a mood of better charity once he sees you're one of us.'

I wasn't entirely sure I wanted him to realise that, at least not yet. It was all still so novel and unnerving. But I was grateful for her generosity in arranging it all. 'Thank you, Theo, that was good of you to think of us. But you do know, Miss Brown is not of the same persuasion, don't you?' I felt terrible for lying after all her efforts, but I knew if I felt so out of my wits intimidated by these unfamiliar surroundings, it would be nothing to what Annalise would feel. And whilst I had explained to her about our safety from the law at length, I knew it was not enough to reassure her against the idea of us being found out.

'Yeah, I see that.' But I can also tell you wish it otherwise. It's no use, you know, ones like her, like Letty, they're fine for a little company if you know where you stand, but girls like that can break a tender heart. Be careful.'

'I will,' I said, wondering if Theo's instincts were not as astute as I had credited them, even though I was relieved to have protected Annalise from what I knew would be an unwelcome assumption. 'We are dear friends, though, and I know she would do nothing to hurt me.'

'That's what we all think till we're stung. Till they run off and get married to some fella who can make 'em respectable...'

'Annalise is not like that,' I said a tad defensively and quickly realised that, in my defence of her, I had carelessly given her name away.

'Take my advice, innocent, dabble whilst you're game, but when you wanna settle to a serious affair, get yourself an earnest girl of the same mind. Blondie's a stunner alright, and I don't blame you. But she's not got a Sapphist bone in her body. I'm tellin' yer.'

I stifled a laugh at this. That was certainly not the conclusion I drew from the scene I awoke to this morning, her face nuzzled between my thighs as I stirred into consciousness. 'Is that what you're doing? Is that why Letty's not here tonight?'

'Letty wouldn't be seen in here if I promised her a night of free-flowing gin on my purse,' she laughed incredulously.

'And yet it seems Liv would go anywhere you directed her to,' I teased.

'She's a bit enthusiastic, I know. But she's a good lark, and we go way back...'

'Is that all she is? A good lark?'

'Depends who's asking. If it's you, Queenie—'

'No. I am not asking. You may be sure. But I think you might have a care not to turn out to be the breaker of tender hearts you warn me off, for I think she is very set on you from the little I've seen.'

'Liv's as tough as old boots, don't be fooled over her infatuation. She's sweet on me now, but I give it till as long as she's got her feet under the table with Fortescue 'till she grows tired of me. Anyway, we better get these drinks over. It looks like Blondie's stirring up a crowd.'

I almost dropped the glasses I was carrying, managing to stop them from slipping from my grasp and losing only half the contents as I caught sight of a woman sitting up close to Annalise on one of the sofas. 'What the deuce, 'I declared, pushing my way through the room and hastening my steps.

'Calm down, Queenie, I'll deal with this,' she said coolly and marched ahead of me. Her movements were quick but smooth, placing the glasses down on the table, sliding up next to Annalise on the sofa and slipping an arm about her shoulders, saying: 'There we are, m'love, a small beer.'

Annalise's eyes darted to mine, daggers of consternation radiating from them.

I offered a look of reassurance as I noticed the stranger beside her inch back a little at Theo's intrusion, before standing up entirely upon my approach. – I had hoped she would move away and give up her seat to me and take her leave, but as we levelled with each other, she put out her hand and looked at the rest of our party, 'Well, is someone going to make me an introduction?' she asked coolly, casting her gaze up and down me.

'No need,' I held out my hand to shake hers, 'Queenie, and you are?'

'Enchanted,' she replied in a sultry accent, the corner of her mouth turning up into a smile until all her neat teeth were revealed.

'How do you do?' I said abruptly. 'If you don't mind...' I pointed to the seat she had risen from.

'Perhaps we could both squeeze in together?' she offered. 'Or there's always my lap.'

'You saucebox Misty, let my girl sit down, will you, and maybe she'll think your manners pretty enough to be invited to dance later,' Liv put in.

'That seems a worthy bargain. I shall be waiting upon it, Queenie,' she smiled and slinked away back to her own table where a party of ladies were looking over in our direction.

'Well, that was an unusual introduction,' I said, picking up my glass from the table and taking just a small enough sip to wet my dry mouth. The fires around the room roaring so hot, the air felt arid and stifling.

'You's two had better get used to it,' said Theo, and Liv drained her glass and slammed it back down on the table.

'So, what exactly is this place?' I asked.

'A meeting house of sorts, for outcasts, I suppose you could say.'

'Outcasts?' Annalise said, looking even more unnerved by this description.

'Has it always been for this purpose?'

'Nah, I was talking to the bargirl the other night, said it used to be a coffee house out front and a gentleman's club of sorts, literary types. They'd come and perform their poetry on that little stage over there and debate the topic.'

'I see,' the layout and decor made much more sense to me now. 'So how long has it been a "meeting house"?'

'A few years now. Apparently, the old lady inherited the place and turned it into what it is today.'

'And what about the poets?' asked Annalise.

Theo shrugged. 'I guess she didn't care much for poetry or gentleman,' she laughed into her glass and took a sip.

I was impressed at this lady's enterprising nature and courage to create such a controversial establishment. She hardly looked like someone I would have credited with such a scheme. 'She sews Miss Brown, in silk, didn't you say Theo?'

'Oh,' Annalise said, and I explained that Annalise was a very skilled seamstress.

'I bet you don't sew dildo's though, do yer Blondie?'

Annalise frowned, and Liv burst into a lively peel of laughter. It was the first time I saw her face lighten since we had arrived.

'Is it a type of silk?' Annalise asked, but this only sent the pair into a heartier fit of laughter and left Annalise and I more confounded.

'Have you really never heard of a dildo before?' Theo asked, recovering now, making an effort to hold a serious tone to pose her question.

We both looked blankly at her and shook our heads.

'Jesus Christ, Liv, go and ask the old dear if we can look at some. —Tell her we're thinking of buying one.'

But as Liv rose to leave the sofa, she broke out into an excited greeting and went dashing towards someone behind us. When we turned, we saw it was Jasper, wrapping her up in his arms and squeezing her until her feet were lifted from the floor. This was followed by an exchange of kisses and excited conversation we couldn't quite hear above the din of the room. I was shocked by the casual intimacy the common classes seemed to readily bestow upon each other. It had quite thrown me at our tavern visit in Barnwell, the lack of restraint. No need for an introduction, just perfect strangers ready to speak to you as if you were already long acquainted. Gentlemen daring to touch females they were clearly not married or related to. I had seen many women sitting on the laps of fellows that night and even saw one dare to smack the barmaid's bottom in passing. It had been quite a spectacle of an evening for me, watching all this lewd behaviour unfold before my eyes in so public a fashion. And yet still, it was nothing on this...

'Sit down, and I'll get you a drink,' Liv said, pulling an armchair up and directing him to it.

'Thank you, sweetie,' he said, and sunk into it, noticing Theo now and saying with a finger pointed in the air, 'Now I recognise that face!' he said to her thoughtfully, as if tracing his memory to place her. He certainly seemed in better spirits than we had found him this afternoon.

'Alright Jasper, been a while.'

'Theodora Bradley,' he said as if offering up an answer to a waiting schoolmaster. 'Well, I never thought I'd see you again, I must say.'

'Well, Jasper, that's what everyone said about you when you left the Haymarket with that scene painter.'

'Freddy will be along in a while. He's still painting a scene board he's taking up to Norwich. Anyway, what are you doing here?'

'Working, like the rest of us. Not all of us get swept off our feet by plump pocketed scene decorators, you know.'

'Well darling, what can I say? Freddy's a rare find, a diamond amongst a scuttle of coals. Anyway, what's with you and Olivia?'

'A little reunion, nothing serious. I have my eye on a diamond of my own,' she grinned in my direction, and Jasper turned to look at me for the first time as if a part of the furniture had just come to life. 'Jasper, let me introduce you to Queenie, or Miss Andrewes, I should say, and Miss Brown.'

'We've already met,' I offered, trying to keep the chide out of my tone.

'So we have.—You two pulled me from my bed this morning,' he said, accusing.

'Guilty as charged,' I smiled.

'Well, I'm not one to hold grudges. You should have said you were a friend of Theodora and Olivia and—'

'You might have remembered your manners?' I said, unable to resist.

He smiled, amusement dancing in his pink-rimmed eyes, 'Hmm, I like her Theodora. She's got pluck, and the fair looks to contradict it. Well, I apologise, Miss Andrewes, Miss Brown, but I am not at my best on rising. Perhaps we may start over?'

'Happy to,' I said, lifting my glass and listened distractedly as he and Theo spun off into an exchange of questions about people and places, I knew nothing about. A trend that exacerbated when Liv returned from the bar and joined in. I hardly minded. I was so intrigued by my surroundings I could have sat all night just watching. Trying to work out who was a Molly and who was not. Sometimes the distinction was readily apparent and sometimes surprisingly ambiguous. But the greater share was certainly of the female persuasion. I cast surreptitious glances at ladies I caught sight of, openly displaying affection. One pulled another into her lap, and they sat chatting with the rest of their party in this pose with the easiest of airs. Another pair were holding hands beneath the table, and most, just conversed teasingly, sitting close, exchanging hot sultry glares that conveyed their meaning with little need for any further tactility. I could tell Annalise was as fascinated as I at the display, even if still stiff in her seat and ill at ease. Which was why I did not suggest we dance when a small string band set up on the little stage and the music started up. I knew she would hate the idea of being watched by strangers in so vulnerable a circumstance, and yet I would have loved nothing more to invite her to dance with me. Take her by the hand and pull her onto the crowded floor and show the room that this was my girl. My love. My everything...

But it was for those very reasons I refrained, the want for her comfort greater than my want for dancing with her. Certainly, these dancing styles were like nothing I had ever seen before and would cause the most seasoned waltzers to blush. Close. Embracing. Too indecent for a public exhibition, and yet, it thrilled me. Made me long to be back at our hotel in the privacy of our room so I could devour her in private. And so, when Misty came to demand I dance with her, I took it as a timely moment to take our leave and bid our company an early farewell. Liv, the only member of it, seeming pleased at this announcement.

Theo walked us out to show us the exit door, since we were not permitted to exit through the tearoom because it was now 'closed' to protect the club from any undue attention or potential raids. We were led through a narrow corridor where at the end of it, an impressively well-dressed Molly was waiting, with chatelaine in hand, to unlock the door and let us out into an alleyway, with the instruction to follow the young lad outside, who would convey us back to the market square.

A rush of cold air met my cheeks, and we stepped up quickly behind the boy lighting our way through the darkness with a heavy-looking oil lamp held out in front of him. We stepped furtively over rotting vegetable peelings and oily-looking puddles that shimmered in the lamp's glow, the scent of mould and wet animal fur catching in the breeze as it whistled its way through the narrow cleft between buildings. It was not the most civilised of places, I considered, even if I liked the concept of it immensely. A more comfortable and respectable saloon would better serve the purpose. Not haughty or exclusive, but a more pleasant setting and a slightly less informal behaviour code. – Not so tightly reigned as to spoil all the fun, but nor quite so tawdry as to give off such a lewd and predatory air. I knew it was at least part of the reason for Annalise's apparent dislike of the place.

For a moment, I caught a glimpse of the perfect setting in my imagination. A dignified room, not unlike the one at our hotel lobby, stylish and neat but not overly formal; perfectly comfortable for spending time conversing and sipping on drinks. Drinks, now they would need to comprise of a far better offering than ale and spirits. Good tea and chocolate, coffee and cordials, as well as French wines, and perhaps even some dining options so that one might dine with a prospective companion. Then another room, entirely separate from this peaceful and civilised lounge, set out in the style of a small ballroom where dances could be held now and then for those who had a fancy for a livelier evening. On other evenings, a violin or pianoforte player could be hired to offer a pleasant backdrop to the lounge. Then as the image of it crystalised almost portrait-like in my mind, I realised that was it! That is what *we* could do. Not move into a pie shop in Carshalton or find a little hideaway dwelling somewhere obscure, not knowing how we would meet our expenses when the money from the trinkets ran out. We needed to open our own establishment. Create our own stream of earnings. And put our efforts into something industrious and forward-thinking.

'ere you are, misses, that way to Buttermarket and that way to Kings Road,' he said, stopping and pointing.

I paused the thought, minded to return to this more seriously later, found a shilling in my purse for him and thanked him, grateful as we stepped onto the cobbles to be on cleaner, well-lit ground and in walking distance of our hotel.

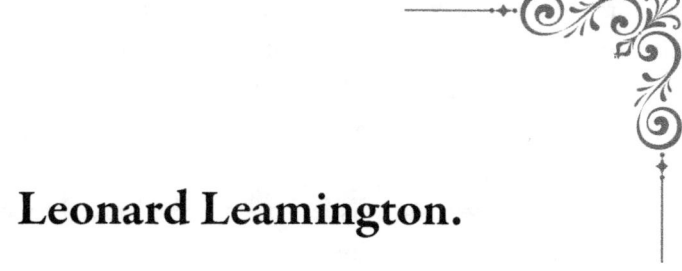

Leonard Leamington.

January 1822. - Annalise.

Annalise woke early the following day, sitting in one of the easy chairs in their pleasant hotel room, watching Bury begin to rise. Street cleaners with push wagons travelling below the large window overlooking the square, stopping to sweep a pile of horse dung up. It was a pleasant view, with the rugged wall of the Abbey gardens facing her, the Abbey itself rising proudly up into the early morning January mist of a sky. A pretty arrangement of box hedges bordering the walls, being tended by a pair of warmly clad gardeners, scraping wet leaves from the beds. It seemed to her not such a pleasant job at this season, having always envied the gardeners at Cuddington for being out all day in the sunshine. In winter, it must be little more than living in damp socks and clearing soggy debris from the land.

She often thought of Cuddington and the shop in Carshalton, her friends and her mama's grave, with a sense of deep longing. She liked the quiet country life at Stapleford, the small family of staff that had taken them under their wing, and above everything, she loved living closely and freely at Eleanor's side. She only wished she could scoop it all up, take it back to Surrey with her, and have everything dear to her in one place.

But the time of her visit drew ever nearer and helped to sustain her. She would soon have more than Miss Lockheart's letters to rely on and would see for herself how her friends were, and how the shop was coming along. If they had settled to it nicely and made a happy home of the blank canvas she left behind last year. The letters had slowed lately, and the pages grew briefer, owing—Poppy had mentioned—to how busy they were finding themselves now that the Pie Shop was up and running. In her last letter, she had sought Annalise's permission to take on another staff member since there was more work than two could manage. She had written back directly, encouraging her to do as she saw fit and sending her on the money draft to pay Mr Benson's bill and staff wages. There was not much left to do to conclude the building works now, by the sound of it. Painting the extension parlour was underway, and the garden would have to wait until spring when the ground was less boggy. She looked forward to seeing the progress, although the prospect of moving into the place seemed evermore unlikely. She knew she and Eleanor had crossed a point of no return lately. This new intimacy and lifestyle had bonded them so closely she could not see a life without her anymore. That such simplicity as having a good roof over her head amongst friends would not be enough now she knew what it was to feel such deep companionship. And yet she also knew the place was not fit to bring her to, not just on account of its humble nature, but its locality was too risky, and on that basis alone, she thought it unlikely she would ever be more than a holidaying visitor to number sixteen Carshalton High Street. That her friends could benefit from it was consolation enough at present. But it saddened her to think the sewing parlour might never come to fruition. That so much money and work had been wasted in the provision of something looking more and more unlikely, she would ever need. She was confident it could be put to some other use though, maybe to let out to another seamstress. Perhaps being a landlady was the most she could expect in this venture now, and so long as her friends were happy and the place became capable of sustaining itself and them within it, she knew it would prove worthwhile.

Such grounding thoughts of ordinary concerns consoled her after the strangeness of last night at *The Mermaid*, which had caused her hours of sleepless musing before she finally exhausted herself into slumber beneath the weight of Eleanor's limp arm. It had been an uncomfortable and disconcerting affair to be taken to such a place and with no prior warning to mentally prepare for such a shock. When Theo had said she was taking them out, she suspected another low tavern, not a place where she would feel as vulnerable around a party of women as she had sometimes felt around young men. It did not seem to her in women's nature to behave in such a predatory manner, and yet it was not only common to Theo, as she had first thought. The eyes her own had met within that room were equally, if not sometimes more explicit in their intention than that which she had observed in the way she often caught Theo looking at Eleanor. It was abundantly clear to her why Theo was being so helpful and enterprising in doing her utmost to please Eleanor, even if Eleanor could not see it herself.

It had been the maid bringing in a note for her this morning that had woken her so early, despite settling so late. It had been from Theo, advising Eleanor she had secured Jasper's services as a dresser, and she could call upon him today, so long as it was after the hour of four-o-clock. Since their stagecoach tickets had been booked for noon today, she knew that attending Jaspers would mean extending their trip. More time in the company of Theo and *The Mermaid*.

The prospect hung heavily over her as she sipped her morning chocolate and watched Eleanor sleep, oblivious to all that had unfolded in these daybreak hours. This news would please her in the same measure it caused Annalise to feel anxious. It was true, an effective disguise would be safer for her to go out under. But such a disguise might offer her a false sense of security too. Would give Eleanor the license to poke about the proctor's business and risk getting found out in London. Yet, she knew the scent of danger would not be enough to throw Eleanor off the idea. She seemed to have quite a habit of getting into scrapes, and it was not difficult to see why now she had come to know her so well. It was almost like she had an appetite for it.

She would of course, have to go along with it all, however much she wished it otherwise. The disguise. *The Mermaid* and its patrons. She could not deny Eleanor this novel discovery when it seemed to bring her so much revelry and joy. But nor could she deny to herself how much it had the reverse effect on her own feelings in equal measure. She was not sure why she didn't feel the enthusiasm and excitement Eleanor did in this matter, only that she knew where Eleanor gained a sense of comfort or belonging from meeting these "likeminded" ladies; it only served to make Annalise feel more alienated from her sense of self. She did not need to belong to a collective, not anywhere but at Eleanor's side, anyway. She did not need to befriend these strangers with questionable habits to feel at ease with the world. She only needed Eleanor's love to feel at home with herself. It was enough to have each other and live quietly as they had been. She did not want to be openly intimate before the eyes of others, regardless of whether it met with their approval or not. Their intimacy was a private matter, and she was convinced she would feel the same whether Eleanor was a man or a woman, for Annalise did not love Eleanor *because* she was a woman...but because she was Eleanor. Because her heart had given her no say in the matter. Because she was the only person on this earth that had ever made her feel this way.

THEY REACHED THE HOUSE in Westgate Street at a quarter past four, having extended their stay at *The Angel* and rebooked their stagecoach tickets for tomorrow. It was just as Annalise had expected, and she said nothing to dissuade Eleanor from this altered course. One more day and they would be back safely tucked away at Stapleford, just the two of them. No Theo or lecherous eyes following her about in the dimly lit confines of the secret mermaid room.

'Ah, ladies! Good to see you again!' Jasper declared when he sent for them to attend him in the drawing room. There was a note of irony about his tone as if he was making up for the poor reception they had received only yesterday.

'Good afternoon,' Annalise offered, Eleanor taking a more casual approach and saying: 'Jasper! How good of you to see us today.'

'Well, we are friends now, and I am not such a shabby character as to turn away a friend in need. Now, Theo tells me you are after a cunning disguise. You have some serious business to undertake by the sound of it.'

'Yes. Is it possible? To render me unrecognisable, even to eyes that know me?'

'My darling, you are talking to the artist that made Jane Merriweather look like a beautiful Venus upon the Drury Lane stage in her thirtieth year, and did such a convincing job of turning Drake Clarke into the likeness of a gorilla that a great number of females swooned in the pits, thinking it a real wild animal let loose upon them! So yes, I can transform you beyond recognition. The trouble,' he said more thoughtfully, 'is that you shall need to be able to replicate the look yourself without my assistance, and that is where we find our duplicity constrained.'

'Well, could you explain how to replicate the art once we have settled on something suitable? Annalise can help me achieve it if you show us how.'

'Yes, yes. That's all very well, but I cannot simply show you what has taken decades of accomplishment to master in but a few hours and expect you to pull it off adequately, my dear. However keen and quick-minded you are to learn. There are recipes to prepare, equipment needed and most importantly, a skilled and talented eye.'

'Well, what do you think we could learn by the end of the day?'

He chewed his bottom lip and said with a wave of his hand: 'Stand up in the window's light. Let me look at you better.'

Eleanor did as bid, and a shaft of mottled wintery sunlight caught the side of her profile, the smooth lines of her black widow's dress standing out against the lace.

'I had in mind an old lady. I need to be able to disguise my youth and my looks. The proctors have a penchant for locking up fair young ladies they don't know. But an aged lady should be above their notice or suspicion, if it can be done.'

'Hmm, well, it can be done. But it is a messy business greying hairs, setting out convincing wrinkles from egg whites and gelatin, and painting heavy eyelids with subtle flair – it simply won't be feasible for novices. And it would take hours to perfect each time you required it. No, I don't think that will do. We need simplicity to pull this off in such limited time. Give me a moment to think on it. Will you join me at the port? I need to get the creative juices flowing. Or, I think we have a little sweet wine in the cellar if that is more to your liking?'

'Oh, no, I thank you. It is too early for wine with my constitution. Tea would be welcome, though, or chocolate if you have it?'

Annalise nodded her assent to this proposition. Despite the many months since Eleanor's dependent spell on the liquor, such offers always made her nervous of a repeat.

'Tea? We don't have tea in the house. Coffee we can manage. Sandro, coffee for my friends and bring my port. —It is never too early to warm the blood. Now, I trust you can manage the purchase of the garments you shall need? We may borrow from the theatre dressing stock, for now, to try out some ideas, but once we have decided upon them, you shall need to go and procure your own in replication.'

'Yes, naturally, once we know what to buy—'

'And your hair, how long is it?'

Eleanor levelled a hand at bosom height to indicate, although Annalise was sure it was a little longer than that when unpinned.

Jasper nodded. 'And your curls, I assume they are achieved with the irons?'

Eleanor shook her head. 'No, they are natural.'

'Hmm, that's trickier to resolve. Well then, it would seem our options would be a dye or a severe cut to its length, both perhaps. But if you are precious about it, then I suppose a wig would do. There is a fine wig maker in London I can give you the direction of—'

'No need. I am willing to accept it cut, dyed, whatever will best work to our advantage. It will grow back, after all.'

'Very well, a black henna. I think your skin too olive-toned to be convincing of red hair. And a *mouche la galante* is always good for showing age, in brown velvet, yes. A little outmoded, but great for a false distinguishing feature you can whip off.'

'A what?' Annalise asked, puzzled. She had translated the French to: fly the gallant, and was none the wiser for it.'

'A little false mole, my dear. We could do the same with the brow line, square it out and harden your features, these are simple enough to be stuck on the skin with a little Arabic gum, so it shall prove quick and easy enough for you to manage yourself.'

'Velvet eyebrows?' Annalise said incredulous.

'No. Those we shall have from the wig maker, a nice bespoke pair to match the hair once it's dyed. But we will have to make do with whatever we have here for now. Now, for the body, we could make you fat around the middle with a little quilting suit. We have one in the theatre you can try that was used to play Prinny before he was King. I doubt it will see much use now he's been crowned. Simple enough to make with a little calico and feather stuffing and comfortably warm too, at this season.'

Annalise was beginning to think this sounded like an awful lot of work to undertake, and they would only have a couple of weeks to achieve it if Eleanor meant to travel into London with her and visit Lady W. She was not keen on the idea. As much as she knew she would miss her on her visit to Carshalton, she didn't think it worth the risk of discovery, however remote.

'You can use a little candle wax upon the face too, to create some imperfections on it. If mixed with a little pigment or arrowroot, it can be made to look like a convincing wart, or an angry boil or scar if you dab it with a little rouge.'

Annalise was finding it hard to believe that these ideas would amount to anything passable for everyday looks. It all sounded garish in the extreme and surely would be seen for what it was in the light of day, unlike in the soft glow of dim theatre light where such tricks may be passable. Surely such a look would serve to draw attention to her, rather than divert it away.

However, when they finished their coffee and headed over to the theatre, she was unexpectedly impressed at the transformation of Eleanor into something of a puff-guts old hag, with a number of unpleasant skin disfigurations upon her face. She thought it proficient enough to keep the proctors away, but doubted it would fool anyone who knew her looks. Her eyes were too striking in their colour and almond-slanted shape, and whilst the false brow worked from afar to alter them, from a closer distance, they looked young, striking and as vibrant as ever. Anyone who had ever looked into them would recognise them in an instant. And then there were her plump lips set at such a pronounced and defined bow at the peak that they, too, would give away her youth. Elderly ladies sported pale, thin lips, and she could see no means of turning her into such a style.

'Well,' Eleanor said, turning in the looking glass, 'What do you think?'

'It is certainly impressive, but I'm not convinced it will do for London,' Annalise said.

'Hmm, she has a point,' Jasper agreed. ' We're not quite there. Here, chew on one of these,' he said, pulling out a tin of pomfret cakes, 'they should dull your teeth a fraction. Failing that, you could always try a good claret.' He fumbled about in a drawer, then pulled out a pair of spectacles and handed them to Eleanor. 'Better,' he declared at the grey-tinged teeth and spectacled eyes which went some way towards obscuring their shape.

'It is an improvement,' Annalise agreed.

'Hmm, there's something still quite off. I can't quite put my finger on it. We need a second opinion. Wait here – I'll see if Freddy's still about.'

They had already made Freddy's acquaintance on their way in. Unlike Jasper, who seemed much in the effeminate style, not only by his fashion and looks but also by his mannerisms and speech, Freddy had no trace about him that could give away his inclinations. He looked like any other fellow, perhaps slightly more particular, with well-groomed hair and neatly trimmed fingernails, but nothing to raise suspicion.

'Come now, Freddy, you will notice what is missing,' Jasper said, pulling him into the room. He was wiping paint from his hands onto an old rag.

'Well, you certainly don't look like the lady I met earlier. But yes, there is something not quite right.'

'But what is it, Fred?'

He circled her. 'She's in too much of a bloom of health. It belies the aged features you have placed over such a rosy complexion. The combination is an odd one.'

Jasper sighed relief. 'I knew your fresh gaze would spot it. 'Well, powder and egg whites, it will have to be. Although this is no easy art, it shall give you away if you overdo it or over-wear it.'

'No, I don't think that's the answer,' Freddy said thoughtfully. 'If the aim is simplicity, then surely you must work with what you've got.'

'She cannot look young and fair, darling. It would throw the whole scheme off.'

'As a woman, she cannot look young and fair, but as a handsome young fellow perhaps?'

Jasper clapped his hands together. 'That's it. Why didn't I see it before? You shall be a boy. A rather pretty boy, but there is no harm in that.'

'Oh, I don't know about that,' Eleanor replied, and Annalise suspected it was on account of her increasing waistline. To be sure, it was too subtle to be noticed beneath her dresses, but in pantaloons or breeches, it would surely be less easy to obscure. In an ageing fellow, it may be taken as little more than a fondness for the ale house, but in a young fellow, it would be out of place. And what of her breasts? They were not modest enough to pass beneath even the slackest of greatcoats, and they, too, seemed to be increasing with her belly these days.

'Whyever not? It's perfect! You become the inverse of those who might seek you out. Just think how freely you can roam those Cambridge streets if you are a young man. We must be sure to make you distinctive enough not to be considered one of the undergraduates, though, unless, of course, that would allow you better access, in which case you must see about procuring yourself a gown.'

'No. No, I think that might be pushing my luck a little too far. But, I am willing to try at an ordinary-looking fellow if you really think it will work. And I suppose you shall not need a disguise if I appear to be chaperoning you about,' she turned and said to Annalise.

'Excellent,' he declared with his customary clap of the hands. 'Well, we better pack up here and head over to the Gentleman's wardrobes!'

THE GENTLEMAN'S WARDROBE was full of all kinds of costumery. Whereas the ladies wardrobe tended to consist of one type of dress or another, be it shabby or chic, medieval or modern, the men's had a variety of styles in the impression of sailors and military men, chefs to chimney sweeps: an array of trades and office's displayed on over crammed hanging rails. Jasper browsed through them with quick, nimble hands, occasionally pausing to pick an item and hold it out to study briefly before replacing it with something more to his liking. This continued on and on for what felt like an exasperatingly long time, before, finally, he decided on two outfits: one a redcoat's uniform and the other the simple dress of a fellow of modest means. A plain tailored pair of tawny breeches with boots, an ivory muslin shirt, a little yellowed about the cuffs, a brown calico waistcoat with a neck scarf and shabby looking heavy winter overcoat. He made her try both, tucking her hair beneath hats but suggesting—to Annalise's horror—it easier to simply lop it off and spare herself the struggle.

'Len, not your hair,' Annalise cut in at this suggestion.

'Len?' Jasper asked.

'It's a nickname,' Eleanor explained, wrapping her hair into a top-heavy bundle, to make the hat fit more snuggly.

'Well, I have to say, I think you make a very handsome redcoat indeed. But perhaps a little too handsome if you want to remain low-key. Redcoats have a way of catching one's eye, and you are at risk of having a brood of young maidens pursuing you if you go about town like that.' This was met with all round agreement that the simple outfit would better serve the purpose. With that matter settled, Jasper took her over to the dressing table and fitted her with a pair of heavy brows, sideburns and a thin strip of a moustache. 'Hmm,' he declared, standing behind her and checking her reflection in the glass. 'Just a little more detail,' he added and began mixing something up in a small dish. 'Now, this is a kohl mix with a little oil, you shall need to get yourself a couple of artist's paintbrushes, good hair, preferably goats, but horse will do. One for dappling as so...' he demonstrated, tapping it into the mixture, taking the excess off on the back of his hand and then patting the blunt brush end against Eleanor's cheeks. 'Now, you want to go light. We are attempting to create the impression of a little bit of shaving shadow, not a painted beard. So, dapple it, and before it sets completely dry, just a light dusting of powder to dull it down.

'My goodness,' Eleanor declared, peering closer to the mirror when Jasper reloaded his brush for the other side of her face. 'It really does look convincing, doesn't it.'

Annalise agreed, trying to take in this strange new appearance of her beautiful Eleanor, evermore looking like a young man. A *handsome* young man.

'Now, go just a touch heavier about the border of the sideburns and jawline and keep the shadow looking sharp and angular to deceive the eye of your softer features, then blend out sparser and lighter as you work up from it, and just a little way down the neck.'

This feature looking perfected, Jasper proceeded to draw on with a thin brush, strokes of eyebrow hair that seemed to almost join the brows lightly in the middle, giving her eyes a harsher and more masculine frame.

Annalise wondered where they might go to get her clothes in this likeness since there would be no time to make them before their journey to London. Besides, Eleanor meant to do her *Spinning House* investigating ahead of their trip, in order she might report to the Society all that she could find out, in time for her clandestine visit. If they were back in Surrey, she would know just the right market stalls to go to find such garments, but here? Here she hadn't a clue where to begin.

'Right then, I think we finally have success. Now stand up and let me see you. Ta-da! Quite the transformation! There's only one matter left to address sweetie, and that's these buxom beauties of yours!' he said, talking to her breasts. 'These are perhaps your weakest point, but let's see what binding them can do.'

'Binding them?'

'Yes, wrapping them up in stiff bandages should do the trick. You shall have to dispense with your stays and attempt to work to the opposite effect. Now, since we've no lady dressers about at this hour, either you shall have to try, or I shall. As much as I can assure you, you could not be in safer male hands than mine; we might both prefer you make an attempt under my instruction. – Miss Brown, will you help her?'

It took some doing, even with his instructions. Annalise had a vague notion of what he meant, having heard of nursing mothers binding to stop their milk, but she had never actually seen it done. The difficulty was not just in squashing them into a flatter shape, but the obvious pain it was causing Eleanor when she wrapped her successively tighter as each previous attempt failed to achieve the effect. She knew her breasts were often sore and tender since her pregnancy, and she had grown used to keeping her touch feather-light in their lovemaking since Eleanor had begun to complain of the ache in them. So as Eleanor bid her pull tighter, eyes watering with the discomfort, Annalise winced, but said nothing and did as bid.

Eventually, they could do no more, and whilst a slight bulge was visible through the muslin of her shirt, by the time her waistcoat, overcoat and necktie was in place, it could not be readily discerned.

'Go a size larger on your clothes when you get them. You shall need to keep to baggy and shapeless if you are to disguise all those curves. And don't take off your coat in public, and learn to tuck your scarf into your waistcoat like this. That way, if anyone catches a glimpse of a bulge, they shall put it down to it being the ends of your scarf rising from beneath it. Nothing suspicious in that at such a wintery season.'

'Won't it look curious if I wear ill-fitting clothes?'

'Perhaps if you were attempting to mimic a gentleman, but the class you imitate often wear ill-fitting garments for they don't have good tailors to wait upon them. No, nothing to worry about on that account. Well, young sir, all you need now is a new name.'

'Yes, I suppose I shall,' Eleanor agreed, and Annalise wandered how they would ever keep up with all these aliases. 'I've always been fond of the name Maxwell.'

Jasper said, with the note of a laugh, 'Maxwell? No darling, not at all fitting for a man of this class.—Now what was that nickname you called her earlier?' He asked, turning to Annalise.

'Len?' Annalise replied.

'Yes, now that's more like it; Leonard. Leonard...what's the name of that spa town? Leamington! Leonard Leamington. Now that fits.'

Eleanor seemed unconvinced and Annalise thought it would at least be easier to remember.

'Well, I think it's time to test out your disguise.' He wiped his kohl-covered hands with a cloth and checked his pocket watch. 'Fortescue's troupe should be on the stage rehearsing now. Let's have their verdict. Besides, you must work on your gait and mannerisms. You walk too tall and elegantly for a boy, even for a Molly. So, I suggest you call on *their* expertise in mastering that aspect.'

'Thank you, Jasper, for all your hard work. I am so very grateful. You have done such a fine job. I am astonished at how convincing I look,' Eleanor said, turning about in the full-length looking glass and checking her reflection from different angles.

Annalise had to agree. The old lady would have given her away, but this, this was quite a remarkable feat. And it was simple enough for them to replicate, so long as they could get the right clothes and Eleanor did not rely on her cosmetic skills to handle the face paints. She might have come a long way since the days of Camille's chiding instruction, but it was hardly her speciality and had taken her months to perfect a little subtle rouging of the cheeks and lips.

'Now, Jasper, you must allow me to settle my bill with you. I know you said you did not want for the money, but it would not be right for you to go without pay, having spent hours at work in this. And I have money enough, so you needn't offer me charity.'

'Well, I can't accept money from a friend. But I can accept that the drinks are on you at *The Mermaid* tonight. How about we agree upon that?'

'No. That shall not cover it.'

After a bartering exchange on their way down to the stage area to meet the troupe, it was settled that Eleanor would buy them dinner at *The Angel* and take care of the drinks at *The Mermaid*. At this, the compromise was met, and Annalise was grateful for an end to their protesting and counteroffers. Even if somewhat less thankful, for having dinner tacked onto what already seemed destined to prove, another long night ahead.

They came in through the side wing where the troupe was singing around a pianoforte, some comical ditty they appeared to be learning the lines to as they crowded around a chalked board to see them as they sang.

'When the song ends. I want you to distort your voice as low as you might manage, tap one of them on the shoulder, tell them you are the new lamp lighter and have lost your way and need directions to the stage manager, alright?' Jasper whispered to Eleanor.

Eleanor nodded, and Annalise bid her to practice her voice.

After a few attempts that made them all break out into spontaneous laughter, she said to them below the hubbub of the singing: 'Umm, 'scuse me, I'm the new lamp lighter and need to find my way to the stage manager, if you please.'

'Not bad,' said Jasper, '...perhaps a tad more colloquial.'

Eleanor nodded, cleared her throat and stepped onto the stage as the music faded. It was impossible to hear what was said from the wings, but Annalise could tell from her reception that they had not recognised her.

'Forty,' Letty shouted down to the pits, 'Whereabouts' is the stage manager's office in this place?'

Jasper put a hand on Annalise's shoulder and bent in towards her ear. 'They're buying it!' he said delighted, watching them—hawk-like—across the stage.

It seemed all well enough until Theo turned about and paused, squinted, and looked Eleanor up and down with a quizzing eye, then declared loud enough to reach out to the wings: 'I know that face,' she pointed an accusatory finger. 'My, my, my. Well, what a handsome job Jasper's done on you,' she said, circling Eleanor now. Examining her from hat to boots and up again. All to the confusion of the rest of the troupe who hadn't made the connection, until Liv stepped up to the pair and said something that made the rest of the actors' frown in disbelief, and gather in to make their own examinations.

'Well, looks like the cat's out of the bag now,' said Jasper. 'Come on, let's have their opinion,' he pulled Annalise out onto the stage with him and then, in exaggerated volume and tone, began: 'Ahem!' May I present to you, Mr Leonard Leamington.' And with this dramatic introduction, he bowed, ready for his applause.

Annalise was fast forming the impression that whilst Jasper himself was not an actor, his theatre-based career had rubbed off on him and lent him towards a theatrical air in whatever he did. It seemed strange to her that he had never been inclined towards the stage with so much natural animation to his character and confidence that bordered on cockiness.

He accepted his applause from the troupe and a few jesting comments: 'Those Gaynesford brothers, got nothin' on Jasper. Think you should stick around here and work with us.'

'Yeah, she looks more of a fellow than you!' Theo added, before leading Eleanor off the stage, Annalise trailing behind them. 'You gotta come to *The Mermaid* in character tonight,' she was imploring Eleanor, who was shaking her head at this proposition.

'I can't. How will I be admitted to my hotel afterwards looking like this?'

'You can always come back to ours. They won't notice with a group as big as us. We're at the *Half Moon Inn* on Buttermarket.'

Annalise let out an inward sigh of relief when Eleanor declined this offer and said, 'I thank you. But these clothes are on loan and so I cannot. I only wished to test it out for efficacy, and now I know it works; well, I just need a little practice in manly speech and manner. I thought perhaps you could help me with that, Teddy?'

'Alright, I'll try, but it's not easy to emulate God-given manliness,' he said, flexing his biceps in exaggerated poses, to which Theo gave him a little shove of rebuke.

'Look,' said Theo, 'We got a couple more songs to learn this afternoon before Fortescue lets us clock off. Why don't you come back then, and we can go through a little play-acting, and then we can go straight onto *The Mermaid*?'

'Well, I am taking Jasper and Freddy out to dine as a thank you, and you and Olivia may join us if you like? My treat for talking Jasper around to helping me.'

Annalise tried at a smile.

'Well, I can't decline a dinner invitation with a handsome chap like you, can I now,' she winked. 'What time?'

'Seven-o-clock at the *The Angel* on Angel Hill.'

'Swanky,' she said teasing. 'Better pick out me Sunday best.'

IT PROVED A DRAWN-OUT taxing night for Annalise when they finally returned to *The Angel* just before midnight, their cloaks soaked through and their boots soggy from the rain. Annalise stripped down to her shift and held her frozen toes out to the fire, feeling the icy burn of heat begin to thaw them. After enduring an hour of Teddy schooling Eleanor in vulgarly masculine traits (the scraping his throat and spitting at the floor being the most poignant to her memory), she had then had to tolerate the next two hours at the table with Theo's bawdy jokes and lecherous eye set at Eleanor, and Liv's scornful glare set at Theo. By the time they arrived at *The Mermaid*, she had decided to turn a blind eye to all the lively flirting and over-excitement, and chatted with Freddy for most of the evening, who seemed to her, to be the only one of their party capable of calm conversation and ordinary manner. Even Eleanor could not be relied upon for her usual civility in such company: taking to the dances with a little persuasion and then marching her out to some discreet back room to decide upon the purchase of a shocking-looking item called a dildo, which Theo then proceeded to parade about the place with, making obscene gestures and jokes.

She was not against a little funning, but this unrestrained wildness was a little too much to bear, especially amongst the company of strangers. And it was all Annalise could do to hold onto the fact that this was their last night here, and they would soon return to civility.

There had been a suggestion that Theo and a couple of the troupe, might come down to Cambridge soon to help them in their *Spinning House* investigations, but since Fortescue was holding them to a relentless rehearsal schedule, it seemed unlikely it would be anytime soon. – Certainly not within the coming weeks. She hoped that between the two of them and Eleanor's new disguise, they could undertake the business before Theo sent word of them having a holiday granted and that there'd be no need for them to come at all.

'Shall I send for a tray of tea or chocolate?' Eleanor asked, joining her at the fireside and helping her out of her wet clothes.

'No, thank you. I am tired. I want to warm up and get some sleep before our journey back tomorrow.'

'I'm sure I can think of a way to assist you in both quarters...' Eleanor teased, throwing her discarded stays to the floor, drawing up behind her and kissing the plane of her shoulder.

Annalise pulled away. 'I'm too tired tonight. It's been a long day. I'm going to get to bed. Goodnight,' she said, pecking her on the cheek as she passed, lifting the tightly tucked blankets lose, and climbing into the bed. There was no way she would consent to trying out that dildo if that's what she had in mind, however much the others had barked on about it. The look of the thing was abhorrent to her—frightening even. Was their lovemaking not already perfect? She had undoubtedly always found it so. What could some offensive and inanimate piece of stuffed silk do to improve upon something that required no improving? To her, at least. Did Eleanor find their passions lacking and in want of some redress? She was the more experienced of them. Perhaps there were things Annalise did not understand about those experiences. Eleanor had always spoken of them with an air of discomfort and regret, yet it was not so long ago that she sought out Richard's company of her own volition...

She pushed the thought away. She had made so much progress since then that the idea of re-conjuring the memory felt more effort than it was worth. In the early days, it had been exhausting. She had poked at the images in her head like you poked a sore in the mouth with the tip of your tongue to see how much it stung. It had long since failed to sting with any zeal and was replaced now, with a dull resilience, like venom that had lost its potency. This deadness of emotion was welcome after so much self-inflicted mental torment, and she had no mind to resurrect such horrors that had since been laid to rest. And whatever these new associations had unleashed in Eleanor of late—an enchanting fascination of sorts—she knew Eleanor had no interest in Theo, or any of the sirens at *The Mermaid* that made eyes at her. It was that, which made it easier to bear the obvious intent of others towards her love. To Eleanor, it was all a big adventure; harmless camaraderie and a lust for knowing and belonging that motivated her, not desire for any of these women. If the past months had taught her anything, she knew how to perfectly read the flame of desire in Eleanor's eye, and it had never been fixed in any other direction but her own. Of that, she felt convinced.

Fleet Market.

January 1822. - Annalise.

The fortnight back at Stapleford had been busy and fruitful in preparing for their London-bound trip and sourcing the materials for their disguise. The clothes they had managed to procure from the local rag and bone man, but still required a fair amount of alteration to fit Eleanor in a convincing enough style. The wear on the clothes even added to the authenticity of the look, Annalise had persuaded her, at her reluctance to put on such shabby attire that Eleanor was convinced must be flea infested. Once she had given the clothes a good soak and press with the hot iron, declaring not a single trace of any critters having resided in the seams, she accepted to try them on and permit Annalise to pin them for alterations. It was only the moustache and brow wigs they had been unable to procure in Cambridge.

Still, they had managed well enough with the sideburns Jasper had let her keep, and the finely brushed and powdered kohl strokes, that they decided it would do suitably until they got to London and could visit the wig maker he had recommended. Annalise's disguise was to comprise of only a hair wig of brown or red in order to conceal the distinguishing brilliance of her blonde tresses, which Eleanor insisted made her stand out amongst the crowd far too easily. She was unwilling to have the henna put to it as Eleanor did, thinking how her mama would turn in her grave to see her alter the locks she had always admired. Of course, her brief position as Eleanor's lady's maid would not render her widely well remembered amongst Eleanor's associates, but they were to take no chances whatsoever.

Today, as they rattled along in the stagecoach down the Old North Road, Annalise felt a mixture of excitement and anxiety at their return home. The coach had been fully occupied by inside and outside passengers leaving them little opportunity to talk beyond casual matters, and since Eleanor was still nervous about the conviction of her tone, even this, she wished to keep to the minimum. They had agreed to pose as brother and sister on this occasion since only Eleanor had a wedding band to wear. Annalise had tried it, to find it too big for her. So Eleanor had promised to procure one for Annalise during their visit in order that they could pose as man and wife for the remainder, and also enjoy matrimonial protection from the Proctors upon their return. It seemed this would be the better sham, since already Annalise had attracted the unwanted attentions of one of the coach guards, and Eleanor spent the journey with a young maid casting smiling eyes at her and receiving the chides of her platter-faced chaperone, sitting opposite them in the carriage.

Annalise had little else to do but sit with all her thoughts as she gazed through the small coach window at the wintery planes of countryside they passed through at a speed she was not entirely comfortable with in such an icy season. Eleanor had insisted they try out the journey on *The Star of Cambridge*, which advertised an impressive four and a half hours to reach Ludgate Hill. This, of course, did not include the better part of an hour it had taken to reach their alighting point at the *Hoop Inn* in Cambridge, which Mrs Duckworth drove them to in the trap this morning. But as this promised four and a half hours turned to five, and London was still not on the horizon, it had proved just as Annalise had expected: a rather outlandish claim.

Six hours later, in the wet drizzle, they pulled up at the *Belle Sauvage* with apologies from the driver that the slippery roads were to blame for the delay. This was met with equanimity by most of the shivering passengers, but a couple of the more disgruntled, dared to express their disappointment with the time discrepancy, vowing to travel by the *Tally Ho* or the *Royal Regulator* next time, and save a couple of shillings if there was to be no improvement on the journey time.

Annalise wasn't sure, as they stepped out onto the muddy street, if this part of London seemed ugly and disagreeable to her because she had been in the contrast of the countryside so long, or whether the dismal weather was to blame for casting a particular shade of gloom over the crowded

London inn yard. In either case, she was glad that they were not staying long in this district, and they hailed a hack promptly to convey them to Fleet market where they were to visit the wigmaker, and Eleanor procure herself a haircut from a barber, ahead of their meeting with Lady W and Mrs Neal, who had offered to host the visit at her house in Cheapside, in case Grosvenor Square was under the gaze of spies.

'Well, that's the wigmaker over there,' Eleanor said, pointing through the crowded market street to a small shop beyond them with bowed windows and wigs on dummy heads behind the glass.

'I shall get my hair cut, and I'll see you there in an hour, alright,' and with that, she pecked Annalise on the cheek and disappeared into the throng. Of all things, this was part of the scheme Annalise most disliked. She loved Eleanor's long chestnut curls that trailed her back, and was already missing them now she had applied the black henna dye to them. It seemed too harsh a shade and washed all the warm bloom from her cheeks. Now she seemed unusually pale, and her long black curly hair made her look reminiscent of a young King Charles the second, from afar, even if exceedingly more handsome, Annalise decided. But what would she look like with it all cropped short? Yes, it would grow back, as Eleanor had pointed out, but she could not help but dread the result as she set off in the direction of the linen drapers.

She intended to find some new fabrics since they were here, with which to make new dresses for Eleanor before she grew too large to fit into her usual ones. She also meant to make her a new shirt from the off cuts to replace the one she was wearing now that she complained of being too coarse. And then perhaps she might make a few baby caps and dresses. However, this was not a proposition she could put to Eleanor, who was entirely closed on the subject of the babes arrival. She was sure it was the anxiety to blame for this refusal to acknowledge that there would be a baby at the end of this pregnancy. *Her* baby. But avoidance of the matter was not going to alter the fact, nor that it would need to be clothed, swaddled and nursed in the interim between the birth and being placed with its new family. Whoever that may turn out to be. —The best of homes, Eleanor had insisted. A life where her child could be free of the shame of its birth. Yet Annalise could not help but think that the shame of one's birth would prove the lesser evil in the bargain, where a mother's love was to be the price. She knew. She had lived with the shame of an illegitimate birth, and yet nothing would have been worth the deprivation of her mother's love and care. However difficult it had turned out, she knew she had been blessed to have such a mother and could think of nothing worse than never having known her.

It saddened her deeply to think of the fate that awaited this unsuspecting little life growing beneath Eleanor's skin. She wondered if Eleanor might feel differently when the time came. Want to keep her child—to the devil with the consequences. No, that wasn't all. She didn't only wonder. She dared to *hope*.

After all, if her own mama had managed to bring her up independently of a husband, surely between the both of them, they could do as much. It would have the care of two mothers, even if no father. She had no direct experience or real knowing of what was involved in a mother's work, but she did know that love was the most important nurturer, and that, they had in abundance.

As she went from draper to draper, collecting bundles of good linen, she wondered how Eleanor was getting on. She could not help being nervous of these charades and for a female to dare to enter such male domains was a bold and risky step. This, she knew, would thrill her deep down. To go where she was not ordinarily permitted to. To gull them into thinking her one of them. She only hoped no one would detect her and that she would be at the wigmakers on time to meet her in an hour.

The Lark.

January 1822. - Eleanor.

I stood outside the barber's shop for at least twenty minutes, too nervous to enter it. Every time I came close to plucking up the courage, another gentleman would walk past me and push the door open. I was hoping to catch the barber alone so that at least if he did suspect me, there would be no audience to witness the fallout. But before I knew it, a queue was forming on the wooden benches inside the window, and I knew if I wanted to get my hair cut today, it was to be now or never.

I bought a newspaper from a passing paper boy and headed in, doing my utmost to remember the briefly practised gait that had won the troupe's approval. It felt contrived and unnatural to walk with such a casual swagger. Still, I did my best to embrace it as the bell rang out above my head, and the seated men looked up briefly and nodded in something of a gesture of polite acknowledgement, before shuffling up a fraction to make room for me on the bench.

I took my seat and spread out the rolled-up sheets of the paper, which I only noticed now was a shameful and inappropriate purchase to flaunt beneath the noses of the merchant class men I was amongst. *John Bull* was boldly printed across the top, and I rolled it back up as quickly as I read the title case and tucked it beneath my arm, hoping no one had chanced to peek at it. Gosh, even I could not stand this Tory hack, the poison pen that had vilified our Queen with such relentless satisfaction in the years before her death. She had been the best thing our Royal family had to offer since Princess Charlotte, as far as I could tell, and whatever else, the public opinion of the same could not be rightly called unjust on this topic. I could think of nothing more offensive to these humble men than the political rhetoric of such a pompous swine as John Bull.

I had hoped to pick up a copy of *The Morning Post* to check who was reported to be in town presently, whilst sinking behind the pages until my turn in the barber's chair came about. Now I was to try to comport myself as best as possible without looking out of place amongst them.

I cast furtive glances about the parlour, taking in this strange environ: its unusual smells, consisting of the woody scent of male cologne and talcum powders masking undertones of sweat and the damp coats of tradesmen. Of the one who sat closest to me, I caught the scent of wax and tallow and considered he might be in the chandler's business. Another, the scent of the meat market, clung to his sheepskin coat, and another, a scent I knew all too well; the smell of the stables. Oh, how I missed that smell. How I missed my Samson, pelting along Rotten Row on his back in the spring sunshine. I looked ardently towards our reunion. As soon as we found someplace to settle permanently, I would send for him. Although, whether we would have the space or means to keep him might be an altogether different matter.

I listened to the casual chatter set against the vigorous snipping of hair and the scrape of the cutthroat razor. There were two barbers at work in this parlour and another one who was taking his patrons out to a back room to have their teeth pulled. I tried not to flinch at the groans of pain and cursing that rose out of that direction from time to time, as some poor fellow faced the barbary of the iron pliers prising out a stubborn tooth. I half listened to the chatter and occasionally put in a nod of agreement if it seemed the popular opinion of the room, but on the whole, I tried to stay quiet and observe the behaviour of the others in order to better inform my own.

By the time my turn in the queue came about, and the barber brushed down his chair and gestured me into it, I had already learnt the cost of the haircut by watching other men pay. The protocol of having a linen cloak draped about one's shoulders to protect your clothes from the falling hair, and to be offered the service of a shave at the end of the cut, to which I must remember to decline on account that my stick-on sideburns would give me away. I must decline the customary tap on the cheeks and neck of cologne if I was not to have the kohl stipple marks wiped away by it too.

'Well, I don't think you've visited us for a time,' the barber jested as he untied my hair, which I had put in the style of a back ponytail in order to keep my hat on better.

'No,' I said simply.

'Well, what will you have today then?'

'I want it all gone. As short as you might.'

'Quite a drastic change then, lad. You sure you don't want me to cut it down in stages and see how you like it first?'

'No.'

He shrugged. 'Would fetch a pretty penny from the wig maker if I cut it off in one neat bunch. I can have it tied with string and wrapped in paper for you for an extra threepenny if you are certain?'

'Yes, quite certain. Thank you, sir. My wife wants it gone, so she shall have her wish today.'

'Newlyweds, are yer?' the barber asked in a tone of surprised amusement.

'Yes, last month, as a matter of fact,' I said, having hoped this explanation would prove a conclusion to the topic, not an opening to another.

'That explains it then,' said one of the waiting men upon the benches with a little laugh. 'Enjoy it whilst it lasts, young fella. In a few years' time, you'll be putting more effort into escaping her nagging, than bowing to please her every whim.'

'I doubt that, sir,' I said with more affront than I meant to, which was met with a peel of laughter from everyone in the parlour, save the latest screamer in the backroom.

'Ah, to be young and rosy-eyed again, eh,' said the barber, pulling the lengths of my hair out from beneath the cloak he had just fashioned about my shoulders.

'Aye, it's hard to imagine I was once like that. My Betty and I can barely stand the sight of each other now, though.'

'How long you been married, Reggie?' The barber asked, as he began to trim my curls to neck length.

'Twenty-two years too long, but the first one doesn't count amongst them because I liked her then,' he laughed out loud. 'I'd 'ave sold her after the first year, when she was still worth a pretty penny before the children came and she lost her figure, had I known what I'd be in for, for the other twenty-one.'

'Well, I too am to be a father this year, and I could not care a fig how my wife's figure alters, for I love her now, and I shall love her all the more for bearing me a child,' I said, trying to moderate my tone whilst maintaining my manly voice. I could tell the inflection wanted to rise naturally with my infuriation.

'Romantic notions, nipper, but I'll wager you'll be of a different mind altogether when the time comes about. And even if she manages to keep her figure, I doubt she'll manage to keep her nagging tongue if she's already dishing out orders to have your hair lopped off.'

'Leave the boy be, Reggie,' said the barber. 'Let him enjoy his honeymoon without the taint of your ill fortune.'

'Hear, hear!' said the man in the chair next to me, who had been unable to join the conversation before now, since he was holding still for the barber's blade. Now he patted his cheeks dry with the offered towel. 'Just because your luck is down, don't mean to say romance is dead for the rest of us. I've loved the same woman for nigh on twenty years, and it only increases with the passing of time.'

'I didn't know you were married, Barney,' said his barber, who was pouring cologne into his large palms.

'I'm not...yet,' he replied. A reply that sent the room up in a raucous fit of hearty laughter.

'Well, there you are then, that's why – she ain't your wife!' Reggie declared, as if that proved his point.

'She shall be soon, though, you may be sure.'

'And there you will begin your journey to understanding what us knowing folk are talking of. All women seem a handsome enough proposition, until you marry 'em.'

'That's may be for you, but I have waited an age for this opportunity, and I shan't be put off by your bitter talk,' Barney retorted as the barber delivered a slap of cologne to the cheeks.

'Aye, but don't say I didn't warn you. These womenfolk are cunning little wenches.'

'Well, mine, sir, is the fairest of beauty and heart,' I cut in, and was glad that I had defended Annalise's honour, even if I could not openly defend my own. Is that really what men thought and said of us in our absence? I hoped this was but a poor representation of their sex, for I was not sure how well I could uphold such a pretence if I was to be subjected to such insults.

But the subject seemed to die off with a hint of stale discomfort hanging in the air for the following few minutes, until the barber beside carried on his conversation with the shaved man, to which I did little more than listen in on, for the remainder of my time there. It was pertaining to some bad business about a shipwreck that occurred on the Thames estuary earlier this month, where the crew perished with it. The Captain leaving his wife and four young children to mourn him. It sounded like a dreadful circumstance from what I could make of it. Although the fellow in the barber's chair beside me seemed of a mind that one's man's loss was another man's gain, and he meant to go and pay this grieving widow a visit and propose to her, for she was the object of his heart. – Some abbreviated tale of a lost love of his youth was given, and now it seemed to his mind that fate had afforded him a second chance. The other fellows in the barber shop chided him, just a little, on his eager timing, but he was not to be put off. Saying she never did love the Captain anyway and would not be sorry about his loss.

There was a time when I would have thought such talk insensitive and false. But I knew now what it was to have a husband I would prefer dead over alive. I could think of nothing better than to hear that Giles had been shipwrecked on one of his sea voyages and to be rendered forever free of him. Free to live out my days with my true love without ever having to look over my shoulder again. Indeed, shipwrecks were reported in the papers with such regularity that surely it was only a matter of time before one of his journeys went ill. I could but live in hope, I supposed, and asked, just to make sure: 'What was the name of this ship that sunk and for where was it bound?' For all I knew, he might have set off for Venice by now, or made one of his trips across the Irish sea.

'The *Lark*,' came their reply.

135

'And where was it bound for again?'

'Newhaven, the very same direction I am headed for this very day!' said the fellow beside me, the barber untying his linen cape and brushing loose hairs from the nape of his neck.

It seemed an unlikely route for Giles to take, but it was not impossible.

'WHERE ON EARTH HAVE you been?' Annalise demanded when I finally arrived at the wigmakers a quarter-hour late, and found her at the dressing parlour with an assistant unpinning a mousy brown wig from her head.

'Sorry, the barbers were busy.' I did not mean to elaborate beyond this explanation in the company. Nor did I want to show her my haircut with an audience, so I kept my hat on despite her asking me to take it off. 'Have you found anything suitable here?'

She nodded and proceeded to show me the selection of wigs she had been trying out whilst the assistant brought me a range of moustaches and brows to look at. I held them up to my face in the looking glass until we agreed upon the most convincing, and we waited whilst the assistant made small trimming adjustments to better fit me before sticking them on with a paste of Arabic gum. I told him I was an actor and he seemed to pay no marked interest in my odd request. Only asking me if I might like to consider the purchase of their own fixing gum, which was renowned in the theatres for holding much better.

'Thank you very much, sir, I shall take two jars. Now, my dear sister here would like to take the brown plaited wig, and that will be everything. —Oh, and the barber mentioned that you might be interested in purchasing this?' I pulled the paper-bound knot of hair from my pocket, glossy and thick with ringlets twisting beneath the string ties.

Annalise cast a mournful glance at it.

'Your own hair, sir?'

'Indeed. Freshly cut but a half hour ago. Yours for the bargain, if you wish.'

'Right, well, I shall just have a word with my superior—'

'Of course.'

He took the bundle of hair out to a backroom of the shop and returned a minute later declaring that he would take it off our hands for ten shillings redeemed off of our bill, to which I—knowing no better as to whether this was a fair bargain—accepted the offer and paid the remainder, glad to have spared some small coins for the rest of our journeying. All this hiring of coaches to get from one place to another was such a dreaded inconvenience; the booking of tickets in advance and making sure to have the right change in my purse at every moment. I had never before travelled using such public methods, and I could not claim to prefer it. The Ashlyn coach and four was a luxury I had never before appreciated until being shoulder squeezed up against all sorts of persons with no room, no warm blankets at my lap, and some suspiciously odd smells arising from time to time. It was a luxury I would be sorry to part with, but at least when my term was over, I could take to riding again. I should prefer the option of travelling on horseback or driving my own vehicle, above all public alternatives. However, getting Annalise comfortable with horses, let alone teaching her how to ride, might yet prove the greater challenge.

We stepped out of the shop straight into a downpour of murky drizzle and not a hackney cab in sight, arms full of Annalise's purchases from the linen warehouses and the wig box tucked beneath the heavy sleeve of my greatcoat. As if that wasn't enough to contend with, a cart horse decided to halt, and empty his bowels directly in our path. I hailed a crossing sweeper to spare Annalise's skirt hems, and he led us all the way through the market and back to Ludgate Hill, where at last, we were able to wave down a cab to take us onto Mrs Neals.

I knew Cheapside was not far from this district and was likely walkable if I consulted my *Cary's* pocketbook. But the weather was grim, and we still had our travelling bags to collect from the *Belle Sauvage* on our way through.

The groom hopped down and lowered the footplate for us, held his arm out to help Annalise into the carriage and simply doffed his hat at me. It took me a moment to register that ill manner was not to blame. I was a young man now in the eyes of the world, requiring no such assistance, and I searched for something to hold onto to climb up before he closed the door behind me. I could not help laughing just a little at my own absurdity in expecting him to convey me up.

'What's so funny?' Annalise asked, frowning as she tucked her linen parcels neatly on the seat beside her.

'Nothing, I just came close to making a little faux pas, that's all.'

She nodded. 'Well, are you going to take your hat off and show me your haircut at last?'

'But I know you shall hate it.'

'Of course I won't hate it. Besides, I shall see it later anyway, so what's the use in prolonging it?'

Reluctantly, I lifted it, prepared for a horrified gasp or some such reaction. Instead, she turned her head at an angle and said: 'It's not so bad as I feared. It suits you in an odd, manly sort of way, I suppose. —Do you like it?'

'I regretted it the instant I saw it.' I did not tell her that I was so distracted with my infuriation at the derogatory speeches I was subjected to in that place that I failed to notice it until it was cropped to just above my ear, where at that point, I intervened to bid him stop there. 'It feels wonderfully light though, *that* I like.'

'Well, as you said, it shall grow back.'

'IT CANNOT BE!' SAID Lady W. holding a palm to her chest, when we were admitted into Mrs Neals house on Watling Street. The shock was genuine, and I knew that she would otherwise have failed to recognise me if it were not for Annalise.

I flung my arms about her and squeezed her tight. 'Oh, how I have missed you, my dear friend. And Mrs Neal, it is good to see you too. How well you both look. Thank you so much for inviting us here.'

'You are very welcome, my dear. Why don't you let Hobbs take your coats and hats, and we shall go into the drawing room and have some tea to warm you up. You look chilled to the bone.'

We readily accepted this, grateful to get warm and comfortable and shed our damp coats after so many hours bereft of a good fire. We spent a lively half hour catching up and exchanging news before discussing the *Spinning House*, which surprised them both a great deal once I had explained all I knew of the place. They knew nothing of such schemes, but since my writing to Lady W. on the matter, she had undertaken some enquiries and consulted her legal man who, himself having been tutored in Cambridge in his youth, was all too familiar with the way things were done there.

'It seems this royal charter has been in place for over three hundred years, pertaining to both Oxford and Cambridge, and so it is nothing new it seems,' Lady W. said, turning pages in her journal where she had taken notes. 'But, it appears to Mr Noakes that the University authorities are misusing it, and that if there happened to be sufficient proof of this abuse of their authority, then indeed it may be possible to bring a case against them. Most salient, he feels, is the use of what appears to be a private prison and the dubious circumstances of *reasonable* grounds for apprehension in the first instance.'

'The townspeople are well aware of these abuses. Young girls scared to walk about the town, and mothers worried about their daughters being plucked from the streets and having their reputation ruined or catching some deathly disease from the filthy place. I am certain I can gather evidence now we have the cover to move around in disguise. It has been too risky to try before now.'

'Well, that would be the better way to approach it, quietly for now. Gather as much as you can up there, speak to the local women, anyone who has been unfortunate enough to be on the receiving end of the proctors and willing to testify. Down here, I shall consult with Mr Noakes on whatever you discover and find us a man with the gall to take up such a case. He shan't be persuaded to challenge them publicly, but he is willing to assist me in finding a man who can. A young-blooded liberal, not afraid of a scandal, who would like to make a name for himself, he thinks would best answer for the task. If it goes to court, it is likely to cause quite a scandal for the University and may even incite the rioters of recent years, if the public mood is riled. So, we shall need a brave fellow willing to take on the risk.'

'Does Mr Noakes think we have much chance of finding such a fellow?'

'Well, if we shall anywhere, it will be here in London, and if all else fails, there is always a good old-fashioned monetary reward, which seems never to disappoint in its persuasive power.'

'I don't have much money anymore. Not without—'

'Ah, but you see, I do, and we may raise some too as often we do for the Society. You have a band of experts in that art right behind you, do not forget, and whilst we have not announced the topic in our monthly meeting as of yet, those we have entrusted to this information are far from happy about the goings on up there and are ready to rally. But we have to have a care, you see. Some of our supporters are mothers who entrust the guardianship of their sons to these institutions and may not share our views. We don't want to cause division amongst the Society, so our recruitment to the cause may need to be quietly selective.'

I had not thought of that. I could imagine mama being outraged by such a notion as to reduce the proctor's power, and in her mind at least, leave her darling sons exposed to the dangers of lewd women. That they were the procurers of such services would not be up for discussion. That they managed to find ways to make up amply for it when away from the proctor's protection would not be spoken of either. I would have liked to believe that Society women would be of sound enough judgement to see things for what they were, and not hide behind such myths of ignorance and denial, but I knew most of them too vaguely to be any sort of judge.

With the preliminary plans for the scheme settled, we moved into the dining room where Mrs Neal had taken the trouble to furnish us with the finest-looking feast I had set eyes upon since leaving for Stapleford last year. I had never really appreciated the grandeur in which I had been used to taking every meal in, until late. Not that Mrs Duckworth's fare was to be grumbled at in the least. Quite the contrary. But it was simple home cooking, tasty and nutritious enough to be sure, but there was no turtle or sautéed pheasant in foie gras, or white truffle to be seen upon the table there, and the offering of it now seemed something of a novelty too good to pass up. I filled my plate with a helping of each. Annalise, on the other hand, glanced at my plate with a suspicious eye and settled for sliced beef and vegetables. I could tell she was uncomfortable at the table. She had become accustomed to dining privately with me but never at a grand table like this and in such company. I made a pointed effort to indicate my choice of cutlery and plate to guide her blank-faced confusion. I should have taught her before now, but there had never seemed the need. Of course, our company was well aware of Annalise's position but had no qualms in admitting her to the table and treating her with all the civility and generosity that was offered in my direction under the circumstances. The guise of this being on account of assisting in the false story Mrs Neal had given to her servants: that she was to be visited by a twice removed niece and nephew today. I had wondered at this being a little over-cautious since neither of us were known to Mrs Neal's household, but its necessity soon became clear when our plates were cleared, and Lady W. pulled out a wad of newspapers and spread them out upon the table in front of us.

'Now, my dear, you know I am not one for stirring up a panic, and I have to say, having seen you now so drastically altered, I feel a great deal more at ease that not a soul would notice you. But I have to show you these.' She slid papers towards us, and to my horror, an article had been placed, marking me as missing from my husband since last year, offering up a reward for my safe return and sporting an impression of me that looked suspiciously reminiscent of my coming out portrait taken last spring. I could hardly believe my eyes, and when I looked up from it, Annalise's were equally horrified. 'The devious blackguard!' I declared. 'Forgive me, ladies,' I added quickly, remembering my company. Annalise had said that I had been too long in the company of the vulgar tongued, and it was rubbing off on me. I knew she meant Theo and the troupe, and whilst I had denied the accusation at the time, upon reflection, I had begun to realise that perhaps she had not been entirely unjustified.

'Choice words my dear, but fitting, I don't deny. Now, as far as I can tell, these have been printed consistently in the London papers for the past two days. I cannot vouch for any further afield, but it seems reasonable to suspect tomorrow's prints may well contain the same.'

'Surely it would cost him a small fortune to continue printing in the papers day in and out.'

'Well, he has plump enough pockets, my dear, and it seems he is unwilling to let you go without putting up a fight. That is not all. It seems he served papers on Mr Richards only last week.'

'No. Are you certain?'

She nodded, and from my peripheral view, I saw Annalise's gaze set on the tablecloth and took a moment to think before I spoke. 'Have you had it directly or—'

'On the rumour mill, until Saturday evening when he approached me at the duke's hunting ball dinner. He was playing there, you see. Doing very well for himself and can be expected in any fashionable ballroom or concert hall, for how long now, remains to be seen. My advice to him was to take a holiday abroad for a little while and wait for the storm to settle. Whether he shall take me up on it or not, I cannot say.'

My heart sunk in a welter of guilt. *He did not deserve this.* He was finally making a name for himself, and it should be me, the mother of his child, who would be his undoing. I tried not to let the sadness show upon my face. I hoped its odd disguise might help to better conceal it. 'Do the scandal brewers believe it for fact or suspicion?'

'From what I can gather, purely suspicion as it stands. I have not seen anything reported on it. I believe that cousin of his has been busy fuelling that fire.'

'Mariella,' I said through gritted teeth, biting down on them to prevent myself from speaking in profanities again.

'Your parents are reported to be most displeased, but that's to be expected.'

'And now this,' I picked up the article with my face staring up at me from the page, 'they will surely have seen it by now. My papa is back at Westminster, so they are likely at Berkeley Square. My mama always has the *Morning Post*. Perhaps I should arrange to see her whilst I'm here. Secretly, I mean.'

'No. Don't do that, my dear. They are likely being watched. I know I was, until of late.'

I felt a tear bleed down the length of my cheek and dampen the whiskers of my faux moustache. 'I'm so sorry, Lady W.'

'No need for that, my dear. You are not to blame for his actions, and you may be sure I have given these shady fellows quite the runaround; their heads must be in quite a spin. I suspect that's why they have given up on me of late.'

I smiled through my tears. Annalise's gentle palm was already resting lightly against my back. I stared at the image in front of me, its carbon ink slightly smudged from my tears but clearly and faithfully depicting me, despite it. 'I don't understand how he obtained this painting of me. My parents would have never permitted him into the house, and that portrait is far too large to be taken out of it without notice—'

'I daresay he didn't undertake to try. But it is not very difficult to send an unknown man, is it? A few shillings to a willing servant for a peek inside the family gallery. A request to the housekeeper for a tour whilst your parents are away in town. Even someone known to the house. It could all be made to seem innocent enough, I'm sure.'

The idea of all this sneaking and surveillance made me furious. Turned my stomach. He thought he had the right to stalk my friends and family, advertise me publicly like a lost hound or stolen filly and recapture me for a few Guineas. *What was the reward?* I scanned the small print again to find it was not stated. It read only:

"A handsome reward to be bestowed upon the bearer of information leading to the safe recovery or whereabouts of this wealthy gentleman's beloved wife."

Two vindictive paths of scheming were forming in my mind. The first: was to set him up and contrive some faux reply stating a sighting of me in some distant part of the country, or even on the continent, to throw a rub in the way. The other was to hatch a plan to take the reward for myself and contrive a way to escape and flea with it at the last. Perhaps Mr Leonard Leamington could make enquiries with him. The address given in the advert was not one known to me, and I assumed it to be that of his legal man or some such man of business.

'Eleanor?'

I looked up to see Mrs Neal offering me a handkerchief and a jar of smelling salts. 'Thank you,' I said, accepting both, realising as I mopped my wet cheeks that I had rubbed the kohl paint off, staining the white cotton.

'Would you prefer to stay here for the night, for the duration of your trip perhaps? I think you will be quite safe with us for a time,' offered Mrs Neal.

'It might be for the best. Surely Carshalton will not be safe now—' Annalise added, eyes pleading with me.

'No. No, thank you, Mrs Neal. You are very generous, and I thank you for it, but I mean to undertake my trip as planned and not permit him any further satisfaction at my cost. I shall be safe enough in my disguise, don't you think?'

'I do,' said Lady W., 'Providing you keep your head and do not attempt to contact any of your connections, however secretly.'

I nodded. 'Of course. I was not thinking straight.'

We spent a little longer at Mrs Neals, sat about the fire whilst she sent her manservant to arrange the hire of a coach and horses from a nearby inn. She would have her own horsemen drive us back so they knew we had reached there safely. It seemed too risky to them, under the circumstances, to permit us to travel by stage or hack or any so public a means that close to home, where the locals were undoubtedly well aware of my picture and status as "missing". However well disguised I was, nothing was entirely failsafe, and I could not deny that despite knowing how altered I was from that picture in the paper, I no longer felt the confidence I had arrived with. All the creeping pangs of paranoia and anxiety rushing back through my veins like I had never left at all. Like even from afar, he had managed to pull the veil from me and expose me to the world. My face on every breakfast room table in London, perhaps beyond.

Half of me was minded to head directly back to Cambridgeshire, the other defiant and determined to visit Annalise's premises. I had wanted to see them from the moment I learnt about it. I was proud of her, and I wanted her to see it for herself. I wanted her to understand that I was serious about a change of lifestyle after the child was born. That I meant to settle for more humble ways of living with her beside me. A trade-off my heart was already long decided upon.

We patched up my face paints, put on our dried and brushed coats and hats. and exchanged an emotional farewell with our dear hosts as they waved us off from the mews.

An Unannounced Fiancé.

January 1822.- Annalise.

They pulled up at Carshalton High Street under cover of darkness and disembarked as quickly and quietly as possible.

Annalise was relieved when they stepped inside, and she closed the door behind them, with no one about the street to take notice, from what she could tell. The heat rushed over them instantly, and the smell of the day's cooking lingered in the warm air: Beef dumplings and parsnip soup, she thought, as she turned the key to lock the door and lifted her travelling bag back up off the floor. The shop parlour was in darkness, but a thin veil of moonlight cast just enough light to make out the outline shadows once their eyes adjusted. No more an empty carcass, she knew it much altered as they stepped around tables and chairs and were careful to avoid knocking any of the chinaware from the surrounding counters and shelves as they lifted the countertop to pass through to the back parlour. She tapped gently at the door, not wanting to startle Poppy if they were sat on the other side of the partition wall. But no answer came, and she nudged it gently open and was rendered astounded at the cosy, homely look of it. She felt instantly close to tears.

The fire was roaring in the grate, two mismatched armchairs set on either side of it and a low upholstered bench seat opposite. There were wooden side tables in reach of each chair, an empty mug upon one of them and a folded-up newspaper. Annalise knew what this must mean since neither Poppy nor Maggie had their letters. They must have seen the article. Perhaps Miss Lockheart had told them of it.

She sank down into the chair beside it and picked it up. The *Surrey Gazette*, page two and there it was, the article they had seen at Mrs Neals. It was not only the London papers then.

'Annalise, this is marvellous. I cannot believe it is all yours!' Eleanor said, standing in the doorway, looking about her and taking in the shape of the room and everything in it.

'It's in here too,' Annalise said, holding up the article to show her.

'I suspected it would be. No doubt every press all the way to John o' Groats.'

'Sit down, warm up,' Annalise bid her.

'I will in a moment. I just want to look about the place.'

Annalise nodded, returned to the paper, then threw it into the flames, watching it smelt down to ashes. When she looked up again, Maggie was in the kitchen doorway screaming, 'Housebreaker!' at Eleanor, and Poppy came running out behind her with a heavy saucepan in her hands, lifted, poised, ready to strike.

'No!' Annalise shouted, bolting into view and in front of Eleanor, who had jumped back a fraction and was trying to talk to them through all the noise.

Poppy dropped the pan onto the floor in surprise. 'Annalise?'

'Yes, it's me. S-he's with me too. There is no housebreaker.'

'Oh, fank the lord! That didn't 'alf give me a fright,' Poppy said with her hands clasping her cheeks, which were scarlet red with heat.

'Sorry, Poppy, we didn't mean to frighten you. I did knock, but there was no reply.' Annalise had not had time to send word ahead of them to say they would be arriving before the stagecoach they had been booked to journey in. Everything had changed so quickly at the last minute.

'No need to knock, luv, it's your 'ouse. We weren't expecting you so early, that's all. We were just trying to get tomorrow's preparations done, so I could sit up with you tonight. Well, come 'ere then, aren't you gonna give me a hug?'

It wasn't a question. She charged forward and scooped Annalise up in a bear hug. 'Oh, I missed you, luv. Let me look at you. Don't you look in rosy health! All that country living's done you good. See that: skin as soft as kid. That's escaping the kitchen, that is. Look at my poor cheeks!' She laughed.

'Well, are you going to pay this fellow and send him on his way,' she nodded in Eleanor's direction.

She must have supposed him a luggage bearer awaiting his veils and dismissal. She quickly considered what the less of evils was; to entrust this secret to them or to offer a Banbury tale. They had discussed this on the journey to Carshalton at length, and Eleanor had insisted that she entrust them with the truth and bring them into their confidence. Something that Annalise would not have second thought in usual circumstances. But these were *not* usual circumstances. There was so very much at stake. She knew neither of them would intentionally betray their trust, but Maggie, Maggie, was the sweetest yet most unreliable when it came to keeping her sense and her tongue. She reasoned that one could not accidentally let slip what one did not know. So she braced herself for Poppy's surprise and said: 'This is my companion. Poppy, Maggie. I give you Mr Leonard Leamington. He shall be staying with us. I hope you do not mind. We are engaged to be married.'

'What?' Poppy replied.

Annalise was so preoccupied with Poppy's jaw-dropping horror and Maggie reeling off excited congratulations and all sorts of wedding fantasies, that she did not see Eleanor's contorted expression. She looked up when Eleanor quickly dipped to a low bow and said:

'Ladies, so very charmed to meet you. I have heard so much about you from Miss Tullier. It is very kind of you to have me here.'

Maggie stepped up excited and shook Leonard's hand vigorously, saying: 'What a handsome 'usband you shall have, Anna! He speaks like a true gent!'

Poppy was still too stunned to say anything more but softened her expression, offering a thin-lipped smile and dropped the slightest of curtsies before eventually saying, 'How do you do, sir.'

'Very well. I thank you. What a lovely establishment you have here.'

'Well, thank yer. Should I make us some tea or fetch some beer?' Poppy offered, at a loss for what else to say to this stranger, seemingly conjured into her parlour from thin air. No doubt about to make himself at home here, with or without her blessing.

'No. Please do not go to any trouble on my account. I am quite well. I was hoping Miss Tullier would be so good as to give me the tour, so we need not disturb you from your work.'

'Poppy looked suspiciously between Leonard and Annalise and nodded, saying: 'Well, perhaps a bit later then. I 'ave got my kidneys on to braise – they should be ready now. If you'll excuse us,' she said, picking up the empty copper saucepan from the floor and grabbing Maggie by the wrist and pulling her in the direction of the kitchen.

'What the deuce—' began Eleanor when the kitchen door closed behind them and the sounds of the kitchen stirred back into life.

'I know, I know. I can explain,' Annalise said, palms held up in front of her.

'I suggest you do! I thought we agreed—'

'Not here. Let's take our coats off, and I shall give you the tour,' she said pointedly, and Eleanor did as bid, lifted her greatcoat off and hung it upon the back of one of the dining chairs, placed her hat upon the tabletop.

It was only then Annalise noticed through the back window, the shape of the new extension building jutting out into the garden yard in shadow. She picked up an oil lamp and said: 'Let's start in here. I have not seen it yet,' she indicated towards the door she had once thought a cupboard. Opening it up now, she was met with a door through to the extension room, which seemed so much larger than she imagined it would be. Maybe it was owing to its emptiness, nothing but the flat lines of floorboards and lofty glass windows to frame the empty space. It near brought a tear to her eye, seeing it here, ready, waiting to be furnished and brought to life with industry. *What was to become of it now?* It hardly seemed worth troubling herself with thoughts of the furnishings and layout, even though her mind leapt instantly to such imaginings.

'Well?' Eleanor said, drawing her attention back to their current predicament. 'Are you going to tell me what all that was about? I thought you were of a mind that honesty amongst friends was paramount, and here you are cutting such shams—'

'Keep your voice down,' Annalise hushed her, seeing the glow of light beyond the kitchen backdoor through the condensated windows of the extension building. The slightest sound seemed amplified in here. 'I'm sorry. I had no choice. When we decided to bring them into the scheme, we didn't know if the news had reached this quarter, and now we do. Now everyone will be talking about it, since it is so very close to home and your family so prominently known.'

'Well, we knew it was a possibility.'

'Yes, but you don't understand. Maggie. She is the sweetest, most harmless of souls for the most part. You will see that for yourself soon enough. But. She does not think before she speaks and speaks a little too freely and honestly to anyone. It is perhaps her only fault, but it can be a perilous one when anything serious is at stake. I assure you, if we were to tell her who you really were, it would be all over the village tomorrow and not out of any sense of malice or intent, but simply unintended carelessness, and then what?'

'And Poppy? You said you could trust her—'

'I can. But I shall have to tell her privately when Maggie is not about to hear it.'

'I suggest you do that sooner rather than later. She looked appalled at you. I cannot imagine she will appreciate such trickery. Why could you not just say I was some sort of manservant as she had assumed me to begin with? Or a friend, a long-lost relative. Your fiancé Annalise? By gad, we are playing with fire.'

'And insult my friends by bringing an unknown male stranger beneath their roof without warning and calling their respectability into question in view of their neighbours and customers tomorrow? I had no choice but to tell them you were my fiancé, for it is the only respectable excuse I could find for a young man being present here at all. It is not as though we have service quarters where it would not be questioned. And as for playing with fire. I have never known you to do otherwise since the day I met you! I told you to stay at Stapleford. Then you declined Mrs Neal's sensible offer to remain with her—'

'Alright. Don't get into such a fidget. I'm sorry. I see you are only trying to protect us all. I was just taken by surprise. What, oh no, don't cry. I'm not trying to upset you. Forgive me, love. I'm sorry.'

She felt Eleanor gather her up in her arms, and it was enough to invite the tears gushing forward now she was at last at liberty to let them fall. It had taken everything to contain them today, but they would be contained no more. They sprung hot and furious from her now and bled into the fabric of Eleanor's neckcloth. 'I'm scared, Len,' she eventually said when she recovered her breath enough to speak. 'I'm scared that people all over the place know your face. That he has spies out watching your family, your friends. How long before this closes in on us and we—' she whimpered the words out:' We are parted by him. I cannot bear it. The thought of you being forced back to that brute, the thought of you leaving me...'

'Come, come. You must not think that way. Nothing shall ever part us, Annalise, and I shan't go anywhere with him, no matter what.'

'But what if he—'

'Hush. You are letting your head run away with you. It's been a long day, and we are both tired. We shall feel better in the morning after a good night's sleep. Come here,' she said and pulled her into a kiss at the very moment Maggie walked through the door and said in excited accents: 'Oh, sorry! I didn't mean to...interrupt!'

They both stepped apart in surprise. 'You did not disturb anything, Maggie,' Annalise said quickly, knowing it was already too late. —That Maggie would rush off into the kitchen to convey a dramatic account of what she had just witnessed to Poppy, no matter what she tried to say to dissuade her.

'Oh,' she said, with a knowing grin on her face. 'Well, Poppy wanted me to ask you what the sleeping arrangements would be. For she's very sorry, but she only made arrangements for one of you, and she wants to put everything in order before bed.'

'Yes, yes, of course. I will come and see her directly once I have given Mr Leamington a tour.'

'Alright. I'll go and tell her then. Oh!' she clapped her hands together, 'It's all so romantic!' and backed out of the room, her footsteps dissipating in an excited frenzy.

'Damn!' Annalise said. 'She's going to tell her the whole.'

'Meaning you have the choice of continuing to keep Poppy in the dark now, or bringing her far closer into your confidence than you had planned—'

'I can't do that. We shall have to keep it up. Let's get this tour out of the way and work out where to sleep tonight. This day is full of unwelcome surprises, and I should like to put an end to it!'

Eleanor nodded, followed her out of the room, into the tiny hallway, up the winding staircase, and into the bedroom that had originally been meant for her. To Annalise's amazement, she found it comfortably furnished, the bed she had bought off Dr Shaw, dressed in bright white linens and soft woollen blankets. A side table she had not seen before but went perfectly with the chest of drawers and heavy wardrobe Mr Benson and his son had struggled to turn in the stairwell. On the floor, there was a sheepskin rug, the pile soft and un-trodden. At the windows, a heavy set of drapes in dusky pink velvet and upon the fire mantle, a freshly picked bunch of snowdrops in a vase. 'It's beautiful,' she gasped, taking it all in. Remembering her last impression of the room, partially bare and her belongings piled up all over the place. Poppy must have put them away neatly, for it was all perfectly uncluttered now and yet with enough homely finishes to make it feel complete.

'It's charming,' Eleanor agreed. 'Is this your room?'

Annalise nodded. 'It was supposed to be. But it was much a blank canvas when I left; now it is; a *real* home.'

'How many bedchambers do you have here?'

'Three.'

'Ah, I see the difficulty. Perhaps, I can take the sofa, it looks very comfortable.'

Annalise hadn't even spotted the fine Chinese sofa against the wall behind them. The one that had been meant for her sewing room. She wondered how they had managed to get it up here and hoped Poppy had not made the attempt herself at moving all the rearranged furniture about. 'No, that won't do. You shall stay here, and I will go in with Poppy.'

Eleanor frowned uncomfortably at this proposition. 'But I shall miss you beside me. I shan't be able to sleep.'

'There is nothing else for it. It is bad enough that I have to extend this sham with Poppy. I can hardly have her think me so bereft of propriety that I will share a room with a fellow out of wedlock, even if she does think him my fiancé.'

'Alright. Look, I shall do whatever you ask of me to make this as easy for you as possible. Gosh, if I had any idea how ill this would turn out, I would have stayed behind just to spare you the anguish. I hate to see you like this.'

'I know. I think we must make this trip briefer than planned. Perhaps we could take the stage back tomorrow.'

'No. No, I shan't have your visit spoiled on my account. I shall go back tomorrow alone. And you shall follow on after your holiday, and all will be well. I only wanted to see your home, not cause you grief. I am so proud of you, my love. And I want you to know that even though I realise it cannot be here, I want nothing more than to settle somewhere just like this, with you, for the rest of my days. I have been quietly planning for such a future for us, and when we are back in the country again, I shall explain it all. Perhaps we can find such a place together, just as you have managed to bring this all about so cleverly. For you see, I don't have the first notion of how these things are managed. But you can teach me, and we might have it all worked out by the time the child arrives. Then we never need live like this again. We can begin anew on our terms. But for now, I shall retire so you can have some time alone with your friends. And tomorrow, I shall set off early on the stage.'

'No. I don't want to be parted from you, Len. I have had this terrible gut feeling ever since Lady W. showed us the article. It's like I can *feel* him on our tail. Like this inexplicable horror inside me is whispering: run and do not leave her out of your sight beyond a moment.'

'That's just your mind doing what it always does when given something to puzzle over. He cannot know where I am, or he would have intervened by now, hmm? Look at how many people we have been about today, and not a single sign of anything suspicious. So long as I stay as Leonard and keep myself quiet, there is no reason to think anyone shall be the wiser. Don't you see? Poppy doesn't know who I am. The disguise works. And what with my haircut and facial hair: I am quite beyond recognition now.'

'Oh Len, what were we thinking setting out like this? We should have just stayed where we were. And what if the papers in Cambridgeshire have been publishing your image? We have been so freely about the town and even up at Bury, and then you were not in disguise. Think how many people shall recognise you now.'

'Well, we have certainly not seen it in any of the papers before leaving, have we? And even if it has, by now, been printed there, well, it's simple. We are nearly a ten mile from Cambridge anyway and further still from Bury. From now on, I promise I shall not so much as leave the grounds of Stapleford for any purpose whatsoever, unless I am in the character of Leonard, alright?'

Annalise nodded and fell into her embrace again. What did it matter now if Maggie was to barge in again? The damage was already done. Poppy was to think poorly of her for kissing her male fiancé or her female lover. She would have to brace herself for an ear boxing either way. So for just a moment, she wanted to feel the comfort and warmth of Eleanor's embrace before she faced the music.

ONCE ELEANOR WAS TO bed, and she had conveyed their travelling bags upstairs, Annalise braced herself to face Poppy, who was still busy in the kitchen from the sound of all the clatter of pots and pans. *Is this how late she worked now?* Not much of an improvement upon Cuddington, she considered, checking the clock to find it was now a quarter past ten. She could not decide whether to go in and disturb them or wait quietly in the back parlour until they were done. She dithered between the two, walking up to the kitchen door momentarily, then losing her nerve and padding back to sit at the dining table again.

There was a beautiful ambience about the main parlour now, however humbly furnished. Poppy had breathed life into the place with all her little additions. It was the small things that brought it about. The pots of herbs upon the windowsill. The lacework doilies laid out on the dining table to spare the polish of the wood. The pewter candelabra at the centre of it. She had even found some more pictures to hang on the walls. Was that? Yes, it was, a sketch of this very house looking on from the street. If nothing else positive had come from this trip insofar, she was grateful to see how well settled they were here. How far it had come since she had fled from it that November morning, fearing herself too late.

She sat about, taking in every detail of the room for another ten minutes before resigning herself to put an end to this fretting and go into the kitchen. She could hear their voices rising from behind the door; the other sounds quieter now as if their work was drawing to a close.

'It's not romantic!' she heard Poppy say, exasperated. 'Don't you see what this means?'

'That we shall need a new frock for the wedding breakfast?'

'No. Not that! He will be wanting to move in here, won't he? He will become master here.'

'But I thought Anna owns it?' Maggie said, in puzzled accents.

'Yes, she does now, you nincompoop. But when a woman marries, everything becomes his, don't it.'

Annalise tapped at the kitchen door. 'Can I come in?' she said, thinking it better to warn them to curb their conversation than startle them again. Poppy opened up the kitchen door and bid her in.

'Mmm, something smells delicious.'

'You hungry, luv? Shall I fix you something?' Poppy asked, slinging her tea cloth over her shoulder and wiping the table with a wet cloth.

'No. No, we have supped already. But it smells divine in here. What have you been cooking?'

'Well,' said Maggie, chiming in, 'we have steak and kidney pudding, game pie, chicken and leek – that's our best seller so far, so we have to make more of them than anyfing else. And then there's potato soup for tomorrow and the plum cakes, pound cakes, apple pie—'

'Alright, miss, I think she has the picture,' Poppy intercepted. 'Get yourself off to bed, won't you. Annalise can help me with the last few bits.'

Annalise nodded, understanding that Poppy wanted to speak privately with her.

'Oh, must I? I wanna hear all about the wedding.'

'Tomorrow, Maggie. We shall speak then, alright? Make the most of an early night whilst you can, eh?' Annalise persuaded her.

She nodded, threw down her cloth, and bid them both goodnight, leaving Annalise and Poppy standing face to face, not quite knowing where to begin.

'I'm sorry, Poppy,' Annalise said. 'I wanted to tell you before, but—'

'Who is he?' she said in that no-nonsense tone of hers Annalise understood perfectly.

'He is Eleanor's groom at the new house.'

'Well, what's 'e doing here?'

'We have become attached—'

'Yes, to his face, if what Maggie said is anything to go by!'

'I did not know she was there, Poppy. I would never have—'

'And I suppose he's up in your bed?'

'Yes. But I shan't stay with him if that's what you are worried about. I was hoping I could stay in with you?'

'What I'm worried about, Annalise, is that you've been gone for a few months, and suddenly you are throwing your future away on some fellow you don't know from Adam and have never so much as made a mention of.'

'I know it must all seem terribly sudden. I wanted to tell you. That's why he has come, to meet you all and gain your approval before—'

'Before you hand over everything you have to a fellow you barely know.'

'No. Poppy, we mean to have a long engagement, to be certain of each other before anything is settled. I am not as feather-headed as to rush into the matter.'

This seemed to subdue her somewhat, and she started popping the resting pie mixtures into the cooling cupboards. 'I never thought you one to lose your head over an 'andsome face...'

Annalise picked up Maggie's discarded tea cloth and began to help. 'I've missed you, Poppy. I have waited an age to see you. Can't we move beyond this and start afresh?'

'Oh, I've missed you too, luv. I don't wanna be on bad terms with yer on our precious few days together. I—I wasn't expecting this, that's all.'

'I know. And I take the blame for it. I should have written, but I didn't want Miss Lockheart to know, anyone to know but you, for now. It is too soon for such announcements when one of us may yet still change our minds and break off the arrangement.'

A flash of hope glittered in her eyes momentarily at this proposition. 'Well, there is one small problem with that.'

'Oh?'

'Well, I've no choice but to tell you now, though it was s'posed to be a surprise: I've arranged a little party for you tomorrow evening once the shop's shut. Our friends will be here at five o clock—Well, how was I to know you would be in such company? Oh my, poor Will. He shall be sorry to hear this news...'

'It's alright. Leonard will be returning home tomorrow morning. He does not like to impose. He only wanted to see me here safely and meet you, show his face.'

She seemed satisfied with this. 'Well, I wish I never told you now. I've spoilt the surprise. You will have to pretend!'

'I will. I shall do my best surprised look alright?' Annalise agreed, thinking she had become such a fraud of late; what would one more deception matter to add to the growing list? 'I daresay Maggie would have let the cat out of the bag tomorrow, anyway.'

'That's true.'

'Well, are you going to tell me how you've been?'

'Let me fetch us a brew, and we'll go and sit by the fire, eh? I need to take the weight off my poor feet. It's been non-stop since six this morning.'

'No,' Annalise said, taking the teapot from her hands. 'I shall make a brew, and you shall go and put your feet up this instant.'

IT TOOK UNTIL THEIR cups were empty for their familiar ease to return to them once more. She was sorry that she had caused Poppy so much undue shock and disappointment, but was happy to be here at last and hear all about how her friends were getting on. How the business had taken off so well around Christmastide, they had hardly had a moment's rest since St. Stephens day. That not only could they rely upon a full set of tables come noon each day, but Maggie also had to go about with a basket, dropping off orders to local patrons. *The Greyhound* had a daily standing order of a selection of pies for their dining customers. The builder's yard on Mill Lane often sent a lad to fetch a batch each afternoon. And then there were the customers who would have one for their supper but did not like to dine out in the cold season, so Maggie would go from door to door, saving them the bother. It was this she needed an extra pair of hands for. It had started out with just the odd delivery, but quickly turned into such a list that Maggie was often gone for hours when she could hardly be spared for one, leaving Poppy and the local day maid to manage the kitchen and dining parlour alone.

'Miss Lockheart thinks it would be sensible to give the job to a boy who could make the deliveries, and, in between them, take a push wagon about the busy spots in town, like the stagecoach points and the parklands, perhaps even along the fishing lakes when the sporting men are about.'

'It sounds like an excellent idea. Have you anyone in mind?'

'I 'aven't had a chance to think on it since she mentioned it.'

'Well, how about the Bartlett's boy? He would be perfect for such a job.'

'But don't they live towards Epsom way? How will he get here each morning? He'd have to be here by nine to make a start.'

'Well, you were planning to look for a boarding maid, were you not?'

'Yes, but I can't expect her to share with a boy, can I?'

'You could if it was to be his own sister.'

'Oh, the one you're to make a sewing apprentice, yes, I suppose that could work out, but, well, how's there to be room for us all? I mean before, I supposed me and you might go back to sharing, but if you are to be married—'

'Poppy, to tell the truth, there is something more serious I wanted to talk to you about whilst here. I don't think I will be coming back, not to live, anyway.'

'Because of Mr Leamington?'

She shrugged noncommittally. 'If things were to turn out well between us, we would likely move into his family home, you see. And if they don't, I expect I will remain with my mistress for as long as she needs me.'

'I see,' she said, seeming to weigh this up as she took it in.

Annalise suspected she was partly relieved to hear that Mr Leamington would not be elbowing his way in here as master, but sad to hear she would not be joining her as they had spoken so excitedly about in those days before her leaving. It upset Annalise too, but she knew now it was to be the way of things. She and Eleanor would eventually have to find someplace to settle, somewhere far from here if they were to live without the fear of her husband always on their tail. So what was the use in pretending otherwise and stalling progress here? Poppy needed the boarding space for staff so she was not worked off her feet from morning to night, and the Bartlett's children needed work. It all made perfect sense. 'Here's what I suggest, and you do not have to accept it, for you know best since your hard work has got things here. But the reality is, I do not need that room upstairs. Convert it into a dormitory for the young staff so you may take as many on as you need. I don't want you working your fingers to the bone, alright? The plan was never to trade one life of hard toil for another but to have an easier lot now. Half the work and thrice the reward, remember?'

She nodded.

'I'm sure there is room for at least four single beds up there, maybe five at a squeeze?'

'I don't think we need that many luv, not yet anyway.'

'Perhaps not, but you can build it up as you need to. Besides, you can have three young apprentices for the price of one established maid. And just think, you are giving them the learning to secure themselves a future, taking the burden off their parents by providing them board and still leaving them something to send home and keep for themselves.'

'But what about when you come to stay? There'll be nowhere for you and Mr—you do mean to come and visit, don't you? Take holidays with us at least?'

'Of course I do. As many as I can once things are more...certain. And who said Mr Leamington has to come? I can come and stay in with you, if you don't mind?'

'Don't be daft. I'd never mind a bit.'

'Well then. All that's left to consider is what is to be done with the new extension now. Have you any ideas?'

'Well, I suppose it would make a very nice dining room or servants' hall if we are to have so many staff as that. We'll hardly fit around that table comfortably. We already have to use it as an extra space for peeling and chopping when I'm baking in the morning as there's not enough space for all the cooling racks and for us all to be at work out there.'

'Well, yes, that's certainly an option, although I was thinking of how to put it to work for us to cover some of the bills. Rent it out, perhaps to another tradeswoman. A seamstress or Milner or the like, who hasn't a workspace of their own.'

'My luv, I don't think we'll need to. You see, well, you know I'm not good with me letters, but I've always had a head for counting, and I s'pose I got better at it since I have so many orders to tally and coins to count up. But anyway, it's all in my head. So last time Miss Lockheart was here, I asked her if she'd write it all down for me so I could make sense of it all and—I'll fetch it for you on our way up to bed so you can see for yourself—but she says we are already making a handsome effort from what she could tell. I told her the cost of all the merchant bills and coal and candle costs, wages and so on, and she said, we make on average, near to two pounds a week in...what was the word she used? Profit, yes that were it.'

'Two pounds a week in profit. Poppy, are you certain?'

She nodded. 'Yeah, I thought there must be a mistake in the counting, but she checked it all through with me, and it was all correct. I'd been trying to work it out meself before Miss Lockheart wrote it down, but because we've had so much to buy, between the ingredients, the furniture and all the new crockery, well, it's in and out the money jar in a flash. So I hadn't really been able to keep proper account.'

She was impressed. She had supposed there would not be a penny of profit to be had for quite some time. Mr Harrison had explained to her at length that new businesses often lose more money than they make to begin with, until their trade picks up and becomes established. And yet here they were, two pounds in profit within weeks of starting out. It certainly seemed a promising start. 'Well, Poppy, I am by no means an expert, but it certainly sounds like you have started with a bang.'

'Miss Lockheart reckons that at the rate we're going, we'll be doubling it in no time. Especially if we put our prices up a little. She thinks they are a bit on the low side. Says these ain't no penny pies we're selling but "artisan fare". And it's true enough. You'll find no broxy, cat meat or clay crust in our pies. She says the shop in Epsom charges about two pence more a pie than we do, and theirs ain't half the size or quality to boot. I s'pose I 'ave something to fank Mrs Simpson for, if nothing else, she taught me proper.'

'Well, I shall leave it to your judgement Poppy. You have certainly judged things well enough from what I can see. It sounds like it's time you took some wages for yourself.'

'Not yet, luv, we still have things we need here, and besides, what do I want for now, eh? I've every comfort to hand. I've never lived so well in all my years. You know, I've even put on weight about me hips, which I never managed before. I 'ave figure now, I'm told.'

Annalise laughed. 'By who, I wonder?'

'Ah, no one like that,' she waved a dismissive hand. 'But I've had a few of the lads pay me a compliment that's made me blush.'

'But tell me, Poppy, are you happy living here?'

'Happy? It's the best thing that's ever happened to me, and Maggie's the same. The girl hardly stops smiling from morning to night, no matter how much work we've to contend with. I s'pose it's being free, in't it? Not having anyone to answer to and breathe down your neck like Cook always did. And we've such lovely customers, a real friendly bunch, so it's always a pleasure to serve them, unlike those hoity-toity Ashlyns. And we've made friends of our neighbours. The bakers a bit stuffy, but other than that, all the rest of us go along nicely. Oh, Annalise, you'd love it here, you would. I'm sorry you're not coming. I really am.'

'I know. Me too. But for now, my mistress needs me where I am—'

'Oh yes, you know 'er face is all over the papers, don't yer?'

Annalise nodded. 'Yes, I saw the papers in London.'

'Terrible scandal. Apparently, that 'usband of hers is often seen about the village. A regular at the *Greyhound,* the innkeeper's wife told us when she popped in yesterday.'

'When? When was he last seen about town?'

She shrugged. 'I don't know, luv. Never seen him meself. Why? Are you worried he'll try questioning you over her whereabouts?'

'It's possible. I am one of the few persons that know it.'

'He doesn't know you own this place, does he?'

'No. At least, I hope not.'

'Well, he ain't never been in asking, and none of the gossips have made mention of you. They seem to think you're Mr Harrison's niece, so I told everyone that you were. I thought it for the best, given all the talk of the bad business.'

'Thank you, Poppy, you did right to. No one must know of my connection to her. It could be dangerous.'

'Well, I don't want you to be putting yourself in danger, luv. If she's fled from him, that's up to her to decide the risk. But I don't want you getting tangled up in anything dangerous.'

'It's not that simple, Poppy. He is a violent, unkind man and has treated her very badly.'

'That's not how I had it.'

'What are people saying?'

'That she's a deserter. An adulterer who has brought shame upon a respectable family.'

'It's not true, Poppy. He is a lying, scheming scoundrel. He used her so badly. I saw it with my own eyes—'

'You did?'

Annalise nodded. 'I can't tell you more, Poppy, for I am sworn to secrecy with my mistress, but I need you to trust me. She is the victim in this, not he.'

'I do trust yer, luv. No doubt about that, and if you say that's the way of it, I believe yer. No one'll get a peep out of us. You may be sure.'

WITH A FEELING OF NAUSEATING anxiety at her making the journey back to London alone, Annalise waved Eleanor off from the *Greyhound* the following day, knowing it was for the best. She was to take up Mrs Neal's offer and wait the next two days there for Annalise to finish her holiday, meet her from the stage, and journey back up to Cambridgeshire together. Eleanor had not seemed to mind the retraction and only regretted that she should have to miss her, but insisted she was happy, so long as Annalise got to enjoy a holiday with her friends and she could put the house back at ease again by way of her departure.

It could not be denied that it had done so. Breakfast had been uncomfortable, with Leonard trying hard to engage Poppy in polite conversation and getting very little back in return. Maggie, of course, filled the void, levelling all sorts of questions at the pair of them: how many guests were they to have at their wedding breakfast? Would she be invited to attend? Perhaps she might have a new frock for it, for she had nothing suitable, and her Sunday clothes would not do for such a high occasion. How did we meet? How many children would we have? And might we have one soon? For she was fond of babes, and yet no one she knew had any for her to play with.

If Eleanor had thought her play-acting skills had been tested that day at the Barnwell Theatre, it was nothing to what Maggie had subjected her to over breakfast. It seemed a relief to all but Maggie when Annalise walked her down to the stagecoach as the breakfast plates were cleared away.

That was, at least, until she watched it drive away, and that creeping feeling of concern over Eleanor's safety, returned to haunt her.

She tried to put it out of her mind. She had promised Eleanor she would make the most of her time here, so she meant to. She was to spend the morning helping the pair of them in the kitchen, then going about with Maggie to join her on her deliveries. Then she had some errands of her own to see to, and then it would be time for her *surprise* party. She also meant to stop in at Old Mill Street before she left, not just to see her old friends, but to bring the happy news that she had work and board to offer Jane and Thomas. She knew the weight it would lift just having their food and board alleviated. Two less mouths to feed was no small relief when money was so hard to come by. Then there was the extra space they would have, no longer six of them to one bed of crates. And she meant to pay them well too. If they were in profit already, it seemed they could afford to. And wasn't this the very reason she wanted the place to start with; to do some good by way of her own good fortune? To give others, who might not otherwise have it, the chance at a better way of life, just as she had been given. Then after the Bartlett's, she would pay an overdue visit to her mama's grave. It suddenly seemed so busy and more than capable of keeping her diverted from her worst fears over Eleanor's safety.

MIDWINTER.

For a while, it seemed she might forget her other troubles and enjoy the company of friends.

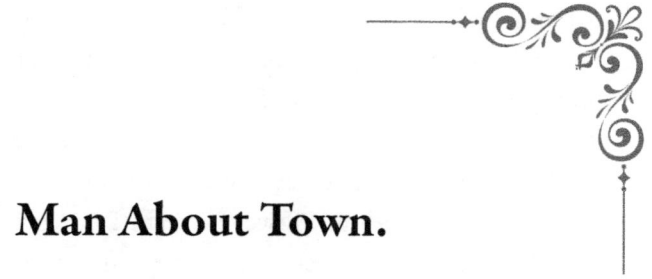

Man About Town.

January 1822. - Eleanor

Being so close to home had put me a little out of sorts for the first half hour of the stagecoach journey back to London. Watching pensively for any sign of a familiar or suspicious face, or anyone casting such looks in my direction. But it had proved needless. Even as I watched the tradesmen in the coach reading their morning papers, there had been no comments made about the article, and it seemed to me it was already yesterday's news. The men spoke on other current affairs without the slightest interest in me as we rattled into London in thick morning fog.

It was this restoration of my feeling of anonymity, that revived my confidence to entertain the idea of what I chose to do next. Something wild and reckless. Something I would likely never get the chance to do again.

So when the coach pulled up at Charing Cross, I did not hire a hack to convey me to Watling Street as planned, but instead, slung my bag over my shoulder, walked to Piccadilly and booked myself a room at *Millers Hotel* on Jermyn Street. It did not seem to me the type of hotel the haute ton would frequent, yet it seemed more genteel than any inn I had yet come across on my travels. It was one thing travelling the stages alone, and another, feeling safe enough to sleep alone in an inn. But a hotel of better standing, I was willing to take my chances on.

It had all been perfectly straightforward as Leonard Leamington. No fusty explanations to make up to the hotelier to procure myself a room. I was a man now, and need not find excuses for lone travel, or explain my business to anyone. How simple and liberating it was to live on such easy terms.

After a little doze upon the bed and putting my things away in the cupboard, I touched up my face paints, put my greatcoat and top hat back on, and headed out towards St. James' on foot.

I had always wanted to walk down that very street in abject defiance of the notion of male districts, ever since that day I saw Mariella walking by from the carriage window. However much I had grown to hate her, I had always admired her boldness and courage in doing such a frowned-upon thing without a hint of care. Of course, I knew I could never do the same as myself. But today, I was to go as Leonard, and feel the thrill of being where I knew I should not be, even if no one else knew it.

Since I now knew he had not gone down with the *Lark*, I avoided the clubs and anywhere I thought Giles likely to frequent. Although whether or not he was in town, or some other place on business, or attempting to discover me elsewhere, I did not know. It certainly seemed he had left the dirty work of my detection to men in his employ. I must be sure to have a care not to converse too freely with anyone I brushed shoulders with whilst in town, for aside from Digby, I did not know the faces of these men and could accidentally chance upon one of them. Perhaps the article and all the evidence of his determination to stop at nothing to track me down, should have made me frightened and flee into hiding. But it had an altogether different effect on me and fuelled me further into defiance. There was a sense of justice in flaunting myself about town in plain sight, knowing he was combing the streets for me. I suspected he must have thought me to have fled with Richards to some secret love den and was concentrating his efforts on keeping eyes on him. It was comforting to think of him following such a false trail, yet worrying to think of him pursuing Richards with such vengeance. I hoped he would be alright. I hoped he would take Lady W.'s advice and take a holiday. If he was lucky, his new connections amongst his powerful patrons, might go some way to protecting him now he was established. Giles might have had more money than some of the ton, but he would never have their respect or gain true admittance as one of them, and that, I hoped, would be enough to render him little support amongst them in this matter.

I might be a pariah now in the eyes of the ton, but I was still a pariah of Ashlyn stock. I was sure that however vilified I was over the scandal broth parlours of Mayfair, my parents and the rest of my family, would be looked upon with sympathy and deep-seated allegiance against a family like the Craythornes. I was sure these public antics of spying and advertising for me would be considered a vulgar display to society and that he may even earn himself more disrepute than I, in conducting himself in such a manner. Of course, I could not be certain, but I felt relatively assured of their response from what I knew of their ways. That was one advantage I had over him: I *knew* society inside and out. All its peculiar rules, nuances and foibles. I might not have played by them, but at least I knew how to recognise a whopping faux pas when I saw one.

My first stop was to be the *Cocoa Tree Club* Coffee House on St. James' Street, one I often heard the men in my circles refer to as one of the best in town. I wanted to see what all the fuss was about, so I looked it up in *Cary's* and headed down Piccadilly with my gaze kept low when passing anyone too closely. My eyes were declared my biggest giveaway. Not my tightly bound bosom, my slightly protruding navel or my feminine hips – all of those had been obscured in artful costume trickery. And, of course, my hair was no longer a feature of distinction either, a cluster of black curls limp with Macassar oil combed to a peak on top of my head. But my eyes were a liability I could do nothing to alter. So I kept my top hat pulled down low and averted my gaze from any that settled on me in close proximity, staring instead at the straw-strewn cobbles and slow-draining puddles of rain that pooled in them.

I walked casually past the coffee house before entering it, trying to ascertain through the window glass if I noticed anyone of acquaintance. It was too difficult to tell, and after a few minutes of repeating the anxieties I had felt walking into the barbers at Fleet Market yesterday, a renewed downpour of rain encouraged me in. I walked with my best-contrived swagger, and whilst I could not spot anyone I recognised amongst the patrons hunched over tables and coffee pots—plumes of smoke curling above their heads—they seemed so surprised at my arrival, I immediately feared my disguise had been detected by means unknown to me. I took a peripheral glance at my attire to make sure everything was in order and not revealing some tell-tale clue. I could find nothing out of place, then instantly feared it must be my face at fault. I was sure the generous brim of my top hat had shielded my stippled cheeks from the rain, but perhaps I had been mistaken. *Maybe they had begun to run?*

'Can I help you, sir? You seem lost,' came a voice. When I looked up at the sound of it, I noticed a manservant standing in front of me carrying an empty tray in one arm.

'Oh, no I am not lost. I had a fancy to take shelter from the rain over a cup of your fine coffee.'

This was met by poorly stifled peals of laughter from all but he.

'Well, sir, I am afraid we are full. Perhaps you might try the *Finnish* at Covent Garden?'

I ignored the uproar of laughter that erupted at this suggestion, even though I couldn't understand what was so funny, and pointed at the vacant table and said: 'But half your tables are empty.'

'Oh those, those are reserved for luncheon, and that is not served until two-o-clock—'

'Chivers, I think you have forgotten your manners. This man is here upon my invitation. Now be so good as to take his coat and fetch us a fresh pot of coffee, will you?'

I looked over to the man who had risen from his seat in a tiny alcove to the right-hand side of the room to address the manservant. I had not noticed him tucked away there. He was a black-skinned man, and I was quite surprised to see him, and knew immediately that we were not acquainted.

'Well, my apologies Mr Richmond, had I known...' The manservant replied in more cordial accents than he had afforded me and gestured with an arm: 'Follow me if you will, sir,' and led me to the nook where the man had been sat, with an open paper and half-filled coffee jug upon it.

I handed my hat over but refused my coat, nodded and sat down opposite this unlikely stranger who appeared to be the finest dressed in the room.

'Thank you. You didn't have to do that, but I am grateful,' I leaned in and whispered to him, glancing at his paper, grateful for no sign of my picture today.

'Well, it's raining hard, and you look like you did not realise the type of den you were entering.'

'A den of snobbery, it seems. How poorly I judged my choice.' I really should have known better than to rely on the preferences of the men of the ton for a recommendation.

'Well, if it makes you feel any better, he doesn't much like my presence any better than yours.'

I assumed he meant on account of his caste and did not mean to question that assumption, although I was curious about his standing. He certainly knew how to put them in their place. Perhaps he was the owner? I had rarely come across dark-skinned persons that were not pages or commoners, and his smart dress and exemplary manner told me he was neither. He was a handsome-looking fellow of about mid-forty, I estimated. Neat white teeth and eyes of tawny brown hues. His hair sat neatly cropped in tightly spun black curls, and he cut a burly figure in his tailcoat that suggested him a sporting man. 'I can't say that it does,' I replied, 'but it is certainly worth remaining long enough to see him thrown out of countenance.'

He laughed a little at this and said, 'Precisely my line of thought. Bill Richmond, pleased to meet you, young man.'

I reached across the table to shake his hand. His were so large mine almost disappeared into the grip of his palm. 'Leonard Leamington, very pleased to meet you, sir. I think I owe you a coffee, in the least,' I said, taking up the bill of fare the manservant brought back with the new coffee pot.

'Son, you don't owe me anything. A wise man once told me; kindness is its own reward. I was too young to understand it then, not much younger than yourself. But life has a way of making better sense of things as it goes along.'

'Yes, yes, I suppose it does. I shall try to remember it when that stiff-rumped manservant is waiting for his tip.'

He laughed. 'So, are you new to town?'

'No. But I'm not too familiar with *this* district.'

'I thought as much.'

'So I look as green as I feel then,' I said, pouring myself a steaming coffee and cupping its warmth between my hands. 'I suppose that's why they found me so amusing,' I gestured with my head in the direction of the loud bunch of fellows seated by the window, who had moved onto a new topic of ridicule now, having spotted Romeo Coates passing by.

'It don't take much to amuse small minds,' he said wisely, topping up his own cup. 'So, what brings you to this district, Mr Leamington? You here for the prize fighter's benefit?'

'Oh, no. Curiosity, I suppose... and a little time on my hands.'

'So what do you mean to do with it, son?'

I shrugged. 'I'm not entirely sure. I might have a bit of a wander about. Find some nice eating houses—ones with more cordial servants. Maybe see what's on at the theatre. Nothing too taxing.'

'Well, why don't you come along to *Five's Courts* on Thursday? We've got a benefit for two of the most promising upcoming fighters.'

'No, sorry.—I'm not much inclined for prize-fighting, to tell the truth.' I was surprised that he was. He seemed such a kindly and polite man. I would not have thought him the type to enjoy such violent amusements. But then it was the same with my aunt and uncle. They always had a taste for such questionable sports and were perhaps the nicest of my family's set. It was a peculiar paradox I had never really understood.

'Well. Why not give it a try since you're at a loose end? I mean, it's an amateur sparring, but it will be a great opportunity to see the upcoming champions of your generation: Jackson's protégé against my own.'

'That's very generous of you, sir. But I'm not sure I have the constitution for all that blood.'

He laughed again. 'So what do you do for sport then?'

'Riding. I'm an excellent whip, I confess.'

'Do you hunt?'

I shook my head.

'Too much blood, huh?'

'I prefer more peaceful pursuits. I don't deny it. Blood sports, fighting, well, it's never appealed to me, in truth.'

'Well, each man to his own.'

We turned to more ordinary topics thereafter, having established no common ground in sporting matters, and I enjoyed a convivial hour of conversation once we moved on to other things. I took my leave of Mr Richmond in much better spirits for his kindness and good company, and

I had entirely forgotten my troubles as I perused the rest of St. James' offerings at my leisure. There was not much relevant to me; gentleman's outfitters, boot makers, watchmakers, barber shops, tobacconists and liqueur merchants. But the novelty of it sustained my interest long into the afternoon until I found myself hungry and in want of a place to take my dinner. I supposed I could have taken it back at my hotel, but it seemed a waste to forego the license of staying out past the hours I was usually permitted, and I fancied to know what altered in these streets beyond dusk that forbade us ladies to be out on them. It didn't take long to have an answer. On my way back from *The Thatched House Tavern* where I had dined on mutton and grouse for less than half a guinea, I was accosted by several rouged women on my journey back to Jermyn Street. I was offered all sorts of services, ranging from a quick spell in an alleyway for fifteen shillings, hand relief in a carriage for ten, and a night I would "not forget in a hurry" with a handsomely dressed lady for two guineas. I was certainly not green enough to be surprised to see such women about the town at this hour, but the boldness of their address had taken me quite aback. I had always thought such affairs occurred discreetly, in shady brothel houses or low taverns. Not be so openly flaunted on the streets. Men— some more than a trifle disguised—disappearing into the night, or sometimes just down an unlit walkway with a woman or two upon his arm. Carriages slowing briefly to permit a harlot to step in. No wonder our sex were forbidden to wander this district after dusk; half the ladies of the ton would likely find their husbands or sons in such a fashion, if they dared.

I SLEPT WELL THAT NIGHT, even though I lamented the absence of Annalise's soft arms about my waist. The adventures of the day and the many steps trod along the London cobbles, had tired me sufficiently to fall swiftly into oblivion the instant I sunk into the mattress.

I took a light breakfast in the hotel coffee room, feeling refreshed, and set back out on my Piccadilly adventures, enjoying a little morning exercise and fresh air. It had been difficult to get enough exercise recently at Stapleford in the muddy country sludge of winter. But here, so long as I remained to the paved and cobbled pathways, I was free to roam about without the need for patens or fear of getting stuck in a marshy bog. Besides, I had not the hindrance of skirt hems to consider now, and my coat, albeit a heavy thing to wear, was much more weatherproof than my winter cloaks and jackets, and permitted me to manage outdoors far longer. All in all, it made for a welcome change, and with the sun out bright, despite the icy chill of the air, it was a pleasant morning sojourn about the district. Though it did feel odd to be so close and yet so distant from all the people and places familiar to me. How I longed, at weaker moments, to chance a quiet visit over to Berkeley Square to have news of my family and the few friends I still cared for. I wondered if Martha had birthed her child yet. How Bethany and Mr Dickenson went along. If Delores and the squire were well.

It would have been an easy enough scheme to pull off, if I took a hired coach directly to our mews at the rear of the house and went in via the back door. But I did not give in to the temptation. Annalise had made me promise that I would not make contact with any acquaintances beyond Mrs Neal, and so I heeded it. I knew she might not be best impressed with my choice to stay about the town alone either, though she had never made me promise not to. But I hoped she would see there was no harm in it, and I meant to give her the whole when I met her coach tomorrow.

I had a few things on the agenda today, given it was the last of my adventures. The first, I conducted straight after breakfast: which was to pop into *Floris* and buy Annalise a gift of their sweetest smelling toilette waters. The next was to find somewhere to buy her a wedding ring so that we could pose as man and wife in our Cambridge enquiries. And finally, the thing I had been most excited to set out to the moment the idea had sprung to mind last night, was to walk to Hyde Park Corner and visit *Tattersalls* on the only occasion I would ever be admitted to the place. Of course, I knew I couldn't afford to buy a horse for Annalise right now, and there was hardly a rush whilst I was unable to teach her how to ride, but to be amongst the horses for the day, get an impression of the cost, would be delight enough.

I knew instantly it had been worth the walk when I entered the auction yard. The smell of the place: damp horsehair, worn leather and manure, comforted me in its familiarity. It had felt like an age since I set off in my habit and headed for the stables. I walked about the bustling veranda until I found a good spot to see the horses from, and though I could not access the subscription rooms or make a bid, I felt excited to be here all the same. There was every class of fellow here from what I could tell, and I was pleased that this peculiar mix of classes and clothing would not render me particularly noticeable after my reception at the *Cocoa Tree* yesterday. I had taken better care since then, to judge my choice of establishment, accordingly, reminding myself that my license as a man to roam so freely, did not necessarily admit me into *every* male domain, whilst I was dressed in the style of a tradesman, anyway. But it seemed it had been the right choice to make, for there was another thing I had learnt since bearing my disguise in this district: that the tonnish and gentry folk looked right past you when in common attire, as though you were not there at all. And so, I no longer slid my gaze to the cobbles as I walked about the streets, or turned my back to a party of well-dressed persons or coaches bearing coats of arms. For I knew they could not see me: I was invisible to them, and they would not even attempt to look. The only looks I had received that had made me feel uncomfortable, were that of suspicious proprietors and shop assistants, that seemed to think I was minded to steal their wares, by virtue of my very presence. It puzzled me, until I had worked out what it was. But now I took a little satisfaction in their hawkish anxiety, and toyed with them just a trifle, before pulling out my purse to pay for something, or leaving an over-generous tip to shock them and wipe the poorly stifled contempt from their smug faces.

But here, in the auction yard, it seemed I was perfectly welcome whilst remaining perfectly invisible to the gentleman amongst the crowd. My initial wandering beneath the colonnades before the horses were brought out to parade the courtyard and the auctioneer began chanting his speeches, had given me no cause to think I was amongst anyone of acquaintance. And when the crowd started raising their bids, I kept an eye on their direction to be certain, which, until at least an hour had passed, I was sure I did not know a single face amongst them. I had grown comfortable in my surroundings, distracted by the horses parading and trying to gauge the going rates, complacent in sharing the occasional few words with a nearby fellow once in a while. But then a bidding war started over a handsome young filly, between a Gentleman beneath the opposite colonnade, and one standing right in front of me. The sight of him had done nothing to alert me, since he looked akin to any well-dressed gent from the back of his tailcoat and top hat. Indeed I was sure he had been there with his companions the entire time.

It was his voice that alerted me to my familiarity with him, although for a fleeting moment, I could not place it. I stepped back behind a taller man to the left of me, to create a buffer between us, whilst I figured it out. Listening hard, to hear the conversation between him and his companion, a fellow I could see enough of a side profile of his face, to know I did not recognise. I listened for him to call out his next bid before I knew unequivocally who it was. The last person I had even considered it possible I would bump into here. I had not seen him since last year. The last I knew of it, he was bound for Malta with his regiment. I supposed they must have returned now.

My stomach sunk as I took it in, memories of our parting moments creeping out of undisturbed corners of my mind as I tried to match them against this figure before me. I pulled the brim of my hat down a fraction and went to leave, when, at the precise moment I stepped out to pass him; he turned about in my direction to reply to his friend. I froze on the spot. Not wanting to stay, but fearing to provoke his peripheral attention by moving against the crowd, who were eyes fixed on the courtyard. My reaction to seeing his face caught me most by surprise, his familiar blue eyes flashing with determination as he appeared to be rebuffing his companion's attempts to persuade him to pull out of the bid. It was getting rather high now, even if it was a very fine horse.

I thought I would still feel bitter at the sight of him, but this was only a mild undercurrent to the sadness it provoked in me to look upon the face of my childhood friend, my once-betrothed... and remember. How. It was all turned to ash in the space of a season.

A habitual part of me had missed him, despite myself, and wanted to go up to him now, press him into a hug and bid that we forgive each other the transgressions of last year. I was ready to forgive him, now I had moved on. Now I had found happiness. My love for Annalise had shown me for certain that Sheldon and I were only ever meant for friends and never lovers or spouses. Now I knew how ill he had suffered and come close to losing his way in the world from the fallout of it all, I felt sorry. He had suffered enough. I hoped he had recovered now, that his time abroad with his regiment had brought him to his senses. He looked in good health from the glimpses I caught of him.

The bidding war continued as these thoughts and old emotions crossed my mind, and by the time it was over, and he had secured the chestnut bay for twenty-one guineas—a price the crowd gave me to understand exceeded anything expected—I realised I had stood still there all this time when I had meant to make a dash. I was not quite sure why I had remained. Why even now, I wished to better hear his conversation and try to gauge his spirits. I suppose the part of me that cherished his long-esteemed friendship wanted to know how he did, whether his broken heart had mended now, as mine had.

I caught only fragments of what was said: A few nearby fellows congratulating him on his winning bid, telling him it was a fine piece of horseflesh he had got himself there and that Mr Scriminger's stables were well renowned for handsome breeding. But it was his answer that struck me hard when he replied to the man, saying: 'Yes, I know. I had one of his bays for the past thirteen years, and I knew nothing else would replace her other than her very own line.'

Delilah! Why did Delilah *need* replacing? Oh no. My gut had already given me the answer. She must have perished, for he would never sell her, and if she had fallen ill or past her prime, he had no need to do more than retire her, for he had other horses he could ride. I felt a tear roll down my cheek and remembered at the last, not to attempt to wipe it and smudge my face. *Poor Delilah. What had happened to her?* She was too young. She should have at least another decade or two to look to.

My thoughts turned instantly to Samson then, her big brother, whom I had missed sorely these past months, but consoled myself with the prospect of our happy reunion once I could ride again. What if something terrible happened to him in my absence, and I, – I could not bear to entertain the thought, but was distracted from it at the very moment by hearing Sheldon say, 'You go on without me. I will catch you up this afternoon once I have settled my affairs here. Where will you be?'

'We're staying at *Steven's Hotel*. We might dine in tonight before heading to *Cribbs*. I'll send word to you by five if I do not see you before,' came his companion's reply, and with that, he departed, leaving Sheldon speaking to his groom.

It took everything for me to hold back from marching over to him and asking him what had happened to Delilah. I knew I mustn't. He would certainly recognise the eyes he had once gazed into so ardently. And even if he did not, Leonard: a common stranger, would have to explain his reasons for asking. I stood watching him until he went off with his manservant in the direction of a pair of double doors which I presumed led to the auctioneer's office, or the Jockey Club subscription rooms. And then, with heavy tears welling in my eyes, I decided to flee, find a cab to convey me back to my hotel and let them out in privacy.

The life-long link between Samson and Delilah was to be forever extinguished.

I HADN'T INTENDED TO sleep away the afternoon and felt muzzy-headed when I woke with a start, to the sound of some commotion out in the street. The room was shrouded in darkness, and I staggered my way clumsily out of bed and went over to the window, using my arms to guide me about the furniture. I could hear raised voices rising from the street below and lifted the weight of a curtain just a fraction, so I could see, without being seen.

It appeared a couple of the hotel liveried staff were conversing with an overexcited watchman, claiming that guests of the hotel were up to pranks, and had turned his box over and retreated here. They were disputing his claims that any such fellows had taken to hiding out in their establishment, and that their hotel was a respectable place, and he must be mistaken.

It seemed he was not to be persuaded and demanded he be permitted to enter the hotel and conduct a search of these premises, to which the hotel staff refused on account of disturbing their guests' privacy. I hoped they would not let him in. The prospect of being subjected to an inspection and having to answer for my identity would be a precarious business, since, presently, everything about me was a fraud. But if I had learnt anything about it these past few days, it was that it was a very *convincing* fraud, at least.

With renewed confidence, I looked forward to getting our *Spinning House* investigations underway upon our return, having tested out my disguise in the metropolis and grown further into comfort with the charade I had to maintain as Leonard's character.

I pulled my shirt sleeves down to my wrists and walked over to the fire. There was an arctic draft coming from the closed window, and the fire had burned down to the lowest of embers. It was my own fault. On my return, I had told the concierge that I did not wish to be disturbed, and so the maidservant's evening visit, where they built a good fire to burn down gently into the night, had been forgone. I strained my eyes to find the coal bucket and stirred a few into the embers, hoping to revive it, but to no avail. I would have to call for a maid. It seemed there was an art to building a good fire, and it was one I had never been schooled in. Instead, I took a candlestick from its holder and held the wick to a lump of glowering coal until I managed to coax it into flame and lit the others about the room. I checked the clock, expecting it to be late into the night, but finding it was only half past six. My stomach growled with hunger. I had not eaten since breakfast, and realising it was still early enough to remedy it, I decided to re-dress and find a place to sup.

I hadn't consciously intended to pass along Bond Street as I meandered about looking for somewhere to dine, but I instantly recognised the name of *Steven's Hotel* as I passed it. There were saddle horses and tilburies clustered all about the front of the place, and I had to squeeze my way between them and a few military men, to pass by it. I wondered if Sheldon had joined his companions there, or if I would be admitted into the place to dine if I attempted it. I did not want to make a spectacle of myself again, and I doubted my luck would stretch to chancing upon Mr Richmond twice, to rescue me. I continued walking on past its facade at a slower pace, trying to catch a glimpse beyond the windows, when suddenly, I felt myself crash into the wall with the force of a body of weight. Dropping to my knees, my top hat tumbling from my head, and for a moment, I was too dizzy to understand what had happened.

'Forgive me, sir, I did not see you,' came a voice I recognised instantly, even before he took me by my arm and pulled me back upright. I could feel my temple pulsing with pain, and, yes, blood, I realised when I pulled my prodding fingers away to examine them.

'You are hurt?'

I shook my head, not wanting to meet his eyes, and said in the lowest reverberation of tone I could manage, 'It's nothing, sir, I am well.' I took back my offered hat, which he had recovered from the ground.

'You are bleeding fellow. Let's get you inside and have it looked at. I am terribly sorry. I was fleeing from that dashed whip driving races all over the place!'

'No, no. I will look at it at home. I'm sure it's just a scratch,' I protested, hoping he would not recognise me in the dim light of the streetlamps. But he was too preoccupied, calling the concierge over and explaining the occurrence, bidding him take me in and fix me a brandy whilst he found one of his army medic friends to look at my wound. I knew it a bad idea and wanted to set off at a dash, but the pain was throbbing smart, and I felt a little unsteady. The reluctance of the concierge to admit me into the place was swiftly overcome when Sheldon gave his title, and I was pushed through the doors and taken into a private parlour where I was sat down, and a manservant was given orders to fetch water and clean cloth for my wound. Of all the people I could have got into a scrape with...

I kept my head bowed to the floor, hoping Sheldon would leave me to the care of the staff now. The light in here was much better and too risky to be examined beneath his watch. It had been as much my fault as his, I supposed. I had not been looking where I was going either, too consumed with trying to spot him through the glass when he wasn't even inside the place. I watched him leave the room and was left in the care of the servants.

I was given a cloth to cull the bleeding and a glass of what looked like Brandy when the footman returned, and I swiftly poured it into a potted palm tree when he was not looking and held the cloth against my temple, already able to feel the lifted end of my stick-on brow flapping about the tender flesh which throbbed beneath my fingertips. 'Have you a looking glass?' I asked the servant, and he pointed to one hung at the wall behind me, to which I went instantly over to. The wound did not seem very bad to look at once I had dabbed away the excess blood from it, which made it look far worse than it was. I had a small split on the bone beside the corner of my eye that looked like it may require a stitch or two, to stop the bleeding. This was all I needed now. The last time I had had stitches was when I had fallen from my pony and gashed my elbow on a rough stone in the stable yard. I had swooned before Dr Reeves had even put the needle to my flesh. Although I had been only nine years old at the time. I hoped my constitution was a little stronger now, or I would certainly give myself away.

I considered I had better do away with my faux brows too, if I did not want that discovered, or worse, mistaken as my own skin and stitched down with it. So, holding the space beside my wound steady, I peeled back the brow wig, gasping as it tugged stubbornly against my gaping skin, and shoved it into my coat pocket. The other eye proved easier, and I spent just a moment spitting onto the cloth and wiping the gummy residue and kohl strokes from my face, in order to look more ordinary before I was examined. The upshot being that my agitation of the wound had set the bleeding off far worse than before, and when Sheldon came back in with some other man, he gasped and said, 'Oh dear, it looks very nasty indeed. Patch him up, will you, good fellow. This is Captain Langham, an army medical officer of great experience. I assure you, you are in excellent hands Mr—'

'Smith,' I said quickly, covering as much of my face with the cloth as I could as I returned to my chair.

'Let's have a look at it then, Mr Smith,' said Captain Langham, and I closed both my eyes against the peripheral sight of Sheldon as the Captain tilted my face up skyward.

'Hmm, nasty little gash you have there, but nothing a few stitches won't put right. Now, how's your head? Any dizziness?'

'A little.'

'Your sight? Does it pain your eyes to open them?'

'Yes,' I lied, grateful for an excuse to keep them shut.

'Hmm, could be a touch concussed. Shouldn't be anything to worry about, but it might be an idea to have someone sit up with you overnight to keep watch should you take an ill turn.'

'Where do you live, Mr Smith?' Sheldon asked.

'In the provinces. I'm staying at a hotel for the night.'

'Anyone with you who can keep an eye—'

I shook my head, forgetting how painful it was for a moment.

'Keep still there young fellow, you'll make the bleeding worse. – Right Shelley, I think you'll have to have them set him up a room here in that case.'

'No, no, I will go back to my hotel. If you could just set me to rights.'

'Hmm, perhaps you can get a maid to sit with him at his hotel then, would that suit you better, Mr Smith?'

'Yes,' I agreed.

'Very well, but we can't stitch this here. Let's get him up to a room then footmen. One on each arm, as quick as you like. And send my valet for my medical case, please, Shelley.'

It was a wasted attempt. The hotel was fully occupied, and so I was set out upon a cleared parlour table and bid to take off my coat. I protested and claimed I was too cold to remove it, and in the end, it was put down to shock and they began with my coat still buttoned up. I was encouraged to take several lugs of Brandy as the Captain set out his utensils, and I heard the cold clink of metal and dared not even glance in the direction from which it came. Then with a few bracing words beforehand, I felt the mighty sting of some spirit flushing out the wound and felt ready to vomit with the burning agony.

Pies and Profit.

January 1822. - Annalise.

'**D**'you see 'im off alright?' Poppy asked when Annalise came back into the shop with the chill of both her short outing and her pensive apprehension carrying in with her.

'Yes, he is on his way now,' Annalise replied, pulling her remaining hand from her muffler and untying the ribbons of her bonnet.

Poppy was busy taking chairs off the tabletops and setting them back beneath them now the floor had dried from its daily scrub.

She took an apron from its hook, tied it around her waist and joined in the effort.

'What you doing, luv? I thought you were out with Maggie this morning on her deliveries?'

'Oh yes,' Annalise said, half hoping that detail might have gone forgotten given the taxing over-excitement of Maggie's mood earlier at breakfast. 'Well, I can help you for a bit. She doesn't seem to be ready yet.'

'You don't have to go if you'd rather not, luv. You are on a holiday. You can put your feet up or get on over to Epsom if you'd rather.'

'No. I am happy to pitch in, Poppy. I shall do that in the afternoon, as planned.'

'Alright. Well, cheer up then. We'll soon 'ave customers at the door and I don't want them frightened off by your blue mood. He's only been gone five minutes and you've a right Friday face on yer.'

'Sorry. I have a lot on my mind. I shall snap myself out of it, and you may be sure that the first customer will be greeted with my brightest smile.'

But when she looked up at the bell ringing and bestowed it upon a young lady who burst in breathless, as though she had been running all the way, her face chaffed scarlet by the cold, she turned out to be the day maid, frowning at the sight of Annalise behind the counter and turning swiftly to Poppy to offer a thousand apologies for being late.

'Again, Ruth?' Poppy looked up from wiping the table.

'I'm so sorry. It shan't happen again.'

'That bairn had you up all night again?' Poppy asked, going over to her. She nodded. 'He's cutting a tooth.'

'Jesus, your frozen. Go fetch yourself a brew and warm up by the fire, will yer.'

'But—'

'Don't worry about this. I've got an extra pair of hands today. Ruth, this is Miss Tullier, the proprietor.'

'Oh,' she said, looking frightful at the first impression she had given now she could put a name to this unknown face. She swiftly dropped a curtsey and offered, 'How do you do, ma'am?'

'Ruth,' Annalise said, gently, 'It's nice to meet you. But there's no need for all that. Why don't you go and warm up and then we can get better acquainted later.'

She nodded. 'Thank you, miss.'

'Call me Annalise.'

'Thank you, Annalise,' she said and headed into the back parlour.

'She has a child?' Annalise asked once she was gone.

Poppy nodded. 'Six-month-old boy. Jolly little nipper.'

'Who looks after him when she is here?'

'She pays a neighbour to mind him till she's home. Her husband's a coachman for the inn, so he's rarely about and the poor luv's left to manage between it all. Do you disapprove of me taking her on?'

'No. No, not in the least. I only find it a shame she can't be about to take care of him.'

'She needs the money, luv. Does her best.'

'Do we pay her enough?'

'Aye, handsomely, and she is worth the coin. We'd be lost without her. She's my second pair of hands, and I can trust her to any task without worry. She's just rarely in on time. That's the trouble.'

'Well, maybe once I've been to the Bartletts today to see about the work for the children, perhaps you could give her a later start?'

Poppy nodded. 'Would be doable, I suppose. If the youngen's could see to the floor and the jobs out here, I could manage well enough for another hour or so.'

'To be sure they could, Jane often helps her mama scrub the floor and set the table, and I'm sure Thomas could help before he went about with his wagon. I suppose we shall have to see about getting one made.'

'Leave it to me. I know just the fellow. One of the carpenters who come in from time to time.—Anyway, you better make ready, sounds like Maggie's set to leave.'

And in she came at a song, basket in arm, mitten clad and smile bright at the sight of Annalise making ready to join her.

THE FIRST HALF HOUR of her morning rounds with Maggie was every bit as fatiguing as she had suspected. But once she grew distracted with her customers and furnishing Annalise with a rundown of who that was, what she knew of them and where they were to go next, the frequency of all the wedding questions began to wane and they both became distracted. It was the burden of the lie that made it difficult to bear. The innocent enthusiasm and genuine delight Maggie displayed was an energy that rarely failed to brighten her. And it had always proved a welcome antidote to a stagnant mood, whatever her troubles. She supposed the thing that made it so very hard to bear was just how much she wished it was true—wished that she could celebrate her newfound happiness with those dearest to her. How many times she had longed to seek Poppy's counsel and perspective on some matter or another but had not been able to. How often she came close to answering Maggie's questions more earnestly and saying, Yes, my heart is truly taken, and I want us to settle together like a real family. And yes, she would very much like to have children, at least three or four to fill the house with merry spirit and watch over them attentively, as her mama had done for her. Go on birthday outings to the seaside, watch them paddle in rock pools, gather shells up in their pockets...and so much more. But she could say none of these things because she grew increasingly doubtful that they would ever get to know such a life. And even if they did, it would be a clandestine existence, not one where her friends could be part of the story.

Still, by the time the basket was empty and they were on their way back, Maggie's effervescence proved contagious and Annalise felt lighter and more buoyant in her steps, as she began to piece together this novel little world Poppy and Maggie had created in Carshalton. Already well known and liked about the place. Already familiar with the swiftest shortcuts to take and where the best views of the river could be gleaned. It heartened her to see their contentment in their endeavours, the pride which was taken in even the smallest trifles of detail, from the gleaming scrubbed doorstep as they approached it, to the little vase of snowdrops set upon the centre of the tables.

It was a hearty hive of chatter when they pushed through the door and into the warmth of it. Patrons filling nearly all the seats, a few standing at the counter as Ruth chatted familiarly with them and packaged up their orders.

'There you are. I wondered where you'd got to?' Poppy said when they found her in the kitchen ladling stew into bowls and setting them on trays.

'Maggie wanted to show me about a bit,' Annalise said. 'I didn't mean to keep her. What can I help with?' she asked, hanging up her coat. 'Shall I take these out to the tables?'

'No, Maggie can see to those. If you could cut up another loaf to go out with them, that'll be grand.'

So, she washed her hands in the bowl beside the stovetop and set to work. First, on slicing generous wedges of fresh malty bread for Maggie to take through with the stew. Then she helped roll out more pastry, set another pan of bones on for tomorrow's broth, peeled more carrots, and shelled more peas in an hour than she was sure she had in her entire career as a kitchen maid. But it was happy work with Poppy to chat away to as they stood over the table, finding their way back into full comfort again, almost like she had never gone away. And she felt easy at last. Far removed from her troubles now. So comfortable in this companionship and the busyness of the work she lost track of the time entirely and was only reminded of her trip over to Epsom when Maggie came rushing through to say the hackney driver was waiting for her outside. She had ordered it this morning, along with Eleanor's stage ticket and had long since forgotten the hour she had booked it for.

She packed up the parcelled meat pie and heavy stoneware flask of piping hot stew, Poppy had set aside for her to bring, grabbed her coat and bonnet, and rushed out to find her hack.

AFTER A WELCOME RECEPTION in the doorway of the Old Mill Street cottage, she took her seat at the Bartlett's table and acquiesced to their insistence she partake in the offering with them whilst it was still warm. She agreed to take a small helping to save her appetite for her own supper later. But she would have rather they set her portion aside for themselves. To be sure, it was an ample pie, and the stew would last another meal if they kept it by. But there were many mouths to feed about the cramped little table, and from what she could tell of the minuscule fire and scantly stocked pantry shelves Rosie fetched the plates from, they were having a difficult spell.

'Well, look at all this, oh and the smell!' Mrs Bartlett sang out as she cut the pie open and began distributing it to the waiting plates.

Mr Bartlett rubbed his hands together. 'You do spoil us, Miss Anna,' he said gleeful. 'I can't remember the last time we had meat on 'table, can you, Rosie, love?'

'Christmastide, we did,' she said as if nearly six weeks without meat was nothing to answer, ''ere, let's 'ave your plate Jane.'

'And Mr Tilney bought me a calves foot on our way back from the brickyard the day he let me go.' Thomas added in support of his mama's point.

'Aye, guilty conscience,' said his father.

'Are you out of work, Thomas?' Annalise asked.

He nodded briefly, distracted by the steamy scent of mutton rising from the plate his mama had just slid beneath his nose. His eyes peeled back wide with delight and she saw the smile in them.

Annalise said nothing more to this yet. She thought it better to speak to their parents privately to give them a chance to consider her offer first. She knew they would be grateful for the opportunity of work, and it seemed they had fallen into the regular winter spell of hardship they often did, when the kind of outdoor labour they relied on generally dried up for a time. But it would be hard on Rosie to part with them for live-out work. She remembered how she had sobbed when her eldest left, however much she knew it necessary.

'It ain't Mr Tilney's fault if there's no work to give em, love. And he said to try with him again after the cold spell, didn't he.'

'Aye, he did. But theys saying we might 'ave snow in the next couple of days and who knows how long that'll last for.'

'Snow?' Annalise said, distracted by the size of the portion Rosie had passed to her and swapping it for the tiny wedge she had apportioned for the babe, who was sat on Annalise's lap slapping her palms against the table and trying to reach for the cutlery. She had grown so much in the months since Annalise had last seen them. A swaddled little bundle she'd been then. Now she had passed her first birthday and was capable of all sorts of mischief if she was set down from someone's lap for but a second.

'Aye, the farmer says so this morning when I went to take him the coal.'

Annalise suspected they had resorted to selling it to feed themselves, remembering the large stock they ordered at the end of summer with the money Eleanor had gifted them. She'd hoped they would at least fare well this winter after struggling so ill over the last, barely managing to keep a fire lit for long enough to cook a supper. She made a mental note to have some sent over for them before she returned to London tomorrow.

'Right then,' Rosie said, putting her arms out to her daughter, 'give her here love, so you can eat in peace.'

'It's no trouble. She can eat with me, Rosie.'

'I'm not having your pretty clothes spoiled with mucky mitts.'

'Honestly, I don't mind a bit. They will soon wash out.'

'Uh-uh, she'll 'ave you wearing half the plate,' she said, and picked her up, carried her back over to her seat and tied a rag beneath the babe's chin to spare her clothes.

MIDWINTER.

Then once they were all settled, Mr Bartlett said grace, looked up brightly and declared everyone tuck in. The room fell delightfully quiet for a spell as they did as bid, and save little Lilian's gargling, and the initial wave of compliments on Poppies fare; there was nothing above the crackling of the grate and occasional clink of cutlery to be heard. Such moments, Annalise had always found difficult to bear up to, the conflicting sense of satisfaction of their want appeased, set against the creeping dread that it would likely be a short-lived respite of circumstances as usual to them, as rare to her. She silently chided herself for her neglect of her dear friends over the past few months. She had been so caught up with Eleanor and their recent concerns, that she hadn't taken a moment to consider how they might be managing without her regular visits and baskets of alms. She had been so self-consumed it disgusted her to realise it now. She must do better from here on. Out of sight must not equate to out of mind.

Once they'd finished eating and the older children were set to the chores of washing the plate, Annalise braced herself to put the scheme to them.

'There was something I wanted to talk to you both about whilst I am here.'

'What is it, love?'

'It seems the pie shop is taking off in quite unexpected style.'

'How happy I am it's working out for you. Though, I'm not surprised with that supper as the example,' Rosie said, and her husband nodded his agreement and added, 'to be sure, there's a talent to good fare like that.'

'Thank you. I shall give Poppy your compliments. The thing is, she's run off her feet trying to manage it all, and though she'd work her fingers to the bone if I let her, I want her to have some help, so it's not so hard on her. We are looking to hire two apprentices. We need a boy who can go out with a push wagon, making deliveries and selling to passersby, and a girl who can learn kitchen work and keeping the parlour. I wondered if Thomas and Jane would be suited for it?'

'Oh Anna,' Rosie gasped, clasping her hand about her mouth in disbelief, 'really?'

Annalise nodded. 'There is one matter though, which is they would need to live in as we're so far and the work starts so early, and I'm not sure if you are ready to part with them yet?'

She nodded slowly and I could see she was in conflict on this head.

'But if you were. They would have their board and lodgings, a room they could share, and three shillings each a week.'

'Three shillings each?' She said, surprised, and I understood her wonder at this, for I had doubled the number Poppy had put forward only hours ago. I imagined Poppy's face would be an equal picture when I confessed these altered arrangements.

'They shall have to toil for it and be keen to learn their duties, for it is a very busy place and timings run tight to see everything ready. But they shall go early to bed and can come home every Sunday when the shop is shut. —Oh Rosie, I don't want to upset you.'

'Oh love, you haven't,' she said, wiping her streaming cheeks with the corner of her apron. 'You've answered our prayers, that's what.'

Annalise reached across the table to squeeze her hand and was sure even Mr Bartlett was welling up as he patted Rosie's back.

Annalise was relieved to see they were happy tears and not the same she had spent her visits comforting for such a time when the other children had left home. It was a relief to find them amenable to the scheme, but it caused her to question how hard things must have been to be willing to take it up. Then through her teary outburst, Rosie explained that the rents had gone up last quarter coinciding with Thomas outgrowing his boots and old coat, and what with the winter laying off and the baby she was due to birth anytime next month, it had all been quite the strain. No, she didn't truly want to part with them just yet, but she seemed to feel that way no matter how much they grew, and it wouldn't be so bad if they could come home every week. And to know they'd be in a good house, learning the ways of something beyond scraps of hard labour here and there, well how could she deny them such a chance as that? How could she deny them a good meal to sup on every night when of late, they'd had only bread and broth to look to. And at least they'd have each other as a comfort if they grew homesick. Yes, so long as the pair were willing, they were to go and have a chance of a better way, and yes, they could start as soon as next week. She might need

Jane's help for a few days when the new babe came, just till she got back on her feet, but if Poppy wouldn't mind it, then it could all be settled just as soon as we liked.

WHEN SHE TRAVELLED back, she reflected on it all with a sense of profound relief and gratitude. Not only for being able to help, but for remembering precisely what it had all been for, accepting Gint's draft and procuring the dwelling shop. Lately, she had forgotten. It had felt something of a wasted effort with how abruptly she'd abandoned it all. But coming home again, witnessing how it had transformed Poppy and Maggie's spirits and seeing how it could do the same for the Bartletts, brought back all the fire in her belly that had first initiated the scheme. And when she passed through Ewell village in the coach on the way back from her mama's grave, she cast a glance out of the carriage window to the road that led to the Hurley Street house and felt at greater peace to be reminded of the alchemy of the blessed-curse of her parentage, and how something good was possible to come out of something she had only been able to see as bad, until now. Yes, when even darkness was touched by the light of love, how even those works could be made to serve the greater good.

She was still looking out of the window when they reached the boundary of the Cuddington estate as her journey progressed along the Ewell Road. She had found it odd, passing it on her way up earlier, remembering her very first visit to the estate for her interview and all that had since come to pass. She reflected on the good memories and those she was not so fond of too. She wondered whether cook had learnt to mend her ways with whomever had come to replace them all, thought briefly of the gallery in which Eleanor's coming out portrait had been hung and wondered how Giles had managed to access it. She hoped none of the staff had been knowingly turned to serving his ends. An image of Fanny then bloomed into her mind, and just as she considered this, she saw someone walk out through the wooded clearing she had often used herself when leaving the estate. Was it? Yes, she was sure it was Will, dressed in his Sunday clothes and the brown tweed cap he wore as part of the outfit. Perhaps he was making his way over to Carshalton already. It was probably not so far off the hour of their gathering, and it was hardly a quick walk over from here. She might risk being late herself, having stayed at the cemetery so long, until the light fell indigo over the headstones and she remembered her commitment. Poppy had been firm with her about keeping to time. 'The shop shuts at 4-o-clock, and they're all to come for five. If you can arrive ahead of them all and keep to your room, we can still carry it off as a surprise,' she had said.

She had not heard the church bells chime for a while, she could only hope her timing wouldn't be off and she'd flub Poppy's arrangements. She probably shouldn't have the coach turned back to offer Will a ride either, not only on account of blowing the surprise but also on account of travelling alone with him. They had left on civil terms, but it would be awkward, especially with the threat of Maggie letting the detail of Leonard slip, still hanging over her. But it was cold outside. She would not be surprised if the farmer had been right and snow might yet fall. And it was a long walk, above three miles, she considered. Then as they rattled on towards the crossroads, she tapped the coach's roof, and the driver slowed.

'Hang on if you will, please, driver,' she called out from the carriage window. 'I need to pick up that fellow back there to journey on with us.'

So, the coach pulled aside and waited as Will absentmindedly headed towards them, the collar of his coat pulled up tight as he made swift strides, only slowing to check the traffic as he approached the crossroads.

'Will,' she waved him down, and he looked up and paused to work it out, and then when he had recognised it was she, set off at a run to meet her.

'Anna!' he said, snatching her up in a bear hug. 'What you doing about here?'

'I've just been to Epsom and I was passing through.' She permitted a brief moment of embrace before pulling back. 'It is so good to see you again, Will. Were you going to walk all the way there?'

'Aye. Eh, how'd you know where I'm headed for?'

'The cat is out of the bag, I'm afraid, but you shall have to play along in it too now if you want to ride back with me?'

'Well, that's an easy bargain. It's bitter out here,' he said, opening the carriage door, handing her back into it, and pulling it closed against the chill as he settled opposite her.

'So, how have you been?' Annalise asked as he tucked his hands beneath his armpits to warm up.

'Getting along, considering all the barmy business that goes on there nowadays. Your departure was well-timed. It's all gone to pieces since those good ole days. —I was lucky Grantley permitted me the early finish tonight. He's been in such a foul manner lately. I thought I weren't gonna be able to come. I daresay he wouldn't have let me if the family weren't to London and there's no one about to wait upon.'

'What barmy business, Will?'

'You must have heard, seen the papers? All this scandal with your mistress.'

'Well, yes, but what has happened at Cuddington?'

'As you'd expect, the Ashlyns are in a fury over it all and miffed as to how the picture was obtained. And to be fair, it's hardly a small thing to carry off without being noticed.'

'It was taken from the house?'

'Aye, though no one knows how.'

'Well, it was obviously that monstrous husband, since he has put out the advert.'

'Well, we all know it, but no one can prove it. That's the trouble. Besides, he covered his tracks with that, had it returned to the Ashlyn's last week, claiming that having put his man on the business of foiling the crooks that he claims to have taken it and having them apprehended. So, he's come out of it looking the hero all the same.'

'That is not what they think, is it?'

'Course not. They know he's toying with them in plain sight. But what can they do? Except for firing all the new staff and sending everyone a severe warning, apparently.'

'What?'

'Yes, three of them gone all in a day. No characters to take with them either, poor blighters.'

'You do not think they had a part in it?'

'Well, someone must have, there was no sign of any housebreakers, but I doubt all three of 'em were guilty. Mightn't have been any of them, for sure. Anyway, never mind all that. I'm happy to escape the place and forget the whole affair tonight. So tell me, how are you? How's Scotland faring?'

'Alright. Certainly less eventful than it seems down here.'

'So, have you missed us then?'

'Of course, dearly,' she admitted. For now she was home, she had realised just how much.

'Good. Hopefully, you'll not stay away too much longer then.'

Annalise smiled. 'Perhaps by the summer solstice, all being well.'

He looked crestfallen at this. 'Well, better make the most of it whilst you're here then.'

And it was exactly what she decided to do—putting all the bad business aside, all the haunting concerns over Eleanor's safety out of mind. The worry of whether she had reached London safely and was lying low. They would be reunited tomorrow. But for now, she was to enjoy the reunion of much-missed friends.

And it took no effort at all as she sat about the shop parlour with them that evening, supping on a banquet Poppy had somehow managed to pull off, despite the demands of her customers keeping her to task. Mr Harrison and Miss Lockheart arriving together just a whisper after she and Will had stepped down from the hack. Maggie kept busy minding Ruth's baby for the most of it, and I saw that Poppy had been wise in that scheme. Permitting Ruth to bring him back with her, not only so she could join in the fun and grow better acquainted with me, but to keep Maggie so occupied she might manage to keep her tongue over Leonard. And surprisingly, she did. And it made me easy again, for even through the merry party of chatter, the clink of plates and cachinnation owing from a few too many cups, she could still see the fire in Will's eyes for her, casting warmly across the table all through the night. He had not surrendered his hope that she might be brought to come around to him in time. It was one thing to know that she would not, and another to have his hopes shattered so cruelly by hearing of Leonard. Especially when she had told him, she didn't mean to marry or settle down any time soon.

MIDWINTER.

How strange that shift seemed to her now when she longed to do just that. Settle down to family life and all its simplicities. Perhaps that's what love did to you? Made you long to lay down foundations and bask in all its simple joys.

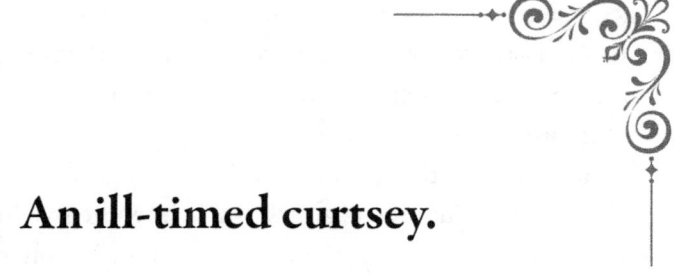

An ill-timed curtsey.

January 1822. - Eleanor.

I awoke thinking it had all been a terrible dream, conjured from my odd chance meeting at Tattersalls and the tragic news that Delilah was no more. But as I rolled onto my side and saw a maidservant sitting in the chair beside my bed, I started and realised this was not the shape of my hotel room. 'Who are you?'

'Oh, you're awake, sir. I better tell the master.'

'The master? Where am I?' I sat up to look about me, but the room was cast in shadow with the only light coming from the glow of the fire, which was distorted by a firescreen.

'Oh no, you're not supposed to sit up, sir. Doctor's orders. Lay down, won't you, and I will go and fetch my master.'

'I did as bid and felt the injury at my temple throb with the movement. A tentative prod with my fingertips discovered a spongy swelling with the spiky ends of stitching strings poking out from it, although I could not recall them being done and supposed the Brandy, however reluctant I was to take it against the mothers' manuals advice, had served me well in that regard at least. I presumed I had been conveyed to one of the rooms at the *Steven's Hotel* after all, and though I was not best pleased to have landed myself in such a dangerous scrape, I was relieved that I could slip away early in the morning and collect my things from my hotel room, and be waiting at Charing Cross for Annalise's coach to come in, without any real harm done. Oh, how I missed her now the hours of our separation had grown so vast. I hoped she was having a happy time with her friends in Carshalton, but I would be glad to have her back in the morning.

Footsteps came along the hall, and I expected the medical officer and the maidservant to arrive back in the room. I was not expecting Sheldon to come into it behind her. I turned my face instantly away.

'Mr Smith, how are you feeling?'

'Much better, I thank you,' I replied in my gruffest accent.

'I fear your injury looks all the worse now the swelling has set in, that's quite a shiner coming up there, but Captain Langham says it all looks nice and clean and should heal agreeably. I am terribly sorry, fellow. It was entirely my fault, and I hope you will permit me to make amends—'

'You already have, sir. I thank you for the rest and seeing my wound tended to.'

'Well, it really was the least I could do after all. Anyway, I should let you rest. Tell the maidservant if you need anything for the pain or anything else. She will stay up with you for the night.'

'Thank you,' I said, relieved.

When he left, I asked the maid for something to drink and to know what the time was. She turned up the light to better see, and helped me sit up just enough to take a few sips of water from a glass, and told me the hour was a quarter past eleven as she stretched into a long yawn, then asked me to excuse her.

I felt better for the water. The Brandy had rendered my mouth as dry as chalk. 'You needn't stay, you know. I am perfectly well enough to sleep alone.'

'Oh no, sir, my master would be unhappy if I did that. He's been worried half the night that he'd done you a serious harm. I daren't chance to leave you, and you have another one of them spells.'

'What spells?' I asked, realising that frowning was a very ill idea presently.

'Well, when master brought you home, sir, you'd been out clean for a good hour and couldn't be woken.'

'What? Hold on, did you say, brought me home? Where am I?'

'Oh no, don't sit up, sir, if you please. You're at Park Lane, sir, in my master's guest quarters.'

What the devil? 'But I was at the hotel. I don't understand.'

'Yes, yes you were, I believe. But there were no rooms for you there, all full to the brim with everyone pouring into town for that boxing match tomorrow. So he had no choice but to bring you home with him since you were concussed and needed nursing until the doctor comes in the morning to examine you.'

There was no way I meant to remain here long enough for that encounter. Not under this roof, in any case. It was bad enough having to run the risk of Sheldon discovering my true identity without the Viscountess and Lord Elmbridge to add to the number in the morning. No. I would wait a little while for the house to be to bed, then slip out back to *Millers*. It was not very far from here. I could walk it in a quarter-hour. Although I was not certain if the entirety of the route could be relied upon to be lit with gas, and I didn't much fancy the attempt in complete darkness. We were a little too close to Half Moon Street for my liking. I had been careful in my ramblings to avoid that street and its immediate junctures, just in case Giles was in town. I had no reason to think so insofar, but I could not rule it out.

The maid stifled another yawn with a cupped hand and apologised again.

'I really don't mind that you are tired, you know. You can't help it. If you are not willing to abandon me, then why don't you at least lie down on the chaise and get some sleep. I shall stir you if I need to.'

'Oh, I really mustn't. My master—'

'Seems like a fair-minded enough man not to scold you for having a rest.'

'He won't, sir; it's not that. Only, well, I don't want to worry him unduly if you do take a turn. He's had such a worrying time of it, and now he's finally back in better spirits—'

'I understand. Has he suffered some ill fortune of late, then?'

She nodded. 'But he's back to himself. Better, his mama says, now he's married. In such a bloom of health.'

Married. I hadn't seen any announcements. 'Well, you know what they say, if there are three things to make a man happy, it's a good table, a good wife and a good horse.'

She nodded. 'Are you married, sir?'

'Soon to be. I'm engaged to a charming young woman. She used to be a maidservant, too,' I told her with an excess of pride borne of rarely being able to speak such words in ordinary circumstances. It was not a deception, but the truth as my heart knew it. The world may have only understood the sanctioning of such unions through ecclesiastic approval and legal contracts, but our hearts knew that on everything but paper, we were bound as fast as any husband or wife.

'Did she?'

'Yes, a kitchen maid at a grand country house.'

'I'd like to go to the country one day. I'd like to get married too, but I'm not sure if I'll ever get to do either.'

'Why shouldn't you? What is your age?'

'I've just turned nineteen.'

'Well then. Young, fair, your whole life set before you. Anything is possible.'

She blushed a little at this, and it pleased me to cheer her. 'I don't know, sir. I suppose things like that don't seem to happen to girls like me.'

'Yet! But there is time enough. Life has a funny way of surprising you. You often think it is heading in one direction, and then you discover it has something altogether different in mind. Sometimes things you never even thought possible. When two hearts are meant for each other, they find their own way to gravitate towards each other. So why shouldn't you find your sweetheart out there someday, hmm?'

'I never thought of it like that before. —Oh, are you alright?'

'Yes, I just need the pot. I don't suppose you would mind stepping out for just a moment to let a fellow keep his dignity?'

'Oh, right. Yes, of course. Perhaps if I just help you to your feet then.'

She did so, and I was glad to get a moment's privacy to undertake this task. I was relieved that only my coat and boots had been removed from me and I was still otherwise fully clothed. On the whole, I found men's attire far more practical than women's and certainly at such a season as this. But if there was one complaint I had, it was the inconvenience of having to strip my lower garments off to use the pot when it required nothing more than a quick lift of skirts ordinarily.

Once I was finished, I walked over to the looking glass above the fire to examine my face and almost jumped back with fright at my reflection. *Good grief.* My left eye was the size of an orange, and my purple eyelid refused to open beyond a narrow slit. No wonder it smarted so. With this monstrosity answering to the task, I would certainly not require much disguising tomorrow. *Oh my. Annalise.* She would be horrified at first sight of me in the morning. Any hope of trivialising it was certainly out of the question now.

I stepped light-footed over to the window where the curtains were drawn and lifted one a fraction to see out onto the street. If I wanted to find my way out of the house before sunrise, it would help if I had a notion of where I was within it. I had only ever been here to dine a couple of times and did not know the house well or its layout beyond the first floor. The majority of our families' mutual entertaining took place in the country.

I wiped the misted glass with my sleeve so I could see. The street outside was quiet: a few windows still lit up amongst the terraces and the streetlights casting amber auras over patches of frost glittering pavement. I hoped it would be cleared by morning for our journey back to Cambridgeshire. Having such a close brush with my discovery tonight, I was keen to get swiftly on my way now.

This was not to be an easy feat. When the maid returned to the room, I attempted all manner of ways to contrive my exit, only to find an obstacle at every turn. She was certainly not to be swayed into assisting my quiet departure, and the more we spoke, the less I felt inclined to put her in a position of calamity should she get the blame for my disappearance. But it was not only her I had to overcome either. Upon asking for a plate of supper, I discovered that she was not the only one keeping watch. There was a manservant stationed outside the room, too. I supposed to keep watch over the porcelain and silver, should I prove a rogue. So as the clock turned into the early hours, I began to realise that the only way I would get out of here tonight would be a direct appeal to the master himself. I had already ascertained that his parents were not present, and for that knowing at least, I felt at slightly greater ease. I was still unsure if Sheldon could be trusted to keep his silence should he discover who I really was, now so much bad feeling had marred our once reliable understanding of each other's character. But I did know Lord and Lady Elmbridge would have no incentive to hold a secret on my behalf, and could be here by tomorrow.

So with this in mind, I weighed up my options and eventually decided to persuade the maidservant to wake Sheldon from his bed and bid him to release me. It was by now a quarter past two, and I was growing concerned that the doors at *Millers* would be locked up if I left it much longer. It certainly seemed that fellows came and went late into the night, but I didn't know if there was a curfew.

He came into the room in his bed jacket, his face still carrying the shape of his slumber. 'What is it, lad? Are you alright?' he asked me.

'I am, sir. I feel perfectly recovered and well enough to depart now if you please.'

'In the middle of the night?' he said, puzzled.

'I'm afraid so. You have been very generous to me, and your staff have looked after me so attentively, I wish it otherwise. But I'm to travel home early in the morning, so I must pack up my things at my hotel and be ready for my journey.'

'To be sure. Though I would feel better if you could wait to see the doctor—'

'No need. I'm as fit as a fiddle now.'

'Well, if you will be good enough to allow me time to wake the groom, we shall convey you back to your lodgings.'

'Generous of you, but no need for waking anyone else up tonight on my account. It's not far from here, and I wouldn't mind a bit of fresh air.'

'As you wish then. My man will sort out a little something for you in the way of compensation. I hope there will be no enduring damage to your health and bid you well—'

'Please. You have been generous enough.'

He nodded in acquiescence. 'Mr Smith,' he held out his hand to shake mine, and I felt uncomfortable at the notion of us touching, especially since we were both un-gloved. Hesitantly, I lifted my hand from my side and offered it in return, and in that moment of our hands clasping lightly, for only the briefest of seconds, something altered, and he looked up sharply at me, a question in his eyes. I turned mine instantly away from him and asked the maid for my coat and boots.

'Where did you say you were from again?' he said after a moment of brief contemplation.

'The provinces, sir, far from here.'

'And the county?'

'Suffolk.'

'Not so very far then.'

'It is by wagon, sir...'

'I daresay. Funny though, you don't have the accent.'

'Travelling. It does that to a fellow. Something wrong, sir?' he had stepped in close to me, which urged me to hurry on with my boots.

'Have we met before?'

'Not likely, my first time in the metropolis.'

'Then elsewhere, I wonder?'

I stood up, and the maid held my coat out for me. I slipped an arm into the sleeve as he studied me intently. 'Don't think so.'

'You remind me of someone I...once knew.'

'Often said; I must have one of them faces.'

'Yes. I daresay. I am tired. Forgive me. I should let you get on your way.'

I nodded and put on my hat, turned to the maidservant and said: 'Well, thank you kindly for your good care of me Potts,' and too late to stop myself from making such an instinctual error, I dropped a curtsey in Sheldon's direction, before I could correct myself into the low bow I had managed to remember on *every* other encounter since my theatre practice in Bury. I turned to see if there was any chance at all he may have missed it. I knew instantly he had not. He was stunned. Speechless for a moment, and I meant to seize the pause to head out of the door, when he said, 'Wait,' came upon me and asked with a searching glare: 'Who are you?' It was barely a question. I saw the recognition in his eyes before he spoke again. 'El?'

It was useless to persist. It was beyond recovery. He *knew*. I dropped my head and asked the servants be dismissed. I did not yet know what would pass between us, but to contain it, was the most I could hope for now. News of his recent marriage and return to better spirits gave me hope that this was the man I knew before it all turned ill. I could only pray I was not about to change it for the worse. He had been courteous to Mr Smith. The truly honourable gentleman I had always known him to be, before last Season, alas.

'It is you, isn't it?' he said when the door clicked shut behind the footman.

I nodded.

'What the devil?'

'I'm sorry, Sheldon. I didn't want to deceive you. This was the last place I expected to end up tonight.'

He shook his head and paced the room. 'I can't believe I didn't know it right away. I see it now. My god, look at the state of you.'

'That was the idea.'

'So your face is splashed over all the newspapers, and this is how you answer to it?'

'I had to do something.'

'Dress in the like of a man? What were you even doing in that district? At *Steven's*?'

'Looking for somewhere to dine.'

He laughed sardonically. 'You have gone queer in the attic, to be sure.'

'Sheldon. My husband has spies out looking for me, and if I wasn't already well enough known here, now everyone who's had sight of a newspaper knows it anyway. What else was I to do?'

He shrugged. 'I don't know, El, stay in Scotland under Caitlyn's protection, I suppose.'

'I never went to Edinburgh. It was a decoy.'

'Well, perhaps you should have.'

'Yes. You are probably right.' I put my top hat on. 'I will be on my way now. I didn't mean to upset you, Sheldon— truly.'

'No. No, don't just leave like that. I'm sorry, this has caught me quite by the cuff.' He sat down in the chair Potts had been sitting in and sighed into his palms. 'Look, I have had so many conversations with you in my head since...our parting. None of them included this one, I must confess. But I hoped that one day you might hear me out, and though I doubted it would be anytime soon, well, you are here now—'

'I'm not sure that would be any better an idea than me walking about St. James' in a greatcoat.'

He laughed just a tad at this, then said more seriously. 'Please, El. I know I don't deserve to ask anything of you after how dreadfully I treated you...

I could see the pain in his eyes at this recognition.

'But if you would grant me a chance to...clear the air between us.'

It was all I needed now after such a day, and yet, I knew he was sorry, and I knew that I, too, had treated him abominably. I had realised it more and more the further in love I fell with Annalise, just what a callous torture I had subjected him to in my naive ignorance of matters of the heart. I had since realised I had never been in love with Sheldon, but I knew he had been in love with me. And whilst his injury to me was grotesque and overt, mine had been more subtle and prolonged, but still despicably grievous. 'Alright,' I agreed. 'But promise me that you will permit my leaving at any time I choose.'

'You may walk out the door unhindered whenever you wish and know that no one will hear of your ever having been here.'

'Thank you.'

'Shall we go somewhere more appropriate?'

'But your wife...?' *Dash*, I had not meant to let that slip. It seemed now I had been thrown so off the mark, I was making more reliable blunders than anything else.

'How do you know about my wife?'

'Someone mentioned it.'

'Who? Hardly a soul knows of it here.'

'Don't be cross with her, Sheldon. The maid let it slip. She meant no harm.'

He seemed relieved at this. 'Shall we go into the study?'

I nodded and followed him out of the room. Realising as we trod the corridors and stairs that it would not have been all that easy to get out of here tonight anyway.

He had a fire lit and a tray of coffee sent for, and we took our seats opposite each other in front of the fire. It was so strange a turn. I could scarcely believe we were here.

'Where is your wife?' I asked when we were settled and left alone again.

'In Malta.'

I frowned.

'It's a long story, and if you want to hear it, I will tell you. But first, tell me why you're on the run from your husband.'

'I thought it old news by now.'

'Not the scandal brewers version. I want to hear it from you.'

I explained to him an abbreviated account of things, leaving out the more intimate details, only describing Giles as having attacked me. I could tell he was torn between feelings of *I-told-you so* and genuine horror. I hoped the latter the more ardent of the two, but he said very little, listening attentively to my account, still looking at me oddly from time to time, observing some detail of my altered appearance, perhaps trying to align it with the image of me he knew. What a sorry picture I must have posed to him in both looks and story. And yet the irony was, despite it all, I had never been happier.

'I'm sorry, El. They set you up for a mighty fall. I always had a bad feeling about Miss Craythorne, though I could never quite put my finger on it.'

'You don't have to say that. I'm sure in your mind, I got only what I deserved. I mean, everyone warned me to stay away from that family—'

'No,' he laid a hand upon mine, which was resting on the arm of the chair. I flinched at the surprise of it, the awkwardness.

'Forgive me,' he said, withdrawing it. 'Nobody could have known they were up to such a scheme as that. Who could even think to contrive such a crack-brained idea?'

'Well, certainly, I did not see it coming. A loveless marriage, yes. A decline in status, naturally. But this...Oh, Sheldon, it is such a mess, and my poor family have suffered the most for it. For even though I am ruined, I do not care for that; only that I am free of him.'

'You may be sure that every door it is within my power to close to that family—'

'It's not your fight Sheldon. Though I thank you for the sentiment. It is my problem, and if nothing else, I take responsibility for having made a poor choice.'

'But you were not with child El, don't you see; we cried off for nothing more than a sick-minded prank. What fools they have made of us both—'

'Well, it's true enough, but if it hadn't turned out that way, you would not have met your wife for a start. Tell me about her.' I did not tell him that despite the phantom pregnancy, there was now a genuine one on Richard's account. Besides the fact that it was my closest guarded secret, I knew he hated Richards and had always been aware of his fondness for me from the beginning.

He smiled now. 'She's beautiful and smart and a little fiery – not altogether unlike yourself. And, what can I say, El? She stole my heart when I thought I had no heart left inside of me.'

I understood perfectly. 'That's beautiful, Sheldon. I am truly happy for you. For you both.'

'Thank you, El. That means a great deal, from you especially. I fear you shall be in the minority of well-wishers, however. You are not the only one to have dashed your family's high hopes.'

'Why?'

'She's poor, El. Her birth is legitimate, but low. She hadn't a penny for her dowry. She lives in the provinces of Malta. Her father is a donkey farmer with ten children to provide for. And to top it all, she's Catholic. My mama's worst nightmare, it turns out.'

'So how on earth did you manage to gain your parent's consent?'

'Well, that's just it. I didn't. I married her in Malta without it. That is why no one beyond a few of my close friends in the regiment knew of it before I returned. Now it is only my nearest family.'

I was stunned, Sheldon, of all people. The most dutiful of sons.

'I came home at Christmastide to spend—what I thought might be the last I would ever be permitted—at Nork Park. Then I gave them the news of my marriage. I told them I was ready to surrender my Viscountcy, be disinherited, and disappear quietly from society to save them the ignominy. No one need ever know. They could say whatever they thought would answer that would spare them any further grief.'

'And what happened?'

'Well, their initial reaction was everything I expected it to be. But, after a time, they had a change of heart, said that I was their only son, a much-loved son, and they were unwilling to lose me. Perhaps the thought of my cousin inheriting it all was too much.' he jested.

'Don't be daft. Your mama would never be parted from you, not for anything.'

'So it seems. And well, I am headed back from my leave in a fortnight. During that time, my mama will make the announcement of our engagement, and when I return for Lent, we will be married here and Caterina will be given a new story that mama thinks society will find more palatable. That's why I must ask you to keep your silence, for it's anyone's guess what mama will come up with to try to save face, but it will certainly not be the daughter of a donkey farmer.'

'I shall keep an eye out for an announcement of your engagement to a Maltese Princess or some such,' I teased, then said more seriously, 'No one shall hear anything from my lips.'

'Thank you.'

'You must really love her to be willing to give it all up.'

'With all that I am. I can't explain it, but, well, just her simplest smile can lift me from the lowest mood. When I'm with her, everything feels possible, worth living for...I know I should have done it for you, El—put you first. For what it's worth, I regretted not marrying you despite it all, every single day until I met Caterina.'

'Maybe you needed to discover what was most important. Perhaps in some peculiar way, it taught you to.'

'It did. There's no question. When I lost you, I felt I had lost everything. I lost my way. I lost myself. But she helped me find my way again, even though I was not looking. Even though I was on a path of self-destruction.'

It stunned me how parallel our stories run. It was like he was telling me the story of Annalise and I's coming together: unexpected, unlikely and yet somehow destined against all the odds. Of course, I could not say as much, so I simply nodded and listened.

'You will always be my first love, El, and a part of my heart shall never forget that. But, well, it's different with Caterina. She makes me want to be a better man. She brings out the best in me, and I think she's as head over hills for me as I am for her, and well, it was never like that with us. We seemed to bring out the worst in each other. I didn't like who I became with you, El. I am ashamed. Disgusted. Embarrassed. There was no excuse for my conduct, so I will never ask for your forgiveness. But I want you to know how truly sorry I am. How much I have revisited those monstrous memories and wanted to swallow my own pistol—'

'Don't say that, Sheldon. I *do* forgive you.'

'You do?'

I nodded. 'I confess I did not know it until today, but yes. I expected I would feel angry if we met again, but I suppose what I felt most was sadness. Sad at how sour we turned such a happy friendship. I always thought of you as the big brother I would have liked my own brothers to be. I have so many fond memories of our youth. I find it hard to align them with what passed between us...'

'I know. I thought of you only last week. You were the one person in the world I knew would understand my grief, and I had no best friend to turn to.' He choked up.

'Understand what?'

'Delilah. She's gone. I had to put an end to her misery. We were on the hunt and she took a nasty fall. Her leg broke and became infected and—'

This time it was me that put a hand over his and held it lightly as he wept. 'Poor Delilah,' I said softly, trying to hold back my own tears.

'I did everything I could. We had the best veterinarian treat her, but it was too late. The infection had turned her blood septic. She was suffering, in so much pain. It was tormenting to see her in such sorry straights. I could subject her to no more trials. She just seemed to get worse with every attempt to make her better. I saw it in her eyes—the pleading. She could bear no more.'

'Oh Sheldon, how dreadful...' I, too, was crying now. 'She was too young to die.'

Without realising how, suddenly, we were holding each other, trying to comfort one another through our outpouring. Perhaps it should have felt uncomfortable or odd, but it didn't now. Something had shifted. Cleared. And it felt like I was hugging my old friend again.

We stayed that way a little while, and then he turned his face to meet my gaze and said: 'I can't tell you how much comfort it gives me to share that with someone. Thank you, El. Tell me, what can I do to set things right between us? There is nothing I wouldn't do to have my best friend back in my life again. I miss you, you know. And I don't mean like *that*.'

'I know. I missed you too.'

'Really?'

'Of course. When you went on your tour of the continent, I cried for weeks. I missed you so sorely. Then when I would get one of those letters you'd send me with the odd foreign stamps on them, how I longed to write you back and demand you come home or return and take me with you,' I laughed at the memory. 'But I never could. You never had a return address for long enough for the post to relay a reply, and, anyway, when you came home last year, I looked forward to having you back. I had no idea how impossible it would be in those few years for us to return to what once was. To grow so far apart and so much altered.'

A tear rolled down his cheek, and I knew this one was not on account of Delilah. 'How I wish we could return to that day in the stable yard and erase all that came after...'

'Well, I daresay we have both learned much since then, for better or worse.'

'Tell me, what can I do to help you in your predicament?'

'Not very much, other than promise you won't blow my cover, not to a soul. Not even to your mama.'

'I shan't. You have my word.'

'Then I am grateful. But the truth is, I may be gone away some time until I can achieve a separation from Giles, and since he is unwilling to grant it to me, I don't know whether it shall amount to months or years. But I will write to you once in a while if you would like it? Just like those non-replyable letters you used to write to me from the continent.'

'I'd like that a lot.'

'And when I do return, I look forward to meeting Caterina.'

Snowdrift.

January 1822. - Eleanor.

'Oh my goodness! I knew I should not have let you go off on your own. He's found you out, hasn't he? Where is he?' Annalise said without a breath between her words as she came bounding out of the stagecoach with an expression that turned from happy anticipation, to abject horror in a single glance at me. In the couple of hours of sleep I had between returning to *Millers* and setting out to meet her this morning, my purple eye had grown larger, weepier, and now extended—albeit in a slightly lighter tone of severity—along the breadth of my cheekbone. It had made quite a lark of trying to get my faux sideburn to stick to it this morning.

Annalise's appearance was unexpectedly altered, too. She stepped out wearing the brown wig we had procured from Fleet market. I had not had the chance to see her try it before, and so the sight of her came as a surprise. Her face remained unaltered and as pure and vibrant in beauty as it ever was, but the concealment of her defining gold tresses beneath these mousy unexceptional locks, rendered her plainer at first glance. It was undoubtedly a good thing. Ordinarily, she was too easily marked out of a crowd. Today she would blend amongst it.

I was so happy to behold her again after such an odd couple of days. The sight of her was immediately grounding. I waved off her flapping and cooing over my injury. I could only smile and take in the sight of her. 'No, I am fine. Let's get into the coach, and I will explain. I don't want to cause a scene here.'

She accepted this and handed her travelling bags to the groom in the hack I had been waiting in, ready to convey us on to Ludgate Hill to catch our stage. I explained everything in the time it took to reach our next coach – even the unlikely reunion with Sheldon. *No secrets,* I reminded myself as she began to reel off a rather passionate reprimand for almost everything I had done since leaving her at the *Greyhound Inn* that morning. I knew I was to expect a vexed reaction to such confessions, and, upon reflection, I could see the validity of her point in some matters, but I was a little tired and fragile after so little sleep, to tolerate it as well as I might usually. Still, I knew it the less of evils. I'd sooner have her ranting and reprimanding me for some honest (even if disagreeable) account of things than deserting me for withholding something from her. That was a lesson I need never repeat, so I accepted her scolding tones and cold reception as we waited for the stage to set off for Cambridgeshire.

We were the first to board, being a quarter-hour early. It was not usually permitted more than five minutes before departure, but a couple of shillings was sufficient to persuade the groom to let us board whilst he was still rigging up the horses. As much as all had gone exceedingly well with Sheldon's discovery of me, it had brought to mind the sobering realisation that he might not be the only one capable of seeing past Leonard's facade. So I did not mean to hang about in public view where it could be avoided, especially in busy coaching alighting points like this, where there was a continual flow of people stepping on and off the footplates.

'Look, see what I got for you whilst I was here,' I said to Annalise, awaiting a sufficient pause in her complaints to present the wedding ring to her.

She pushed it away. 'No, don't think trinkets shall make amends for your carelessness.'

'It's not. It's a wedding ring, part of our disguise, remember? Will you let me put it on your finger? We shan't look so queer travelling about if you do.'

'Fine,' she held her hand out to me in a flippant wave, 'though why you trifle over such a detail when you've been flaunting yourself all over the metropolis like you've nothing to concern yourself with, I don't know.'

'Come, Mrs Leamington,' I said in a teasing tone as I slid the ring over her knuckle, 'aren't you going to permit a husband to kiss his new bride?'

'It's not a joke, Len,' she said, snatching her hand back, 'What if *he* had recognised you, just as your *friend* did?'

'He was not in town for all I could tell. But I know it isn't a joke, and to be sure, I shall be more careful now that's happened. I promise,' I said in earnest. 'Now, how about that kiss? I have missed you.'

Her features softened. 'I've missed you too. But not here. Someone might see us through the window.'

'So what if they do? Can't a fellow kiss his new bride?'

She laughed, and I saw a hint of relent in her expression as it brightened, and she leant forward to accept my waiting kiss. I gathered her up in my arms and took in the smell of her, so glad of our reunion and desperate to get her home where I could make amends in private.

We moved slightly apart when a couple of passengers boarded: an older man who was fond of his own voice, and a prim-looking lady dressed in the style of a governess with a dark dress and cloaks and neatly pinned chignon. Her expression seemed to be as severe as her dress, as Annalise's smile, and my doff of the hat, was met with the thinnest smile of acknowledgement. I supposed she must find her company very low. Unlike my own fall from grace, hers was most likely forced upon her by circumstances beyond her control. To know a genteel way of life and then be forced into the harsher and harder-to-navigate world of the common folk would indeed prove a difficult transition if it were anything but voluntary. With my Annalise to offset the hardships and woes, it was a worthy price to pay in my calculations, but otherwise, it might seem very hard indeed.

It seemed they were to be the only passengers joining us, with no sign of the customary clambering up of outside passengers at the last, before the coach pulled out of the *Belle Sauvage* yard and scuttled its way through the traffic along Ludgate Hill. It was nice to have a little more room to stretch out on such a tiresome journey with two spare seats. It might have been a little more peaceful, too, if the old fellow wasn't minded to talk to us all uninhibited. I didn't mind, to begin with. I was so relieved to be on the move again and drawing closer to the sanctuary of Stapleford that I paid only a half mind to it. The occasional smile, nod or friendly word, I had no objection to. In fact, it appeared to be the custom on these public means of journeying. But as the fellow prattled on about the coming snow that was forecast today, which accounted for the lighter than usual passenger load, then proceeded to recount all the bad winters he could remember in his sixty years, I began retreating to gaze out of the window. In contrast to our passenger load, the London streets were busier than usual, with persons rushing about their business and stocking up on essential wares to try to get ahead of any snow drift that may keep them contained to their houses. What would become of the boxing benefit at *Five Courts* that all the sporting men had poured into the city to see tonight? —He asked me then. Followed by a jest that I looked like I should be heading to *Five Courts* myself on account of the great shiner on my face—was I a prize fighter, or had I just come off unlucky on a night at the tavern? I laughed at this but offered nothing more than a shake of my head in reply. I wanted to keep quietly to myself for the rest of the journey. My scrape with Sheldon, however cathartic and peaceable it had turned out, had given rise to a fresh paranoia I had not previously felt since disguised as Leonard. And whilst I had no confirmation that Giles was in the city, his love of sporting and this prize-fighters benefit being such a hurrah amongst the male sex, I thought it highly likely he was by now, or at least, heading into the district on account of it. With this close at mind, I was keen to return to less risqué ground and Stapleford's quiet, anonymous sanctuary.

When we reached Tottenham, I slowly regained my usual composure and began to relax as I watched light showers of snow peaking and falling over the country landscape the further North we travelled. It had failed to settle insofar, so I did not fear for the viability of our journey, until we reached the Hertfordshire plains and un-trod hills and meadows began to transform into white-capped carpets of powdery snow, with no sign of relent. The roads, at least, were still passable, the traffic disturbing them enough to interrupt its sporadic attempts to settle. But if it were to go on much longer, I was concerned we might have to break our journey more often than usual to change the horses, at least. This weather would prove hard for them at length, even if the roads remained drivable. No doubt by tomorrow, they would not be, once all had turned to slush and ice. By then, I hoped we would be snuggled safely around a warm fire amongst our Stapleford family. I had much missed them, their simple care and company. Watching Mrs Duckworth about the kitchen table and trying out some novel task she might permit me. It seemed curious to me that I should after such a short spell, but we had bonded in these short months in a way I could never recall doing with anyone but Nanny.

It soon became apparent that the prospect of reaching there today was looking more and more unlikely as we stopped for yet another change of horses in Buntingford.

'Is everything alright old chap?' the old man asked the groom when our routine stop turned from the usual ten minutes to a half hour and counting. If I had known at the outset how delayed we were to be, we could have at least gone to the tap room and taken tea to warm us. Usually, there was barely time for a scalding sip in these frenzied turnarounds.

'Not sure yet,' the groom replied. 'The drivers in discussing it with the London-bound crew. Apparently, there's a heavy blizzard headed south and on its way towards Royston, perhaps beyond. He got down here by a whisper of it chasing his tail.'

'Dash it,' I said aloud, to which they both turned about and looked at me. I lowered my tone and said more gruffly, 'You don't suspect he'll cry off the rest of the journey, do you?'

The groom shrugged, 'Not for me to say, sir, but if it's as bad as all that, then perhaps it will be for the better if he does. We took a near few slides as it was on the way up here, and I doubt anyone would wish to risk the carriage turning over.'

'No indeed,' replied the old fellow. 'Reckon there's time then to take a little hot toddy in the tap room?'

'I'll find out for you, sir.'

It was not he, but the chief driver that returned from the private parlour and addressed us as we lingered in the hallway.

'I am sorry to tell you that we shan't be making our departure as planned,' he began.

The governess broke her silence for the first time and said to him, in the cultivated accents I suspected of her, 'But sir, you surely cannot mean to leave us stranded here? I am to be collected at Godmanchester in but three hours and must change coaches in Royston first – they may not wait for me.'

'I'm very sorry, ma'am, to be sure. But the matter is out of my hands. The Innkeeper won't hire out his horses going North on account of reports of a nasty blizzard making its way south. My only choice is to convey you back south on his horses or, to rest ours a few hours and see if conditions improve adequately to continue on to Cambridge.'

'A few hours!' she declared in a tone of objection.

'Yes. In the least. They are cold and tired, having been pushed so hard to get us here in such conditions. I can ask no more of them without a good rest.'

I could not object on this point. Even a few hours of restoration seemed scant, given the journey they had endured. I was not best pleased with being delayed either. I was eager to reach safe ground and put this adventure behind me. But there was nothing to be done but accept the circumstance and bear it as best as we could. 'Come on,' I said, nudging Annalise along the corridor.

'Shall we have some tea?' she asked, following me.

'Yes, we might as well enjoy a warm fire whilst it's on offer.'

'But the tap room's that way.'

'I know. But I don't mean to take it there. It's busy. I shall see about a private parlour so that we might be at ease and give our ears a rest from our company,' I whispered, casting a glance in the direction of the old fellow who was detaining the driver in further conversation. At that moment, a maidservant came by, carrying a tray of dirty mugs in her arms.

'Excuse me, miss,' I hailed her. 'Who do I see about hiring a private parlour?'

'Mr Higgins, sir. I'll fetch him for you. If you would wait in the common room down the hall.'

After ten minutes of pacing the floor in the common room, the queue of waiting customers gathering thicker by the minute, finally, the Innkeeper joined us, red-cheeked and flustered at the demands levelled at him upon his arrival. He threw his palms up in the air and said above the din: 'I can't hear anyone if you all speak at once. Now, who was here first?' he asked. The maidservant indicated a fellow who had already been present ahead of us.

'Right, sir, now what can I do for you?'

'A private parlour, if you please, and a table in the tap room for my servants.'

'I'm afraid the last parlour has been taken up already, and there are no departures scheduled presently. You have the choice of a table in the tap room, the dining parlour, or a seat in here.'

'The gentleman looked about the room indignantly and said, 'then the hire of a boarding apartment, sir.'

'Will you be stopping the night?'

'No.'

'Well, I'm afraid I can't help. We have only two apartments left and parties of twice the number who may yet be stranded for the night, who shall be in greater need of them.'

This sent the gentleman into a fitful protest, demanding to know the whereabouts of a 'decent' inn in the locality, where the Innkeeper knew the customary respect due to a man of his station. It had also sent the common room into a buzz of panic in overhearing this. I, too, was put a little out of countenance by this news. If the weather did not improve, as was hoped, we would be stranded in an inn with no rooms for hire or forced to head back to London. Neither of those options appealed to me, so when our turn came about, I asked directly for a boarding apartment, which was granted, upon satisfying him that we were one of the "stranded parties" referenced and that we would—in all likelihood—be staying the night. Of course, if that were to change at the last, on account of better weather, I was willing to lose the money for this immediate convenience since he insisted upon paying him upfront for the room in full anyway.

The problem which emerged next was how to pay for the thing. I had been a little frivolous in London with my purse, not expecting to have to stretch beyond our journey home. I was unsure of the typical cost of a night's board at a coaching inn. The last we had stayed at in Barnwell was courtesy of the theatre troupe, and the hotels I had frequented in Bury and London, being of an altogether higher class of place, was naturally a little on the pricey side. In any case, twelve shillings for a room with supper, breakfast and attendance, was more than the three shillings sixpence I counted into my palm.

'What is it?' Annalise asked when I looked up, a little puzzled.

'I don't have enough.'

'Then I shall pay it. I have a sovereign Poppy insisted on giving to me as a share in the recent profits of the pie shop. It was fortunate she knew me so well and hid it in the luncheon parcel she gave me this morning, or I would never have taken it.'

'Why not? You are entitled to a share in the profits.'

'Because it's too early. There's still much to invest in. Besides, it doesn't feel right to profit from all their hard work when I have barely lifted a finger to help them—'

'Ahem,' came the Innkeeper's interruption to our little tangent, to which Annalise promptly paid the boarding fee, and we were shown up to our room by the maidservant.

It became instantly apparent why these lodgings had seemed pricey. It was, evidently, one of the more generous apartments, with two adjoining rooms to the main bed chamber. One set up as a small dining parlour, the other as a cosy drawing room, complete with day beds, I presumed to accommodate a valet or lady's maid if need be.

We took off our boots and sprawled out upon the bed with the fire roaring hot at our feet, our stiff red toes thawing in the welcome heat and Annalise cheek-pressed against my chest.

'I've missed you so much, Len,' she said, stroking my belly through my shirt. 'And you too, little one,' she said to my navel. And for a moment, all our troubles seemed forgotten. Having her back in my arms again, snug and warm against me, was enough to diminish all else to dust.

'My god, did you feel that?'

'What?' she said, looking up at me puzzled.

'I think I felt the child moving. Here, give me your hand, and we shall see if it happens again.'

She smiled gleefully and I loosened my shirt from the waistband of my breeches and pressed her palm against the place I had felt the extraordinary shifting beneath my skin just a moment ago. It was a strange sensation, not just physically, but I found myself suddenly emotional. Like this little thing inside me was trying to communicate with me somehow, in the subtlest of languages. I was unprepared to feel so moved by this impromptu sensation. I had tried, at length, not to ponder this strange occurrence that was taking place beneath my very skin. This life forming within me like some unfathomable miracle. I had refused to engage in the autonomous dialogue between my body and emotions, even as I watched my body changing to accommodate its presence. It had been easy to ignore the subtle protrusion of my belly, even the painful swell of my breasts after a time, but this, this slight motion, a twitch beneath my flesh, was not so easy to disregard. It seemed a response borne of instinct, where despite my unhappiness at being pregnant and knowing I could not keep this child at the end of it all, a part of me *wanted* to respond, *wanted* to know it.

I listened to Annalise singing, her head hovering above my navel, my shirt rolled up to my ribcage, her warm palm rising and falling with the contraction of my breath. And then, just as I began to doubt what I had felt, wondered if I had been mistaken, there it was again, a flutter and a shift beneath Annalise's palm.

'I felt it!' she declared, breaking her song, excitement in her eyes as she glanced up at me.

I nodded as another wave of movement rippled from one side of my pelvis to the other, like a bird fluttering from its perch.

'Oh Len, isn't it a wonder,' she said, tracing the movement with her hand. 'Aren't you a little marvel indeed,' she said to my tummy.

'What were you singing? I think she likes it.'

'A French nursery rhyme my mama used to sing to me when I was small. You think you shall bear a girl then?'

The thought had not even occurred to me before, yet it seemed such a certainty now that I pondered it. 'Yes, I think so.'

'What shall you name her?'

I shut down that line of thought as swiftly as it was levelled at me. She was not mine to name, since she was not mine to keep. 'I haven't thought about it,' I said, pulling my shirt back down and nudging her to come back up to me so that I could kiss her.

'You know Len, you don't *have* to give her up... We could give her a happy home with us once we have found a place to settle to.'

Not this again. 'And who knows when that shall be.'

'Well, now we have our disguises settled, we should try at selling those things you buried in the garden at Stapleford.

I had entirely forgotten about the chest of trinkets with all the diversions of late. We had carried it over to a small copse at the estate's boundary where it bordered onto Wimpole and dug a hole four feet deep to hide it shortly after our arrival. It had been back in the time of my initial paranoia that any day, Giles would turn up having found me out and march me back to Beddington against my will. Since, legally, all those trinkets belonged to him, I had thought it better to put them out of reach so we could return for them later if my worst fears came to pass. Now, having been at Stapleford undisturbed for all these months, it seemed an absurd thing to do, however necessary it seemed at the time to make such drastic contingencies. 'I doubt we will have any luck selling them in Cambridge, even in our disguise. It is hardly the place to find the sort of ask-no-questions purchasers we must find.'

'No. But Barnwell is.'

I saw her point. 'Hmm, perhaps, although I saw more taverns than shops there,'

'Well, Leonard might find the taverns just the sort of place to find out what kind of shopkeepers might be interested in his wares.'

'Really?'

She nodded. 'Taverns are where all kinds of business transactions—particularly of a more *irregular* sort—go on. So I am told.'

'Well, it wouldn't hurt to try with something small. I hardly expect to shift a *Gainsborough* down the *Sun Inn*, but perhaps I could try with some of the jewellery or pocket watches. Although I don't much fancy attempting to dig up the chest in this weather. The soil will be frozen solid by now.'

'Then when the weather improves, hmm? I don't want to go on running from him, Len. Being in Carshalton these past few days, I have realised how much I want us to settle properly. Have our own safe house, start afresh and build our own little world where we may live freely. Give this precious one a proper start when she arrives into the world—'

'You know we cannot keep her, Annalise. I thought you understood that.'

'But we can if we have something to offer her. If we can keep her safe. I was thinking about it. No one knows you are with child—at least, no one who would let the detail slip, anyway. Who is to say she is not *my* child, hmm? Then how could your husband ever claim her as his own? It would be impossible for him to prove his claim if there is no evidence to the contrary. If we stay in Stapleford until she is born but go directly to our new home after that, introduce her as *my* new daughter, record it in the bible, christen her as such in the parish church, and give me the story of a young widow, so it's all respectable... Well, in a little while, everyone in the village would be able to attest to the same, never knowing it any different.'

'You *have* given it some thought. But I don't want to talk about it now, alright? There is enough to deal with presently. Oh, don't get upset with me. You know how I hate it when you are sad.'

'Len, don't you see? We will never get the chance to have children again. I want to be a mother one day, and yet I know now, I shall never marry. And I'm certain you'll feel differently in time when you hold her and see she is a part of you, see how much she *needs* you.'

I sat up.

'Len...Just think about it, is all I ask.'

I nodded noncommittally. I *couldn't* think about it. That was the problem. It was all too big. Too messy. Too uncertain. If I wanted what was best for this child, I could not let my heartstrings get tugged into the equation. I would make sure she was safe, free from Giles' clutches. *That* was more important than any other consideration I must take into account, however compelling.

'Thank you. I love you, Len. You're not alone in this, you know. I am beside you in it all. I am here.'

'Not close enough,' I teased, pulling her towards me and kissing her softly. And then, not so softly. Hungrily. Aware of how deprived of her comfort and proximity I'd felt in the days of our separation. Aware of every soft peak and plain of her body as I surveyed it with my palms.

'Take your wig off, will you, now we are alone.'

'Don't you like my new look?' she said, feigning affront.

'No. I long to see your beautiful golden hair again.'

'And I long to see your beautiful face untarnished by that nasty swelling. Does it hurt terribly?' she asked as she sat up and started unpinning her wig.

'No, not too badly now. A little tight and tender, but nothing compared to the monstrous headache I had last night. I must make quite the unflattering picture.'

'Impossible. You never could,' she said, flinging the unpinned wig upon the bed and pulling me up from it to undress me. Exposing my flesh to the draft drifting in from the windows, curtains still undrawn. Releasing the weight of my tightly bound bosom and tossing the binding to the floor.

I followed her example and removed the heavy winter layers concealing her soft pale flesh, warm to the touch, sensitive to my playful manipulation of it, as I unlaced her, brushed my nose against the rising vellus hair at the nape of her neck and paused a moment, to smell the musk of her skin. This unique essence of hers yielded such power over my senses, eliciting a rabid response only she could conjure. These feral stirrings led us back to the bed in a tussle of roaming hands and ravenous kisses. The instant alleviation at the reunion of our bodies as she sank beneath my weight and the warmth of us was captured hot between our skin. *Oh, how I loved this woman with every ounce of me. Every breath. Every heartbeat.*

She never ceased to be a wonder. No matter how many times I explored her with my eyes, my hands, my tongue, it held all the exaltation of the first. It remained a profound honour to be permitted this luxury of our intimacy. To be the one she invited into her deepest places. The one she bared her glorious flesh to. The one to coax her into raptures of delight. I was certain I had near perfected this art now since the early days of our anxious fumbling's. I knew precisely the sequence, the rhythm, the pressure and all its undulations and variations that would bring her swiftly to blissful murmurs. She knew mine too now. Our early winter bedtimes and late morning risings had given us ample practice to grow into this private knowledge of each other. To learn to be bolder with our demands and offerings. To be at ease in our nakedness and ever-evolving entwining postures.

She still shied away from our trying out the silken dildo I had procured at *The Mermaid*. But I had bid her use it upon me in the hope it would bring her closer to the temptation of trying it as she watched my writhing hips and listened to my thunderous groans of pleasure as she thrust me with this curious creation that seemed so incapable of such industry. I longed to ease her open with it, gently, of course, not the way it had been for me. I wanted her to feel no pain. To make a gradual attempt until she yielded, freely, for want of offering me this one untasted privilege that remained to her to bestow.

I thought about it now as I repositioned myself, knees behind her shoulders, face between her thighs as they fell open for me, and I met the gleaming pearl of her with the tip of my tongue. At the same moment, she clung to my buttocks and buried her face between my own. This had become a favourite way of toying with each other since we had discovered it, at top and tail, to pleasure each other simultaneously. It oft became a battle of wills as we toiled for the other's pleasure whilst attempting to resist our own. To no avail, of course. We would peak and succumb in differing moments as one or the other could no longer resist falling weak and indulging in the tongue trickery of the other. I was often the weaker party, dropping back to my hips to perch just above her face as my body gave in to her manipulations. Hovering just a fraction above her as she pulled me savagely down upon her face and sucked at me until I could not prevent myself from releasing torrents of passion and pleasure into her waiting mouth. Using the last threads of restraint, not to collapse upon her, the muscles of my thighs burning with the strain to hold steady as she hooked her arms around them to lift herself closer. Today it took mere seconds to reduce me to a spent and quivering wreck. I had gone too long without her touch to contrive to pace myself.

I dropped down to my elbows and delved back in to appease the momentary neglect. I meant to make it up to her now and prove it worthy of the wait as I tickled her lightly before nibbling on the swell of her. I had believed it to be only men that stiffened and swelled, but I knew now this was not true. When adequately enticed, she would harden like a bud upon my tongue and increase to twice the extent. I knew precisely how to coax her into such a state: the gentle pressing of my lips sealing about the bulge of her whilst pulling back slightly to draw her into my mouth as vigorously as I could. I alternated this with withdrawing completely and tracing feather-light tongue strokes over the frailest frills of skin. The language of her body told me when to make the switch; her buttocks lifting from the mattress to find my mouth, indicated a vigorous spell. Her lowering back down, thighs twitching, indicated an indulgent teasing spell. I had learned to play to the tunes of her body like any good musician would know precisely how to evoke the clearest, brightest tones from his instrument. This was not a purely manual task like those that had gone before with others. This was a reading. A conversation. A curiosity, and yet a knowing, all at once, devoid of any spoken word and yet complete in its meaning. The more we practised this intangible language, the more fluent we became in the art of it, the mastery.

We made love for at least two hours before the wafting aroma of hearty cooking alerted us to the creeping of time. If it were not for the faint hope of our journey resuming today, I would not have been able to convince myself to rise at all, with so much delight and comfort pulsing through me as we rested, tucked snug and warm beneath the coverlet. I forced myself up and instantly felt the coolness of the room against my nakedness as I crossed to the window, lifting the curtain just enough to observe the weather. It was still light outside. The sky pale with snow clouds, and the treetops in the distance capped with a faint dusting.

The panes of glass were frost gleaming at the edges and misted with condensation on the inside, curtailing my view. I brushed away a patch to see out onto the village, which was scantly blanketed in patchy snow drifts from the light but persistent snow shower that rained prettily enough before my view.

'Do you think we will travel today?' Annalise asked me, up on one elbow, head cocked.

'It's hard to say.' I stepped away from the window and picked my shirt up off the floor. 'It still looks drivable presently, but the worst of it may soon be working its way down to us. I suppose we shall have to go and see what the coachman has to say,' I said, reaching into my shirt sleeves and pulling it over my head.

'Well, in the worst case, we can take a little supper before resuming our next act. In the best case, we shall be home in a few hours and have the comfort of our own sheets to warm.'

'You may be sure of it.' I bent down to peck her on the cheek as I collected my breeches and stockings from the rug.

MIDWINTER.

———— ❦ ————

I WAS BACK IN THE STYLE of Leonard, and she in her mousy wig in about ten minutes. Having only one eye to tend to now, had the effect of shortening the task of brushing my face paints on and refastening my wigs. I took her arm and led her down the stairs like any proud and affectionate husband, enjoying the new license this disguise offered us. It was a shame I disliked the look of myself so much in this style, for perhaps this was the answer to all our problems, present and future. Giles would always be looking for a woman, not a married couple. It would overcome the difficulty of my image being splashed all over the newspapers too. And *if* – and it remained a very big *if* – we might consider the possibility of keeping the child, we would be quite above suspicion on any account. However much I lamented my beautiful dresses and pinned coiffure, it may prove a worthy sacrifice to be able to love her freely and publicly for the rest of our days...

We descended into a hubbub of persons in the downstairs hall, thrice as thick in number than when we had left it. We had been too preoccupied to hear the coaches that must have arrived in our absence. We shouldered our way through to the dining room, where long queues had formed outside of it, and hailed our maid in passing.

'Oh yes, Mr and Mrs Leamington, your table is reserved. You may go straight in. But if you wouldn't mind being timely – we have a swift turnaround today.'

'So I see, and of course, we shan't be leisurely about it. Where did all these people come from?'

'Coaches from London that hadn't gotten word in time to turn back. Quite a kafuffle we are in, all over a bit of snow.'

'Indeed. Are there no other inns about?'

'A few, but they're all full now, and we're all in the same boat for the present. Now, if you'll excuse me, sir, I'm wanted in the tap room.'

I was pleased to find our coach crew in the dining parlour when we were shown to our seats which had been reserved amongst them. I would not need to fight back through the crammed halls and parlours for an update now. I was not quite as thrilled to be sat beside our prattling fellow passenger though, particularly now he smelt as strong as a brandy decanter, I noticed, pulling up my chair.

'Ah, Mr Leamington, there you are,' said the coachman, looking up from his plate and acknowledging us. We returned the greeting and extended it about our table, the governess still offering nothing more than a glance of recognition. She seemed lost, subdued, and I supposed that she unlikely had ever found herself in such a predicament as this before, and all alone to deal in it too.

'Have you any news for us, sir?' I asked the coachman once he had finished his sip of ale.

He nodded. 'Yes, we did try looking for you, but—'

'Apologies, we took a little rest in our apartment,' all eyes set upon us at this announcement, and then I remembered the room shortage.

'You managed to obtain an apartment, sir?' asked the governess, putting down her soup spoon.

'Yes, we took the precaution once we realised the possibility of being stranded.'

'A wise choice,' the coachman said rather pointedly. 'We shan't be leaving until morning, I'm afraid. The worst of the blizzard appears to be slowly moving east now but might yet pass over this way before we're clear of it. With all the inns between here and Cambridge full to the brim with stranded passengers, we can't afford to risk a bad decision, having nowhere to stop, should we prove unlucky.'

'Fair enough, it cannot be helped. Have you secured lodgings here for the crew?' I asked, as a bowl of white soup was placed in front of me without warning. I supposed the staff had little time for the trivialities of offering choices under this level of strain.

He nodded as he tore a hunk of bread from the loaf with his bare hands. 'We have rooms in the service wing, and the horses are already stabled, so we are luckier than many tonight. There's about twenty people here who won't have more than a truckle bed or sofa to make do with, by the sounds of it. It looks like we got here in the nick o' time.'

'Did you get a room?' I asked the governess, who was staring intently, eyes watering.

She nodded and, lip trembling, got up from her seat and darted out of the parlour in a fit of tears.

'What did I say?' I asked, amazed.

The coachman lowered his voice and leaned in close. 'She had only the choice of sharing an apartment with old prattle-box over there who has drunk half his weight in spirits since we arrived, or, boarding in with the stable boys in the barn loft.'

'No wonder she's in a fidget. She is a young lady travelling alone and I think not much used to so doing.'

'Well, that's one way o' putting it.'

'Why did the innkeeper not give her the room and ask the old fellow to take the barn space? Chances are he shan't know any better by the time he hits the pillow.'

'He got in first. I told her to go and book in sharp, but she wouldn't have it. Had a right old tantrum, demanding we find a means to get her to Royston by nightfall. She was lucky the old bugger took pity on her and offered her to take the bed and all, but she was not best pleased by it. Though she seems to prefer it over a barn loft.'

I knew instantly what we must do, although I felt more than a tad anxious under the circumstances of our disguise. We must invite her to come in with us. Offer up the other day bed, too, to some other female who may be amongst the number without lodgings tonight. We didn't need all that space to ourselves, however much we might have enjoyed the privacy. And she might be missish and proud, but how could I condemn her for it when I had lived most of my life in the very same manner. I knew no better then. It seemed she was still to learn. But to leave her to share with an unfamiliar man—a very foxed, unfamiliar man—did not seem any more reasonable than expecting her to bunk up in a barn with a crew of stable boys.

After a dinner of beef stew and cheeses to finish, I stole Annalise off into the common room to speak to her about the proposition. As I expected, she was in unison with the sentiment and pleased that I was willing to spend a night in Leonard's character as the sacrifice. It did not take her long to find another female in need of our assistance either. The granddaughter of a gentleman who was grateful to have her comfort attended to, even if in want of his own. We took the pair of them up to the apartment to settle in and arrange their things and finally received a kind word and smile from the sulky governess, who was now gushing with gratitude for this service we had rendered her.

We found the extra blankets and linens in the closet of our bedchamber, and Annalise, being Annalise, insisted on making the day-beds up for the pair of them, which I knew they would be grateful for, remembering how cumbersome I had found the task of making up a bed for the first time the dreadful night I had vomited all over it in my drunkenness. I smiled to myself as I watched her tucking the sheets in perfect neat corners and remembered that there was a time when neither of us much liked the other's presence. It seemed difficult to believe it now. Yet I still remembered her furious face as she beheld me and the nanny-esque way she would speak to me sometimes, like I was a petulant child causing mischief for her. And I could not deny the charge, however ashamed such former versions of myself made me feel upon reflection. I wondered if the governess was feeling the same about her cold reception to us, now she watched Annalise smoothing the blankets over her bed and plumping the pillows for her. Her thanks were given in genuine accents as she held her hands out to the fire's heat and rubbed her palms together.

'We shall leave the key and give you some privacy to settle in and prepare for bed. We shan't disturb you when we come back in. We'll have the maid let us in. I hope you sleep well. Come on, Len,' she turned and said to me. 'Let us go and take a cup of chocolate in the tap room. —Goodnight.'

'Goodnight,' the ladies chorused back, and I picked up my hat off the side table and offered them both a bow.

'We could have ordered the chocolate to our chamber, you know. I doubt we'll find a seat in there with how frantic everything is downstairs.'

'I know. And we don't have to go there. I just wanted to give them a little time to settle in and feel at ease.'

'Of course, you are right, as ever,' I said, kissing her temple before we descended the stairs. 'We might as well take a cup of chocolate then and get an early night ourselves, if he means to set off at first light. Not that it shall be the kind of night I had planned for us.'

'No. We shall be straight to sleep.'

'At least we should be home by midday, and all of this will be behind us.'

We waited in a queue for almost a quarter-hour before we could be seated for our drinks. The privilege of our boarding status in the dining parlour did not apply in the taproom, and we had to make do with perching on the end of a crowded table to take our drinks. It was hardly what I had in mind, fancying one of the cosy little booths or easy chairs about the fire, just me and her. But who knows how long we might have waited for one of those to be vacated.

Night had fallen now, and the light was low in the parlour, bringing a sense of cosy ambience, despite it having the din of a low tavern about it, being so overcrowded. It was at least a pleasant inn. Neat, clean and well-furnished with generous fires and an army of staff. We might have ended up somewhere like the Barnwell Inn and been covered in bed bug bites, or worse. The memory reminded me of Theo. I would write to her on my return to arrange the next stage of our investigations at the *Spinning House,* now I had given my disguise a (mostly) successful test run. I did not take Sheldon's recognition of me as an abject failure, given how long it kept even one of my longest-standing friends from realising immediately. Besides, it was the exception rather than the rule. Across the board, I had been accepted without question as any other man, by all who crossed paths with me. I felt confident we were at last ready to take on the Proctors. Whilst in London, I had thought much of how we might contrive it. Getting one of the troupe to pose as a concerned university servant who had spotted some undergraduates conversing with a party of females, was one idea.

'A penny for your thoughts?' Annalise said when our tray was slid in front of us: chocolatey steam rising from our cups, and a saucer of biscuits we had not asked for, but would probably end up eating since dinner had been a little on the modest side, even if good fare.

'I was just bouncing around ideas for our *Spinning House* coup' d'etat. I mean to write to Theo when we get home and see if their offer of help in the scheme still stands. I have an idea I think will help speed things up...'

'What is it?'

I took a small sip from my cup to test the temperature, and as I lifted my eyes to answer her, I almost jumped out of my skin. Before I realised it, I had allowed the cup to slip from my grasp and was wearing most of my chocolate. Thank goodness I still had my greatcoat on, or else I was sure I would have sustained a scold from it. I had no time to ponder. I apologised to the maidservant who came over to assist me in the mess and said to Annalise as calmly as I could manage: 'We have to go. Now.'

'What?' she frowned.

'No, don't look about.'

'Len, you're frightening me. Whatever is wrong?'

I could barely speak for the constriction of my throat. I cleared it with a cough into my fist. 'He's here,' I managed.

'Who? – No, you don't mean Giles?' she mouthed the name rather than spoke it.

I nodded and tried not to react to the terror that thundered across her flushed cheeks as she took in the shock. I gave her hand a gentle squeeze and said: 'He's not facing us. But Digby, his manservant, is, so we will have to leave as soon as the maid comes back with the cloth and ask her to direct us to the stables, alright.'

'The stables?'

'I'm going to have to hire a horse and trap to get us out of here tonight.'

'But we've not much money left. Will it be enough?'

'We better hope so, or it might just be a horse.'

'No, Len, you know you cannot ride in your condition, and you know I'm of no help. And what about this dreadful blizzard? Surely it would be too dangerous on horseback, even if you weren't—'

'What choice do we have?'

She stared blankly at me, tears welling in her hazel eyes, which darkened now with the glisten of her tears, so they reflected the colour of the chocolate in her untouched cup. 'But the baby—'

'Is as good as lost to us if he catches us here...'

She nodded in acquiescence, and we waited for the maid to return and furnish us with the directions before rising as calmly and casually as anyone might, turning about without looking in their direction and walking out at a leisurely pace, arm in arm.

MIDWINTER.

I was sure I had held my breath the entire journey out to the courtyard as a long exhale blew a fogging cloud before my face. 'Turn about and see if anyone has followed us.'

Annalise shook her head. 'All clear.'

We walked on to the stable buildings, found the farriers cottage, and knocked.

'Sorry to disturb you, but I want to hire a horse and trap or some such vehicle. What is the charge, please?'

'Depends where you're headed.'

'The next town, Royston.'

'No can do. We're only hiring out southbound.'

'Alright, then to the next place south of here. Where would that be?'

'Puckeridge,' he said. 'Twenty shillings for one horse and a choice of cart or wagon. Or a pair of horses and a small coach for two pounds six. Plus, eight pence for each postilion.'

'Whatever is the cheapest will do.'

'The cart then. a total of twenty shillings eight pence to Puckeridge.'

I remembered then we had paid upfront for our lodgings and didn't have enough left for even this. 'What about just a horse?'

'In this weather? You dicked in the nob or somein?'

'Then a hackney or some fellow who will convey us for a fee?'

'No chance. Not in this. I'll have enough trouble getting the postillions to go out for collections.'

Annalise stepped in before I lost my temper. 'Forgive my husband's impatience, sir. We've just received some terrible news of an emergency at home, but find ourselves on a budget. We are looking to find the fastest and most economical way we might set out. You see, my grandma has been declared to have only hours to live...' she began to weep now, and I patted her shoulder consolingly and watched as the farrier grew uncomfortable.

'Where's home?' he said eventually.

'Godmanchester,' Annalise whimpered, and I knew she shared in my desperation to tell such clankers. I was grateful for her quick thinking and display of feminine sensibility though, she seemed to be bringing him about. I supposed I was unlikely to have the same effect on him in Leonard's likeness.

'Best bet is to take a single horse as far as Puckeridge. You can probably hire a trap there for half the price if you can stomach the half-hour ride over in this. Higgins doubled our rates since this snowstorm hit this afternoon. But I can do you a good strong bay for five shillings and a two-pound deposit, which will be returned to you when you drop him at the *White Hart* in Puckeridge. I can do no more, Mrs, truly.'

'Thank you,' she gathered him in an impromptu hug and whilst it took him a little aback, I could see he was not immune to her charms and accepted her display of feminine gratitude with a fleeting blush. We had the five shillings, the problem was how to find the rest of the money for the security deposit. My brain raced over the options, and it occurred to me there was a way. It was a reach, but worth a try at this point in these desperate straights.

'Well, you wait here, and I'll go and tell the groom to have him saddled up for a double, alright,' he said, fetching his hat and coat from beyond the door and stepping out.

'Thank you. We shall go and get our things.'

'Oh god, Len, how are we going to pay him?' Annalise said the moment he disappeared. 'I had thought about offering him my pearl broach, but I'm not sure it would be enough.'

'It's alright, don't cry, my love. I have an idea. Now, are you willing to go back in without me? I shall watch you through the glass from outside, and if I see anyone take notice of you or follow you about, I shall report him as a rogue to the Innkeeper, alright?'

She nodded.

'I want you to go and get our bags, then speak privately with the gentleman's granddaughter. Wake her if you must and set this proposition to her: We are willing to sell our room to her grandfather for two pounds.'

'But Eleanor, that is more than three times as much as we paid for it and without the meals. It isn't right.'

'It doesn't matter. He can afford it and shan't care a jot for the sake of a comfortable night. Bid her, put it to him, and tell her she must hurry, for someone else has already offered us the sum, but you wanted to give her first refusal since her grandfather would benefit from the comfort of a good bed. The only proviso is, they must let the governess stay, alright.'

She nodded, and I squeezed her, kissed her on the cheek and watched her through the glass as she vanished up the stairwell. Thankfully, the crowds had thinned out somewhat now, and I could get a clear view in to see if anyone was watching her. I saw no sign of anything suspicious and considered she must have reached the room by now. It was only one flight up. I paced the cobbles outside as I kept watch. I had begun to shiver already with the cold creeping beneath the sleeves of my heavy coat. How would we manage a horseback journey in this? I wondered if I *was* leading us into danger.

For my own part, I considered it to be worth the risk, but I did not mean to expose Annalise to danger, not for anything. Perhaps she would be safer left here? He did not know her after all. And she was not alone. She had the other ladies' presence to reassure her and raise the alarm if need be. Oh god, no, I couldn't leave her here alone. Perhaps we should give up the idea and just stay put and remain in our room, hoping it was purely by chance and not by design, that he was here. He was always travelling about, after all. It might be nothing more than an unfortunate coincidence. Certainly, no one seemed to recognise or suspect us, and we hadn't been followed, as far as I could tell. Digby must have seen me drop the cup if no one else. But I saw no sign of recognition on his face as he returned to his conversation. But perhaps that was the ploy, to act oblivious, to make us feel at ease, so we did not try to flee. Then tomorrow, if the roads were drivable, who knows.

How could anyone have tipped him off about my whereabouts? Had I been travelling about as myself, it was likely with a handsome reward on offer. But I had not spent a moment out in public without the protection of Leonard's character. And no one knew...except Sheldon. *No. Impossible. He would not.* But hadn't I said the very same of others I had once mistrusted, himself amongst the number? He knew I was in character. He knew I was to travel from Charing Cross this morning, even though I would not disclose to him where to. It would not have been too difficult to ask after the coach I boarded, given the description of a fellow with a whopping great shiner on his face. It was the Elmbridges, after all, that sponsored the Craythornes way into society for reasons I could never quite make sense of. There was all that sinister talk he gave me about secret circles in which they held power of some kind, although he was evasive. *Oh, Sheldon, I thought you were in earnest last night. I thought we had made amends.* I brushed a tear from my lashes before they had a chance to fall. Not now. Now was not the time for sentiment. Instead I fixed my interest on a frozen spiderweb that had crystallised in a corner of the inn's signpost and shimmered in the lantern-light, in the pattern of finely spun lace.

Champion

January 1822. - Eleanor.

By the time Annalise returned to me, about a quarter-hour later, I was trembling with cold and a nervous wreck. 'Was everything alright?' I asked her instantly, taking up one of the bags she carried out with her.

'Everything's fine. I have the money. It all went just as you said it would. The grandfather was more than happy with the bargain and to relinquish his truckle bed in the common room for the premium. I took this too. '

'Well done. What is it?'

'A blanket.'

'Annalise, you cannot steal. People go to prison for taking less than that.'

'Well, I'm not stealing it. I shall send it back freshly laundered once we are home. I'm not having us freeze to death out here tonight.'

'Annalise, you don't have to come with me. I know horses make you nervous, and it might be a treacherous ride. If you stay here, I can ride straight on to Stapleford tonight and send Travers back with the trap for you when I arrive.'

'You think I am leaving you to set off alone heading into a blizzard? Perhaps you *are* dicked in the nob.'

Somehow, through all the palpable anxiety, she coaxed me into a laugh, despite our circumstances being anything but humorous. 'You are certain? I won't pretend it is without risk. If we are hit by that blizzard, especially on an unfamiliar horse and, well, I shall be a little rusty after –'

'I know. We take a risk in going. We take a risk in staying. I'm not losing you, Len, not for anything. Come on, let's get going. We no longer have a room, so it seems this is our only choice now.'

'It was true. I would take the careful option and drive south as far as Puckeridge, trade in the horse there and see what could be done with our two pounds deposit in the way of getting back to Cambridgeshire in the morning when hopefully, this snow spell would have blown itself off east. Of course, I did not know what way Giles was heading, and I could not rule out that if this was a mere coincidence, we still might meet him on the way back up if he was setting off in the same direction. Perhaps it would be safer to return to London for now, seek refuge with Mrs Neal and be conveyed back up to Cambridgeshire by private coach when we better understood how things stood. I could send a courier up to Stapleford to ask Mrs Duckworth if anyone had come about asking after me. Make sure it was still the safe little retreat we had left only days ago, before returning there.

These circular and unanswerable thoughts did not stop spinning until we were saddled and had ridden at least a mile off into the night. Annalise clinging tight to me as we galloped through feathery drifts of snow that grew lighter and more intermittent the further on we went. But it was arctic, despite the extra layers we had added to our dress before climbing up on Champion's back. He did at least live up to his namesake, ploughing sturdily on down the dark lane as if it were merely a balmy spring afternoon. *Thank you, boy.* He did at least have a sheepskin mat fitted on his back to protect him from the worst of it, and then there was the extra insulation offered by the saddle bags, plus our own body heat – if we actually still possessed any such thing. I was numb from fingers to toes and had no sense of warmth beyond the fogging of my breath as I exhaled and it blew back against me. Our saving grace was that according to the Farrier, we should make the journey in under an hour if the roads were quiet and passable.

They were not just quiet but entirely derelict, not a sign of a soul about insofar. Coupled with the presence of the snowy landscape and the windless night sky, it created a sinister sense of calm. A stillness that was almost too quiet, that seemed difficult to trust in its unusual serenity. At least it would be easy to distinguish any attempts to follow us on a night such as this. Although we would leave clear tracks in the snow to be followed by, I considered. I had kept to the road edge to be on the safe side and ready to make off through the woodland should we need to. There were few advantages to being on horseback on such a night, and certainly, our speed would be no match for a coach and four if Giles was in his usual carriage. But we had the facility of being able to set off through woods and meadows at a trice if we needed to. I hoped we would not have to. I knew nothing of this area, and the light was exceedingly poor now we had left the village behind us. Aside from the occasional farmhouse set aglow somewhere in the distance there were no other buildings in sight. Childhood tales of Dick Turpin rose to mind and sent me on another course of anxiety. I had nothing capable of protecting us should we need it. I could only hope even highwaymen took a night off in bad weather, even if for no other reason than the lack of coaches to prey upon.

AT A QUARTER TO TEN, we finally reached the *White Hart* without a trace of anyone having followed us here. As I slid down from Champion's back, inflexible, stiff as a wooden sewing dummy, I could feel nothing but deep gratitude for having got to safety without a dozen potential horrors having prevented us. 'Thank you, Boy', I said, patting Champion's haunches with a numb hand and gathering Annalise up beneath my arm as we set off into the inn. I exchanged my security ticket with the innkeeper and received our two-pound deposit back. Unsurprisingly, this could not procure us a room or a method out of the place tonight since they were full and had nothing left to hire out. The stables were half empty and all the horses posted were at rest.

They did, at least, have a private parlour we could use and a good fire still burning bright from its last occupants, who I presumed had taken off to their bedchamber. It was like an oasis in a desert after the evening we'd endured, and I accepted it readily and paid for it to cover us till morning. We found a space on the sofa to make for a bed and re-ordered the mugs of chocolate we had never got to drink earlier, but were in need of now.

At half past eleven, the maidservant came to stoke the fire and remove our tray. She also took pity on us and came back moments later with a pillow and spare blanket for us, and there we huddled together beneath it, grateful for this small comfort and, moreover, having succeeded in our great escape.

I WOKE WITH A STIFF neck to the smell of coffee rising beneath my nose.

'I thought you might need it, sir,' said the maidservant, who had placed a tray of coffee and cups for two upon the side table. She was the same who had brought us the blankets last night.'

'That's very kind of you indeed, thank you.'

'You're welcome, sir. Breakfast is available in the dining parlour in twenty minutes if you would like me to hold a table for you?'

'Yes, that would be very welcome. What is your name?' I asked.

'Mildred, sir.'

'Mildred, do you happen to know if there has been any new guests since we arrived last night?'

'No, sir, there have not.'

'Thank you,' I said feeling relieved, 'and for the coffee. What a credit you are. If only all the inns showed such courtesy as yours.'

'Happy to be of service, sir. Twenty minutes. The dining parlour is down the hall to the left.'

I poured us both a cup with cream and sugar and took a sip, watching Annalise stir a little at the disturbance before settling back into sleep again. I knew she must be exhausted to sleep so soundly in such an uncomfortable fashion, and had we not been in a rush to move on from here, I would have let her be a while longer. But the mission to return to Stapleford had reset today, and I was determined that one way or the other we would get there this time, and with the coast seeming clear there wasn't a moment to lose. So I pressed a kiss to her cheek and stroked her hair from her face, which of course, was the mousy wig that had slipped just a fraction as she slept. 'Annalise...'

'Hmm, what?' she sat up, squinting.

MIDWINTER.

'It's morning, love. Here, there's a coffee on the table for you. I'm just dashing off to use the privy and to see if there's any news on travelling out this morning.'

After breakfast, I managed to procure two outside tickets on the mail coach that was due in for a change of horses at noon. It was my least preferred way to travel, but beggars could not be choosers, and it had two advantages at least: it was fast, the tollgates already being opened for it, meaning we would make good speed without needing to stop, and the armed guard that escorted the Royal Mail. Giles would not wish to interfere with the Kings mail, I hoped. And so it felt like a safe choice, even if not the most comfortable.

The blizzard had been reported to have crossed the East Anglian coastline in the early morning hours, having never reached south at all in the end. I almost cried at the relief of this news and had to pull myself together and blame it on my weepy injured eye. I don't know when I became such a blubber, but it seemed of late that it took almost nothing to send me into a fit of tears.

The mail coach was crammed both inside and out. And I understood now why a few of the other enquiring guests had turned down first refusal on the outside tickets I had managed to obtain. We were ushered up onto a crammed back box, the benches hard and ill-contoured for a comfortable ride, and whilst the snow had stopped, an arctic chill in the air remained, turning nose tips brilliant red and eyes streaming in the wind. My injured eye now seemed to be over the worst of its outcry at least, the swelling appearing somewhat shrunken and less angry when I caught sight of it in the dining parlour looking glass this morning. Though whether it would remain so after weather beating it was about to sustain out here, I doubted.

The change of horses was expedient, all arrivals set down and departees loaded, fresh horses at the ready in about five minutes of the mail coach flying into the yard, and we were setting off out of it at a trice. The feeling of relief was indescribable as we rattled along the lane that had seemed so very blank and obscure in the stifled snowy nightshade we had journeyed through last night. I smiled at Annalise as we huddled together beneath the borrowed blanket, trying to get used to the carriage throwing our neighbours upon us—and us against them—from time to time as we

237

traversed a sharp bend or overtook passing traffic. I was glad we were at least not set atop the coach with the speed at which we travelled. I had always fancied myself quite the whip, but these mail coach drivers were of an altogether different cut when it came to keeping up speed, regardless of the obstacles of other traffic. It was as though the horses carried a fanfare as they galloped, saying: "Make way for the Kings mail", swerving effortlessly around slow-moving vehicles barely dropping speed.

WE MADE IT TO ROYSTON just after one-o-clock, a little rattled and exceedingly numb from the cold. But after the impossible mission it had previously proved, and our very close scrape with Giles, we could only feel grateful for having landed at last, however cold and rattled.

We hailed a hackney cab that took us as far as Arrington, then the remainder of the journey on foot, in order to ensure we led no one directly to our door without knowing it. But the lanes were quiet once we made out of the village and beyond the occasional passing carriage or push wagon, few villagers dared to venture out on foot. The snow had set much thicker here. Drifts swept to the roadside turning to dirty slush, but inches of neat, bright un-trod snow blanketed the meadows and hills, our footsteps carving virgin tracks in them as we veered off the main lanes to take a shortcut of a public bridleway through the farmer's fields. This way, we would be made aware of the presence of unwanted eyes should we be followed, as well as less inclined to slip on ice as we might on the roadside.

Thankfully, we came across no more than an occasional farmer attempting to shovel snow from some patch of land he needed access to. It seemed a shame to disturb it. There was such a majesty about the downy scene; so pristine and smooth, hiding all the imperfections of the barren winter landscape. And with the serenity of the view came a serenity in the silence of it, the stillness of the crisp air. That minute pause between an exhale and an inhale protracted out above the treetops.

Then as our tracks drew meandering lines behind us that faded far from view, we came through a clearing and met the driveway of Stapleford, boots crunching first at the layer of snow, then as they sunk fully with the weight of our steps, the second crunch of disturbing the gravel. We shared a smile of relief as we traversed it. Nobody had been here by the look of the undisturbed driveway. *Stapleford was safe and we had made it. We were home.*

I suspected, from the lack of disturbance to the Stapleford grounds, that the staff had kept quietly to the house in our absence and I was pleased with the thought of them taking a little respite from our care. As much as they made it seem quite the contrary, I knew it must have been a little taxing for Mr Fulton and Mrs Duckworth to return to waiting on us after so long on board wages, and in their advancing years. I supposed mother would have pensioned them off by now, had she been about to see the twisted joints of Mr Fulton's weathered hands and the pronounced curvature at the top of Mrs Duckworth's spine. Of course, the younger staff took the brunt of the hard labour, but I couldn't help but feel the pair of them were of an age where they should be waited on, rather than waiting upon others. I should never like to offend them with such observations but once my time here drew to a close, I would tell my mama and see what might be done for them.

Before we reached the house, we took a detour to the gardener's shed so I could change out of Leonard's character before arriving there. It would be enough of a shock to turn up with the injured state of my face without confusing the staff, who were not in my confidence, beyond Mrs Duckworth.

'OH, I'M SO GLAD YOU'RE back,' said Mrs Duckworth, ushering us into the hall and fetching up our hats and cloaks. 'I've been worried sick. Oh my! You are injured!'

'An old injury. I took a little tumble, but I am recovering well now.'

'Glad to hear it, it looks mighty sore. Oh, and look, you're frozen stiff. I can feel the chill carrying in with you. Let's get you into the drawing room before the fire, and I'll fetch you both a hot toddy, eh, warm up your blood. Are you hungry? Daisy, Daisy, go and put that broth on to heat, will you. Mistress is home,' she called down the corridor as we passed through it and were ushered over to the fireside chairs in the drawing room. We were so cold it stung to be too close to the flame to begin. I had visions of the spitting sizzle I'd seen in the kitchen when Mrs Duckworth cracked an egg into a hot pan. Instead, we opted for fresh blankets and cloaked them around us, moving to the sofa furthest from the fireplace.

'Now, milady, I don't want to alarm you,' Mrs Duckworth said, lowering her tone, 'but 'ave you seen the newspapers whilst you've been away?'

'Yes. You've seen my picture then?'

She nodded and looked relieved at not having to be the bearer of ill news. 'And you know I'm not one to pry love, but, well, the trouble is, everyone else has seen it too now.'

I'd suspected as much.

'I want you to know your secret is quite safe with us. Mr Fulton and I have had strong words with the rest of the servants, and they are well aware they are not to utter a word to a soul outside these walls. But I wanted to warn you, they know your real name now and that you have a husband out looking for you, so I've had no choice but to confess that you're Lady Ashlyn's daughter.'

'Are you certain they will not talk?'

'I'd swear my life by it, ma'am. They know it would cost them their place in a very happy home and what's more, they care for you miss, we all do.'

The problem, as I saw it, was the reward on offer was probably adequate to compensate for the loss of their place here if they were so minded. I could only hope they cared enough. 'Thank you, Mrs Duckworth, that means a great deal, and I think perhaps, that given the change in the situation, it might be time I was a little franker with you and the others. You see, I know the article paints me in a very unfavourable light; deserting my husband and going into hiding, but the truth is he is a very dangerous man. He tricked me into marrying him with the most vulgar of cunning schemes. Then on our wedding night, he was unfaithful beneath the same roof. And when I attempted to leave, he imprisoned me, violently attacked me, sodomised me against my will...I was lucky to make my escape at all.'

I could tell Annalise was shocked at my forthright speech. She knew I had only confided these details to but an essential few and disliked so doing immensely. But if I wanted their protection, I knew I must impress upon them the severity of this situation. Ensure they understood that my very life hung in the balance of the cover of Stapleford. Accordingly, Mrs Duckworth looked utterly astounded at these confessions. She crouched down and hugged me tightly. 'You poor love. What a menace...' she said in cooing tones.

'Forgive me the intimate detail Mrs Duckworth, but I want you to know—all of you to know—that I did not take the decision to flee from my husband lightly. I had no choice. I fear if he caught me, I would be subject to more of the same, worse perhaps. You see, this is a matter of life and death for me...'

'And we shall guard it as such, ma'am, be assured on that head. We shall only need to be a little more careful outside of the house, for that is beyond the realms of my control. I'm not one for setting instructions to my betters, ma'am, but I do think it might be best you remain to the house for a time—'

'Yes, that sounds very wise,' Annalise put in.

'Well, I agree that for the most part I shall have to have a care locally. But there are matters I must attend to presently elsewhere, and for those, I mean to assume a disguise, Mrs Duckworth. The very same I used to travel to London in. It may be time to share this detail with the rest of the staff.'

She seemed unconvinced by this proposal, and having already shocked her enough for one day, I felt this was not the time to introduce the rest of the household to Leonard, so I did not press the matter further. But it would be necessary now, to let the household in on the secret. I would need to leave and return under the cover of Leonard hereon if I dared to step outside the house, and I didn't want to give one of the servants a fright should they wonder at the comings and goings of a strange man.

The following day, the news of this went down oddly but with an air of allegiance, all the same. Should anyone enquire after this new fellow, it would be given that he was my husband returned from sea, to throw off any suspicion that I was the sought-after wife printed in the papers. The staff would continue to deny it being anything beyond a striking likeness to me, should anyone ask. Thankfully, beyond the groundsmen of *Wimpole* and the errand boy from the butcher's shop who delivered our meat orders each week, we had no visitors here, and it was unlikely anyone would know my face quite so well as to swear it was me. It was possible that those in the neighbouring towns could recall my face, but it mattered not, since they did not know where I resided. For all they knew, I was a visitor passing through, never to be seen in these parts again. In many ways, it had been a blessing that the ill weather of the past weeks had kept us much shut away indoors. And then I remembered with a haunting sense of anguish, the Christmastide church services we had attended – pews packed shoulder to shoulder. How many locals might remember me from there? Seen me disembarking Mrs Duckworth's trap; forty, fifty perhaps? I had taken such care to stay away from the weekly church services up until then. It seemed right to have made an exception for Christmastide, and how was I to ever know that Giles would pull such a fantastic trick as having my portrait posted over the national press?

My worst fears were confirmed the following Sunday when the staff returned from their weekly service, having suffered several questions levelled at them by some of their nosier neighbours.

'That Lillian Topp has a ghastly wagging tongue in her head,' Mrs Duckworth complained as we sat about the kitchen table that afternoon, waiting for the vegetables to finish roasting for our Sunday meal. 'She had the cheek to ask me in front of the vicar if you were the one in the paper.'

'What did you tell her, Mrs Duckworth?' I asked as I poured spoonfuls of beef dripping fat into the pan in preparation for the Yorkshire batter Annalise was still mixing.

Mrs Duckworth set out a meat platter. 'I laughed and said, we too, had thought the likeness very striking but not uncanny. I gave some detail of the nose being altogether too long and the proportions of your face being quite the part different from the Lady in the picture.'

'Did she believe you?' Annalise looked up from her mixing bowl.

Mrs Duckworth shrugged. 'I daresay she did love, especially when I pointed out that the Lady in the paper was said to be of the aristocracy and our Christmas tenant was only of the gentry. Though I'd be sure to pass on the compliment of the mistake if you were to stay with us again next Christmas.'

'Thank you,' I said, grateful for Mrs Duckworth's quick thinking and willingness to spin Banbury tales for my sake when I knew she prided herself on her Christian values. Though she had herself said that whilst she was not fond of telling tall tales, she could not think the Lord would wish her to be frank in a matter that might lead me into harm's way. That would not seem a very Christian act at all in her mind, and so she took solace in the cause, if not the means.

'But I think on the safe side, love, you should stay a while indoors, give it a chance to cool off. There's been nout in the papers for days now, so let's hope it all comes to nothing and is soon enough forgotten, eh?'

I nodded and slid the oiled pan over to Annalise.

Coup d'état.

February 1822. - Eleanor

I managed an uninterrupted week indoors before I felt the itch of adventure stirring up in me once more, as the fear of Giles' discovery of me finally began to wane. It had been ten days since our return, and there had not been a single hint of anything above the ordinary. Nothing more reported in the news, no more questions levelled at the staff on church days, and nothing reported from London in my latest correspondence with Lady W.

It had been a welcome repose from all the panic, coinciding with my birthday celebrations that had taken me quite by surprise, with Annalise having put the staff up to secretly organising a birthday supper in my honour, that had been as merry as the Christmastide feast we had all enjoyed together. She had also presented me with a beautiful pearl encrusted locket in which I could keep her Lover's Eye concealed within. It was my favourite gift and I attached it to a pretty length of ivory ribbon so I could wear it around my neck. I had also received a draft of twenty pounds from my parents, which I was grateful for, since I had nearly run out of money. Lady W. had snuck a gift of a fur cape into Annalise's care whilst we were in London, quite without my knowing. I received the usual trifles from my siblings; thermal stockings and gloves, toilette waters, a new novel, and a peculiar one from Harri: a set of patterns for clothes for nursing mothers. Something I expected would be useless, but Annalise was thrilled by, incorporating this design into the clothes she had been making for me.

As I watched the snow turn to slush and ice from beyond the misty windowpane, I decided it was time to get back on track with our *Spinning House* plans, now all was well and quiet again, and the roads were perfectly drivable. Besides, if I did not act soon, it was questionable how much longer my disguise would remain plausible with the ever-increasing protrusion of my belly through my clothes. It seemed altered by the day, Annalise already having extended my skirt hems to the most generous degree and now cutting out patterns for even bigger dresses with a greater number of concealed pleats that with some clever crafting, should manage to shroud me into the latest stages of my confinement. It was not only the child's size that had increased but the frequency of its movements too. The stirrings becoming less fluttery and more pronounced and startling in their episodes. However much I tried to ignore the reality of my condition and Annalise's growing attachment to the idea of our becoming parents, it was made increasingly difficult with such compelling reminders. I needed a fresh distraction and to finally put our long-sought plans into action.

In our recent housebound days, I had taken up a correspondence with Theo and Mrs Duckworth or one of the servants would convey and collect our letters from the post office in Royston, since Annalise had objected to my disclosing the actual address. So I waited impatiently for a reply; the one confirming a date when the troupe members willing to help would travel down to Cambridge and assist us in the effort.

Fearing it would not be for some time, I was anxious that I might outgrow my breeches and waistcoat, which were taught at the seams now. I tried them out after breakfast this morning thinking they would last another week at best.

To my surprise, the letter that came back from the post office this afternoon, announced that they would be able to come as soon as Monday next, now that they had rehearsed their latest set well enough to enjoy much of the daytime to themselves.

I wrote back instantly, agreeing that we would meet at the *Castle Inn* where I would procure a couple of rooms so they could change in and out of their disguises in privacy and comfort, and where they could take a meal and wait out their return coach home once our investigations were over.

I was so grateful for their effort and assistance that covering all their expenses seemed the least I could do. I sent a courier to the *Castle Inn* directly, making all the necessary arrangements to receive them.

MIDWINTER.

Come Monday, we were up at first light, dressed as Mr and Mrs Leamington, shocking all of the household staff with how convincing we carried off the guise as we took a light breakfast and waited for the hired hack to arrive. There were to be no chances taken today in giving away my association with Stapleford. Hence, the trap was to remain here, and we were to travel in the privacy of a privately hired carriage and return by the very same.

We were received at the inn without question and advised that none of our guests had arrived yet, although they expected the coach from Bury to pull in by noon. So we spent the hour betwixt their arrival and ours wandering the streets, looking out for any clue of the Proctors or his bulldogs on patrol, then for any likely prey that might attract them. We spotted nothing untoward, but this was no matter since we were to create our own diversion anyway. A plan, even more elaborate than the one I had pondered, being revealed to us when four of the troupe turned up, complete with a trunk full of costumes.

'Ah, it's good to see you again, Queenie, and you too, Blondie!' said Theo, delivering us an enthusiastic hug as the boys carried the trunk up to our rooms. Even Liv was unusually pleasant and helpful today, apprising us of the plan they had concocted. She had volunteered to bait the Proctors all the way to the *Spinning House* if it came to it. Teddy and Theo were to play the role of constables with an escape plan ready to have Liv released should it be necessary, on the grounds that she was wanted by the magistrates for a more serious crime in a neighbouring town. Richard, or Dickie as he preferred to be called, swanning out in his full robes and mortar board, was to play the mischievous graduate in pursuit of Liv. Being something of a sporting man capable of outrunning everyone he knew, with only the exception of a very irked hound having ever managed to catch up with him, he seemed best placed for his part. I did not ask after the circumstances of that event, as he pointed out a shiny pink fibrous scar at his left ankle where it had sunk its teeth into him.

'Then what shall be our part in the scheme?' Annalise asked as Liv passed her a rather frumpy-looking bonnet that seemed more suited to an elderly aunt.

'You two shall play the innocent concerned townsfolk that, upon taking a stroll to the market, happened upon me and Dickie and felt concerned for the graduate and proceeded to duly alert the Proctor. That way, should you be recognised again in the future, it will be as heroes rather than villains.'

I was astounded by such thoughtfulness coming from Liv.

'See, we got it all sussed. Liv's been on it. More eager than you! Even got us a safe house sorted along St. Tibbs Row, should anything go ill. Not that it's likely. You're dealing with professionals 'ere,' Theo winked in that familiar way I had entirely forgotten until now.

'That *is* very generous of you, Liv,' Annalise cut in with an unusual precision in her tone. 'But what if the plan fails and you end up committed to the place, or we cannot get you out?'

She shrugged. 'What's a night or two in the rough? And you'll get what you're after—an insight into how it all works in there—what it's like. Imagine the account you can deliver back to your friends with clout?' she said, looking at me with a spark of delight in her eyes which seemed somehow misplaced.

'It'll not come to all that,' said Theo, 'I told yer, you're dealing with professionals, just you wait and see.'

IT CERTAINLY SEEMED to be the case as we set out in our various guises, looking every part convincing. Theo and Teddy in their constable's uniforms, Liv done up in an accusatory shade of vibrant red lip paint and cheeks so rouged it was enough to make Marie-Antoinette's toilette seem subtle. And finally, Dickie, looking every part the undergrad, in his heavy robes and polished boots and hair combed over neat to one side of his head.

As we dispersed to make our way to our various stations, it seemed our part was such a small one it felt lacking, like our roles were an inadequate contribution to the cause. I felt uncomfortable with them taking on so much risk whilst we remained safely beyond reproach in our role of innocent bystanders. It had not been how I intended it. They were doing us the favour after all, and it suddenly seemed such a hair-brained scheme to

MIDWINTER.

involve them in it should anything go ill. I had visions of Liv being violently dragged along the street by the bulldogs, just as we had witnessed from the upstairs window in the artists' parlour that evening. Theo and Teddy being discovered as frauds by the *real* constables. Dickie, at least, might come out of it unscathed if he really could run off as fast as he said he could.

'What's wrong?' Annalise asked as we pushed our way through the crowded marketplace with the smell of fish and cruciferous vegetables carrying pungent in the chilly air.

'I'm worried we have asked too much of them if it all goes wrong.'

Annalise squeezed my arm. 'Well, they seemed keen for the challenge, excited, I would say. There was no deterring them, and so there is little point in worrying over it now it is done. Besides, think of how long you have wanted to get this investigation underway? By the end of the day, it will be done, and you shall have enough to report back to the Society and have them raise the roof on the matter. – Think of how many will be spared by that, hmm. Besides, if Liv does get into bother, I'm sure we could manage to get her out of the place with you in one of those determined heads. Do you forget the power you yield when you are in such a temper? I shall never forget the look on Mr Honeyfield's face that day...' she nudged me, and I laughed just a little. But the truth was, I felt uneasy. Like I sensed some ill event creeping upon us—nay—like we were walking straight into it of our own volition.

I tried to shake the feeling as we rounded the corner of Market Hill and stepped away from the square to head out towards the Shire House, where we expected to come upon Liv and Dickie. But when we got there, they were nowhere to be seen.

'It was Butter Row, wasn't it?'

'Yes,' Annalise nodded, looking as perplexed as me.

After a while hanging about we headed onwards to turn the corner to see if they were somewhere in the vicinity, but before we made it back onto the main square, Teddy came bounding around the corner shouting: 'Run. Get to the safe house – we've been rumbled!'

There was no time for questions. We followed him at speed along the narrow lane, back through the crowded market and eventually, into the door of a little terrace house that I assumed must be the 'safe house'.

He closed the door swiftly behind us, but we were all too out of breath to speak the urgency of the words upon our lips, so we huffed a moment, chests heaving for air. Teddy bent over and dropped his palms to his thighs to recover.

Then eventually, I managed, 'What...happened?'

But before he could answer, the door began wrapping with violent knocks, and it took me a moment to hear above the huffing of my own breath that it was Theo's voice that broke through the furious pelts upon the wooden door. 'What the fuck Teddy? I know you're in there, so you better open the fuck up!' she demanded.

I went immediately to the front door and opened it, relieved she was alone and appeared to be alright, though the look upon her face, frantic and hard, made me instantly fear for Liv and Dickie.

'What's happened?' I asked her as she barged into the parlour and headed straight to Teddy, shoving him hard so he almost lost his footing.

'Yeah, Teddy what happened? What the fuck was that about?' she demanded, her voice steely and threatening.

Teddy recovered his near fall and stepped back a fraction. 'I don't know.'

'We were set up, that's what! Dickie had barely spoken to Liv before them bulldogs stepped down from that carriage and dragged her into it!'

'Oh no!' I cried at this. 'They have taken her off?'

'In a heartbeat. And this oaf who was supposed to help me and go after them, runs the other way.'

'I was stunned,' he said feebly.

'You were stunned! What about Liv being lifted off like that?'

'She'll be alright. We'll go now to the bridewell and claim her, come on,' he said, urging Theo towards the door.

'We'll come too,' I said, picking up my top hat.

'No,' Teddy said, 'who will be here to tell Dickie where we've gone if we all go?'

'Alright, we'll stay until he gets here and if you have not returned by then, we shall set out to find you.'

MIDWINTER.

WE PACED THE STRANGE room a little while, twitching at the curtains from time to time to look out for any sign of Dickie, discussing in panic-stricken bursts what might happen to Liv, how we might go about getting her out, hoping no harm had come to her. Praying Theo and Teddy would pull off their attempt to transfer her out of the place.

When the door tapped again, it was not Dickie as we expected it might be, but Teddy on his own, looking flustered.

'We need to get out of here. Theo' sent for a hack. It'll be here any minute. Make ready!' he said, and before we could shut the front door, the carriage rumbled down the cobbles, and he ushered us towards it.

Annalise was already inside, and I was poised at the footplate ready to join her, when Theo came darting up the road towards me shouting: 'don't get in...It's a trap!'

My stomach lurched, and I reached instantly into the carriage to grab Annalise's arm and tell her to get out, when a face I had not expected to see again appeared at the door on the other side of the carriage. The shock was enough to make it easy for Theo to pull me down from the footplate, and in what seemed like a flash, Digby had shut up the carriage doors and bolted off with Annalise inside it. I chased the carriage in a stupor of delayed horror as the horses picked up speed and was left folded and breathless at the junction of the street in abject panic. *Digby had Annalise. Giles had come for me. But how?*

I barely felt the tugging of Theo beneath my arm when she grabbed me and pulled me off at a run and down an alleyway, where she pushed people out of the way until we came to a disused shed at the back of one of the shops.

'What are you doing? We need to go after Annalise. They have her.'

'They got her now, love, not much I can do about that on the spur, but I *can* keep you out of the way.'

'Where have they taken her?'

'Fucked if I know. The whole thing's been one enormous fiddle.'

'What do you mean?'

'Liv and Teddy, they set us all up.'

'What?'

'She's been in cahoots with that husband of yours. It seems this whole thing was concocted betwixt them to lure you out of hiding since no one had an address for you.'

I slapped her swiftly around the face. 'How could you, Theo?' I screamed at her and thought I might do a whole lot more had the earnest offence in her face struck me just short of raising my hand again.

'You think I had anything to do with this? Really?' she said, affronted, holding her cheek in her palm.

I knew instantly that she had not.

'I've just turned down forty pounds for you, you know – far more than I'll earn in a year on a good stint. And you: a husband? You told me you ran away to avoid getting leg-shackled.'

'The reward my husband put up for me, that's what this was for?'

She nodded. 'Apparently. Teddy and Liv had it all worked out. Teddy just offered me a cut to turn you and Blondie into him.

'Bastard.'

She nodded to this too.

'So where is Liv?'

'Tucked up comfortably in some swanky hotel your *husband* has set her up in. The whole thing was staged. It was never the bulldogs.'

'By gad.' *How long had this plan been in the making?* Is that why we happened upon Giles at the Buntingford inn? I had assumed him heading back down to London for the sporting, but he must have been on his way up to Bury to concoct this plan and...'

'Don't cry, Queenie, we'll sort this out, alright. If I could just talk to Liv and get her to change her mind, she'll listen to me. If that bastard Teddy will tell me where she is.'

'It's too late for that. They have Annalise now—'

'Yeah, but what good is that to him if it's you he wants?'

'I don't know, but I do know he will go to any lengths to get the whole out of her until he finds me, and I'm not leaving her at the hands of him to suffer such interrogations.' *Or worse*, I considered, knowing what a beast he was. 'I have to find her. I should go to the constable and report her being kidnapped.'

'Fat lot of good that'll do. She's long gone, and the peelers are useless at the best o' times. Our only hope of finding out where they've taken her is to get it out of one of those cunts.' She dropped onto an upturned crate and sat thoughtfully for a while before saying: 'Here's what we'll do. You will stay here out of the way whilst I go back to the safe house and see if Teddy is still about. I'll tell him I've had a change of heart and want in, see what I can find out about where she's been taken. Try to persuade Liv to call off the deal and get her to speak up on what she knows.'

I nodded. 'Whatever he is paying her, I can match it. double it, whatever it will take for her to get Annalise back.'

'I don't want your money, and she'll not have a penny of it by the time I've had my say, you may be sure. Just sit tight, alright? I'll come back for you when it's safe, or send a message to you, alright? Come 'ere.' She pressed a kiss to my forehead. 'If you've not heard back from me by sunset, get yourself somewhere safe and send a message to that inn you booked us, alright.'

I nodded, tears streaming down my face as she took a cautious look through the crack in the door.

'Theo,' I said, before she left. 'I'm sorry I didn't tell you about my husband. Now you see why I had to be cautious. He's a lunatic.'

She nodded. 'Don't blame yer, he is off his nut. But you could have trusted me Queenie. If I'd understood the circumstances better, I might have cottoned on to Liv's sudden interest in the scheme. But I hadn't a clue, thought she was doing it to win my favour. Don't read the papers either, so I never even saw that picture of you until Teddy just showed me it. God, I wish I never even said I'd help.'

'I'm sorry Theo. I have landed us all in the suds...I never meant to.'

She turned back to where I was and hugged me. 'Don't cry Queenie. It's my fault too. You pretty ones are always a bother,' she said in a lighter more flirtatious tone, then before I could anticipate it, kissed me swiftly on the lips, and stepped out into the alleyway.

The sound of her boots against the cobbles dissipated into the sound of raindrops pelting against the makeshift tin roof of this ramshackle place of a storeroom. I began to look about to see if there was something I could make comfortable for a seat whilst keeping out of view, should the owner come into it for some such thing the shelves were littered with. But before I could move enough barrels and crates to make a screen to perch behind, the sound of footsteps towards me was already building.

I ducked blindly behind the stacked pile, and sunk to a squat as I heard the click of shoes drawing close.

'I know you're in here.'

It was not the words but the sound of the voice that made my blood run cold as its familiarity engulfed me. I felt paralysed, like my very heart had stopped beating.

'It's no using hiding, my dear, the game is up now, and I win.'

'You win?' I stood up and said with a ferocity of tone that seemed to leap from my throat without warning.

His eyes slid to mine in the dim light, cold and glassy as they settled on me, and he was taken aback by the sight of me. 'Well, no wonder you had such a good run with the state you are in. Who would recognise you in such appalling garb and what the deuce have you done to your hair? Still, we'll soon have you set to rights prettily enough. Come on. It's time to go home, *my dear.*'

'I'm not going anywhere with you. You might have gotten the message on that head by now. Don't you see how I despise you? That there is nothing in the world that could induce me to return to you?'

'Nothing? Hmmm. Well, it's a shame. I know this friend of yours is banking on you being as willing to save her skin as she was to save yours.'

'What have you done with her?' I demanded.

'Nothing – Yet! She's right here. Fellows, bring her in, he called out, and within a minute, Theo was dragged into the shack hanging between the arms of two hefty-looking brutes who I assumed were the very same that had been commissioned to stage Liv's capture. It was easy to see how convincing it must have looked. But it was not Theo I expected him to produce, but Annalise. I opened my mouth to say so, but before I could, Theo struggled against the men and made murmuring sounds where they had tied a rag about her mouth to stop her screaming.

'Ah, I think she has something to say to you. Now boys, untie the gag. If you scream again, you know what will happen this time. It was then I noticed a cut above her cheekbone that I knew had not been issued by the slap I had dealt her. *What had they done to her?* 'Are you hurt?' I said instantly.

She dismissed the question and said, 'Don't tell 'em a thing, Queenie, and don't make any bargains for my sake, alright.'

'Ah, but that might be tantamount to a death sentence, would it not?' said Giles with a grin curling up the sides of his mouth. 'Impersonating a constable – surely that's a capital offence, hmmm boys?'

'And so is kidnap,' I snarled.

'Hmmm. I see your point, but I'm sure the law will look very leniently on a fellow of good standing, doing his bit to carry out a citizen's arrest upon such criminals.'

'They are not criminals!'

He shrugged. 'Well, if you are not going to prevent me so doing, I suppose we shall just have to call for the watchman and see what he makes of all this?'

'No,' I said, knowing that he was not bluffing and would throw Theo or anyone else that stood in his way, beneath the cart and horse if he had to. And it was not only Theo either, he had Annalise, too, and there was no way I meant to put either of them in jeopardy. I knew I would have to go back with him and put an end to this, even though the very idea seemed impossible to me as I stood face-to-face with him, suspended in a surreal sense of disbelief. I looked at Theo, thought of Annalise in one of her panics and decided that even if it was just for long enough to give him the faux impression that I would accept the ransom until they were released, I must do it. *I must.* 'Fine,' I said more reasonably, 'If I come home with you, you will let them go?'

'Don't do it, Queenie...' came Theo's protest as she made another attempt to struggle from the captive grasp she was held in.

'Well, well. What keen *friends* you have become. So much chivalry and sacrifice...'

What would you know about either? I thought. And then I realised his mistake. He believed that Theo was the one to hold to ransom because he thought *she* was dear to me. *Had they seen her kiss me at the door?* I paused a moment to ponder this. If he thought that much, he would think Annalise insignificant and useless to continue holding. A mere maidservant that could be released, now he had his bargaining chip. 'You will truly let her go?' I said more earnestly, playing up to his misunderstanding of the nature of our attachment.

'Well, of course my dear. I knew you would see sense.'

'Instantly?'

'Well, once we are safely on our way, of course.'

'I want your word Giles, a guarantee.'

'Step into the carriage, and you shall have it.'

I did step into the carriage, using every ounce of determination to force my body to oblige, despite itself. Every step felt like an act of self-betrayal. But I insisted Theo travel in with us and not in the coach that followed behind, which he had intended for her. I could not have her left alone in it with those brutes, and besides, I wanted to make sure he kept his word.

Even the sight of her close by helped me feel some small modicum of comfort against the oddity of my circumstances. How could it be that this very morning I woke up carefree and in the blissful arms of my love, and now, mere hours later, I was *here*? With *him*.

A Royal Issue.

February 1822. - Eleanor.

We travelled some way out of the city, and he would not entertain my demands to set her down until we had crossed some derelict patch of countryside some way beyond Cherry Hinton, where we eventually pulled up at what appeared to be a country farmhouse.

'What are we doing here?'

'Lodgings for the night, my dear. You do not expect us to travel directly to Beddington today, do you? I have been travelling up and down the country for weeks trying to find you. A man needs his rest and a good fire, and the spot beside me in the bed has been cold for far too long'

My heart sank. It took little to work out what he intended for me tonight. I pushed aside the dread and said, 'But why have you brought these along with us?' I gestured to the other carriage where the brutes had disembarked. 'You said you would let Theo go?'

'And I shall, my dear, you may be sure I mean to keep my promise. What – you didn't expect me to set her down instantly and trust her not to dash off and raise a dust? Come, dear...you do not take me for a fool, do you?'

I resisted the urge to raise my brows at him in confirmation. I suppose the truth was, of all the many things I considered him, a fool was not amongst the number.

'We shall rest here for the night, and in the morning, once we have made good headway, *then* I shall have your friends released.'

Friends. It was then I saw Annalise set down from the carriage that had pulled in behind us, Digby holding her by the arm and leading her in towards one of the stone buildings. I wanted to call out to her and ascertain that she had not been harmed. But I thought better of giving him a clue to my true feeling and said simply. 'What is my maidservant doing here?'

'She too will be released in the morning,' he said, giving the nod to one of the brutish fellows to collect Theo from the carriage and take her into the same building Annalise had just been escorted to.

'Well, at least I shall not want for my toilette tonight,' I said nonchalantly, and stepped down to be led into the larger building beside the one they had been conveyed to.

'My dear, don't you know you shall want for nothing as my wife.'

I made no reply to this and walked silently into the place, a million different escape plans forming in my head as I surveyed the craggy stone building, hoping to catch sight of someone about it. But there was no one, not outside or inside it. He had thought of everything, it seemed, and I wondered, as I was conveyed by him to a bedchamber, how long this plan had been in the making.

I WAS SUMMONED TO THE dining parlour after being furnished with a basin of water and new clothes and instructed to wash and change out of Leonard's attire and throw it into the fire. I had to make do with managing myself since he would not be brought to prevail upon Annalise, and there seemed to be not a single servant about the place to call upon. He was not willing to risk anyone being turned to helping me, I realised when a delivery of the steaming pots of pre-cooked dinner arrived by wagon and was brought into the parlour by Digby and one of the brutes. I wondered then, how I would convince him to permit Annalise to remain with me if he was this overcautious, and yet I feared that if she did not remain, I might never see her again. For whatever he said, I doubted he was foolish enough to return straight back to Beddington with me, knowing that I had connections I could readily call upon to assist my escape there. No, I was certain that just as he had found this remote place to lodge, he would have found another elsewhere where I would be equally isolated, for a while at least, until he was sure of me. And so I knew that all I could do now was to make him certain of me so that he might be brought about to grant me at least the provision of my maid. If he thought her nothing to me beyond a useful servant, I felt the chance of it better.

So I kept these thoughts close at mind when he set upon me after dinner with kisses and overtures that I had forgotten the horror of in the luxurious months of our separation, trying hard not to squirm and flinch as I felt his breath upon my face. But when he led me to the bedchamber and began undressing me, I could not continue the pretence and backed away from him. 'Giles, we need to talk,' I said as calmly as I could muster.

'And there will be time for that tomorrow. For now, we shall make better use of our first hours of reunion, my love.'

'No, Giles, it's important. It cannot wait.' I shuffled further away, and he edged up behind me and gathered his hands about my waist, ignoring me. Planting kisses at my neck. Oh, how I wanted to thrust my clenched fist into his groin and make a dash. If it had not been for Annalise and Theo being held captive by those brutes, I would have been unable to resist the urge. *But they were.* I unclenched my balled-up fist and exhaled. I would *have* to behave tonight, and he knew it. 'Please, Giles, it is important.'

'What?' he said impatiently, and I felt nervous at what I was about to confess. It would, of course, infuriate him and might inflame his temper, but it could equally have the effect I hoped for and warn him off of me. It seemed a risk worth taking as I felt him lift my skirts to my thigh. Besides, the secret would hardly hold out for long in any case.

'There is something you don't know. The true reason for my disappearance,' I began, seeing the opportunity to spin the narrative into a more favourable light. 'I had no choice but to run away, you see...'

He paused and turned to look at me with a frown across his brow.

'I did not want to disgrace you or myself, further.'

'I think we know that you succeeded in both—'

'I'm pregnant, Giles,' I said quickly before I lost the nerve.

He stood back, staring me up and down and then, with a ferocious snatch, grabbed the fabric of my new dress and tore it down the middle. I tried to pull away, but he had the shift now in his grasp, the fabric holding me taught from the back until he followed suit, tearing it savage, until I was stood there with my clothes hanging ragged from me and uncertain what he might do next. I tried not to flinch. I was petrified, but somehow, to let him see the manifestation of it seemed a level of self-betrayal to which I wasn't prepared to stoop.

He pulled both layers of muslin to the ground and stared hard at me, at my navel, and I watched the recognition dawn across his face as he followed the altered shape of my body with his glassy narrow gaze. Not even a fool could think me gammoning with the taut pronouncement of my navel rising beyond the usual bounds of my profile. Clothing had hidden it well enough so far, but in my nakedness, the stark prominence was undeniable.

He circled me fully, and the click of his shoes against the boards seemed suddenly sinister. 'How long?' he asked eventually.

I cleared my throat. 'Four months.'

He said nothing, but I could see him calculating in his head the time of the occurrence and then, without warning, he lifted his hand and struck me across the cheek with the back of it, so fast I had no time to escape the blow as I felt my head sway with the force. It was neither as harsh as a punch nor as mild as a slap, but he had caught the side of my nose, and as I lifted my hand to my face, instantly, my nose streamed with hot thick blood. The sight of it seemed to render him more surprised than me. I had always had a sensitive nose for a bleed as a child, knocking it when riding my pony or running about the park with my siblings. It rarely took little more than a tap to provoke a torrential outpouring of blood, making it look far worse than ever it had felt. But he appeared taken aback by the result and seemed to second think any further attempt, instead lifting my discarded shimmy from the floor and handing it to me to staunch the flow with.

Then, as I proceeded to clean myself up and pull a blanket from the bed to wrap around me, he continued to pace the floor as if not knowing what to do next. As if his plans had been derailed, and he did not quite know how to pull them back on course. I, too, was unsure of what to do now. I knew what I *wanted* to do, looking at the hot glowing coals in the hearth and stifling the temptation to reach for the scuttle to launch them at him. Had it been only he to contend with, I might have been incensed and desperate enough to try my chances. But there were the mighty brutes in the next-door building and Digby hovering somewhere about the place to raise the alarm if I went down that path. So I took this moment of uncomfortable silence to consider what other options remained to me, and whilst I could anticipate nothing of use in this instant, when he turned to me and asked: 'Is this Richards work?' I knew precisely how I must play it.

I had not forgotten Lady W.'s report of the crim con papers he had already served upon Richards. 'No,' I replied, and watched the surprise and consternation alter his features.

'Do not lie to me, woman. I know you lay together—'

'It is true, and I do not deny that it happened once as you say...but, well, that was all the way back in the summer, and my courses ran as normal until...'

'Until what?'

'Until I was reckless with a widowed man and fell with child.'

'Who?'

'I cannot say. If I do not speak of it, neither will he, and then both you and his own family shall not need to face the humiliation of another public scandal...'

'You will tell me this very instant, the whole!' he said menacingly, standing over me.

I let out the start of a cry. 'You don't understand. I am sworn to secrecy. The ramifications of my revealing it would be so dire to us that I must protect us from my stupidity. Don't you see? That's why I had to go into hiding. I had no choice—'

'Balderdash! You will speak, woman, or there will be worse to contend with than breaking your oath to this cad!'

'It was no cad Giles, but a man so powerful it would ruin us if it came out. That's why I was forced to flee into hiding, and that's why I couldn't return any of your letters. I feared you would get the truth out of me, and we would all suffer—'

'Damn it! Who? Name him,' he thundered.

I let out another feeble trail of tears before looking up and saying, 'Promise me, Giles, that if I tell you, you won't tell a soul...'

'You, missy, are in no position to strike bargains. I suggest you speak his name now or that poor excuse for a lady friend in the barn shall have the hiding you deserve.'

'No,' I shrieked. 'No, please don't hurt Theo! I will tell you, Giles.'

He gave a satisfied glance, and I was glad that this Banbury tale was working twofold, in taking the focus off of Annalise and Richards. I checked again whether the man I was about to name was the best choice of decoy available to me before speaking it and having no room to rescind. Who more powerful and beyond Giles's threats of menace, interrogation and suit? Whose child would he not dare to place in harm's way? Many could answer, but none so beyond his station to even pose the question than, 'George. King George,' I said with all the sincerity I could muster from my recent acting practice.

He laughed sardonically for a while, then stopped suddenly as if unsure what to make of it.

'I told Henry there would be nothing to worry about, that I need not be sent away, for no one would likely believe such a story anyway, but—'

'Henry?'

'My brother.'

I watched the recognition dawn. He knew, as did anyone, of Henry's days of scandal amongst Prinny's set. Crookshanks had printed many a mocking illustration of the King's set in the days of his wilder antics, and Henry had featured in more than a few. It was true that I had only met him a couple of times and that I was not then, of an age to be in the very condition I claimed. But how was *he* to know that? For all he knew, we were fast friends. Certainly, he would not be able to doubt my ease of access to court. After all, I had only been there last spring for my coming out. It was a world far beyond his reach or experience. The royal drawing rooms did not admit the likes of the Craythornes.

'You expect me to believe— '

'No. I didn't expect anyone to believe it, which is why I told George and Henry that it was needless to send me away. But with the Queen's death having caused so recent a scandal, he felt it could not be risked, the fallout of it all. And he means to provide for the child, there shall be no expense spared, and at the end of my term, he shall have a suitable place found where the child shall be cared for until majority when it can be settled upon, and nobody need ever know. I was going to return to you then, once all the bad business was done with—'

'I think you have lost your mind. You cannot be serious,' he said accusingly, almost mockingly and yet, I could see beyond these words that a part of him was being taken in by the story, beginning to doubt his conviction.

'And that's why I have spoken only to the merest few family members on it, for it does sound ludicrous, I know. Even my parents did not believe me at first. It was only when Henry—'

'Precisely, who knows of this?'

'Well, my parents, my siblings, of course, the King himself and a few of his close aids that have been seeing to all the arrangements. — They are all that know of my condition. Oh, and my maidservant, of course. It's incredibly difficult to hide it from one's maid when you are casting up your accounts each morning. Though she thinks the child is your issue, and it seemed best not to correct her should she decide to leave my employ and break my confidence. Then, of course, there are the few that have their suspicions, and many that were present at the soiree that night who perhaps would be the least surprised to hear of the news after how much we were in each other's company—'

'Enough!'

'Sorry, I thought you wanted the truth—'

'The man must be what, nearly sixty and probably not much less in stones...you really expect me to believe that you would lie with—'

It was ridiculous, particularly given his taste for the older ladies and my repulsion at men of his cut who treated women as appallingly as poor Queen Caro. But, he was also the sort of character where anything he did was unlikely to shock, given his colourful and eccentric past. And there had indeed been enough rumours about his illegitimate issue with Mrs Fitzherbert. What's to say my charms wouldn't have tempted him had I been minded to offer them? Certainly, there were stranger stories told than that. 'He's a very powerful man Giles. It is not so easy to disappoint your King—'

'So where do you say this occurred?'

'At *Carlton House*, it was just after his return from Scotland actually, and Lady W. had an invitation and asked me to attend her. I could hardly decline since I was a guest in her household, and well, he mistook me at first for Caitlyn. He had only just seen her at the drawing room in Dalkeith, and then we got talking about Henry and his wedding and—'

'Does she know of this?'

'Lady W.? She suspects, but I have not confided in her. It is difficult to put a Lady of her standing in such a predicament of knowing such delicate secrets, so I thought it best not to. Besides, the King has sworn me to secrecy, as you know, and I do not think it would be taken lightly should anyone be caught with such whispers upon their tongue.'

'Then who has been harbouring you all these months, if not she?'

'My family stepped in in the end. It was thought best to keep the King as much out of matters as possible until the birth. — Don't you see, in five months, this will all be over, and we can get our lives back together without anyone ever knowing any different, beyond those that are vested in not speaking of it, of course.'

'So you thought you could hide away with your scurrilous little secret for nine months, then return to me as if nothing had ever happened?'

'No, not quite. Well, I hoped we could move on from all this bad business. Start afresh, with no enduring harm done...I was trying to protect us all.'

'Then perhaps you should have kept your legs shut!' The jealous amber hue about his eyes was glowing bright like the fire's glittering embers.

'Well, perhaps if your cousin had done as much, then I would have.'

He said nothing to this. What could he say? All had stemmed from the pair of them.

'Where is Mariella nowadays? Married yet?'

'Not yet, no.'

'I see who has been keeping the bed warm in my absence.'

'Mariella is not the one carrying around someone's bastard, is she?'

No, I thought, which likely meant that she was barren, I considered. But before I put this point to him, he crossed the room and left without another word.

I did not know what to make of that. Had he been taken in by my Banbury tale after all? He certainly seemed adequately disconcerted by the whole affair, and it had kept him from my bed when I doubted anything else would manage it. But it was unlikely to last. Tomorrow I must find a way out of this. I had bought time with my cunning. Now I must use it to think of an exit strategy.

BY MORNING, STILL, I had no answer, no plan. I turned over in the bed to find him still absent. Whatever else I had to brood upon, I was grateful for that, at least. Whether it succeeded or failed in the long run, I could only hope it would continue to do so for long enough for me to get as far away from him as my legs could carry me. I hoped, that now it was morning, he would release the others as promised, and I would be free to make my move thereafter. I did not know what that would be, for I doubted he meant to have us stick around here should they run straight for help. No. I was certain he would not take a risk like that and would have somewhere else lined up, equally as remote. Certainly, if he did not already, he would by now. Whether he believed my account or not, one thing he could not deny was the material fact that I was to have a child and that it was not his issue. Whoever he thought the father to be, it would be too much for his pride for the world to know this truth, and on that account alone, there would be no intention of bringing me back to Beddington for the world to begin whispering.

The thought of being shut up in some remote building like this for the next five months with him was beyond anything. I simply could not entertain something so repugnant to blossom in my mind beyond using it as an incentive to find a way out before it came to all that. If nothing else, we would have to travel to such a godforsaken place, and if we must travel, we must encounter both people and opportunities to escape. I would need to keep sharp-witted now and be ready to seize any such opportunities whenever they might arise.

My thoughts were startled into sobriety when I heard the clank of footsteps on the stairs and the indecipherable rumble of low voices.

'Ah, my dear, you are awake,' said Giles in a congenial tone that told me we were in company before I spotted the long-bearded fellow come in behind him.

I sat up straighter and tried at a smile. This was likely a test and not a good time to try a plea for help. And so I meant to make my most convincing effort at playing nice. 'Good morning,' I said sweetly.

'This, my dear, is Dr Morten. He has come to check your health.'

'How thoughtful of you, husband. Dr Morten, good morning.'

'Mrs Craythorne,' the aged-looking fellow returned, setting down his medical satchel and rubbing his palms together for warmth. 'May I?' he gestured to the chair.

'Please,' I offered. 'You must forgive my undress. I did not know to expect you, else, I would have risen earlier and made myself respectable.'

'No need to concern yourself with that on my account, ma'am. Now, if you don't mind, I'd like to have a little chat with you first and then examine you, if I may?'

'Why yes, of course, Doctor. Would you like some tea?' I offered.

'Not just now, I thank you.'

'I shall leave you to it,' Giles cut in and slid out of the room as quickly as he had come into it. I knew he was unlikely to be far and trying to keep in earshot, so I was pretty with my words.

'Now, your husband tells me you are with child, but you have not had a check since the news, and he would like me to make sure all is well.'

I smiled serenely and played as complacent and frank in my answers as I could when he went over the dates of my courses, movements of the child and proceeded to ask several odd questions about my mood and then, eventually, about the child's parentage. It was apparent that Giles had briefed him that the child was not his kin; I was mildly puzzled by this. I could understand him wanting me checked to verify the dates I had given, but to bring this country doctor into his confidence on a matter so capable of bringing humiliation to him left me concerned. Perhaps he would be paid extra to keep his silence. In any case, these questions levelled at me left me stumbling a little, for I could not choose whether or not to lie to the Doctor and insist the child was my husbands, or lie and say that I could not disclose who the father was. In the end, I opted for the latter, and he abandoned this line eventually and asked to examine me. It was in that I saw an opportunity. 'But, sir, surely you do not mean to examine me without my maid present in the very least?'

He lifted his brows at this, but all the same, tapped at the door and asked Giles to send for my Abigail. I was expecting some excuse. Some long delay whilst Giles dithered about deciding how to play the curve ball I had dealt him. But to my surprise, barely moments later, in come Annalise, neat as a pin. The very sight of her as our eyes met briefly across the room was agonising, however well we both attempted to conceal it with lowered gazes and formal speech.

'Ah, Tulley, good morning. I had wondered where you were with my tea and hot water this morning?'

'Sorry, ma'am. I was not expecting you to rise this early,' she said as evenly as if we had just been thrust six months back in time when she was filling in for Molly.

'No matter, let us not delay the good Doctor. He would like to examine me. If you would be so good?' I said, and accordingly, Annalise plumped the pillows behind my back and loosened the bedclothes from the tail end of the bed to assist the Doctor.

It was in this moment of bodily invasion, where I felt him prod and press my tummy before moving to more uncomfortable quarters, that I at least could look Annalise properly in the eye and mouth to her, 'Are you alright? Did he hurt you?'

She shook her head. 'It's alright, ma'am, all is well. Try to relax. It shall soon be over,' she said, lifting my hand and holding it between her palms.

'Is Theo alright?' I mouthed before the Doctor rose, and there was no time left for her to answer.

'All looks healthy, Mrs Craythorne,' he said, wiping his hands on a cloth and discarding it to the washstand, 'Your date keeping seems well enough accurate to me. You shall indeed bear a child in May or thereabouts.

'Thank you, Doctor,' I said as Annalise fiddled with my bedclothes to set them to rights. 'I have noticed the child is prone to very active movements of late and then at others as still as a picture. Is that normal?'

'Quite normal and nothing at all to be alarmed about. Of course, now you are quick, the movements shall grow further. You only need concern yourself if they were to stop altogether.'

'Thank you, Doctor, I am most obliged. If that is all?'

'Yes, yes. I shall leave you be and go and take that cup of tea on my way out. Good day to you,' he bid as he gathered up his things.

'Good day, Doctor.— Tulley, if you will help me dress. I may as well now I am up.'

'Of course, ma'am, but would you like a pot of tea first?'

ABOUT AN HOUR LATER, when I was, in fact, sat over a pot of tea in another of the new and poorly fitting dresses Giles had procured for me, it seemed that all had gone well enough to placate him since he had permitted Annalise to tend me through the morning. Not that we had had a chance to speak much beyond the perfunctory. Digby – she'd mouthed to me in the reflection of the mirror as she laced my half-stays – was stationed right outside of the door, listening in on us. So we went through the motions of formality and took little risk of any proper exchange beyond the occasional protracted touch of a hand or look of pained endearment.

The only thing I had gleaned from our occasional mouthed utterances was that the Doctor had remained in the downstairs parlour with Giles for almost an hour after he had left my chamber, and whilst she could not get within close earshot of what was being discussed at such length, it was clear that much discussion was taking place. A short conversation was to be expected. No doubt, with Giles grilling the Doctor for certainties of my condition, certainties of my dates, perhaps even seeking counsel on any other *options* on "what might be done" about it. But once a child was quick, it seemed unlikely that any medical man would go anywhere near such an issue, so I tried not to grow anxious on that head.

On all accounts, there was no time to ponder it for long as Digby gave the instruction that we were to make ready to depart in a quarter hour, but as to where, he would not disclose. There was very little to prepare since I had dressed and had nothing of my own with me anyway. The trunk containing Giles's provisions for me was barely disturbed, and other than fishing out a full Redingote coat and hand mittens, there was nothing else to be done. I resisted the temptation to offer Annalise one of the fur cloaks amongst them, even though I feared her being cold in that scant flatweave shawl she had on. Now was not the time to let propriety slip and give us away. My greatest concern at the moment was what he meant to do with her and Theo, now we were to depart.

So when he came into the room ten minutes later, I sought the opportunity to ask him directly. But before I could get a mere word in, he looked at me disconcerted and said: 'Look at the state of you. Have you nothing more decent to put on? The world will be in no doubt of your secret if you go about like that.' He pointed to my belly, where I had been unable to button up my coat over the bump and could only fasten the buttons about my bosom, leaving a gaping protrusion.

'Well, I have only what you have procured for me, Giles, and everything is too small.'

'Well, how was I to know, my dear? This wardrobe was made from the example of your very own clothes.'

'You were not. Few of my clothes fit me adequately now. My Abigail had just begun on fashioning me a new wardrobe to conceal my condition, but of course, I have none of my things with me.'

He turned to Annalise now, who was busying herself making up the bed for want of something official looking to do. 'You can do that?' he asked her.

'What, sir?' she said, looking up and feigning not to have been listening in.

'You can make clothes to conceal my wife's condition?'

'Why yes, sir. I can make them, alter them too in some cases if I have the right material.'

'I see. Then what might you do with this,' he pointed at my unfastened buttons.

'I could put a new panel in either side if I had a fabric that complimented it.'

'And how long would that take?'

'A day or two... if I worked constant.'

'And can you work in a travelling carriage?'

'I own I have never tried, but,' she said, catching a glimpse of my widened glare telling her to agree to it, 'I'm sure I could manage to some degree, even if a little slower on a rickety journey.'

'Well then, so be it. Find something else for your mistress to wear, and you shall begin your work upon it right away.'

'But sir, I do not have my workbox or any fabric to undertake the task.'

'We could stop into my lodgings to collect our things on the journey, Giles. Collect her workbox and fabrics and the few things that still fit me well?' I offered.

He turned to me and gave me a look that said: do you think me *that* stupid? I did not. It was true that would prove our easiest escape plan, for Mrs Duckworth would know in an instant to raise the alarm if she understood us to be in his clutches, however outwardly acquiescent or controlled I was by his presence. She was not one to suffer fools, and I knew it would be enough for her to read my eyes and know that all was against my will. But no, even I was not so conceited to think I could gull him towards such an obvious trap. But I did think that if *he* thought that was what *I* wanted, he might stick more staunchly to his own line of thinking, which seemed to include Annalise in the plan now.

'We do not have time for that, my dear, and I daresay we are not passing back through Cambridgeshire since we have a long distance to cover today. But girl, if you make up a list with Digby of all the supplies you shall need to equip you for the task, I'm sure he can procure them somewhere along the way.'

'Yes, of course, sir,' she curtsied and left the room to find him, I supposed.

'Where are we going, Giles?' I asked when she was gone.

'Come, do you really think I shall tell you that?'

I sighed. 'Fine. But can you at least tell me what you mean to do with Theo? You gave me your word yesterday that if I came with you, no harm would come to her, and you would release her.'

'And I shall keep it. She will be travelling in a different direction to us and will be escorted back to the county border with a little payment for her inconvenience...and silence.'

'She shan't take it, a bribe.'

'So she says. But I fail to see what choice she will have if she wants to get home again and has no other means of doing so.'

'You haven't harmed her have you?'

'No. Why would I? All the while, you learn to behave pretty, what possible need would I have?'

'Can I see her?'

'I don't think so.'

'Please. You need not leave us alone. Just let me see that she is alright. Permit us a parting farewell is all I ask.' I could see how he enjoyed holding this decision over me. I could see, too, how he disliked my eagerness to see her. It was precisely the reactions I hoped to provoke, for whilst he was focussed on that, he was not concerned over Annalise's presence in the least. All the while he thought she meant nothing to me beyond a servant and could pose no risk of harm to his plans, it was less likely he would see any need to separate us. But Theo, he would be happy to part me from, thinking her the object of my affection, and I had no doubt now that he meant to release her as soon as we were far enough towards our destination: Wherever that may prove to be.

'Please, Giles, I beg you. I just want to see that she is alright,' I said, bursting into a trail of sobs for added effect. I did want to see she was alright, though. I wanted to thank her for her valiant attempts to help me and say farewell, given the unlikelihood of us crossing paths again. But when we were finally led out to the carriages, the most I was to glimpse was her waving as she got into a coach with one of the brutes. *Goodbye Theo...and thank you.*

Road to Nowhere.

February 1822. - Eleanor.

We spent something in the order of a good ten hours travelling and were not permitted to leave the carriage, even when the horses were changed at various posts along the way. It was an arduous journey, both mentally and physically. Giles ensuring the blinds were pulled down at every window until nightfall. Annalise and I stiff and anxious as we sat opposite one another, Giles beside me and Digby beside her. The atmosphere was as stale and toxic as a clogged, sooty chimney stack, in the gloom of perpetual darkness and not the slightest idea of where we were, or where we would end up. I had tried, in the beginning, to mentally track the direction we might be heading in. And when we made our first stop and Giles stepped outside, I thought we must be at the county border since no horses were changed and I heard the voice of one of the brutes talking to the groom as we pulled away. I assumed that this was Theo's drop-off point. It seemed one of the brutes had switched to ride atop our coach and perhaps the other had escorted Theo off to wherever she was to be released. I hoped she would be free and on safe ground soon enough. But Giles would not answer any of my questions on that head and said that he was a man of his word, and she would be delivered unharmed and free to return home.

I hoped she would not try too hard to report our kidnap once she was set free. There was little point since she knew not where we were headed and where we even lived. Even if she managed to work out any details from the newspaper articles and find some connection to my family, what good was it by then? We would be shut up in some country cottage again entirely cut off from the world. And in any case, I was his wife. He had every right to make off with me without apology or excuse, and there would be little they could do to intervene now I was under his jurisdiction.

I could only hope. that as the carriage wheels creaked and turned and I stared out into the night through the window—I was at last permitted to look through—he would relax a little once we arrived. Wherever we were bound. If I could keep him onside and placated until then, he may yet loosen his militant guard over me just enough to let someone know where we were. At least with Annalise with me we had a chance at conveying a message and had insofar, been spared the biggest fear that bubbled between us now in these fractious uncertain hours, our forced separation. I pondered this greatly as we journeyed on and on. *Why had he let her remain?* Ignorance and usefulness seemed most likely. He obviosuly wanted someone to tend my wardrobe and would think me far too much of a snob to consider anyone of the servant classes to have any real value to me beyond convenience. And whilst he knew what had passed between Mariella and I, and clearly suspected something of a romantic friendship between me and Theo, I supposed that my dalliance with Richards and pregnant state likely led him to the conclusion that these things were mere harmless, girlish frivolity. *How could he guess we were in love?* He did not even seem to understand the concept of what love was, let alone recognise it between those he must find it most unlikely to arise betwixt. Then I considered whether it was a matter of calculated strategy. Perhaps he thought she was safer to keep close at hand. Annalise would know the right contacts to alert of my disappearance and my family and friends would know her and trust her account. Yes. Perhaps she seemed safer within his sight than beyond it? Then there was the convenience that she was already here, already aware of my condition and, as far as he knew, believed the child to be his. I supposed that seemed easier than bringing someone new into confidence on a matter he wanted hushed up. I supposed it might have been a combination of all of the above. So long as I gave him no reason to understand the true nature of our attachment we would be safe for now, and could be grateful for remaining together until we worked out an exit strategy.

MIDWINTER.

'ELEANOR, ELEANOR.'

I opened my eyes to see Giles before me willing me up from my seat. The sight of him startled me in my drowsy state until I remembered all the horrors of this new reality from which sleep had briefly rendered me respite. I lifted my head from the plush carriage wall where I must have fallen asleep against it and felt the cold rush of air move through the coach as I was ushered out of one door by Giles and Annalise out of the other, under Digby's chaperone. It took me a moment to coordinate my body and find my feet. before my consciousness sharpened and I began to look about to try to work out where we were. It was useless. The night was thick and shrouding our surroundings in a cloak of impenetrable anonymity. When it came into view, the house before us was unknown to me and could have been any house, anywhere. The oddity was that we were not met by the usual line-up of waiting staff I would expect to greet us at a Manor House of this stature. It was larger than Stapleford but nothing of the scale of Cuddington. Nonetheless, a house of this size would require some reasonable level of staffing to keep it running. However much he meant to minimise that interaction with me. And it must belong to someone who was hosting our stay, unless, of course, it was a new acquisition. I felt hopeful as we crossed the gravel and climbed the few steps up to the entrance that we were bound to meet with others soon enough and finally get some gauge on where we had come. Perhaps even the prospect of sending out a message.

But the hope of that did not take long to fade to nothing when the very next day after dinner, Giles sprung upon us that we were to make ready for the coach again, unwilling to divulge where. I had thought this to be our destination. It seemed like the kind of remote cut-off place he would wish to harbour me. Daybreak had rendered me with a view of green plains stretching far into the horizon and no other signs of life or neighbouring buildings I could glean from my chamber window. The house itself – from the limited access I had to its rooms beyond my chamber and the dining room he escorted me to and from – gave away no clue besides the holland covers that remained on some of the furniture in the hall. This small detail led me to believe he might have bought or rented the place. There seemed to be no host about it and I suspected the staff had already been warned to stay away from me. But this unexpected news of our departure confused me. Suggested it was merely another stop along the way. It seemed a drastic amount of trouble to go to for the sake of one night. And despite the presence of other staff in the house this time, neither Annalise or I, had been permitted to exchange so much as a single word with any of them. Catching only the occasional passing glimpse when under the escort of Giles, Digby, or one of the brutes (which it appeared only one of them had remained with us).

In close to twenty-four hours of being here I was only tended directly by Annalise. I learnt in our stifled exchanges that she was not permitted below stairs at all and had been stationed in her own room just up the hall from mine where all supplies such as warm water, food and so on, were left for her in an adjoining dressing room for her to convey on to me.

By afternoon, a new sewing box and reams of fabric were also left there for her with instructions to begin on the alterations to my clothes. She had worked at this studiously, unpicking the hems of my Redingote to fit extension panels of floral ivory silk to offer the concealment my husband was so intent on achieving. *But why? Why did this matter? Why did he make a triviality such a priority?*

It was not odd to me that he wished my condition remain concealed given this child was not his and that whether or not he had been taken in by my account, there was, at least in his mind, the possibility that I was carrying the King's issue. But since it was only a matter of time before no amount of clever tailoring would be able to hide the condition, and the fact that he had taken extreme measures in sheltering me from the view of the world in derelict houses, what difference would a better fitting coat make? I could only conclude that when we did arrive at our final destination, I would be permitted to be amongst others. Others who might glean my condition if it was not sufficiently concealed. A public gaze that knew my face now, thanks to Giles. There was a sense of justice in this backfiring on him. He had shown the world my face and now he wanted to hide it and my shameful little secret, too.

It could not be easy to find derelict buildings for every stop we might need to make and I was sure they would run out eventually. Whilst I had no bearing on our geographical position anymore, it was clear that wherever we were was not far or remote enough for his liking, and who knows how much farther was left of it with such a blanket of secrecy around it all.

By the seventh day of our relentless travels behind blind-fastened carriage windows, I had lost my patience with his silence and the savage conditions we travelled in and could no longer contain my speech. When we pulled in at yet another remote anonymous house that night I refused to attend him at dinner until I had an explanation.

'What is the meaning of this, Giles? I am your wife, not cattle to be kept in such conditions,' I complained, on his command that I go down to the dining room at once.

He looked about him and said, 'I own it is not quite the style you are accustomed to, my dear, but I don't think it's so bad to warrant such violent complaint.'

'I'm not talking about *this* house, Giles, or any others. I am talking about spending ten to twelve hours a day travelling on bad roads without so much as a glimpse of daylight, a proper meal, a stretch of exercise or —'

'Yes, yes, it is far from ideal. But such is the nature of travel.'

'No, Giles. The nature of travel is to make adequate stops at inns for comfort breaks and proper meals, see the countryside views beyond the carriage window and enjoy stops in safe places for exercise and exploration. *This?* I don't know what you mean by this. You know I am with child. Are you trying to cause me a decline in health with this brutal itinerary?'

'No, of course not, my dear. I have taken great trouble procuring you decent lodgings every night so you may be comfortable and well-rested. You think it is easy to arrange such things at the last?'

At the last? So this wretched sojourn was not part of the original plan then. Whatever it had been was now altered, by what? The news of my pregnancy, I supposed. To keep me away from society for a time was likely always part of the plan, but perhaps now it was to be for the next five months and in abject secrecy he had not bargained for. 'So where are we going, Giles? We must have travelled at least three hundred miles since leaving Cambridge. Now, unless you are taking me to John o' Groats, surely we must be far enough away by now?'

'I can't tell you presently. But, I can tell you this: We have but a short journey to make tonight—not above two hours—and from that point, I *can* tell you. So, will you come to dinner so we might make ready to depart, and in the morning, all shall be revealed. I promise you.'

I wanted to be obstinate and refuse to go until he told me where we were and where we were headed. But it seemed foolish to do so now if we really were only a short stretch from our final destination, and all was soon to be revealed. Besides, for some unfathomable reason, he had left me much alone since the night I confessed my pregnancy to him. I did not want to rock the boat and induce him into any absurd or angry outbursts whilst he was keeping a pretty distance. I wondered if the thought of me carrying another's child was off-putting. I hoped so, for if that accounted for him keeping to his own bed each night, I knew it would endure long enough for me to escape. Tomorrow, I would know where we were, which is more information than I had had in almost a week. Surely then I could begin to hatch some kind of plan...

So I agreed to oblige him, with the proviso I would hold him to his word tomorrow morning or refuse to travel another league.

ANOTHER JOURNEY, ANOTHER anonymous stone building arrived at under cover of darkness. Another anxious, exhausting night of missing Annalise beside me in the bed and wondering where on earth we were and how we would find our way out of his clutches, passed painstakingly. In the gaps, I had fleeting thoughts for Theo, wondering how she was doing and if she had reached home safe and well. Fits of almost uncontainable anger for Liv and Teddy and the greedy plot they had conceived to put my safety at risk for a few quick coins. It was true.—there were people who would do anything for money. It was a concept I had much heard spoken of in male circles and one I was convinced could not be true, until I had seen the misery and toil a lack of money was capable of bestowing with my very own eyes. I was persuaded I would be ready to starve, freeze, and endure practically any kind of conceivable hardship than ever exchange my moral fibre for tarnished coins. Yet, even as my resolution hardened, I knew that unless I was ever in such dire circumstances of want, I could not honestly know whether my conviction was for sale...

MIDWINTER.

I got out of bed to use the chamber pot and heard shuffling outside the door as I got back into bed. No doubt I had disturbed my 'guard' from dozing in his chair. If I was not so tired, I might get up and down all night just to wear them to exhaustion and render them easier to overthrow. But I was more likely to founder before them. So I got comfortable whilst I could, then turned my thoughts to other matters. I thought of Mrs Duckworth and our Stapleford family with utter sadness for the confusion and despair our sudden disappearance would have caused them. I wished I had given Theo our address now that all was lost, even if for no other reason than that she could have informed the staff of what had happened, so they did not wait about expecting us. Certainly, I would have expected Mrs Duckworth to have reported my absence to my mother now we had been gone for almost a week. She might have held off for a couple of days, hoping we had broken a wheel or some such inconvenient, but trivial thing. But by now I was sure my parents would have been apprised of the matter and were no doubt making enquiries after Giles, which likely would turn up empty. Even at the best of times he was hard to keep track of with all his business travels, so if he was minded to keep his whereabouts unknown, or to give a cover story to his staff reporting him to be overseas or visiting some far-off district, nothing much could be made of it given its normalcy.

The Promise.

February 1822. - Eleanor.

I felt slightly less dread than I had on other mornings, remembering his promise when I woke. I rose instantly and drew back the heavy drapes to find the view one of forestry all about me. I was utterly confounded. We may well have been in John o' Groats, after all. Except that there was an uncommonly marked improvement in the weather here. The sun casting yellowing rays through gaps in the tall trunked trees and patches of brilliant blue piercing through the lofty treetops. I opened the window to see if it felt as mild as it looked and to my astonishment, found no customary creeping chill to the morning air, but the ambient clemency of a fair spring morning. Yet, it was barely February. We were certainly not in Scotland. We must have headed south.

South West, to be precise. Or so he told me as he permitted me the rare opportunity of a morning walk after breakfast. I knew it was only on account of the particularly remote setting we were in – shrouded in the deep of a forest – but I was glad for it all the same given the dull aching suffering of my limbs from so much travel. Even his chaperone was not so repugnant today, since he seemed willing to answer my questions, at last.

He had confirmed that we were in a place called Bodmin Moor. A Cornish place that I had never heard of, but apparently was well known. He also confirmed that Theo was released in Royston, unharmed, and well enough to spit in the eye of one of the brutes that escorted her once she was released from him. This caused me to stifle a laugh and exhale deeply with relief. She was free. But it also made my heart sink when he said Royston and I realised how close to Stapleford we must have passed, without even knowing it. It took me instantly back to the Christmastide Frost Fair we had visited with such a pang of longing to return to that moment and do things so very differently from that point on, so as to avoid this turn of events altogether. We would have never gone to the Theatre at Barnwell, or to Bury where I was introduced to Liv. But it was no use now. And instead of dwelling too deeply on the missed opportunities, I listened with interest to seek out new ones. He spoke of a visit we were to make today to some nearby place, where I could decide between remaining there, or travelling overseas with him to Venice for the remainder of my confinement.

'I should like to remain here, husband,' I interjected without the slightest hesitation, once he had set the scheme before me. I had no desire to travel anywhere with him. Least of all across seas into some unknown place where I had no hope whatsoever of escaping his clutches, or calling upon friends to assist my escape plans. Besides, if he must go and leave me under the watch of some old harridan, then I was sure I would have an excellent chance of escape without him around to curtail it. Perhaps that was why one of the brutes had been brought along with us. Was he there to act as a warden over me in some clifftop Cornish cottage until Giles returned from abroad? Even if that was his insurance plan, and even if the brute did look fierce enough to prevent my escape, I was sure I would find a way around this. For one, I was a skilled charmer and seductress when I had a mind for it, and I had no doubt I could make something of a pet out of the brute with as little as a few bashful smiles. Secondly, I was confident I would be able to outwit him in a trice and find a clever way of running rings around him once I had the measure of his weak points. I would pay more attention hereafter.

'Well, my dear, do not be hasty. Perhaps wait until we have made our visit this morning before deciding.'

I smiled. 'Well, I would of course prefer to go to Venice with you, husband. And Venice does indeed sound like a fascinating place from the tales I have heard of it, but you see, I am travelling ill enough just these three hundred or so miles. Can you imagine what a trip to the continent will do for my constitution? Never mind crossing the channel.'

'The journey shall indeed be long, and the sea is not for the faint of heart or stomach, more fittingly. But I think you may prefer the option in the end. Let us see.'

MIDWINTER.

The quiet confidence in his tone unnerved me. I imagined he had found a candidate even worse than the likes of Betsy's chaperone, to play guardian and keep watch over me. Or that it was some hard place like a remote lighthouse or some such oddity that he meant to offer me as a home. Maybe stationed on a small island off the coast where nothing could be reached without a boat. Indeed all such prospects would be uninviting and make things trickier, and yet all of them seemed preferable to remaining with him a moment longer.

So as we began to pick our way back through the spindly forestry, the house fashioned from old Cornish stone jutting out slate grey against the greenery, I began to feel optimistic that wherever I was bound for, my mind was already persuaded to accept it, for it spelt an end to sharing a roof with him. I could now begin counting down the hours to our parting, and in this knowing, it seemed easier to play my part of the repenting, obedient wife. However foreign a creature such a character was, to me. More alien than Leonard's, I considered.

So when we journeyed on to this mystery place shortly after returning to the forest cottage, I felt a rising sense of relief. For whether he permitted Annalise to remain at this new house with me or refused and sent her on her way, I knew it would not be too long before we would be freely reunited and back together in hiding. And this time, I would be more careful. Much. More. Careful. Especially now Leonard's disguise had been discovered and my true likeness had been plastered all over the papers. I would have to think of something new... Maybe an uninhabited coastal island or even some foreign shore, might not be such a bad idea, after all.

Annalise had mentioned she had always wanted to visit France and see the village her mama came from. And France was huge if the maps were anything to go by. It seemed like it might prove a relatively easy place to get lost amongst compared to our humbler shores. And we both spoke good French. There was the Americas, too. The free world sounded like a good fit for us, at least so long as peace remained there. Yes. There was much to consider. Much to plan, to ensure that there could never be a repeat of this monstrous captivity again. It seemed fitting to use this time to consider our options for permanent anonymity since there appeared to be little else private to me under his watch now. But my thoughts and my mind were at least beyond his reach.

However, this optimism proved short-lived when we arrived outside a foreboding institutional-looking building that reminded me much of the concept on which Millbank prison was designed, with its odd hexagonal layout. But I knew it was no prison we had arrived at when we stepped out of the carriage. There was no scaffold to be found, for a start. But it was the sign attached to the wall that, as I got closer, read: *Cornwall County Lunatic Asylum,* that brought me to a swift and sobering understanding of his intentions. I was stunned into silence at first, realising how wrong I had supposed it all. *He actually meant to have me committed to an asylum...*

I thought instantly to refuse to go into the place, but then considered in the few moments I had between stepping out of the carriage and being walked up to the door, that I must not do anything that would make me *appear* insane or excitable. So I said nothing at all and walked calmly into the place. The door was answered by a formally dressed servant in a grey pinafore and slightly yellowing apron. The look of the anteroom, although somewhat drab and plain, was not wholly uncivilised. But there was an odd smell in the air. A scent of over-stewed tea leaves and lingering undertones of yesterday's stale supper. This, at least, was preferable to the odd sense of the place, which had an intangible eerie quality to it, despite being unable to assign it to any particular cause. There were no disturbing noises or odd-looking persons, no gloomy brick bare walls like the prisons I had visited, and yet, there was something worse than all of this hanging silently in the ether.

'Ah, Mr Craythorne,' came a voice from beside us. I drew my eyes from the winding stairwell and turned to see a short fellow dressed in formal wear with a curling moustache as black as his neatly combed hair, coming up from one of the corridors.

'Dr Schmidt?' Giles responded.

'The very same, sir, Superintendant here. And you must be Mrs Craythorne?' he said to me.

'Yes, sir.'

'Excellent. I am pleased to meet you. If you'd be so good as to go with matron here, she will take your coat and see to some refreshment. And Mr Craythorne, if you would like to follow me.'

The rest passed in a distant blur of motions as I was led into a small parlour and treated with reasonable civility. But my mind was busy elsewhere, swiftly formulating plans and forecasting potential outcomes, all seeming to present against my favour. I wondered what malady Giles had offered to the medical man to enlist him to his cause and conjured strategies to dispel each potential premise as I considered them. The truth was, I did not know what grounds were adequate for committal to such a place since I knew very little of them. I had a vague notion that vagrant paupers and the emotionally excitable might find themselves at the mercy of such an establishment. But I was neither, so it stood to reason that there must be *other* possibilities too.

After something in the order of half-hour, staring into a pool of murky grey tea in a chipped cup and answering occasional questions from the matron in monosyllabic style, the Doctor returned with a sidekick and sat down at the table opposite me.

'Mrs Craythorne, this is Dr Fitzpatrick.'

'How do you do,' I said evenly, thinking it best to present as civil.

'Very well, I thank you, Mrs Craythorne,' said the slightly younger fellow who seemed in imitation style of his superior in all but face and years.

'Now, Mrs Craythorne, it seems Dr Morten has referred you to us since he had some concerns about your health upon examining you.'

'Dr who?' I asked, trying to place the name, and in this time, I noticed the junior Doctor open out a notebook and begin scribbling something in it.

'Dr Morten, I believe he examined you this week in Fulbourn.'

'Oh, yes,' I agreed, remembering the provincial old fellow that visited us in that derelict house the morning after our capture.

'You remember the occasion?' he asked.

'Yes. I do, sir. I did not forget it. The name took a moment to place since he is not my usual doctor and I only met him on that singular occasion.'

'I see. And, how did you feel about seeing Dr Morten?'

285

It seemed such an odd question. How does anyone feel about having a stranger prod and poke about your body, I thought. 'I'm not quite sure I understand the question, sir. That is to say, I had no particular feeling about his visit, only that I was pleased to hear that all appeared well from his observations.'

'Hmm. Is that what he told you?'

'Why yes, he said, if I recall: 'All seems healthy and that my dates were correct, and he had drawn the same conclusion – that I was likely to birth a child around the end of May.'

'Yes, I do see mention of that in your notes.'

My notes. I wondered what notes he could possibly have since he knew nothing about me and nor did the country doctor.

'Tell me, Mrs Craythorne, how have you felt since you fell with child? Have you noticed any changes, emotionally?'

'Nothing beyond finding myself a little more tired than usual.'

'And, naturally, your husband is the father of your child, is he not?'

'No sir, he has no doubt told you the circumstance of my pregnancy.'

He bit his lip and scribbled something down in his own notebook now. 'Who is the father then?'

'I am not at liberty to say, sir.'

He nodded. 'And why is that?'

'I have been sworn to secrecy on the matter to avoid a scandal for all involved, including my husband.'

'Your husband tells me you believe the King fathered your child. Is that correct?'

'My husband was not supposed to speak of that, sir.'

'Mrs Craythorne, your husband is very concerned for your health. You see, he has explained that since you fell with child, you have run away from your home, assumed a male identity and have the notion that the child he has bestowed upon you is the issue of our King.'

When it was put like that, it did sound rather queer.

'Do you say it is the way of things, Mrs Craythorne?'

'Not quite. I did leave for a time, but that was only to spare my husband the disgrace of my condition when the child is not his, as he claims.'

'I see. Mrs Craythorne, are you prone to imaginings of any marked kind?'

'I do not believe so, sir.'

'Do you hear voices when you are alone or have stark thoughts manifest in your mind that you cannot account for?'

'No.'

'Do you see anything odd—'

'Sir, forgive me, but you are wasting your time. I suffer none of the maladies you propose and I am not insane, I assure you.' *Heaven knows I should be with what that man has subjected me to.* I took a calming breath to steady my tone. 'Please, if you would only contact my family in Surrey, they will be able to attest to the same and provide you with the direction of our family doctor, who has known me from childhood, and will assure you that I suffer from no such irregularities, nor ever have I.'

'Indeed. When did you last see your family doctor, Mrs Craythorne?'

I shrugged, 'Perhaps last year sometime.'

'And it was he who diagnosed your pregnancy?'

'No, not he.'

'Why not?'

'I was out of town when I fell faint, and the doctor of the friend I was staying with was prevailed upon to see me.'

'I see.'

'And did he have any concerns?'

'No sir. Nor has anyone else who knows me. If you make enquiries on that head, you shall find the same to be true.'

'You do not believe your husband's concerns are...justified?'

'Not in the least. Bringing me here is little more than a control tactic to press me into agreement to going abroad with him, to be quite frank, Doctor.'

'And why would he want to do that?'

'That is a question for him, sir. I do not presume to understand his behaviour in the least.'

'Would it not seem reasonable to you that he should seek treatment for you if he believes you to be unwell?'

'He doesn't believe that, sir, whatever he has said to you. I assure you that he knows I am quite well. He only means to punish me for going away.'

'Punish you.'

'Yes. He is rather good at that when he is minded to be.'

'And how does he punish you, exactly?'

'Well, where should I start? In the first instance, he and his cousin tricked me into the marriage in the first place with such elaborate scheming you would be minded to commit the pair of them to your establishment if I told you the whole. Then there was the occasion he had his cousin hold me fast to the bed so he could sodomise me. Then he had her poison me with some draft that caused me to lose consciousness. Then when I escaped to my parents' house, he bombarded me with letters to return, had his snake of a valet spy upon me, and recently he has had my picture printed across the national press and kidnapped me but a week ago –'

'Mrs Craythorne, these are very serious allegations indeed. Have you reported these matters to the authorities?'

'Of course not. How could I subject myself to such degradation and ridicule to have these grotesque details made a matter of public consumption? My family are very well respected, sir, and any such talk would do them much harm.'

'Indeed. Well, I can see you are growing distressed, and it is not our intention to distress you, Mrs Craythorne, quite the contrary. So I thank you for obliging us in this interview, but we shall draw it to a close now and leave you to your tea.'

'And that's all? I report several abuses by my husband, some of which I know to be criminal and what – you men of profession do not see fit to help me? To report this to the local magistrate?'

'Mrs Craythorne, we certainly do mean to help you if we can. But we are medical men, not men of the law.'

'I see. Then I bid you a good day, sirs,' I stood up ready to leave, only to catch a glimpse of the Doctor's flashing glare to the matron, who promptly got up from her seat and ushered me back into mine, more than a little firmly.

'Now, Mrs Craythorne, there's no need to get excited. Sit down and have your tea, won't you? Dr Schmidt will call upon your husband,' she said in a gentle tone that ran contrary to her actions.

'So you mean to hold me against my will?'

'We would prefer it otherwise, ma'am. If you would just be at ease.' She slid the cold cup of tea across to me and I promptly slid it back. It would not have surprised me in the least if it contained some sedating elixir to encourage my complacence.

Within but a minute or so, Giles came into the room and excused the matron, and once the door was closed behind her, it took all my restraint not to reach for the cup of tea and launch it at him. 'How could you bring me to such a place, Giles? Seriously. I thought this too low for even you.'

'Come, my dear. You cannot be surprised. Your behaviour has hardly been consistent with that of a good-tempered wife. You have indeed been out of character for quite some time now, as I'm sure society would attest to the same.'

I stood up. 'And why is that Giles? Because of you and that twisted cousin of yours. Before you two were present in my life, all was well.'

'And it can be well again, my dear. The choice is entirely yours. Now Dr Schmidt suspects you may be suffering from an excess of imagination and hysteria, possibly brought on by your pregnancy. He thinks it might be an idea to admit you for observation to see what might be done. But I have told him that I wanted to see how you felt about that before agreeing to the admission. Now, you may prefer to remain here, *or,* you may prefer to return with me and set out for Falmouth to catch the ship to journey on to Venice with me...'

'I would rather stay here than go with you.'

'Hmm, well, you will indeed prefer to go with me than I have my legal man serve these upon Mr Richards.'

He handed me a roll of papers and I untied them. When I recognised them as legal papers I sat back down and scanned the pages. They were amended court papers attributing the pregnancy to him. 'But I already told you, Richards is not the father.'

'You did. And in that very same conversation you also confirmed that you had lain together.'

'I shall deny it if I must, just as I shall deny the issue of the King.'

'It matters not. I shall speak with Richards myself if I must, help him to see sense.'

'He will not speak to you!'

'I think he will once I have these delivered to him.'

'You would truly wish to have our private affairs made public. For the world to know this is not your issue?'

'Oh, what choice have you left me when you refuse to travel with your husband and fulfil your part of the marriage bargain?'

'I am not at liberty to travel, I told you. I carry the King's child and I am to hand it over to his aids in five months' time.'

'You shall do no such thing.'

'But I must. Will you have me commit treason? You will have us both hung!'

'Not if we are abroad, my dear. Your King has no say there.'

'Oh, and are we never to come home again?'

'It's all quite simple, my dear. Either you refuse to sail with me and you remain here. In the meantime, I shall serve these papers on Richards, or—'

'What possible gain is it to you to sue Mr Richards for damages when you have so much money and he has nothing worth the taking!'

'What is worth the taking is not the money, but the damage it will do to the very little he has. Your little revelation has handsomely elevated my suit for damages now. and I've no doubt he shall lose everything on account of it.'

'You vile creature. It amazes me how you continuously strive to stoop so low. Just when I think you have reached the epitome, you delve lower still.'

'Well, I will not have to if you agree to sail, will I? I shall withdraw the case entirely.'

'You think I would rather sail into the unknown with you than be committed to a Bedlam when you show me how cruel-minded you are? Nay, direct Dr Schmidt that I am ready to be committed and go and sign the papers.'

'Eleanor, let me make myself very clear. I do not only have witnesses to your own testament that you did lie with Mr Richards, but unless your King is willing to step forward and claim otherwise, it will be considered on the balance of probabilities, a fair assumption that you carry Richards's child. I shall win my suit, and he shall suffer very ill for it. I suspect he'll be destined for debtors prison unless he has plump pockets to pay off my suit for damages.'

I thought I would collapse. 'What nonsense. I told you it is not he.'

'Yes, yes, it is the King. The trouble is, whether or not what you say is true or credible, the King shan't take responsibility, shall he? He may even be grateful for a common scapegoat like Richards to take the blame for him.'

'You hateful man.'

'Eleanor, you understand that whilst we both know that the child cannot be mine, in the eyes of the law that child is my property, and as soon as it is born, I will have every right to claim it, whomever planted the seed. Now, we can go abroad together and treat it as our joint venture, or I shall have it collected from this hell hole as soon as you have birthed it and do as I see fit.'

'I would sooner make a counterclaim against you for buggery and petition divorce than permit that. Yes, you might throw around your civil claims, but did you think I was not aware that what you did to me was a capital offence!'

'So you did a little homework, but I know you will not get so far as to bring about your charges once Mariella explains the unnatural advances you made upon her. Couple that with your crying off from Mr Elmbridge and then taking up with me, carrying Mr Richards bastard, cross-dressing, being committed to an asylum. I wonder if anyone will think you capable of speaking a single word of sense or truth. I wonder what your dear mama would make of reading the whole in her copy of *The Morning Post*? I am reliably informed she was not best pleased to find your picture in it.'

And I knew then there was no way out. He would not let anyone alone until he had what he wanted. He had barred every egress. All roads led to hell under his direction. And I could not tolerate any of those things. Humiliating my family so cruelly when I had already brought so much to bear upon them. Nor could I permit Mr Richards to lose the very little he had at last brought to fruition. And above all, I could not abide the idea of this child being under his sole command. I stared hard at him. 'What do you want from me? You must know I could never love you after all of this?'

'And I do not ask it. I am not a romantic fellow. But I do expect my wife to do, and be seen to do, her duty by me.'

'And how can I even trust that me, or this child, would be safe under your roof after what you and that crackbrained cousin of yours did to me last time! The pair of you require Dr Schmidt's treatments, not me!'

'I suppose you cannot. What is life if not one great risk? One toss of the die that could land a number of ways. But, if you honour your part in the bargain, you will not find me lacking in mine. Of that, I can assure you.'

And so, with the heaviest sense of foreboding and running against the very grain of my being, I agreed to travel with him, on the condition that all suits against Mr Richards be withdrawn and that my Abigail could go with us. He accepted the terms without complaint and smiled triumphantly as he tapped the door to deliver the news to Dr Schmidt, that his services would not be required, after all.

I did not cry. I did not give into the temptation of attempting to flee from the carriage as we set on our way. I resolved that I must think my way out of this before it was too late. I would soon be amongst the public again if we were to sail. I would have to see what opportunities this may present, and make ready to seize it the moment it arose.

The Resourceful
Seamstress.

February 1822. - Annalise.

Annalise was busy to work in her bed chamber sewing heavily lined panels of silk brocade into Eleanor's winter dress. She had finished the extension to her new Redingote at last, but there was ample fabric remaining to adjust her other clothes with. Her hands were sore from the relentless work, but she was grateful to have something to keep her mind diverted from all the horrors that had set into it this past week. Busy hands, quiet mind, her mama would often say. And she needed to find some calm amid the chaos of her head. It had been harrowing beyond imagination, and it was all she could do to keep her focus from the torture of the circumstance. The latest being the concern over where he had gone with Eleanor this morning.

It seemed an odd turn to her, given that they had all journeyed together insofar. Yet today she was made to remain at the house with Fletcher, who seemed synonymous with a gaoler, always escorting her from room to room and watching her as she went about her duties, creeping up on her when she thought herself alone. But he said little, and never actually behaved ill to her since the first day when they had abducted her into the carriage and refused to set her down from it. It was the other of the pair that disconcerted her the most. Theo had warned her that Fletcher was not so bad, but Boyle had dealt her a nasty blow to the face when she had put up a fight to flee from them upon her capture. She was grateful *he* was at least gone now, though oddly, she missed Theo's presence. Whilst she had been held captive with her, it seemed less lonely to have a companion in misery. Not that they were permitted to talk much and had only managed a few whispering exchanges when the thugs were distracted in talking to each other or falling asleep on their watch. But since she had been gone, it had felt so odd to be kept under such close guard alone. She was, of course, grateful to be back in service to Eleanor so that they had some contact once more. But it was difficult to bear under the strain of so much surveillance when all she wanted was to hold her and find out how they were to contrive to get out of this mess.

She less liked how she had lately been ushered into service of the rest of the household however, especially Craythorne himself, whom she abhorred from the moment he first spoke to her. He was a slithery, arrogant creature which, even without knowing the full brutality of which he was capable, she would have taken a staunch dislike to in the immediate on account of his countenance alone. He was not to be trusted in the slightest. She knew the day he summoned her from the barn and ordered her to dress neatly and play pretty to the doctor and serve her mistress, that he was up to no good, although what, she could not fathom. Only that she felt so very odd about him setting off alone with Eleanor today. She had fleetingly considered whether he had hatched a scheme to have the child aborted from her in some clandestine establishment, or perhaps, procured a draft to induce her into miscarrying. She had suspected something similarly disconcerting the day of the country doctor's visit when she caught glimpses of the passing of papers and what seemed like the clink of too many coins to account for a simple doctor's check-up. But she had checked regularly with Eleanor that the child was still moving, and so it seemed, she may have been mistaken. What else could she conclude when she had nothing more tangible to go on than her suspicious thought trails and these piecemeal clues.

She checked the window periodically for any sign of their return, but was met with no hint of their coming and a growing sense of despair as the clock turned over another hour. *She must be coming back.* Why else would he have sent for so many sewing supplies if he did not mean for her to remain with them? She shrugged and returned to her hem work. She didn't know what to think anymore. Everything that had seemed certain to her had been upturned and rearranged in such unexpected style that she was not sure anything could surprise her now. At least, that was until they finally returned before sunset, and Eleanor announced in whispers over her toilette, that her husband was taking her abroad.

'And you will go?' Annalise hissed as she noisily sloshed about water in the basin to drown out their speech.

'I have no choice, Annalise. He blackmails me. He took me to an insane asylum today, ready to commit me to it if I did not agree to travel with him.'

'What? Ghastly creature, what a thing! I knew he was up to something...'

'He says that if I go to the continent with him before my condition shows obvious, we can carry it off as his child abroad and when we return, society will be none the wiser.'

'So he will accept the child as his own?'

'He says so, but only on the condition of my going with him. But if I do not, he will collect it from the asylum upon its birth and do whatever he sees fit with the child.'

Her stomach leapt with anxiety. 'Then you must go with him, Len.'

'I know. But I made a condition of my own too.'

'Oh?'

'That I can bring my maid. Say you will go with me, Annalise? I know it is a great deal to ask, but –'

She felt the tears sting hot in her eyes. 'I will go. You know I shall...'

'Oh, Annalise!' She said, her voice breaking to a cry as she leapt up and squeezed her without an iota of restraint for fear of someone listening outside the door, or the threat of them coming in at any moment. It was the closest proximity they had been in for a week, and it felt dizzying to feel her arms about her, the breathy caress of clumsy kisses at the side of her face. 'I know it is not what we planned, nor is it much short of a living nightmare,' she wiped her tear-streamed cheeks, 'but we will be together, and we can figure it out, a way out, together.'

They would have to, Annalise thought as she clutched at her with both hands and made the most of this stolen moment of reckless abandon to feel the reassurance of the comfort of the other. It had torn her to shreds having to watch on the side-lines as this fiend got away with their kidnap and false imprisonment. Fearing separation at every moment. Fearing his violence upon her love beyond the closed doors she was not permitted to traverse without his say-so. If they could not overthrow him, they must outwit him. Somehow.

'No more tears, my love,' Eleanor cooed in her ear, sniffing back her own. 'It will be alright, in the end. We are to travel, so we must soon be among the public. *You* especially might be permitted to mix amongst the servants. You must not let him know you can read or speak French or any such clever things as you are capable of, alright? He must think you simple if he is to believe you to be no threat.'

Annalise nodded. She had already thought of this and played this meek and non-threatening character in all her interactions with the enemy. It would be nothing to extend the charade. It was close to effortless since people of their station made the presumption so readily. It took almost nothing to confirm it to them. This time, their ignorance would be to her advantage. She would look for a way to send out messages for help at the first opportunity whilst they thought her incapable of it. And with this, her first idea was contrived. She wrote down with her dressmaking chalk upon the insides of her underskirt the addresses that could be sent to for help. Eleanor dictated a list, starting with relatives and ending with Lady W. And when she was sent back to her quarters whilst Eleanor was made to dine with her husband that evening, she did not sew in any more silk panels or unpick any more fitted seams. Instead, she began sewing messages into torn-up pieces of her shift that would serve as paper.

"Help! Kidnapped by G. Taken to Cornwall to sail to Venice or else be committed to the lunatic asylum at Bodmin. E.x"

She kept her writing as small and neat as her most intricate stitching would permit, in such a rush. It was the addresses that took the most time to embroider. The messages in their repetition, quickly became habitual and rhythmic. She prioritised the ones to go to Cuddington and Lady W. in the first instance, thinking they were the most important and most likely to initiate a swift response. A rescue attempt if they were lucky. Though she had no clue how long it would take to arrange such a feat from this many leagues away. It had taken them a week to get here at a cutthroat pace. Would they have another week to spare? And that was without the allowance for the post to convey the message. Expedient as they were nowadays, it was many miles to be covered.

She tried not to dwell on the obstacles that presented to her as she worked at a speed she had never attempted, as evidenced by her continual finger pricking and needlepoint blobs of blood spatter over the muslin. There was no time to be precious. If they were to keep to their usual routine, they would likely be uprooted again after dinner and taken to another place tonight. She must do what she could whilst she was at liberty to.

BY THE TIME THEY WERE loaded into the coach that evening, Annalise had managed three embroidered notes and had started on the fourth, when Fletcher burst into the room and bid her to pack up and make ready. She had taken the trouble of out-sprawling her usual sewing work upon the table, and had her fabric letters hidden beneath it so nothing looked out of the ordinary. When he left, she folded each of them into the ankle of her stockings where the seam of her boots would hide any bulging clue should any suspicion be raised. She was often made to empty her apron pockets and undergo a peripheral search when moving from place to place, though why they bothered was beyond her. She suspected the valet named Digby enjoyed the power. Fancied himself something of an aspiring constable or gaoler. However, not a very good one, since she had already hidden the blade of a broken pair of scissors in the boning of her stays and sewn a selection of needles into a hair ribbon that ran its course through her heavy looped bun, rendering any sign of the spiky metal pins swathed in thick hair. She did not know what she would do with them or how they might prove useful, yet, but she felt better for having them all the same. Perhaps they could poke out an eye at close range or be utilised to pick a lock? She was by no means violent in nature or thought, but the terror of being dragged away in a coach alone had frightened her so terribly that all sorts of things had come to mind since then, that she had never before entertained. When she saw Theo's swollen face that first night in the barn, she began looking for objects she might use to defend herself should she need to. There had been an old wagon wheel she had leant up against, where she managed to prise a loose spoke from it in the barn on the first night. The trouble was, it had been too large to take with her. She had found a good sharp shard of flint that she had tried to carry about in her shoe, but it had cut a painful grove into the sole of her feet which persuaded her to abandon it, once she was provided with a sewing kit. These new items of weaponry were far easier and more nimble to conceal and carry about. Though it seemed ever less likely she would use them. Her captivity, now she had grown accustomed to it, was of an altogether different form than its violent beginnings. Subtle and stifling rather than audibly aggressive. The veiled threat of some menacing outcome always lingering behind an intimidating instruction or composed interrogation, but nothing explicitly manifest beyond it.

Besides, it seemed they were to remain together now and whilst she could not feel relief at the prospect of remaining under Craythorne's power, she was at least grateful Eleanor was not to be torn away from her, after all. She was unsure what to make of being taken to foreign lands with such a party. She knew very little of Italy except for famous paintings of grand cathedrals and ruins, and much rumour of civil conflict and colonisation. She knew not a word of the language either. Nor had she ever sailed upon a ship. The whole idea seemed too daunting to conceptualise. But she would be with Len. *What else mattered more than that?* Nothing anymore. She was her everything.

So she focussed on that rather than the finer details. And perhaps some miracle turn of events was yet to spare them if she could find a way to get these notes sent on. If that failed, there was always the possibility of writing to Poppy to have her send some money they could use to get passage back. Surely once they were abroad this level of surveillance could not continue day in and out. Some normal rhythm of life would surely have to resume in so many months. Besides, she had said he was to go there on business. It seemed that might keep him distracted enough to give them some extra room for contrivance, if all else came to nothing.

In any case, when they arrived at another house late that night after a couple of hours journeying, she kept a low light burning and sat up over her sewing until her eyes could take no more of the strain.

By morning, she had five hand-sewn notes completed and ready to send. If only she had someone who might send them for her and some money to make it worth their while. Alas, she had not a farthing nor sight of even a hall boy about the house to put to service. So when she was given the usual command to be ready to leave that afternoon, she settled on doing something she would never consider under ordinary circumstances.

Her room was, as usual under this regime, not in the servant's quarters as it should be but in the main bed chambers of the house.—The rest of the place being out of bounds to her unless she was under escort or tending her lady directly. It meant the furnishings were always finer than what would usually be within a servant's reach to pilfer. And whilst these houses were not grand houses like Cuddington, nonetheless, they contained items of more value than an average house. And so she had spent the day considering the worth of the items around her room. What was less likely to be noticed as missing and light enough to carry about undetected. She had dismissed the obvious items of value: the pewter candlestick holders, the brass mantle-clock and a few fine porcelains dotted about, on account of impracticability. But then, she stumbled upon what might answer well enough to her cause if she could convince herself to take the risk. There was a black lacquered side table of oriental style with painted images in vivid colours quite striking in its day, she imagined, though aged and worn now. Its overarching theme was that of a peacock depicted upon its surface, its tail studded with what appeared to be real mother-of-pearl marquetry overlaid with some precious blue stone. But surrounding it, several white marquetry flowers caught in the light of a flickering candle bloom as she sat over her sewing box. She had not noticed these before. Whilst removing them from the peacock's tail would be obvious, the flowers, she considered so abundant and much smaller, would surely not be so easily noticed.

And so, with a thick needle to lever them, she set about prising the pearl flower stamens out as gently as possible, and was pleased to find it took less effort than she expected—the table being aged and the lacquer not what it once was—giving them up easily to her nimble fingers. She knew they would not be worth a great deal, and she would have to cover the cost of postage and enough to pay for the trouble of her mystery aide, so she decided to take the lot.

Once she had gathered the handful up, she sewed them into a concealed pouch she fashioned from the lining of her heavy winter petticoat, positioned in an area she knew neither Digby or Fletcher would dare to pat down in one of their searches. Then looking at the pillaged tabletop, took her teaspoon from her saucer of—long-since drank—chocolate, wiped off the chalky residue on her apron and melted wax from the candlestick directly onto the spoon. Then from it, pouring small droplets into the empty stamen holes and running a needle tip through the surface to provide a little marbling, before it dried. It would do well enough, she decided, standing back from it and studying it for signs of plunder. Had it been new and retained a good polish or sheen, it might have been noticeable. But it had not been greatly preserved and had a general lacklustre finish about it, anyway. The paints drawing the eye more vividly than the pearl, and the peacock tail the greatest sway on the eye.

Despite this rather convincing feat, she felt sick with the reality of what she had just done. She vowed never to steal so much as a pin after taking wine from the cellars for Eleanor in the early days of their acquaintance. And here she was, stealing pearls from some unknown person's belongings. *Forgive me, mama. Please do not be ashamed of me. If I was not desperate. If there was any other way...*

For the rest of her time in the house, she shuddered at the slightest creak of the floorboards outside and winced every time she glanced at the floral patterning and was able to discern the subtle difference between the wax and the pearl. It was because she knew it was altered, she reminded herself, that she was able to tell it apart. To an unknowing eye, she was confident it would not be noted. But then she began to worry over whether the wax would melt in the heat and give away what she had done. Then she reminded herself that it was still winter and the room a draughty one at that. If it was likely to melt at all, it would not be until warmer weather prevailed in the springtime, and by then, they would be long gone.

Still, she opened the nearest window. Put out the fire to keep the room chill. And sat shivering beneath her woollen cloak until she was finally called to depart—for what they were told would be their final stop until they boarded their ship at Falmouth.

She had never been more relieved to set upon another of these onerous coach trips and leave the Truro cottage with the peacock table behind her. Her heart racing as Digby patted her down and made her turn out her pockets.

Thin Walls.

February 1822. - Annalise.

When the coach pulled up this time, she realised that all her hard work and risk had led her to this moment. Unlike every other night of their nocturnal travels where they had pulled up to a derelict house in some isolated district, today, it seemed would mark the exception to the rule. Before they were set down from the coach and the blinds lifted, Giles said to them both with that polite but uncompromising accent she had come to read as more of a warning than a statement: 'Now. We shall be boarding at a hotel tonight. I expect you to engage with no one and leave all the talking to us. The slightest sign of any mutiny shall result in Dr Schmidt's carriage being sent for at first light and you being taken in for treatment, my dear. Have I made myself clear?'

'Quite clear, husband,' Eleanor said in a tone of submissive equanimity that would likely have fooled anyone else, but she. Annalise knew her too well to be taken in by her practised speech and saw the flicker in her eye for but a millisecond as Giles' words registered with her. It was the flicker of an eye that saw an opportunity, even if she had not yet decided how it might be best utilised...yet. Annalise realised as she said meekly to Craythorne's raised brows in her direction, 'Yes, of course, sir,' that she was already minded to exploit such an opportunity the moment it appeared.

Despite the place being well-lit and attended by staff, it was disapointingly quiet at the Hotel. Likely owing to the hour of their arrival, which proved to be a little after midnight, according to the clock in the anteroom they were shown in to by the staff.

'Ah, Mr Craythorne, I trust?' Came the hotelier in a strong Cornish accent that Annalise struggled to make out. She had not expected such variance in the tongue of her own countrymen. She had once known a Scottish scullery maid at Gint's who she could not understand well, and had noticed a strange ring to the words of the dairyman who delivered to them, who was Welsh. But it had seemed sensible that folk from other countries should have a different way with words. But Englishmen, she had suspected, must all talk alike across the realm, with the exception of variation owing to class, at least. She stood corrected and was certain that if she could be this much put out by a Cornish accent, she would surely struggle to manage overseas when she did not even know the Italian tongue.

After some discussion on the allocation of rooms, of which there seemed to be some mishap in the arrangements, meaning that Digby would have to board with Mr Craythorne, they were shown up to their respective lodgings with quiet expedience. She had hoped that since there appeared to be a deficiency in their accommodation, she would be permitted to board with her lady just as Digby was with his master. But this proved a disappointment when she was directed to a room next door. So this was why Digby must share. The missing room would lead to someone having to, and he was that intent on keeping them in isolation, he would sooner bunk in with his staff than permit them an opportunity to contrive anything together.

She was at least permitted to tend to her lady's toilette, even if Fletcher was sat outside the room on a chair, keeping watch.

'We have to find a way out of here tonight, Annalise,' Eleanor whispered, as soon as the door was closed snug behind them.

'Hush, Len, we will be heard. You could hear a pin drop in here. Everyone else is to bed.'

Eleanor nodded then they both turned to the door. 'Did he just lock us in?' Eleanor asked, perplexed.

Annalise nodded, 'It sounded like it.'

'Damned blockhead,' she scolded, flinging her Redingote to the bed and walking over to the window.'

It appeared they were on the highest floor of the place as they both stood peering out of it to assess it as a potential escape route.

'Do you think it impossible?' Eleanor turned to ask her.

'Without a broken neck, yes.'

'I bet the contemptible knave arranged it especially.'

Annalise shrugged. 'Well, we might not be getting out tonight, but I have managed these.' She bent down and pulled the folded fabric notes from her stocking to show her.

'Good work. The trouble is he says we are to sail tomorrow, so I fear it will be too late, even if we could find a way to convey them.'

Annalise's heart sank. She was so consumed with being found out with them, she had forgotten that detail. He really had left nothing to chance. This time tomorrow they would be on a ship in the middle of the sea somewhere, and far beyond the reach of any help, whether they managed to get one note out, or all five.

'Don't cry, my sweet,' Eleanor cooed. This was followed by the comfort of a soft palm against her cheek and the press of a tender kiss at her forehead.

'Oh Len, what are we going to do? It is impossible.'

'We are not going to give up, that's what. There must be a way...'

'He has us under lock and key, quite literally.'

'I know. But we are amongst others now. This is the first time we have had that chance and in the morning, this place will be alive with other guests. There will surely be an opportunity to seek help then. Here, give me half of those letters so we both have them to hand should we find the right moment to pass them on.'

Annalise handed her a share of the notes and a share of the stolen pearls, so they both had the means to pay for them. Eleanor was grateful for her quick thinking in obtaining them since Giles had stripped her of anything of value beyond the wedding band he insisted she wore. 'We will send a banker's draft to the Truro cottage to cover the cost, once we are out of this mess and can set things to right.'

It seemed the very least of their worries, and though Annalise wished she could share her optimism, she could not help but feel already defeated. And as she settled into her bed next door, she could do nothing but weep with despair as the curdling reality of their circumstances loomed closer and ever more certain.

THE HOPELESSNESS SHE had fallen into sleep with had remained with her through the night and she woke with the very same sense of foreboding. But she had no time to dwell on it as she sat up in bed to hear what she was sure was Craythorne's raised voice through the wall. She had not paid attention to the fact at the time, with so much else running through her mind, but she had been placed between his room and Eleanor's. And it seemed the walls were very thin. It was an old timber frame building. She supposed it likely, given the poky size of the rooms, that the space had been further divided by makeshift walls to get more rooms in after its original build. And those were always easy to hear through.

She padded out of bed, took the untouched tumbler from beside the carafe, and pressed it to the wall.

'Tell your commander it is an outrage. What kind of operation is he running? My yard could have such a repair made in as little as a day, and he, being entrusted to carry the King's mail, cannot do as much in less than three!'

'I will tell him, sir, to be sure I shall. And apologies, once more. I shall come again as soon as we have an update on the rescheduled sailing.'

With that, she heard the click of the door and assumed that the messenger had departed and was about to get up and make ready to deliver the news to Eleanor, when she heard him say:

'Digby, you will have to get me ready and keep watch today. I will have to go down to the harbour myself and see what else is sailing out next. We may have to change our course again. Blast it.'

'You may rely on me, sir. I shall make sure they remain to their rooms until you get back. I will have breakfast sent up on trays.'

'Yes, very good. I will be as quick as I might. If I have no joy, you shall have to set about making some enquiries on alternative lodgings in the area, private, of course. We can't stay here a moment above what we must. We are in the centre of town, and it will soon grow busy. It is too risky above the night we intended. Typical this proved the only damn inn available in Falmouth, and it shall likely remain that way given the delay.'

'What about Selley's place at Greenbank, sir? Shall I try there? Always was rooms aplenty and much more remote than here.'

'Don't be ridiculous, Digby! Every captain on these shores will be boarding there. We shall be recognised in a thrice. No. We cannot take that risk until we are boarded. You shall have to enquire after some private rooms. Failing that, you could try the other Falmouth inns again for two rooms if they still have not three. – We can manage in two if we must. Better square another night here with Mr Wynne though, just in case we are unlucky.'

'Yes, sir. I shall get right to it.'

Annalise was of precisely the same mind and got dressed in record time and wrapped against the door to be let out of the room. It took more than a few petitions before a bleary-eyed Fletcher unlocked the door and let her into Eleanor's room. 'Good morning ma'am,' she said, as Fletcher locked it up behind her.

She, too, was up and ready, bar the loose lacing of her stays and the buttons at her back. 'Good morning, Tulley,' she replied. 'I thought you would never come!' She added at a whisper, when Annalise drew closer to her.

'What is the rush?'

'To get down to breakfast and see if we might suss out an exit strategy, or at least try and get a message out.'

'It's no use. Breakfast is to be sent up on trays.'

'What?' she said, deflated.

'No, it's a good thing. I just overheard a conversation from your husband's room. It seems there is some problem with the ship and we won't be sailing today, after all.'

Eleanor's eyes widened with joy. 'You are certain?'

Annalise nodded. 'By his tone and irate mood, I cannot believe myself mistaken. I woke up to the voice of someone in that strange Cornish accent conveying a message about it. Craythorne was angry. His voice was raised, and he sent him away with a complaint to the company. Anyway, he says he must go directly to the harbour to see what is to be done and that Digby will be keeping watch over us in his absence. But he shall be busy making enquiries for us to move to other lodgings, so I expect he will be leaving us to Fletcher's watch for a time.'

'Then this must be our chance, Annalise. Where is Fletcher?'

'Still outside the door, but looking very worse for wear. I think he has slept in the chair through the night, and poorly, I'd imagine.'

'Yes, I thought so. When I screamed in the night, he responded in a thrice. I suspect he hasn't moved.'

'Why did you scream?'

'The sound of that horrendous gun blast scared the wits out of me.'

'Gun blast?'

'You did not hear it?'

Annalise shook her head.

'Goodness. You must have been tired to sleep through such an irregular raucous in the dead of night. Anyway, it turns out it is a regular feature here, sounded when the posts come in and out, so it was nothing to be concerned with anyway.'

'How did you find that out?'

'I sent Fletcher to summon Giles and explain what was going on. No doubt it is not just Fletcher worse for wear this morning. But never mind all that. My prayers have been answered. We have an opportunity today under Fletcher's sleep-deprived watch. I *knew* something would come through Annalise. I just knew it.'

'Well, we do have a little more time. Though I'm not sure what is to be done with it if they plan on keeping us shut up in our rooms all day.'

'Listen.'

'What is it?'

'The stirring of the hotel. There will be people all over the place upon the hour—staff tending guests, guests rising for their breakfast and packing up, moving along these very corridors.'

'Well, of course.'

'Don't you see? All we have to do is wait for Giles to set out on his way and for Digby to begin on his enquiries, then we can raise a raucous of our own until someone comes and lets us out of here. Look,' she ran over to the window and opened it. They were on what appeared to be the side of the building. The corner plot occupied by the Hotel faced directly onto a busier main street, with their side facing onto a smaller one, which met the former, just a little way on. 'Before long, the streets shall come alive and grow busy. We can shout from the windows if we must. Someone will help us. I know it.'

They were interrupted then by the turn of the key and instantly jumped back from the window. Annalise made busy with Eleanor's lacing just in time to paint an ordinary scene of attending to her buttons.

'Excuse me!' Eleanor snarled at Digby as he slid into the room. 'If you don't mind, I am getting dressed, and you do not have leave to walk in on a Lady during her toilette!'

'Forgive me. I shall turn away. Girl, come and take these breakfast trays,' he said, holding one out in front of him with his head turned towards the door.

Annalise relieved him of the trays one by one and took them to the table, whilst Eleanor continued to scold him and accuse him of un-gentlemanly conduct. He did not stay a moment beyond what he must, and though she was sure they were probably meant to dine separately as was usual, Eleanor's protest seemed to have distracted him from habit.

When they were sure he was gone, they sat over their plates, clinking the china with the cutlery to create a convincing backdrop to their whispers, though neither of them had an appetite and sipped only on their cups in the gaps of hushed conversation.

By the time their cups were empty, they had a plan.

Jago's Slip.

February 1822. - Eleanor.

Once Fletcher came in to remove our breakfast trays and Annalise was escorted back to her chamber, I sat with my chair beside the window, looking out for a sign of Giles's departure. The room's height did not make for an easy view onto the nearside of the street below, so narrow the cleft betwixt the buildings. Since we had not seen the full view of the Hotel in daylight, I was unsure of its arrangement or whether we had entered from the front or rear of it. There might have been a way for him to exit without passing the view from my window, and as the time ticked on without sight of him, I began to think this more likely.

But reliably, the beckoning day had stirred the town into life and wagons and hawkers were passing the winding lane beneath, as fishermen and sailors traversed the one intersecting it in distinctive clothing and carrying bags upon their shoulders and tin flasks in their hands. The rumble of thick Cornish accents rising from below as familiar folk bid each other good morning, or made a purchase from a street vendor selling hot offerings from their wagons. The occasional seagull squawking as it flew past my open window, before swooping low to pester the food pedlars for their wares. I wondered how close we were to the sea. I was sure I could hear the rushing of the waves not too distant. Taste the briny tang of sea air in the breeze. It would not take Giles too long to reach the harbour from here, and yet it seemed not quite the right moment to strike.

So I continued watching and waiting. And the sea merchants and tradesmen began to be joined by other folk. Women on donkey's carrying bushels of goods upon their backs, servants with empty baskets swinging from their elbows, and the occasional more finely dressed couple or family who seemed out of place. I put them down to being tourists or other travellers bound for the boats.

Now was the time to take advantage of the stirring streets below. The creaking floorboards and staircases within the hotel walls.

Accordingly, I took the teaspoon I had stolen from the breakfast tray and the (partially full) porcelain chamber pot from beneath the bed. I carried it over to the wall that adjoined Annalise's room and tapped the spoon against the china in three bright clear strokes, to give her the signal. Then I lent as far as I could out of my window until I could just see her pale arm stretched out of hers, holding a candlestick to indicate that she had gotten my message, and was about to begin.

I drew in a steadying breath, praying that all would go to plan. Then I took the blade of the broken pair of scissors Annalise had given me earlier, passed it through the flame of my candle, gave it a few seconds to cool and then, cut a gash diagonally across my upper forearm between the fleshy edge and the elbow. It was more difficult than I expected, to compel myself to perform this self-inflicted injury with a significant enough depth to produce more than a thin score of blood. So I thought again of the consequences of this plan not coming about: a picture of Giles' smug face blooming in my mind's eye just an instant. Then went over the bloodline again with so much force – for a fleeting moment of panic – I thought I might have instigated a genuine emergency as blood flowed freely from it now. The flesh gaped slightly toward the elbow-end of the wound. I pinched it to let it flow a little more, picked up the chamber pot, and walked towards the door before letting it crash to the ground with all its unsightly contents splashing out onto the boards. Then as quickly as I could, I lowered myself to the floor and screamed.

Perhaps he was dozing in his chair again, but after a slight delay I heard the turn of the key, and Fletcher came bounding into the room, looking dumbstruck at the scene before him.

'Help!' I said to him, clutching my arm to my body, blood running down it and the carefully selected shard of porcelain I had pre-stained, held out in my hand. 'I've just pulled this from my arm, and now it won't stop bleeding.'

'What 'ave you done?' He said, closing the door behind him and stooping to the ground to try to lift me.

'Do not!' I whimpered. 'Can't you see I am injured?' Then his eyes widened with the sight of my blood-soaked sleeve that had absorbed the worst of it. 'Fetch my husband at once. I need medical attention before I bleed to death!'

He looked wild with panic. 'But he's gone out, misses. I can help. What shall I do?'

'Call a servant for a start. They can deal with this mess and fetch me some clean water and bandaging, whilst you get Digby to send for a doctor. This is going to need stitches.'

Another wild look confirmed that Digby was not at hand either, and I silently gave thanks for choosing the most opportune moment to orchestrate this scene. 'Quickly now! Will you have me bleed out or suffer a ghastly infection on account of your delay? My husband will be most aggrieved if I'm declared unfit to travel and our sailing is delayed —'

'I can't do that, misses,' he shook his head despairing, and I almost felt sorry for him, he was in such a panic.

'What? Call for help?'

He nodded. 'Let you speak with the servants.'

'Then do not. Pray, put me next door with my Abigail if you must, she will know how to help me. Then you can lock us in and go and fetch the staff to clean this up and bring supplies for my wound.'

He contemplated this less of evils before resigning this to be the better option, just as I had been counting on. Taking his offered hand, I pulled myself from the ground and took his escort out of the room. 'No funny business, misses, I mean it.'

'Do I look like I am in a fit state to conduct any "funny business" to you?' I glared at him and he unlocked Annalise's door, and right on cue, as he turned the handle, she came bounding out into the corridor screaming: 'Fire! Fire!' at the top of her lungs.

The smoke gushed out with her, and I, too, joined in the chanting effort of calling 'Fire' whilst Fletcher jumped back enough at the shock of the smoke to lose his grasp on me. 'Put it out before the building burns down!' I cried, before Annalise and I, ran along the corridor chanting, until disturbed guests began to emerge from their rooms and staff came bounding up the stairs.

We seized the moment and meandered through them on the staircase, rushing down as they clambered up, and without looking back to see where Fletcher was or knowing how to navigate our way out of the place. We just kept darting on around another flight, another corridor, until we finally found our way to the lower floor.

It was then we saw Digby come in through the doors we were planning to make an exit from, and knew instantly that he had clocked us. We turned about so sharply we ran directly into a maidservant who was trying to stay a gathering crowd of concerned guests in the breakfast room from going up the stairs to investigate the panic.

'Please help us!' I said, holding out my arm. 'We were hurt in the fire. We need help. We need a doctor!' I implored her as I felt Digby's presence drawing closer and heard him shouting out behind, 'Wait!' as the crowd began to utter, "Fire?"

She looked at my bloody arm and the stains upon my clothes with a pang of despair and said, 'Good Lord, miss, I can't be in two places at once. Go and sit in the parlour through there, and I'll send someone to you as soon as I might.'

Then from the crowd of guests who had gathered about me now to gawp and gasp, shrouding me from any view of Digby, came a voice, saying: 'I can help,' and I caught sight of a young lady, barely adolescent, pushing her way towards us and ushering us through the breakfast room and into the parlour.

'Close the door!' we cried out in unison, and a little bewildered, she shut it up behind her, came over to me, and reached out for my arm.

I gave it to her with a curious sense of wonder at this innocent seeming waif of a girl who did not flinch or squirm at the sight of it and, having looked it over, said simply, 'It looks worse than it is. Once we've cleaned it up, it shall need a few stitches, but you'll surely live.'

Annalise, who was back pressed against the door in case Digby had seen the direction we had headed, glanced peculiarly at me and shrugged.

'You seem to know what you are talking about,' I said more calmly now.

'Well, o' course I do miss, my pa's a naval surgeon and I've seen a lot worse than that before.'

'You have?'

She nodded in earnest and her large widening eyes seemed incongruous with the confidence in her tone, and wisdom of her countenance.

'Well then, how fortunate we are to have your help. I suppose you shall require some supplies,' I said, hoping to prompt her to leave the room. I had already spotted the window and thought we must try to make a bolt for it before Fletcher or Digby found us out.

She looked between us both curiously. 'Perhaps *you* could go and seek them,' she said to Annalise.

'She can't... she is still in shock from the fire herself,'

She was not convinced.

'Why don't you tell me what's really going on?' she said more severely.

I didn't know whether to laugh or be affronted. 'Pray, child. We are injured, that is what.'

'Pardon me, miss, but I can see that. What I don't understand is why you bolted from that fellow in the Lobby –'

'Alright. You're a clever thing aren't you, so I shan't try to gull you. Well, how about if I explain our calamity, in truth, you agree to help us?'

She mulled it over. 'I might if I think it right to,' she counteroffered.

'Very well. You have us at your mercy...what's your name?'

'Nancy. Nancy Troon, miss.'

'Well, Nancy, my name is Eleanor, and this is my maidservant, Tulley. The truth is, we are in quite a fix if that fellow in the Lobby finds us. We have been kidnapped. And there are two other fellows working with him. One of them a very large brutish-looking fellow, and the other a gentleman. If any of them catch sight of us, we shall be spirited away in a flash and taken off captive, as we have been for the past week.'

She seemed satisfied at my earnestness and not nearly as surprised as she ought to be. 'Then I think, Eleanor, we must move elsewhere before we see to that gash. I'm not sure how though if there are three of them looking for you.'

'We shall exit through the window and make a dash.' I crossed the room and opened the window sash hopefully, to find that it opened directly over an area of excavation work where the ground had been dug down to a deep cavernous cleft and sandbags stacked around it to prevent anyone from falling down the hole. 'Dash it,' I said aloud, 'we're not going to get out of this window with a drop like that.'

The pair of them came up beside me and peered out.

'What are the bloody chances?' Annalise said.

'I have an idea,' Nancy crossed the room and opened up a mahogany wardrobe that I supposed served as a coat cupboard for any occupiers of this private parlour. 'It looks like you could both squeeze in at a push. You could hide in here whilst I find my pa and get him to bring his medicine bag. He's here to tend a sickly patient, but he might be finished by now. He'll be able to call the magistrate for you and get these felons taken off! Then you shan't have to run off anywhere.'

'No, please don't do that. The thing is, we can't call the authorities. For you see, one of those felons is my husband—'

She furrowed her brow. 'But you said you were kidnapped.'

'I was, by him. We have been separated for months owing to his brutality. My family were keeping me in a safe house in Cambridgeshire—'

'Where?'

'About a week's journey from here. Anyway, he discovered me and captured us, and now he means to put me on a ship and take me abroad where they shall never get word or sight of me again. Can you imagine if someone did that to you, how sick with worry your pa would be? Well, that's how it shall go for my family if he succeeds. Look,' I pulled Annalise's embroidered notes from inside my décolleté where I had hidden them. 'We have been trying to get a message out for help, but you are the first person we have spoken to in a week.'

She unfurled the crumpled linen, then looked up at me, 'It says you are for the madhouse at Bodmin.' It was the first time I noticed her falter and look a little unsure.

'Yes. That was his threat to me if I refused to sail. What was I to do? I am not insane. I swear it. Listen, I do not expect to involve you in our troubles. If you can simply tell us if the coast is clear, we shall get on our way and I will deal with this once we are safe.'

'It might only be a nip, but you could get a nasty infection if you don't have it cleaned and sewn, miss. One fellow off a wreck last year had to have his whole leg sawn off for the very same reason.'

'By gad child, are you trying to frighten me? How can you even recite such tales?'

She shrugged. 'S'what happens when you live in Fal. Wrecks and smugglers,' she paused, and mouthed, 'get inside the cupboard.'

We did not hesitate and let her push us inside it. 'I'm going to lock it, alright,' she whispered, and then we heard the opening of the door.

'Who are you?' she said.

'I'm looking for a lady, an injured lady. I was told she came this way.'

It was Digby's voice.

'Yes, she did.'

My heart sank and Annalise squeezed my hand.

'She went out the window with the maid. I tried to stop her. I thought she'd fall to her death down that cavern. But they walked the ledge around the building, climbed down onto the sandbags, and got safely onto the street. —Look, they've just turned onto Market Street.'

The thud of hurried footsteps thronged right past us making the mahogany wood shudder against our flanks.

'Where?' he asked.

'Just across the way by the pasty woman, see. —Oh, too late, the packhorse has just crossed the view of them.'

Footsteps thudded back past us and my heart matched the frantic pace. Then moments later, she whispered, 'he's gone,' and unlocked the cupboard door.

'Are you certain?' I asked, tentatively poking my head out to survey the room.

She nodded.

'Thank you,' Annalise and I repeated several times, pressing a palm to our chests and regulating our breathing.

'You really ought to at least bind that arm up. It shan't stop bleeding if you don't. Here, hold it up in the air at least. That should slow it. I daresay it would take a mighty long time to bleed to death from such a nip, but all the same.'

'Nancy,' Annalise said, folding my soiled sleeve back on itself as I held it up as instructed, 'Do you think you might find us some supplies? We don't have long to spare...'

'We don't have time for that,' I insisted. 'We need to go now, whilst the coast is clear.

'Have you a clean shift on?' Nancy asked.

I nodded, and without invitation or explanation, she lifted my skirts and tore a strip of it with her bare hands and used it to bandage the wound so tightly it felt like a vice around it. 'That should hold up for long enough,' now, I want you to promise me somein'?'

'What?'

'If I help you to safety, you promise you'll do as bid and not cause any trouble for me?'

'Of course not,'

'Fine. There's a cottage up the fishing lanes near Jago's Slip. *Merrin Cottage*, with a blue door and a birdcage in the window. Now, the owner's away till the *Mary Pelham* comes in, due tomorrow sometime, though we shan't know when 'till it comes in. Anyway, I looks after his birds when he's at sea, and I knows where the spare key is. You can hide out there till then. Sort your arm out and bunk up for the night if you need to. So long as no one sees you or knows you're there, and you are gone by midday tomorrow.'

'Oh Nancy, you really are a diamond of the first water! Bless you,' I hugged her with my good arm. 'Thank you. I promise we shan't be any trouble and will leave it just as we find it, to be sure.'

'I know. You have earnest eyes', she said, then she took off her hooded cloak and held it out to me. 'Take this, and draw up the hood. You can leave it at the cottage, and I'll pick it up tomorrow when I come to feed the birds.'

'Are you sure? I may get blood over it.'

'It was a present at Christmastide from my pa, so try not to.'

'I shall take care of it.'

'I don't have any money, so I'm afraid that's the best I can do.'

'Nancy, you have done enough. You're an extraordinary young lady. What you have done for me today, I shall never forget. You may have just spared me from the very depths of Hades.'

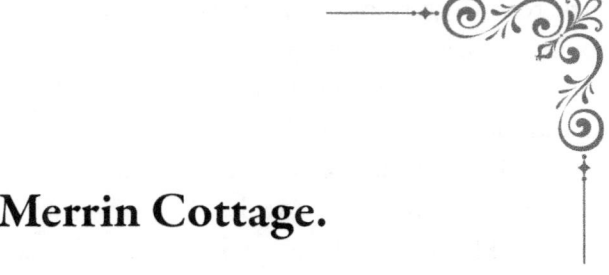

Merrin Cottage.

February 1822. - Eleanor.

We managed to get out of the hotel easier than expected, beneath the cover of Nancy's cloak and her checking the way ahead for us at each turn. She led us to the basement through a service exit that opened onto the rear of the building, and we were soon fast amongst the throng of townsfolk. But when she left us, the cottage turned out trickier to find than we expected, though we followed her detailed instructions and it was not very far away. I huddled beneath the cloak whilst trying to keep my eyes peeled in every direction. But we were anxious. Prone to making wrong turns and missing the landmarks she had referenced from time to time in our heightened anxiety. The bustling streets helped to provide cover to some degree, but hindered us too, sidestepping when spotting the occasional tailcoat or top hat amongst the multitudes that was in the like of Digby's. It was not only Digby either. There was the possibility Fletcher was combing the streets too. And that Giles might be travelling by coach or horse from the harbour by now, and we risked being spotted every time one went by. I, at least, was partly concealed. But Annalise had not so much as a woollen shawl or bonnet to take cover beneath. All we could do was make fast and stay close to the shadow of others, in the hope we would not stand out and attract attention.

We had walked right past *Merrin Cottage* twice already before we realised our error and retraced our steps. Though Nancy had told us the door was up an alleyway, we had not realised what a labyrinth of little nooks and turns these little fishing village lanes comprised of. But we found it eventually and had no trouble getting in unseen, owing to the obscure little recess it was poised in, and we lifted the plant pot beside the doorstep to find the key, as promised.

'Oh god, Len, we made it!' Annalise cried as she shut the door behind us and slid the bolt across it.

I smiled my relief back at her. 'We did.'

'I thought us done for, truly—'

'Ye of little faith. Don't you know that miracles can appear when you are least expecting them? How do you think I found you?'

She smiled bashfully. 'I think Nancy was heaven-sent, to be sure.'

'Bless her. I don't think she was a day above fourteen but she had the head of someone twice her years. I wonder what kind of life begets such wisdom; shipwrecks, smugglers, amputees...'

'Land Ho! Land Ho!' Came the oddest sounding voice and we both started and turned about to see two parrots in a cage beside the window, then laughed out loud as we realised the source of it.

'She did say she came to feed the birds,' Annalise reminded me.

'She did, although I had not expected the talking kind, and yet it seemed the least important detail. Aren't they beautiful? Look at their vibrant tail feathers,' I said, walking over to them to see them closer. 'Hello birdies...aren't you pretty little things.'

'Hello birdies, Hello birdies!' they squawked, and we let out another laugh, which seemed heightened by the strange shift in energy from the fractious despair of our escape, to the instant relief of this sanctuary. 'Oh, Annalise,' I said when our laughter waned, 'What have I embroiled you in?'

'Hush. Nothing I have not chosen to be embroiled in,' she said, coming over to me and pulling me into her embrace. 'Although, I never thought myself capable of arson...'

'Oh, Annalise, I'm sorry for it. For all of it.'

'I'm just funning. There was no real harm done. I'm sure the proprietor shan't miss half a quart of whale oil and an old tin scuttle bucket.'

'To be sure, so long as they put it out quickly enough.'

'I left my wash basin right beside it. So long as Fletcher had the sense to pour it out upon it, it should have been doused out swift before we even reached the bottom of the stairs.'

MIDWINTER.

Like my staged "fall" and injury, the fire had been orchestrated. Annalise had emptied the fuel for the oil lamps into the scuttle bucket and set a petticoat on fire inside it. Providing they had put it out promptly, there would be nothing a good airing of the room would not set right. I gathered her in tight. 'God, it feels good to hold you. Properly. Freely,' I sighed, and closed my eyes to savour the moment. How many times this week past had I longed to feel the comfort of her. How much I seemed to have taken for granted the luxury of her arms in all the months before our capture. It felt like now I had it back, I might never release her. I had, at one point, when sitting in that curious parlour at the asylum, wondered if I would ever get to hold her again.

'I know. Let's take a pause, rest out the night and consider the best way out of here tomorrow when our heads our clearer.'

It seemed she was of the same mind. 'Yes', I nodded my assent. Then the parrots started up again with "Land Ho", and we stepped apart and took in the view of our refuge for the night.

The cottage was the humblest size, only marginally bigger than the Old Mill Street terraces. Walls of rugged un-rendered stone and a fireplace fashioned from the same, with timber beams of mahogany stain cutting through them over doors and above our heads. Uneven flagstones covered the floor, with a rug made of some kind of woven reed laid over half of it. A rudimentary timber table with board benches for seats, dominated the greater share of the space. One frayed armchair, sagging at the centre with a woollen blanket folded over the arm, positioned right by the large fire, which was as cold as the old ash that lay in the un-swept grate. Above the fire, a timber mantle displaying a clutter of mismatched items that appeared exotic and out of place in the plain cottage, adorning the otherwise bare and rudimentary furnishings. *A collection, perhaps, from the seaman's travels?* Then beyond the bowed rise of the fire was a door, which on closer inspection, answered to something of a recessed pantry area where little more than a tarnished oak bench counter, shelves of bottled foodstuffs, and a few chipped pieces of crude crockery sat scantly upon them. A tin bath tucked beneath, and wooden buckets for collecting water sat empty and dry upon the floor. 'I think we'd do well to get comfortable with being hungry today,' I said as we scanned the peculiar offerings. Most looking no more appetising than the murky contents of the specimen jars of a scientist's laboratory.

'Well, he's obviously not much of a cook. He must buy in his meals when not at sea. Let's see how hungry we get,' Annalise said, curiously eyeing one of the jars of pickled vegetables as she led us back into the main parlour.

'Really, do people do that?'

She shot me one of those questioning glances she gave me when it was clear I was asking—what seemed to her—a very stupid question. One of the few reminders of the gulf between our histories. 'Of course. It's not unusual in the common classes to eat from street vendors or other folk who have a flair for a hearty receipt. Why do you think *Poppy's Pie's* is doing so well?'

'Well, yes, of course, I thought it might answer once in a while, but in place of a home-cooked meal, all of the time?'

'Not everyone has the time or skill for cooking or can afford the equipment, or the vast quantities of ingredients often needed to make a worthwhile effort. Sometimes it's easier for folk to find a penny or two for a good pie or a mug of hearty stew after a day of labour,' she shrugged.

'I suppose. Though judging by these unusual collections,' I said, gesturing to the fire mantle now, 'this seaman would not be short of the means. Some of these things look valuable. Not so different to the collections at the British Museum.'

'Well, he either does not know their worth or has the means and chooses to seek his meals elsewhere... Anyway, we had better get you out of Nancy's cloak and see to your arm,' she said as I picked up an odd-looking doll in the image of a man with an elaborate feathered headdress. I had entirely forgotten about my wound amongst all else. Even the pinch of the tight binding had long since dulled. I put the doll back on the dusty mantle and untied the hood ribbon. 'Yes, I suppose we better see what we can find to answer whilst we have the benefit of daylight at our disposal if we are not to put on any lights and give ourselves away.'

'I think we can put on a light and the fire if we cover the window – there is only one.'

'Actually,' I said, looking above her shoulder and towards the right rear corner of the room, 'I think there may be another beyond that curtain.'

Annalise followed the direction of my stare and we walked over to the heavy curtain, pulled it back, and found a small square of corridor behind it. A staircase on the right-hand side and another door directly opposite us.

It transpired that the door opposite led to an underground cellar filled with (mainly empty) ale barrels and casks of various wines and liquors, with odd names and engravings in foreign languages we could not decipher. The staircase above led to a humble bedchamber poised directly over the main room below. Like the rest of the cottage, it was rudimentary in form and furnishing, with a bed, a fireplace, a rocking chair and a few old trunks set against the rear wall. Contradicted by an incongruous collection of exotic articles scattered about the periphery. Wooden carvings and rich tapestries, even some unusual-looking portraits of distant shores hung haphazardly on some of the walls.

Annalise drew the scrap of curtain across the bedchamber window and hung a blanket over the curtain rail. 'That should blackout any light and permit us to burn the fire up here,' she said, prodding the coals into position.

BY NIGHTFALL, WE WERE settled in and somewhat recovered from the anxieties of the day. Annalise had cleaned my wound with spirits from the cellar and sewed the gash together with one of the needles she had hidden in her hair ribbon, and some unpicked thread from my shift. It had put us both through our paces. Me trying my best not to scream or pass out with the pain, she, trying to keep focused on a task she found far trickier to work than any fabric she had ever dealt with. It was an episode we were both glad to see the back of, and when she finally bandaged my arm in a fresh length of shift-muslin, we were relieved the matter was dealt in.

We supped on a barely edible plate of jarred pickles and bottled jellied eels when the hunger grew too distracting. It was perhaps the meanest meal I had ever suffered. Though once the ordeal of it was over, the pangs of hunger from a day of unintentional fasting finally abated enough to be comfortable again, and we lay upon the bed coverlet in each other's arms with the warmth of the fire making us drowsy and content. For having been deprived of liberty and each other, we were both poignantly aware that this was the magic that made everything else worthwhile.

However wretched the day had proved with all its anxieties and trials, we could only feel grateful for this moment. Both vowing we would do the same again, to have the reward of our freedom and comfort of each other restored to us. And whilst we had not yet figured out just how we would make our exit, having no money or contacts to prevail upon in time, we knew we *must* find a way. That it was worth every effort.

WE ROSE EARLY BEFORE the first light had dawned across the staggered rooftops of the fishing village cottages, owing to being so exhausted that we had fallen abed not much past six o'clock the day before. The clock downstairs now drew close to the hour of four, and we wondered what was for the best. Should we set off directly under cover of the inky sky, unlikely to be seen? Or did we risk standing out without a crowd to burrow amongst? We also had the difficulty of coming across any benevolent folk who might permit us to hitch a ride out of the place on the back of a cart at such an hour, either for free or for the scant worth of the few pearl trinkets we could offer. We had not a single thing else to make use of. He had stripped us of everything that may have proved valuable. Even one of the expensive pocket watches I had bought from *Rundell & Bridges* and furnished Leonard with as an insurance policy should we ever be caught in an unexpected difficulty. Not that I ever had conceived of one quite so dreadful as this. Crossing paths with Giles, yes, having to escape him too. But never had I expected to be kidnapped and spirited off to a place so far away it might as well have been another country, or to be forced to the continent, or facing the madhouse. How limited my imaginings had proved in never foreseeing such a calamity as this. How ill-prepared we were for this turn of events. And then I remembered that I still had my gold wedding band on my finger. The sole thing he had permitted me to keep. How lucky I had been wearing it as part of Leonard's character when we were captured. I prised it off my finger and set it on the table where we were breakfasting on a plate of pickled eggs and bottled herrings.—However unpalatable, it seemed a sensible course, given that we didn't know how long it would be until our next meal and that we would surely need our strength to sustain us in what could prove miles of walking in the cold damp air. So we spooned down what we could manage, Annalise finding it far less offensive than I could come to terms with, whilst we sounded out plans between mouthfuls.

'What do you think we could get for this?' I asked her, sliding the ring across the grainy wooden tabletop.

She swallowed down her mouthful. 'I'm not sure, but if it is real gold, it must be worth enough to set us on our way at least.'

'Of course it is real gold,' I said, lifting my fork to attempt another mouthful of soggy herring flesh. 'It's my wedding ring.'

'Oh, I thought it was part of the costumery, like mine.'

'No. It was my *real* wedding ring. It seemed no more significant than a costume prop back then...'

'Well, we have something to bargain with. If we get out to the next town or village, we could try taking it into a pawn shop to see what they propose. It should be enough to offer us some options.'

'Yes, let's do that. Find out where the next village is and if we cannot get a ride, we can walk before the roads get very busy. We can find out then what the cost of a stage ticket back to London will be – I haven't the faintest clue given how many miles we must have travelled to get here. But even an outside ticket would be worth it if we could scrape the fare together.'

'I'm not sure that we could raise enough for both. But that matters not, the main thing is that we get you out of here as quickly as we might.'

I put down my fork. 'Don't be ridiculous. I'm not leaving you here for anything.'

'We may not have a choice.'

'We always have a choice, however meagre. Look what we are eating.'

'So what do you suggest if we cannot cover both?'

'Well, we could look at the rates for hiring a horse—'

'What, for three hundred miles? No, Len, I'm not having you ride again, you are farther along now, and the risk to the child is too great. And then there is your arm, how is it today? We should probably wash it again before we go.'

'I think not. That was agony enough the first time. It looks alright. A little pink and inflamed, but it has held together and there is no more blood.'

'Fine, perhaps we will find some old man's pepper or marigold flower in the fields along the way to stuff the bandage with. That shall help if you won't let me clean it.'

'Pardon me, old man's what?'

'Um...yarrow plant.'

'At this season?'

'Well, the climate seems favourable down here, perhaps not quite spring, but almost.'

I shrugged. 'Anyway, here's another idea; if we cannot get passage for our coin, passage for us *both*,' I said pointedly, 'then perhaps we can raise enough to get a little further on our way and cover the cost of some simple lodgings whilst we convey on a message for help. Wait out to be rescued.'

'I think our money would run out before the message even reached London.'

'Perhaps we could find some work – just enough to fund our fare and keep a roof over our heads in the meantime?'

'Perhaps, that might be possible,' she said vaguely, and I sensed her doubt that I would be capable of any such thing.

'Annalise, I'm willing to do whatever it takes to get us both out of here safely. I'll do anything.'

'I know, and so am I. It's just, your condition is starting to show. It may not be easy to find someone who will employ you.'

'What, even for rough work?'

She nodded. 'But perhaps it's different in these parts. Much is,' she said more optimistically, sensing perhaps, the desolation rising in me. I had tried, so far, to staunch the tide of it for fear of it sending me into an untimely spell of pitiful inertia or despairing panic. But it was growing harder to cling to hope as it seemed ever more impossible to see a way out. I looked up to find her hand resting on my forearm.

'We'll work something out, alright. First things first, we'll get out of here when the streets begin to stir. Once we are in a safer district, who knows how fortune may favour us.'

I smiled thinly, swallowing down the forming lump that could not be attributed to the bottled eggs or herrings.

WE WERE CLOSE TO SNOOZING into a second wave of sleep when we were starkly disturbed by what sounded like a tap on the front door. I sat up sharp. I had been lying across Annalise's lap.—She sat in the only armchair, cradling me childlike as we enjoyed the calm before the storm of our next undertaking. 'Did you hear that?' I mouthed to her.

She nodded and it came again, but this time with the hiss of a voice following the three taps. I found my way to my feet and we both crept over to the door to listen in.

'It's me, Nance...' we heard more clearly this time, sighed our relief, and slid the bolt across to let her in.

'Thank god it's you. You scared us out of our wits,' Annalise said, bolting the door swiftly up behind her.

'Sorry. I wasn't sure if you'd still be here, so I thought I'd come early on the off chance.'

'We were waiting for better light before leaving. But how happy I am that we did not go earlier. Nancy, you really are a godsend. Pray, tell me, how can we get to the next town or village? We have no money for a fare towards the usual options, so we shall have to try on foot.'

'You can't do that. You'll be spotted in a trice. The whole of Fal is on alert for you two.'

'What?' my voice cracked, but I was certain it was only a ricochet from the internal fracture that seemed to shatter my last threads of resolve.

'That's why I'm here. Look, I have my pa's tip dray waiting. I can probably get you as far as Penryn before he notices me gone. But we shall have to hurry whilst it's still quiet about town, for you're the word 'pon everyone's lips.'

'Oh Nancy, thank you,' Annalise cried. But I was rendered speechless a moment, learning that once again, he had made me a figure of notoriety to suit his ends.

'What are they saying, Nancy?' I asked when I found my voice again.

'Not very kind things, Eleanor. I think you'd rather not know.'

'I *have* to know Nancy, or how shall I know what kind of reception to expect if we are seen?'

'It's been put about that the town must be on the watch for a madwoman who set alight the *Royal Hotel* yesterday, and is known to be cunning and dangerous and to fashion herself into male disguise. She is destined for the madhouse at Bodmin, and they ask for any sightings to be reported to the constable or watchmen straight away.'

'Dear god,' I sighed into my palms and strained my eyes against the tears that threatened to fall. I could not allow it. If one tear fell, I knew not how to stop the others from drowning me thereafter. So I followed their instructions to lace up my boots and make ready to leave.

'Nancy, was the fire very bad?' Annalise asked her as I guided my trembling hands into tying a knot.

'No. Not in the least. But I only know that direct from my pa. The rest of Fal has an altogether different idea of things and there are all sorts of outlandish versions on the tongues of townsfolk.'

'I'm surprised you have not been frightened off by such accounts of me,' I said, standing up now with my boots on.

'I told you, Eleanor, I see beyond that. I don't think you're insane. Is that not what they call any of us who won't do as told? That's what my pa always warns me anyway, to have a care when amongst society not to come over as headstrong. But I'm not sure I know any other way to be...'

'Oh Nancy, do not change. But for god sake, have a care with who you marry.'

'I mightn't marry at all,' she said defiantly, and it managed to coax a brief smile from even my lips.

'Nancy, this place where you can take us, Penryn? How far away from here is it?' Annalise asked.

'Not very far, really, but it's as much as I can do. I can't risk being noticed helping you. I've my pa's reputation to consider, not just my own.'

'Indeed, and we would neither ask nor expect you to put yourself at risk. Only, we need to know what the chances are of the story carrying off to those parts?'

'It's not impossible, but I think it unlikely to travel that fast. Might be wise to move on quickly, though, all the same.'

I nodded. 'And do you know how we might go about getting to London on a shoestring?'

'Folk always says the cheapest means is the *Russell's London Flying Wagons*, but in truth, I've never even been out of Cornwall, so I am perhaps not the best person to say.'

'And where would we enquire after one?'

'Well, usually they picks up cargo from the ships in Fal, but that'll be no good to you now. You'll have to catch up with it somewhere farther on, though I don't know its route once it's left here. —Exeter, I think, though I can't be sure. But someone shall, and you can't miss 'em; huge wagons pulled by eight or nine horses under guard...'

'What of the fare?'

'No idea. All I knows is that they go every day to London, are as cheap as you'll find passage, but are dreadful slow, and probably not much better to travel in than the bed o' straw on pa's tip dray. I wish I could tell you more. If I had more time I could find out for you, but if you want to get out of here, it as like be now or never.'

'Yes, yes, of course. I'm ready. Oh – here's your cloak back,' I said, lifting it from the coat hook instinctively.'

'Thank you, here,' she said, handing me in exchange, a bundle I had not noticed she was holding beneath her arm until now, 'I thought these might be of use. They are not fine, but they are warm, and they'll cloak you.'

'Thank you, Nancy, that's very thoughtful of you,' I said, unwrapping two heavy wool shawls and passing one to Annalise.

'They were my ma's, but I knew she wouldn't mind you having them in such a circumstance.'

I caught a glisten of painful reminiscence in her eyes that told me her mama was no longer of this world and was about to say something, when she blinked the moment away and added quickly, 'And there's a quart of cider and a couple of pasties tied in a cloth in the back of the dray for you.

You can pick them up on your way out, should I forget to remind you. – Not sure I'll be able to speak to you at all if Penryn's busy by then. You might have to slip out quietly without so much as a farewell if it is.'

'Then we had better say farewell now,' I said, reaching out to hug her, forgetting my injured arm and pulling her in close. 'Thank you so much, Nancy, for all your kindness. May god bless you for taking pity on us.'

She hugged me back, and when I pulled away, Annalise scooped her up in her arms before we made quickly out the door. We followed her up the still-quiet lanes she navigated with speed and knowing, until we were faced with the back end of one of the tiniest looking vehicles I had ever seen, parked up in a dead-end nook, not dissimilar to the one the cottage door had been located. I wondered if we would even fit in it at first when she pulled the tarpaulin cover from it and ushered us into a shallow bed of straw, before covering us back up again. But, cramped though it was, we managed to draw our knees up enough for Nancy to lift the foot end and secure us in. Then we felt the gentle tug of the pony, which was slow and steady, which we were grateful for, given the fact that we would be knocked all over if it had shifted like a bay. And so we held each other close, our hearts racing every time we stopped or heard Nancy bid good morning and how'd you do to someone in passing.

After the first ten minutes, we calmed down and grew used to our new confines and the muffled sounds of the stirring world outside them. And as we trundled along farther and farther, a little relief began to kindle inside me, and I was able to breathe again. So long as the town folk of Penryn were not on the watch for us, this marked our ascent from hell, and every creaking trundle of the dray cart was a step closer to home.

I would not feel genuinely relieved until we had seen the back of Cornwall, the vicinity of the Bodmin Asylum, and the murmurs of the folk-embellished myth of the madwoman he had painted me. But to be gone from Falmouth and its sailing ships bound towards a life of total imprisonment and isolation on the continent, felt like progress enough for this hour. Who knew what possibilities this new town might bring in our pursuit for London? But I was determined that before nightfall, in the very least, we would have trod every possible league away from here and be somewhere so far from the circumference of Giles's search and capture campaign, that he would be little more than a dog chasing his tail as we vanished again, though this time, forever.

'I THINK THE SUN HAS risen,' Annalise whispered to me, 'There is light coming in from the corners.'

'Well, I suggest we head straight for the town centre before it gets too busy, seek out somewhere to sell this ring if we can, and find out about where to get on one of those flying wagons.'

'Yes, but do you think it might be better if perhaps you go and sell the ring and I seek out the information for the flying wagon? We don't want to waste time for the news of us to reach here before we are on our way. And it might not be smart to have you make enquiries for London travel if the news has spread.'

'I suppose it would be best, I just, the last time—'

'Shhh, someone's talking to her,' Annalise hissed.

I held my breath sharp and strained my ears to the sound of the rumbling voices above the creak and clatter of the still-moving cart.

'Morning, Mr Curnow, how's you today, sir?' Nancy said with a volume that seemed exaggerated as if she wanted us to hear it. Was this a warning alert? Could this Mr Curnow be a constable or watchman on the lookout for us? I felt the dray slow to a stop and squeezed Annalise's hand a fraction tighter.

'I'm very well, thank yer, Miss Troon. What brings you up to these parts at such an hour?'

'Oh, a household errand as usual. I saw an advert in the *Gazette* for a handsome pianoforte and thought it worth a gander. Ours is more of a collectable than a useable instrument these days. I was thinking of sending it up to London to one of those auction houses. – I don't suppose you would happen to know, sir, how I'd find out about sending it on so far? I've heard the Russell's wagons are a ready way, but I'm not sure what route they take.'

'Well, from these parts, they go up to Exeter from Fal, through Bodmin, Launceston and Okehampton. Then at Exeter, a wagon will go out to London, but I don't rightly know what route it takes.'

'Ah, I see... sounds like a very long journey. I thought I'd send our footman to see it safely to London, but perhaps it'll be too much of a trial to send him so far. I bet it costs a fair penny, too, for a person to travel such a distance.'

'About a pence and 'alf a mile, last I knew.'

'Well, that seems a fair enough price. Thank you, sir. I shall think about it indeed.'

'Aye, well, I better get this catch up to Bissom. Pass my regards to your pa and mind 'ow you go now.'

'Good day to you, Mr Curnow.'

The clip of hooves started up and faded into the distance.

'There you go, Ladies – Looks like it's Bodmin you'll have to get to if you want to catch the wagon up to London,' Nancy said to us and then started up at a trot again.

'Bodmin,' we both said in chorus. What were the chances? The very place I should never like to see the sight of again and yet seemed to be destined for. 'I think we should see what the Mail stage fares are before we head in that direction.'

Annalise agreed.

We had little time to consider what to do next, as barely five minutes later the cart stopped again, and this time Nancy whispered: 'Right, I'm going to pull up the cover in a moment. There's no one about, so I'd do well to leave you here before we get right in the thick of town and risk someone seeing you climb out. But be swift, just in case someone comes upon us again. Now, if you carry on up the road in the opposite direction to which I shall go, you'll be in Penryn town in less than five minutes' walk. Good luck to you, and god bless. —Oh, and don't forget your cider and pasties!'

'Thank you, Nancy,' we both said as the canopy sprung open, and a sheet of bright light blinded me temporarily. We scrambled up in haphazard fashion and a vision of the overcrowded bottled herrings sprang to mind as we clambered out through the straw bed and ducked behind the cover of a tree, as another carriage came into distant view. 'Farewell, darling girl. I hope we shall meet again one day in happier circumstances, I called out as the dray pulled away and made a turn before heading on towards the oncoming traffic.

'Bless her,' Annalise said, clutching a parcel of cloth in her hands that she had the sense to remember to pick up.

'Is that the pasty?' I asked.

She shrugged. 'What is a pasty?'

'I assume it a Cornish term for a picnic parcel, but I own I do not know.'

Annalise unwrapped it to take a peek as we waited for the traffic to pass on, 'Well, we shall not have to worry about our food today. She has packed enough to feed four strong men. I'm not sure what it is, but it smells fresh,' she wrapped it back up and carried it under her cloak.

'It certainly looks more appetising than anything we've eaten in the last twenty-four hours. Come on, let's make a dash for it now they've passed.'

We walked the mud track road at a pace so fast we could barely talk for more than the odd sentence to catch our breath in between. Annalise had an idea that we might blend in better if we hid our giveaway accents and tried for something more local sounding. So we took turns, as our sharp breaths permitted, to demonstrate impressions of the peculiar accents we had heard in these parts, with more than a bit of hilarity at each of our attempts which were neither accurate nor convincing, but did disguise our usual ones. It was good medicine to laugh amid so much pensive tension, and whilst we agreed that neither of us seemed to carry the style off in a very good likeness, it would certainly not sound like we were from the South East, if nothing else.

When we reached the town centre we were pleasantly surprised by our amiable treatment and general lack of suspicion in our reception. It seemed my notoriety had not yet spread here after all, or that our mock accents were perhaps more convincing than we'd given ourselves credit for. Either way, it eased our fractious minds, and having disregarded the flying wagon, sought directions to the nearest posting inn to be given the fare to London. 'Eight pounds, six shillings for an inside seat or Five pounds three shillings for an outside,' was the answer, and whilst I would never have thought twice over the fare before now, it suddenly seemed outrageously expensive and insurmountable. Whatever this strip of gold was worth, I found it doubtful we would get enough for it, especially from a pawnbroker, and after half hour of wandering the shopping parades in search of one, we began to think we would be lucky to find such an establishment at all. Then as we began to lose hope, we caught sight of a shabby-looking place across the way beside the liquor merchants, with a sign bearing the name: *Uncle Beagles: Loans on every description of valuable property.* We scurried off in its direction with such fervour we almost stepped out in front of a passing carriage. My panic was two-fold – first at the narrow escape of life and limb, then when that anxiety passed, the concern of who was in it. I had noticed that these parts seemed mainly comprised of rustic vehicles, carts, wagons and farm-style contraptions, the occasional donkey or horseback rider, in the towns at least. On the main roads, like that which Nancy had dropped us, it was more common to see regular sorts of carriages, but less so in these local streets. Many of them were ill-suited to their size in any case. But when a gentleman called out an expletive from the carriage window to reprimand us for our foolish mistake, I felt relieved for confirmation that it was not Giles scouring the streets for us. There was a time when I could have detected his coach's approach by the coat of arms, but he had even had the foresight to use hired vehicles for this trip. So we had no way of telling when one rolled by, rendering every coach and four potentially suspect.

'Now, will you come in, or would you rather me go alone?' Annalise asked as we stood outside the place, staring at its window display offerings of various oddities, from silver teaspoons to craftsman's tools and chinaware. I had never been in such an establishment before, and I could tell instantly I would be at sixes-and-sevens to know how to handle such a negotiation.

'Would you mind terribly? I'm not sure I will get the best price for it.'

'Nor I, but I shall do my best,' she said, taking the ring and disappearing inside.

I lingered about the door and watched her through the bowed glass panes as she moved towards a cluttered counter. I could not hear what was spoken from outside, but it was no quick matter, and I considered whether I should have made a try after all. But my status and the clout that came with it, was long since diminished and would not serve in these parts where the name of the Ashlyn's would be unknown. If it was otherwise, I would have had no difficulty heading to the nearest nobleman's house, appealing to his propriety and having him send me back home in his private carriage, for my family's sake, if nothing else. *But who would believe me now?* Now I was branded an arsonist lunatic. I would as like be telling them I was the messiah returned as get them to believe me the daughter of one of the peerage in a moment of crisis. No. Such attempts would be fruitless, worse indeed, and would probably lead to my apprehension and return to either Giles, or the Bodmin Asylum.

'Seven pounds and not a shilling more,' she said when she stepped back out again.

'Oh gosh, we shan't have our fare then.'

'I did try. He started me at five pounds. It was only when I pointed out the hallmark that he seemed to reconsider. I suppose it must be worth a great deal more, and I daresay a London broker might have given us closer to the value, but he shan't budge, and it looks like he is the only establishment in town. —There is enough for *your* fare Len, let us go back to the inn and get *you* a ticket. I will see if they have some work for me there so I can get a week or so's board until you can send for me.'

'I'm not leaving you, Annalise. I wish you would not keep pressing me to.'

'I just want you safely away from this place. From him.'

I gathered her hands up in my own. 'I know, because it's precisely what I intend for you.'

'It is not me he is pursuing Len. I am of no use to him without you.'

'Precisely. If I am not on offer, he has no need of you and will likely punish you for your part in my escape. You do not know him as I do, Annalise, he is a twisted creature, and I could not be sure that you would not suffer cruelly if you were all that remained to direct his wrath. No. Our separation is entirely out of the question. We will work it out. Let's go back to the inn and see how far we can get on that.'

So that is what we did, retraced our steps in full, but with more vigour. We had seven pounds more than we did before, and so it had not been in vain. I was certain we could get *somewhere* farther on. Far enough to be out of danger and closer to getting a message home, at least. And it appeared that I was right. The fare for an outside ticket to a place called Ilminster was the limit of our coin, but it was one hundred and twenty-three miles from here, according to the passenger notice, so it seemed a worthwhile gamble. We would, of course, be penniless again by the time we reached Ilminster, and we would still be many miles away from home ground. But I felt confident our chances would be better there, and his chances of finding us out, far diminished than if we continued walking about in these sparsely populated rural villages so close to Falmouth. We agreed upon the scheme after a quick deliberation and rang the bell again to purchase the tickets, only to be told there was but only one seat left on today's stage and that the next offering of two seats he had available was one outside and one inside, the very next day. It was no use. It would exceed our means to pay the excess on the inside fare, never mind the matter of where we might take refuge until then. The disappointment was too much, and I faltered into a heap of hapless tears upon the last syllable of his answer.

'No need to get upset, lass. We's got rooms vacant if you need to put up, very fine ones,' he said kindly. But I see the finery of my dress had fooled him into thinking that I would have the means to pay for his fine rooms.

'We are in a hurry, sir,' Annalise interjected, no doubt, to spare my pride.

'Well, you could try the *Britannia Inn* in Truro. They're on a mail route up to London. They might still have seats – I couldn't rightly say, but it might be worth a try if you are pressed.'

'Thank you, sir, we will.'

'How far is it?' I asked.

'About eight miles or thereabouts.'

'Thank you, and the direction if you please.'

'Come out of here and head up to Four Cross, then take the turnpike road North.'

'We shall walk there and try the other inn for a ticket. Eight miles is not so very far in clement weather, and it seems to be favourable now the morning dew is burned off the grasslands. What say you? Three and a half hours? Four perhaps?'

Annalise nodded, 'Yes, there should be ample light to see us there if we don't dally.

And so, we set out on our walking journey following the directions given, keeping, when we could, off the direct path of the road and following closely beside it, if a wooded copse or accessible meadow was available to duck into. Where it was not, we walked briskly and kept our cloaks tightly wrapped about our heads. And so, we continued on these winding roads, with no way of counting our progress beyond the occasional milestone. Discussing on the way, our hopes for covering at least sixty miles today. The extra stop we might get to on the mail, by walking these off towards our greater mission. The beauty of the lands here that were quite spectacular to the ones we knew, though they carried the taint of misery in them for us now, and so we were unlikely to ever return to them, which was lamentable, but not to be dwelt upon amid all else. But a growing spark of optimism began to flow from us now, as though from our very steps, and worked to stifle our anxieties of the many obstacles we had yet to be met with. Because we had already overcome the greatest of them all in breaking free from him and escaping Falmouth. After the unlikelihood of that, all else seemed molehills after mountains climbed.

WE MUST HAVE BEEN SOMEWHERE in the region of the halfway mark when our more congenial conversation was interrupted by a sudden throng of hooves kicking up from behind, at a speed too chaotic to account for even the expedience of the mail coach. We both started and dared a look behind us. But the echoing shock of pistol fire sent us both into panic, and without looking back again, we shouted 'run' to each other and began to scramble up the nearside bank of forestry to get off the narrow strip of road where this convoy was headed. Within seconds, all the anxieties I had thought we had shaken off returned ten-fold. My pulse hammered as we heaved ourselves and each other up a muddy incline with only tree trunks to help anchor us against the slope. But there is something about fear, that seems to spur you into high determination and manage what, in other states, would seem impossible. So against all odds, once we were high enough up to look down upon the road below, we clung to the base of the tree trunks for dear life and watched a band of armed guards chasing down a wagon, shooting pistols at the wheels to try to encumber them to a stop. If there was any consolation, it was clear that they were not here for us, but in heavy pursuit of this wagon and perhaps whatever was contained inside of it. Maybe it was stolen goods? The proceeds of smuggling or piracy, as the stories and legends of such sea-faring places often attested to. Whatever accounted for it, the armed guards were hell-bent on pursuing them, perhaps even to their death, I considered, as the ashy scent of pistol smoke caught in the wind and carried to our senses. It sent a chill creeping across my flesh, despite the sweat of my brow and heaving heat pulsing through my body at the effort of fleeing. One thing that was certain, was despite them having no interest in us; we may well have ended up caught in the crossfire of such a vicious pursuit had we not scrambled out of their path. Whether they would have spotted us too late and fired at us, or whether the wagon they were pursuing tore us down in their furious bid to get away, it was of little doubt that our quick responses had spared us our lives.

Now that they had passed us in a thunderous gallop, the question was how we were to get back down again without falling to a nasty landing. 'I think it safer to go up than down,' Annalise said, when I suggested the path seemed clear once more and the sounds petered out at a distance. I looked up to where these peaks reached their summit on a more level forest floor and could not disagree that since we were already two-thirds of the way up, it was likely the better choice of the two. Whether we could get there or not, now the throbbing fear had diminished somewhat; I wasn't sure. So we took a moment to discuss the better-seeming routes that were thicker with trees to reach out to steady ourselves. Had they been of the oak and beech varieties more common to our parts, it would not have sufficed. But these were of an uncommonly tall and thin variety, seeded closely together and possible to pass an arm about to haul ourselves up with and reach out to the next. But now, the pain from my arm had started up in response to my ill use of it, and each and every manoeuvre was twice as hard as the one that came before it. I said nothing of this to Annalise, though. We needed no distraction from the task at hand, and so I managed, with all the outward nonchalance I could muster, to give her no cause to suspect how terribly I struggled, how close I came to losing my grasp and slipping from time to time. And when she reached safe ground, a few tree-spans up ahead of me, her exclamations that, 'It is safe up here and walkable', spurred me on with the final effort until she could reach down and pull me up to join her.

'Good grief Annalise,' I said between recovering breaths, 'what are the chances of such a rare occurrence as that happening on the one and only occasion, we have ever trod that road. I'm surprised it's not a scene of death down there.'

'I know,' she said, brushing forest floor debris from my clothes and shaking out her woollen cloak before refashioning it. 'I wonder how long that can last before the wagon turns over.'

'Not long, I fear. At least we will not be among the casualties. I only hope this track through the forest remains close to the road, so we don't go off course. It's not like we are likely to come across anyone to ask for directions up here.'

'Well, I'm sure we will find our way. – Come, there's a fallen tree we can sit on over there. Let's take a break to steady ourselves before we continue and whilst we are safe out of sight. I feel suddenly quite weak of limb.' Then to my surprise, she pulled out the picnic parcel Nancy had made for us. I had seen her tie it up and around her waist earlier, to spare the burden of carrying it along since she would not permit me to carry my share. But now it seemed an ingenious stroke of fortune it was not to hand, for it would have been lost amongst the tumult of such a scramble as we were forced to make. How it had managed to stay bound to her, I was not sure, but I was grateful for it as we made comfortable upon our seat and set out the food and the corked bottle of cider upon it. I knew that in my condition, I should not be partaking in such drinks, but I was thirsty, and in need of a little steadying, so I took a few sips to appease my thirst and settled upon the unidentifiable offering that seemed like a curious sort of pie.

'My gosh,' Annalise declared, finishing her first bite and examining the pastry-filled contents as they gaped from her bite marks. 'I don't know if it is because we have been forced to survive on those disgusting preserves, or whether this is some ingenious receipt, but this is delicious.'

I sunk my teeth into mine and nodded. I was still in the deeply impressed habits of my table etiquette, having never been permitted to talk before my mouth was empty for fear of some great reprimand. When I finished, I asked her what she thought was in it.

'Well, definitely peppered beefsteak and potatoes, carrots—I'm not sure what these are,' she said, holding up a cube of translucent-looking mush. 'But I will be sure to ask Poppy if she has ever heard of such a pie as this. It would surely do well to learn the method for her trade.'

And then I noted the distant gaze in her eyes as one of longing for that home, that place where all was familiar and safe, and felt such a deep pang of guilt for our current circumstances, that I could not eat any more of mine and wrapped the remainder back up in its cloth. 'When we get home, you can tell her about it and see if we can find out what it is. I shall write back to this place if need be and source the receipt,' I said brightly, brushing crumbs from my décolleté. But I did not feel so bright inside anymore, catching a glimpse of pain in her eyes for the life lost to her. A life in Carshalton with her friends and the sweet scent of Poppies cooking, a daily comfort. It had been wrong of me to permit her to come up to Stapleford and deprive her of the comfortable little life she had built for herself. She was not in chains like me, yet she had been brought to bear the same fate. I should have waited until it was safe to return to Carshalton to be with her then. Then she would not be here in such a monstrous calamity. She would be safe and warm and happy amongst her kin. I swallowed down a forming lump and took another swig from the cider bottle.

When we got home, she was being sent back to Carshalton, and that was non-negotiable. If the forces of love between us were so strong as to pull us together amidst all these obstacles, then they would be strong enough to sustain a five-month of separation until this child was born, and I was safe again to return. For this time, when I got home, I was determined to release Giles' hold upon me once and for all, one way or another. Either I would give my father the whole and see what he could do to prevent this beast from kidnapping me and abusing me again, or I would pay some felon to put an end to his reign of terror upon my life, so that I never need look over my shoulder again. Free to be with my true love and not force her apart from what she loved in the bargain. It hurt me to see the price she must pay for the sacrifice of being with me. It pained cruelly to know that she was caught between the impossibility of living without them, or without me. *No more.* It was all to be settled so that we need not be in hiding forever. – It had seemed to be the only answer before now, to run off and resettle in some unknown place once the child was delivered and made safe arrangements for. But now I saw the error in even that line of thinking. For whilst I could abandon my home and all that came with it with relative ease, she could not. Her heart was still tied to those people and places that were home to her, and I would never want to be the cause of such a vacuous cleft in her heart. She could come and visit me from time to time during my confinement, and in between, we could write, and eventually, the time would pass, even if very painfully for me. But it would be worth it. She was *worth* the wait.

But now was not the time for such discussions. So when we got back on our walking trail, I said nothing of these thoughts and tried to hide the well of emotion bubbling towards the surface, under cover of more attempts at our Cornish accents to lighten the mood. But I was fooling no one. What remained unuttered did not remain unfelt. And we seemed to walk in silence after a while, with our steps haunted by this intangible dread we had yet to face once we had overcome the many obstacles set before us in order to even broach such a conversation. And it was only when the forest path finally came to an abrupt end, that we spoke again, to decide which way to go.

'We must be on someone's private land now.' I said, pausing to consider the possibilities. 'We shall have to find the quickest way off of it if we don't want to alert their attention and be deemed trespassers.'

'How can you be certain?'

'I'm not certain, but look how neat the grass is trimmed and how well tended the shrubbery is. Even at this season. I should not think anyone would take the trouble if it were not theirs to enjoy.'

'Maybe we should go back and see if there was a way down to the road we missed.

'I think we are further off the road than we realise.' It had seemed from my regular observations that the hill we had climbed to reach this ground, rather than diminishing the slope along our way, had grown not only higher, but also farther adrift from the course of it. I had not heard the rush of hooves or the trundle of wheels for at least a half hour.

'Then we must head in this direction. It looks less orderly. Maybe it will lead to cattle fields or more woodland that we can pass along unseen.'

'So long as they don't have a gamekeeper. Oh gosh, what a fix we keep finding ourselves in.'

'Well, it's either that or we risk stumbling upon someone's house and putting ourselves at their mercy to believe we have come by mistake. But even if we are fortunate, they may still wonder at what we are doing and why we are covered in mud. And if they do not pity our circumstances or believe our story, what's to stop them calling for the constable and the authorities making the connection between us and Giles' report?'

'Oh god, I don't know. Perhaps we should retrace our steps.'

'And waste an hour of walking and risk losing the light to make the rest of the journey in?'

'Alright, let's take the way you suggested and see where it leads.' But even as I assented, I felt a terrible burgeoning sense of doubt in this plan. Though logically, it seemed the less of evil's, it deeply unsettled something inside of me that I could not understand, though I felt it growing heavier as we walked on. We soon came across a ha-ha that we had to cross with care, which did signal that we were likely headed onto farmland and not the immediate grounds of someone's home. But even this did not alleviate the trepidation I felt, looking sharply about at our surrounds at every turn or stretch ahead before proceeding. And when about another half hour had passed upon this new route and the gauzy veil of evening light began to fall over our heads, spelling that we had perhaps just a half hour or so before sunset, it was a great relief to hear the not-so-distant sounds of the road return to us at last. We followed those sounds with care, above the occasional din of a passing colony of seagulls overhead or the mooing of the cattle in the fields around us, until the clip of hooves grew louder and more consistent. Still breaking once in a while and causing us to pause until another vehicle passed by to orientate us. We hurried now, racing against the strain of daylight and into the woodland that had been on the horizon for some time.

'It is down there! Surely, it's the same road. I don't think we have come too far off course on our detour,' Annalise said excited as we peered through the trees to see it beneath our view. This time though, we were not set as high above it as before, perhaps only seven feet or so above, and better still, we did not have to face a sharp slanting hill face like our journey up, but could take a more meandering way where the land leant naturally to a gradual decline if we went about it right.

'Thank god Len. I think we cannot be too far off of Truro now if the business of the road is anything to go by. And it seemed so, a vehicle or rider passing us every few minutes now. I was just about to join in her excitement and dare to rekindle the hope that by nightfall, we would be safe inside a mail coach on our way out, when she tripped and screamed but a stride ahead of me.

'Annalise!' I rushed to help and reached down to heave her back up to her feet, but something in her eyes made me pause, a shade of terror about her iris. 'What?' I asked.

Her eyes watered, and her voice cracked over the words as she said, 'I'm in a trap. It's no use.'

I scrambled down to the floor and lifted the hems of her frock to see a horrific-looking rusty iron man trap set snug around her pale un-stockinged ankle. 'No,' I declared. 'Oh god, it cannot be. How could we have missed it?' It was large and obvious now, it seemed impossible that we would had we not been so distracted by the road, perhaps. 'Alright, let's not panic. We are in reach of help.'

'No, Len, we cannot take the chance.'

'We cannot afford not to, Annalise. These things are near impossible to release without a key. Look,' I held up the heavy chain.

'But it has no teeth, and I do not think it is fully engaged, see there is a gap at the lip of my boot.'

I looked closer to see that she was right, and then it transpired that the rusting rot of the thing had caused some deterioration of the spring mechanism, and it had not fastened properly on one side. But still, it looked too risky. At the front view of her ankle, there was a gap, large enough to poke a small stick down, but at the rear, it tapered in, and one false move might be enough to crush the fine bone at the nape of her ankle. 'How tight does it feel?'

'Pinching, though I think the boot leather is taking the brunt of it, for I'm sure it should feel worse than this. —Pray, go and find some large sticks or fallen branches to lever it with. I think I might be able to slip out if it, if you were to wedge it well enough.'

'Annalise, these things are designed to cut through if they are tampered with. I fear wood won't be strong enough to prevent it. We need metal to brace this if we hope to get you out with your foot intact. Please. Let me go for help. I cannot bear it...'

She nodded through weeping eyes, and I kissed her forehead and said, 'I won't go far alright, just down to the road to wave down help. Here,' I pulled the cider bottle from the bundle and uncorked it. Drink this down, my love. It will help the pain.'

'I am not in pain.'

'Not yet, because you are still in shock. Now drink and do not move a muscle beyond that. If you need me, call out, and I will turn about, alright?'

And with both speed and a careful eye and tentative step to avoid another of these evil contraptions, I found myself down at the road's edge within minutes. I began furiously waving my arms about at passing traffic, though it seemed none of them were minded to stop. And then, when my tears were gushing, and I was fraught with despair, thinking no one would, a farming vehicle came by and slowed on its approach to me. 'Please, sir,' I implored him when he called down in such a potent strain of the local accent I could hardly understand him at all, 'My...sister, she has been caught in a mantrap up there, and we need help. Please, have you any tools to ease her out of it?'

He looked over me, questioning and suspicious. 'What's you been doing trespassing on someone's land, arh?'

'We were lost, sir. I speak the god's honest truth. We are not poachers or swindlers, I swear it. We are but two young ladies who made an ill turn and have only just come close to finding our way back towards the road before my sister got ensnared. We have taken nothing from the land or anywhere else. You will see for yourself.'

'And what's to say you 'aven't already had some accomplice take off with the bounty?'

'Only my word, I suppose—my honourable word and oath. Look, why would I need to steal? I have money, see. I will pay you if you help us. Please. I fear she will already be in decline.'

He sighed, then said to the younger lad sitting beside him in the trap, who I had barely noticed until now, 'Tommy, fetch my pistol and my ploughing forks. Now, young maid, 'he said to me, 'if this is a lark, I'll not hesitate to use this. You may be sure.'

I nodded my understanding readily.

'Now, where is she?'

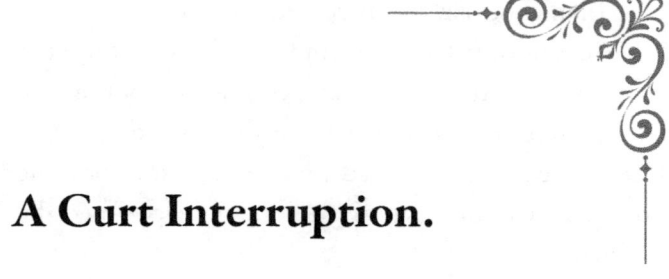

A Curt Interruption.

February 1822. - Eleanor.

Within less than ten minutes of our arrival, he had Annalise prised free from the trap by a careful sequence of sliding a combination of branches and metal forks into the mouth of it. By careful graduations, nudging Annalise's leg further towards the broken side of the trap by adding a length of branch to replace her former position. It was fractious work, and the fear at any moment, we might trigger the functioning end to snap in sudden surprise, was enough to make me nauseous every time we moved her along another fraction. But by degrees of patience in the method, which was devised by this old farmer, steadily, we moved her ankle to the widest extent, untied her boot and managed to slip her foot out of it, without the slightest impediment. 'Thank you, sir, thank you!' we both gushed with relief.

'Aye, well, you're lucky thaat springs rusted away, or there'd been no sparing your foot without the lock being unfastened. Take it as fair warning if I were you, to have a care next time when yous out a rambling,' he said in a tone of mild rebuke as he tossed Annalise's freed boot to the floor.

I stooped to pick it up. 'We shall, sir, certainly so,' I said, crouching down to look at Annalise's ankle. 'Is it paining?' I asked, catching sight of a nasty purple bruise that looked more like one of those rising black pinches forming.

'It is sore and aches some, but I think it superficial,' she said, circling it slowly.

'Well, it likely ain't broken a' least if you can do thaat.' The farmer observed. 'Now, where's you heading? I'm going as far as Tresillian, and can take you in the cart, if you don't mind it in with the hen boxes.'

'Thank you, sir, that is very kind of you.'

'Ain't nothin' to do wi' kindness. She carn't walk anymore, can she?'

'Actually,' Annalise cut in, pressing her foot lightly upon the ground to test the notion, and I shot her a sharp warning glance until she retreated from the effort and agreed that perhaps she could not, after all. We were not in a position to refuse offers of help, especially if her foot proved problematic.

'We are bound for Truro, sir, the *Britannia Inn*. Do you know it?'

'Aye, so. A'right, let's drop you there then,' he said, releasing his iron forks from the mouth of the trap and handing one to Annalise. 'Thaat'll 'elp you hop along.'

I took her by her free hand and steadied the effort.

WE WERE DELIVERED TO the inn without ceremony as night fell thick over the warmly lit windows. The farmer helped us down from the cart and refused our offered coin, which I was glad of. He had spared Annalise's foot and brought us to safety, and if I had had to pay him every coin we had, it would have been worth every shilling, but that he did not want it, I took as the proof of the soft heart beneath his brash exterior and thanked him profusely. But when we got inside the inn, it seemed our fortune was out of favour again when we were told that the mail coach to London had departed just twenty minutes before. It seemed our luck was short-lived and moved in rhythms of ill fortune and despair, followed by the unexpected intervention of kindly folk. Without such kindness, we would not have even made it this far, and so I swallowed the self-pity at this news, enquired after the cost of a room for the night and accepted that we would have to figure out what mileage was left to us in the morning, once we had rested and seen to Annalise's foot. I didn't want to be hasty in purchasing our tickets, risking her injury deteriorating overnight and Annalise being rendered unfit for travel. So I checked the availability, which presently stood at two inside seats remaining and all of the outside ones, and considered we should be safe to delay until morning. I was only glad that they accepted us in without a gentleman's escort or cover story.

Perhaps passing trade was sparser in these parts and a paying customer, deemed a paying customer, I considered.

I declined all the usual offers we would be accustomed to taking for granted, such as supper this evening, breakfast in the morning, and attendance of maid at our disposal. We mightn't have had a choice in having to bed down for the night, but keeping the costs as low as possible was a necessary economy now. Money equalled mileage. And after today's misfortunes, we could see what perils walking such distances could equate to. And so we went straight to our room, the humblest of the inns' offerings, took another meal of our pie and cider, and fell quickly upon the bed in exhaustion.

WE WOKE TO THE INTERRUPTION of the maid, who had not been sent up to us in error as I first assumed, but to ask us to vacate our room if we were not staying another night, since we were over the hour of departure. The clock read a quarter past eleven, and I was surprised that we had slept so many hours without waking. It had been a long and taxing day; week, I corrected myself as we sat up in bed and told the maid we would be out directly.

'It's alright, we have plenty of time to get the coach. He said it leaves at five o'clock, didn't' he?' Annalise said, wiping her eyes and stretching into a yawn that drowned out the end of her sentence.

'Yes, I'm not concerned about that. I just hope the innkeeper won't charge us extra for our un-timeliness. Anyway, let's take a look at your ankle and see how it fares.'

She rolled back the coverlet and revealed an even nastier black pinch that had bubbled to a blister half the circumference of her ankle and an angry looking swelling to the side of her leg, making her ankle joint appear sunken beneath it.

'It looks like it's sprained,' she said, circling it with less fluidity than she had yesterday. 'But it is not terribly painful, just awfully tight.'

She tried at walking with my help, and though she was able, she was at best capable of a slow limp.'

'I don't know, Annalise, could you manage on it?'

'Yes, so long as I have your arm. It's not like we shall be walking much, only to and from the coach. We shall have to sit about a long while in the taproom until the coach comes, I suppose.'

'If you are sure. The problem shall be when we get off the other side. Perhaps, we should change tact. Maybe we should save a little money for another night's board and travel less mileage. I think we are much farther away than before and if we can get just a bit further on, we might be safe to pause for a bit. Spend our money on getting a message out for help, and boarding up to await rescue. That, or seeing if we might hitch any more rides like we managed yesterday, but without the calamity.'

'Let's go and look at the fares and see what our options are, shall we?'

So, we put on our clothes. Which were filthy, but dry at least, and would be mostly hidden beneath our cloaks anyway. Then made a quick effort to make as presentable as we could and packed up the dwindling portion of our pies. The cider was all gone now, so I refilled our bottle from the carafe of barley water, and we set off to make enquiries.

'Morning, ma'am,' we were greeted at the desk.

'Good morning. I wonder if we could settle our bill and see the fare list for the London-bound coach. There are still seats remaining, aren't there?'

'There are, ma'am.'

'Excellent.'

'If you'll take a seat in the parlour there, I'll just be a minute.'

'It's alright. We can wait.'

'All the same, if you'll oblige me, ma'am. I've a coach due in for Penzance, and I can't be in two places at once. If you have a seat and help yourself to a saucer of tea or coffee, I'll be with you just as soon as I might.'

'Very well,' I shrugged and took the door he gestured to. 'Most irregular,' I said to Annalise, sitting her down on the sofa and pouring us both some coffee from the side table.

'Well, we're hardly in a rush, and I could do with a coffee. It seems they need more staff here. Perhaps we should enquire?'

'Not here. It's too close. But the next place we shall make enquiries, to be sure. A week or so should suffice to have our message relayed.'

'Oh, I wouldn't worry about that, though I own I would have taken you for a servant and let you empty my chamber pot—'

We both started and looked to the door at this curt interruption.

'Oh, how the mighty fall...'

'You cannot be serious,' I said agog at the sight of Mariella poised in the doorway with one of those satisfied twists to her grin. The shock caught me entirely off guard, and I was rendered speechless for just long enough for her to step into the room and close the door behind her. It was the confusion on Annalise's face as she looked between the two of us in utter bewilderment, that shook me back into the present.

I stood up. 'What the devil are you doing here?'

'Well, I *was* looking for Giles, but it seems for all his games of hide and seek, he shall come to me now, thanks to you.'

'Annalise, we're going. Now!' I said, and she got quickly to her feet despite her injury, as I barged Mariella out of the way and gripped the door handle.

'Oh, you might not want to do that. You see, the constable has instructions to take you directly to the town lock-up should you try to make a dash. See for yourself.' She gestured to the window, and Annalise limped over to it and nodded at me.

I released the handle and went over to join her, and indeed, there were officials speaking to the innkeeper outside and a jailkeeper's wagon stationed right behind them.

'What the fuck have you done, Mariella?' I said, marching towards her, but then I saw the panic in Annalise's eyes and held back. What was the use in attacking her and trying to flee when Annalise could only hobble her way along and we would likely end up caught and heaved into the back of that barred carriage?

'Oh, it's not under my instruction, so I'm afraid I cannot take the credit for your apprehension. It seems your husband has sent a circular out to all the local posting inns to keep a watch out for you. The fugitive madwoman, I am informed,' she flapped about a scrap of paper, and I snatched it from her hand.

Upon it was the newspaper cut out of my image and a warning notice stating much of what Nancy had appraised us of yesterday morning. 'More of your cousin's desperate fictions,' I said, screwing it up in my palm and tossing it to the grate.

Mariella shrugged, 'Well, you are a slippery little fish, aren't you, sending him all about the country looking for you. Quite the run around you have given him, all the way down to these primitive parts of the country.'

'I sent him nowhere.—Wait, do you think *I* led him here?'

'Well, you are here, aren't you?'

I laughed. 'Yes, because he dragged me here all the way from Cambridgeshire. —You don't know, do you? You think he is here in pursuit of me. Oh, how famous!'

This put her more than a little out of countenance, so I made the most of the pause before asking, 'How long exactly since you last saw your cousin, Mariella?'

'What does it matter? He will be here any moment and I shall see him presently.'

'Not for long. You know he plans to take me to the Continent, I assume.' She needed to make no answer. It was written across her face. 'Yes, he brought me all the way to Falmouth to spirit me off onto a sailing ship. *That* is why we are here. We should have already been on our way were it not for the ship failing and for me escaping him.'

'Nonsense.'

'Oh, you mean he didn't bid you farewell or let you in on his cunning plans this time? Well, you can ask him for yourself when he arrives. Or...you could let us go before that happens and have him all to yourself? A happy reunion.'

'You *are* desperate if you think you can bend me to your will.'

'Why not, if our wills are complimentary? If I am here when he arrives, you won't see him again. We'll be crossing the high seas, and you will be stuck here without him. It's not what either of us want, is it?'

'You're wasting your efforts. You are worth more to me as a capture this time, Eleanor. I haven't spent months on the road for nothing. You know, it's funny. I was about to give up. The trail went cold three days ago and I've been stuck in this wretched place, wondering if it was time to turn back. And then this morning, I am sitting at breakfast, and what do I hear, but a conversation between the servants saying that they are sure the fugitives are under their very roof. No—you are a gift horse this time. I mean to put right my past errors in letting you flee and return you to him. Imagine how pleased he shall be with me when I deliver you up.'

'So that's it; you did not reap the rewards of helping me flee from Beaulieu? He punished you for it, did he? And you think this will settle things between you. What a simple fool you are. Don't you see, he cares not a fig about you, Mariella.'

'He is angry with me. Who can blame him with what a fool you have made of him.'

'And you do not see the fool he has made of you? How he has ill-used you. Abandoned you, it seems, and you think he shan't abandon you now he will finally have what he wants?'

'If he has what he wants, he shall settle, grow bored of you. All this cat-and-mouse chasing is delaying the inevitable. The sooner he has you back in your place, the sooner he will realise what a wasted effort you are.'

'Perhaps, but not here. Can you bear for him to disappear overseas again?'

'He shan't go now you are captured and wanted by the law. Where would you flee to? Even your parents could do nothing for you.'

'He has no choice. Look,' I pressed the fabric of my dress flat against my bump and her face was a picture of horror. 'Yes, I shall bear another man's child, and you think he shall stay in England for the world to know it?'

'But—'

'Yes, you are not the only one full of surprises. So you see, if we go, we shall be gone a *very* long time.'

'Then I shall accompany you. I'm sick of these cold, dreary shores anyhow.'

'I shall forbid it.'

She laughed at this. 'As if you are in a position to negotiate anything. He will be as mad as fire with you. You think he shall have a care for your demands?'

'Well, it's simple. He gave me an ultimatum; travel with him or be committed to the madhouse. Unless you get us out of here before he arrives, on my word, I shall choose the madhouse if he does not forbid your going.

–Yes, I am serious. You may count upon it. Now, are you going to get us out, or prepare to bid farewell to him?'

There was a moment of uncertainty in her expression, as though she was trying to calculate the less of evils, but it was too late.

The door opened, and there he was.

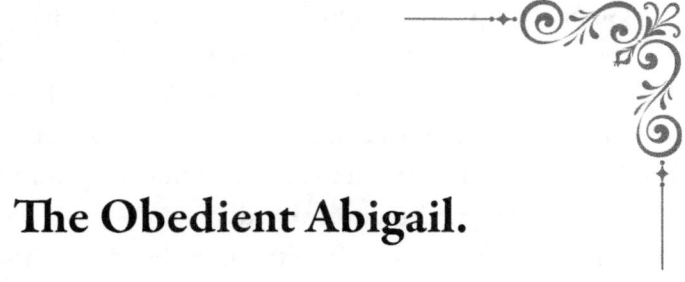

The Obedient Abigail.

February 1822. - Eleanor.

I had expected to be seized from the place in irons and loaded instantly into the constable's wagon, and had braced myself for such a scene. But he was alone and came into the room calmly, surprised only by the sight of Mariella who rushed instantly over to greet him. He brushed her off, came directly towards me and without uttering a word, delivered me the swiftest backhander, which caused Annalise to cry out in despair.

'I'm alright,' I said to her, holding my cheek, but she was weeping hysterically. The blow had not surprised me, only perhaps the candidness with which it was dealt.

'Well, that was long overdue,' Mariella said, biting down on her lip to prevent her grin from spreading.

He ignored her and stepped me back against the wall. 'This is your last chance.'

'For what? To pretend to obey you, Giles. To pretend to be a good wife. To pretend to love you—'

'Eleanor!' Annalise cried, and I heeded her warning seeing her distress.

'I'm not coming with you, Giles,' I said more evenly. 'It's time you understood it. Do what you will. Send me to the madhouse. Call the constables in to arrest me. I don't care anymore. – Don't you see, any of those options equal the misery of your company. They are no better. No worse. That's how much I despise you.'

'Fine. You shall have it your way. It seems you are long overdue a lesson in obedience, and if I shan't deliver it, to be sure, I shall see that it is delivered. —Mariella, call the constable in and bid the innkeeper send for Dr Schmidt at the Asylum,' he said.

'Go on, cats-paw, do as bid!' I said, watching her jump to his command.

He came closer now and I braced myself for another blow. But he only leaned in close to my face, and said, 'You foolish girl. What have you condemned your unborn child to? —Ah constable, yes, it is indeed them. This is the maid who started the fire, and this is my unfortunate wife who I shall be having committed this very day.'

'And this is my abusive, incestuous husband who holds me against my will. But you shan't bother acting upon that, shall you?' I snarled at the contemptuous-looking fellow who marched straight over to Annalise and said, 'You are under arrest. Will you go willingly?'

'What? She hasn't done anything. It was me who started the fire at the hotel.' I sprang across the room and stood in front of her. 'She had nothing to do with it.'

'Eleanor—'

'No, Tulley, you shan't try to protect me anymore. Your duty is done. Now constable, will you take me directly to the Magistrate so I can sign my confession?'

He looked blankly at Giles.

'Don't let her get away with anymore tomfoolery, constable. She did not start the fire. It wasn't even in her room. It was the maid.'

'You weren't even there, Giles, so what good is your testimony? Do you accept the testimony of an absent party or the sworn oath I am willing to make in confession, Constable?'

'She is delusional like I told you. I have a reliable witness constable. He is on his way presently,' Giles told him.

'What do you say, girl?' He turned to Annalise, who shrunk from the question, not knowing what to answer.

'She will try to protect her mistress, of course, but it is needless now, Tulley. Don't you see? I am ready to confess. For you see, my defence to the crime shall be to plead my husband's coercion, and he shall have to answer the charge.'

'Well, if you hadn't just confessed your husband's absence, ma'am, then perhaps it might have carried. But that shan't stand if he wasn't there. So I shall ask you one more time and take you at that answer, was it you or the maid that started the fire?'

'Me!' Annalise and I shouted out in unison.

'Right, miss. You shall go with me now,' the constable said to Annalise, and I blocked his path.

'No. She is lying. I am willing to swear it. Take me to the Magistrate at once and let him decide it. The matter is in strenuous dispute and must be decided by the Magistrate's judgement. Unless, of course, you mean to act above your station, constable?'

'Right, I'm bringing you both in.'

'Let's not be hasty, constable,' Giles cut in. 'If you would, give me a moment to speak privately with my wife.'

'Two minutes, sir, and we shall be on our way.'

'Are you ready to strike a bargain yet?' he said to me as soon as he was gone. 'Or would you rather the maid be taken to gaol, and you be committed to the asylum?'

I glanced at Annalise trembling in hysterics and looked back at him. 'That depends...'

Mariella sniggered, and I shot her a warning glare. 'If you are ready to meet my terms, I will go with you.'

'Name them.'

'First and foremost, *she* is not to travel with us, nor will she have word on where we are destined for,' I said, casting a spiteful glare in Mariella's direction that was powerful enough to wipe the smirk off of her face.

'Done,' he replied, and Mariella started up in protest, to which he stretched out a palm towards her, 'not now, Mary.'

'And all charges shall be dropped against my maid and she shall be given a choice to come with us, or be conveyed home upon the mail coach today.'

'Eleanor?' Annalise said as if mishearing me.

'Is that all?'

I nodded.

'Tulley, what shall it be?' he asked her, and she stopped crying long enough to answer. 'I shall come.'

'Right then. You have a bargain. We sail tomorrow morning.'

I DON'T KNOW WHAT MEANS of bribery or negotiation he employed, but the constable never returned, and we were taken instantly by coach to some obscure establishment. We were we were escorted to what appeared to be some lodging house by Fletcher and Digby, who proceeded to bid us straight to a room within them, surprisingly, together. But no fire was lit in it, and the window had been hatched with an additional batten of timber across it to prevent it from being opened. It was a low-seeming place with well-worn furnishings and a generally drab appearance, but to my surprise, there were two beds in it. I led Annalise straight over to one to prop up her leg.

'Annalise, you do not have to come, you know.'

'How can you say that?'

I sat on the bed beside her. 'Because I cannot bear to think of all the misery that has befallen you because of me. All the misery that shall yet come to pass, if you go with us.'

'And do you think of what misery I shall suffer if I never see you again? What if he never brings you back?'

'Of course I do. I...I just want you to have a choice.'

'Well, I don't, alright. My heart shall be broken whether I come and watch you reduced to his tyranny, or whether I stay and suffer the grief of our separation.'

My voice faltered as the sobs gathered in my throat. 'I know, and I am so sorry for the whole.'

'Len, please don't give up. Not now. After all we have been through, for what? Is it all to be for nothing?'

I could no longer restrain my tears. 'I don't know. I just don't know anymore. How can I fight this, Annalise?'

'We will endure it together. Look for a way out. Who knows what opportunities may yet come to pass when we are not expecting it.'

'Oh, Annalise, we could not even escape from Cornwall, and that was with the help of kindly strangers. How will we find our way back from the Continent even if we get another chance to flee? He shan't give me money or valuable things, especially now we have shown our hand. Look, we are not even trusted with a candle, a fire, or an opening window.'

'He can't keep us so captive on a ship amongst other passengers.'

'No, but where are we to go on a ship but the depths of the sea?'

'Nowhere, I suppose. But who knows once we get off of it?'

I shrugged. 'That reminds me, take this and keep it hidden on you, alright.' I bent down and took the remainder of our money from my boot and passed it into her hands. 'He does not know I have it, so he shan't know to look for it.'

She tucked it into her own boot.

'How is your foot now?'

'Not so bad, in the scheme of things. What about your arm?'

'I haven't looked. It feels no worse. Oh, Annalise, what are we to do?'

'I don't know, Len, but we are together at least, and for now, that shall have to be enough.'

WE LAY HEAPED UPON the bed holding each other in the candleless room. Rueing all the wrong decisions we had made yesterday that had led us to that inn. But what good was it to lament what was already beyond alteration? We had made a try for it, but it seemed futile now to even conceive of another attempt. Tomorrow we would be shipped out of our homeland, perhaps never to return, for all we knew. It was not in our power to decide. Anything.

A point made manifest when Giles entered the room ordering a bath to be drawn and the fire lit.

'Oh, so we are not expected to freeze to death in darkness, after all, Tulley. Look at that! I own I was starting to think this place very similar to the gaol,' I said, crossing the room to stand by the fire Fletcher had lit, pressing my palms out to the heat.

'Tulley, go next door and ask Digby for access to your mistresses' portmanteau. Get her bedclothes out for tonight and something respectable for tomorrow,' Giles said, ignoring my comments. It was all I had left now, the possibility of making my company so irksome that he would not want to be about me. I watched Annalise hobble off out of the room and wanted to forbid it. She needed rest, not to be put to work with her ankle so awful sore. But I could not say anything, for if I did, he would surely work her harder just to wield his long-sought power over me. She was my weakness, and now he knew it. That's why he had permitted her to remain, to be sure of some means of leverage over me. For without her, I might very well have been willing to throw myself overboard into the depths of the sea, or take flight from the window of this very room if the alternative was to remain alone with him. But all the while I had her, I had a reason to go on...and he wanted me to go on, like a long-suffering bondservant.

'Now, before your bath, I shall send down for some tea and make arrangements for dinner. Will you have the mutton stew or a plate of cold cuts for your meal?'

'What a menu from which to choose. I mean, this is a low kind of place, to be sure, but I suppose I should be grateful that it is marginally better than gaol rations. I shall have neither, I thank you. But...I do see some merit in this new low style, Giles. It seems more honest...more fitting to your rank. —Go on, strike me again. I shall look just the respectable part boarding the ship tomorrow black and blue, respectable enough for your type in any case.'

He cast me a piercing arctic stare, and I was certain it was taking all his restraint to contain the affliction of my insults. For I knew his pride was his greatest weakness, and it was easy to get a rise from one so puffed up with such a curious mix of hauteur and veiled insecurity. But whatever his next move was to be, it was startlingly interrupted by a flustered-looking Digby coming into the room. At first, I felt hopeful that Annalise had caused some difficulty, broke free somehow and alerted someone in the building. For I was sure this was a boarding house full of apartments. There would surely be others about. But when Giles said in irritated accents, 'What is it, Digby?'

He replied. 'You're wanted downstairs, sir.'

'Can it wait?'

He shook his head and, giving him a widening glance to indicate the importance of his message, yet clearly not wishing to relay it in my presence, said, 'It cannot, sir.'

'Fletcher,' Giles said, casting his eyes over to me, 'Keep things in order,' and he walked out the room with a parting glance in my direction, which seemed both warning and statement that we had unfinished business.

I took the opportunity offered. What had I to lose in the trying at this point? 'Fletcher,' I said in almost a whisper until he turned about from placing more buckets to boil over the fireplace.

'I'm not to converse with you, misses,'

'Fine. Then I shall do the talking.' I walked over to him until he began to edge back from me. 'Fletcher, I need your help—'

'I can't help you, misses.'

'Yes, you can.'

'You almost cost me my place yesterday. Please, don't talk to me.'

'What if I gave you a better job? One with not just thrice the pay you are accustomed to, but kinder work, more comfort in your lodgings, respect? I know you are not a wicked man Fletcher, not like that other brute or my husband. You must have seen by now what a bad man he is. Hmm?'

'I can't help you. I'm sorry—'

'You must know I come from a very wealthy family, Fletcher. Everything I offer you shall be yours in earnest if you find a way to help me get back home. Your reward for saving me shall be vast.'

'I can't misses. You don't understand.'

'What? That you seem to me the sort of fellow who would rather earn his crust by doing good over evil. I can see that, Fletcher. I see you are not the felon you are painted to be. No more than I am.'

'It makes no difference. We are cast our lot in this, whether we like it or not.'

'So if it's not the money, then what is it? What hold does he have over you?'

He baulked at this, and I sensed I was on to something.

'One last job Fletcher and you shall be set up comfortably enough to never need work for a scoundrel like him again. Never need work for *anyone* again. If you get me to safety, I can make that happen. I shall swear it now, put my name to it upon paper; a binding contract—'

'It's no use, misses, please. If I could help you, I would. But it's more than my life is worth.'

It was me that faltered now. 'Fletcher, please, name your price...don't you see you are as good as condemning me to death helping him to imprison me like this? Then there is my unborn child. Would you have an innocent suffer?'

'Stop!' he said more brusquely this time. 'Stop talkin,' he pressed his huge palms to his temples and gripped his head, and then I did stop because footsteps were once again upon the stairs. We stood apart, he going back to the fire and me over to the window.

Annalise came in first with a pile of folded clothing in her arms and her limp still lagging her steps as she crossed the room to put them down.

'You can get lost,' I said to Digby as he came in after her and closed the door behind him.

'I have orders to keep an eye on you, ma'am,' he said, ignoring me.

I marched right up to him, 'You shall know your place and leave my bedchamber this instant. You think I shall take insolence from a servant? Now get out of here at once!' I opened the door for him. Unlike Fletcher, I could tell there was not a good bone in Digby's body. He took a twisted sense of enjoyment and inflated self-importance in these duties. It was no wonder he and Giles had found good company.

'I shall be just outside the door Fletcher,' he said reluctantly, and as he stepped outside, I slammed it shut.

'What happened? Are you alright?' I asked Annalise.

'Yes, I'm fine, miss,' she said, frowning in Fletcher's direction.

I did not intend to mind my speech with him anymore. He might be either unwilling, or, perhaps in some way that was obscure to me, unable to help, but I did not think he took the same veneration in his duties as the Valet did. 'It's alright. He shan't report on us,' I said low.

'That woman is back,' she barely hissed the words.

'What? Mariella?'

She nodded and proceeded to lay out clothes upon the bed.

'Are you certain?'

'I heard her shouting at the bottom of the stairwell, and he rushed down to deal with her.'

'Well, she will at least keep him distracted, if nothing else. How is your foot?'

'It's alright.'

'You are a terrible liar. Sit down, rest whilst you may,' I told her and began to organise the clothes she had started to set out. And just as I supposed, Fletcher ignored us entirely, our whispering and movements, sloshing buckets of hot water into the tub. Moving loudly and lubberly across the boards. If I didn't know better, I might have guessed that he was doing it on purpose to mask the low rumble of our voices.

It did not last long. Giles returned faster than I expected or hoped and, once the bath was full, dismissed Fletcher from the room and said to Annalise: 'Time for your mistress's bath now, Tulley.'

'I don't want a bath.'

'Well, that's a pity because you *need* a bath. Look at the state of you.'

'As I said, Giles, I was going for a more honest look, so we appeared a better match on our sailing tomorrow.'

'You *shall* have a bath, my dear. Now, if you oblige me on this offer, Tulley shall tend you. If you do not, I shall see to it myself.'

'Fine,' I said, getting up from the chair. 'Tulley, if you will be so good,' I said and waited while she opened the dressing screen where it had been folded into a corner.'

'No need for that, Tulley, nothing I haven't seen before,' he said, pulling the chair over to get a better view and sinking comfortably into it.

I felt my flesh creep beneath his gaze as she undressed me, even though I kept my back to him. She was as conscious of it as I was, as she fumbled nervously with tasks that were as good as second nature to her now. She did her best to make quick work of it, for both our sakes. But between the impediment of her limp, my wounded arm that looked quite frightfully angry when she unwrapped it, and the thick grime upon my skin that took much effort to disperse, it seemed like a very contracted affair.

I did not look at him through the whole, but when I stood to get out, I caught him gazing coolly across her shoulder and once she had bound me in bathing sheets and led me to the fire, he got up and said, 'Well Tulley, you may choose something for yourself from your mistress's wardrobe and use her water, once you have dressed her for bed.

She glared at me, bewildered.

'Tulley?'

'Yes, yes, of course, sir.'

'Thank you, *sir*, is the correct way to respond,' he grinned.

'Thank you, sir. You are very generous,' she said and dropped a curtsey.

Then he walked over to me and lowered himself to sniff me. 'Much better, good work Tulley. Make sure you reward yourself with the finest dress, won't you?'

She nodded. 'Yes, thank you, sir.'

I was close to leaning into the fire to grab a hot coal with my bare hands and launch it at his head. But I looked at Annalise and knew she could bear no more and simply turned away from the sight of him.

'Now, if you are not to go to dinner, my dear, I shall see you once I return from mine. Set up the screen before the bath. Digby shall keep watch until I return.'

'You cannot expect her to bathe in the presence of a male servant!' I protested.

'Can't I? Tulley, what do you say to that? Have you a problem putting up the screen and taking your bath behind it?'

She swallowed. 'No, sir.'

'Forgive him, Tulley. He has no understanding of the proper way things are done in good society.'

'Well, perhaps you might learn a thing or two from the obliging manners of your maid, my dear, since that statement seems to apply as much to you of late.'

HE WAS NOT LONG IN returning, and by the time he had, we were both finished with this ritual that perhaps should have made us feel better, to be clean and fresh, and our bones warmed through. And yet it seemed it had the effect of making us both feel dirtier, instead.

I could not even apologise to Annalise for what she had endured. Digby had not permitted above a whisper to pass between us, instructed Annalise to convey everything through him, and forbade her reply directly to me. And when I began spitting insults at him, he reminded me that Fletcher was outside the door and my husband only in the room beside it. He did at least heed my instruction to turn his chair around and sit back-facing the bathing screen.

It seemed this was to be the preferred way to control me now. Through her. Where I would protest and give trouble, they could rely on the fact that she would not, and, in a roundabout way, achieve the same ends. I saw no way out of this predicament either and began to feel more desolate than my heart could bear at the cruelty of this new way of life that had been imposed upon us.

When it was time for the shift swap and Giles came back in, Annalise was dressed and clearing up the wet linens and I was doing my best to stifle the desolate tears that kept building in my eyes. If it wasn't for the fact that I was determined not to cry in Digby's presence, I would not have been able to prevent them.

'Ah, much better. Digby, send Fletcher in to get rid of this bathing tub, will you. Well, Tulley, how well you look. What an excellent choice of dress. It suits you very nicely,' he said, then cocked his ear to await her reply.

'Thank you, sir,' she said evenly.

'Such excellent manners. Now, Tulley, if you are quite finished, you may go next door and take some supper with Digby, and then you are to tend Miss Craythorne and make her ready for bed.'

I sat up instantly at this offence. 'Why is *she* here? We had a bargain!' I could not give away the fact that Annalise had already told me of her arrival.

'And I shall keep to it. I agreed that she is not to go with us, and she shan't, but we do not depart until tomorrow.'

'Now, who is bending the terms? And where is Miss Craythornes own maidservant? Nay, it does not signify. I will not be inconvenienced on her account. Tulley, you will stay at my bedside! She can go to the devil for assistance!'

Annalise looked uncomfortably between us.

'Tulley, you will find Miss Craythorne is expecting you after your supper. Now if you would be as good,'

'Don't—'

'Miss,' Annalise cut in with a warning glare. 'It is no trouble at all. I shan't be long. Then I will come right back to put you to bed.'

'No need to rush back, Tulley. I shall take care of your mistress. Now, you go and have some food. You must be hungry.'

My heart sank as I watched her go. The thought of her being alone with Mariella without an accurate idea of her company, made me anxious. She was not a stranger to my dislike of that despicable creature, and she had seen enough of her character this morning to grasp something of her measure, but she knew only the half of it. I had never ventured to give her the whole of our sordid past. She understood that Mariella had some warped tendre for my husband and that she had made herself an interference in our marriage, but she did not know what had passed between the both of us in those early days of our acquaintance. The fear rose in me at the idea of Mariella giving up such sordid secrets.'

'My dear, you needn't be so anxious, is everything well?'

'Don't you dare insult me with such nonsensical questions: Bringing that reprehensible cousin of yours back between us and then the nerve to put my staff at her disposal! Is this how it is to be, Giles?'

'No. As I said, we will be gone in the morning, and she will be no more in your sight, I promise you.'

I wished *he* would be no more in my sight. 'Why didn't you just marry her, Giles, and put us all out of our misery?' I said then, thinking more aloud than in expectation of an answer.

'My cousin? I could have no further wish. You have seen yourself: she is even madder than you!' He laughed a little at this, and I glowered at him.

'I do not forget how madly you have stooped to entrap me into going with you, sir, so forgive me for noticing that you seem very well suited to me!'

I saw his colour rise and a shift in his eyes before he sat down in the chair and recomposed himself, lit a cigar from the candle. 'I know you do not share my optimism, but I think in time, we will learn to get along.'

'Oh indeed, famously, I'm sure! There is nothing quite so endearing as to have your husband blackmail you and keep you imprisoned in a bid to win your heart.'

'You think it is your heart I am after?' He puffed out a cloud of smoke that made me cough.

'I don't know. What *are* you after, Giles?'

'Your submission shall suffice for now, and who knows, in time, you may find yourself agreeable.'

'To what precisely, kidnap, blackmail—?'

'To fulfilling your wifely obligations.' He puffed out a plume of thick smoke. 'Now take off your shift.'

'What?'

'You heard me. It's about time you proved worthy of so much effort.'

'But—'

'Take it off, or I shall tear it off.'

'Giles, please—'

'Oh, now you remember your manners.'

'I apologise, alright. Let me ready for dinner. I think I am hungry now.'

He smiled. 'This could be fun,' he said, amusement dancing in his eyes. He stubbed out his cigar on the base of the candlestick holder. 'Tell me, what should you prefer? I have such a cock-stand on I shall have to do something with it before we retire to bed.'

'Giles, please.'

'Well, if it shan't be you, I shall have to prevail upon your Abigail to oblige me. She seems most cooperative and knows her place perfectly well. I don't think she will deny me.'

'What?'

'I'm generously minded, so I shall permit you the choice: Your cunt... or hers?'

I said nothing but stood up and took off my shift, trying to hide my tears. I had expected this to be a price I would have to pay in due course, but Annalise? I lay down on the bed and waited.

A Restless Night.

February 1822. - Eleanor.

'Len, are you asleep?' It was Annalise. 'Len,' she shook me gently by the arm, but I dared not open my eyes and let her see the shame in them. Even all the tears that had fallen would not have washed it away. So I kept them closed and murmured, 'What?'

'Len, I have a supper tray for you. Your husband said you had an appetite now.'

'Please don't call him that.'

'Sorry. I don't know what else to call him?'

'The devil...'

'Len, are you alright?'

'Yes, yes, forgive me. I'm so tired; I think it has all caught up with me.'

'I know. But will you at least take a little something before bed? It's been days since we have had a proper meal, and you have the child to think of.'

'I have no appetite. I shall make up for it at breakfast, I promise. But for now, I need to sleep.'

'If you are sure.'

'Thank you.'

'Well, it appears I am permitted to bed in with you tonight. That horrible madam refuses to let him stay with you, so that is something.

It would have been if it was not already too late to be spared, and had her presence not made me feel more conscious of my ill-used body. There was never a night I would not jump at being curled up in her arms, but tonight, I could not even bear her in the bed beside me, lying within the sheets where he had been.

'Len?'

'Sorry, Annalise. I fear I am near to exhaustion. Yes, take the other bed. It's safer than us risking being discovered bunking in together. I'm surprised we are permitted to even go to bed without a watchman.'

'Well, Fletcher is outside the door.'

Perhaps, I would have seen this as an opportunity given the complaisance of his manner earlier, but I had no fight left in me after that violating episode. And when she bent down to kiss me goodnight, I made it brief and had to stop myself from flinching away, for fear that she may taste the stench of his kisses there.

WHEN I WOKE UP IN THE night from a nightmare, almost as shocking as my waking reality, I sat up and called out to her. 'Annalise, Annalise, are you asleep?' But no reply came, so I got up and pulled back the curtain to see my way over to her bed. But it was dark outside and it made little difference, so I went carefully about the place until I found it and padded the mattress with my palms to find she was not in it. Then the panic set in fast and brought me sharply to my senses. *Please, no.* I scrambled up and found my clothes, making a poor attempt at fixing them before running out to the hall and wrapping at the door.

When I found it unlocked, I opened it and stepped inside, uninvited, and found Annalise sat down on a stool, tears in her eyes and mild amusement in Mariella's. 'What have you done to her?' I screamed, but I lunged for her before she could answer me. This reactionary attack was as much a surprise to me, as I felt my hands tangle in her hair and wrestle her down to the ground. 'You hateful creature,' I bellowed in her face as she tried to paw herself away from me. But she was not going to escape justice this time. I shook her, pulled at her, hit her, and entirely lost myself in a violence so hateful I did not know myself. And then there was blood all over my hands and I thought perhaps I might murder her, and for a moment, I was sure it would be worth it. If I could send both she and Giles to their graves, it would be worth every moment in a prison cell to know they were no more. But Annalise's hysteric pleas reached me through the mist of rage. Mariella's, I had grown quite immune to, as she wriggled and fought to free herself of my grip, to no avail. But in the end, Giles pulled me off her, seeming to come out of nowhere and lifting me from on top of her whilst I still kicked and screamed with a strength that seemed beyond my usual power.

'What the devil has come over you?' Giles demanded, setting me down but keeping a guarded arm across me to keep me away from his cousin. She was scrambling up from the floor, blood running from her nose, her hair wild and on end, cursing me more bravely than she had in Giles's absence.

'She is insane!' She cried. 'Look what she has done to me!' she said, spitting out a mouthful of blood.

'Oh, not nearly as much as I wish to, for you are still breathing!' I retorted, and was shocked to see some unfamiliar fellow and a couple of servants gathered into the room now, staring on agog.

'Is everything alright, milord?' He said to Giles in a West Country accent that told me he was another resident, or the landlord, perhaps.

'Yes sir, I thank you. I apologise for waking you at this hour. My wife is not herself. You will forgive us. If there are damages to your property, my man will settle it between you, you may rest assured.'

He eyed me dubiously as he said. 'Not at all, sir, not at all. Agnes, go call on Mrs Munday to tend to miss here, she's injured nasty,' he said, gesturing at Mariella, and I wanted to tell him not to trouble himself but thought better of it.

When Giles ordered me to leave, instructing Annalise to put me to bed and keep me to my room the rest of the night, I wanted to tell him there was no need, for I wished to lock the door and throw away the key. But I said nothing more and accepted her escort back to our chamber.

'Annalise, Annalise, what did they do to you?'

'Who?'

'Any of them, Giles, Mariella?'

'Nothing. It was you that was violent, Len. What possessed you?'

'I thought they had harmed you, Annalise, that's what.'

'No.'

'Then why were you sobbing when I came in? What were you even doing there in the middle of the night?'

She paused a moment, 'There was an altercation. It frightened me.'

'What happened?'

'I don't rightly know. Only that I woke up to find Fletcher standing over me in the bed, and it startled me. So I asked him what he was doing and he said I was to be quiet and not make a sound, that everyone was to sleep now, and so the going was good. He had tossed the key to the room into the fireplace, and the door would remain unlocked. I should wake you up and make ready to sneak out. He was not going to wait about for the fallout of it all, but he said; you were not to forget your promise, a binding contract.'

'So why didn't you wake me, Annalise, for god's sake?'

'I tried to, but before I could rouse you, I heard noises in the corridor and thought Fletcher was giving me some sort of signal or something, but then the door swung open, and it was Giles, checking that we were here.'

'He knew?'

'I don't know. All I know is that I was ushered into their apartments and told to be quiet. But then I saw Digby marching Fletcher out with a pistol pressed to his head, and I panicked. I grew hysterical at the fright of it.'

'Did he fire it?'

'I don't know. I'm sure we would have heard it if he had.'

'Oh god, this is all my fault. I shouldn't have asked him to help us.'

'You asked him to?'

'Yes. He refused. But I could tell he wanted to. He must have changed his mind. We must go out and try to tell someone he is being held at gunpoint, have the constable called. You say the door cannot be locked?'

'I'm not going out there, Len.'

'Why?'

'Because your husband turned and said to me, "See how I deal with disobedient servants. Take note, Tulley," she started crying again.

'Bastard,' I should have tossed the hot coal at his head earlier as I was minded to.'

'Stop, Len! All this violence! It's too much...'

'I'm sorry. I'm sorry, Annalise.' I reached out to her, and she pulled away. 'What?'

'You are covered in blood,' she said and stood up, lit another candle from her own, poured some water into the basin and threw a towel down beside it.

I looked at my hands and went over to it and washed them. My heart was still pounding, and my head racing to take all of this in. I dried off my hands, went over to her and touched her lightly on the shoulder. 'Please stop crying,' I said to her gently as she busied herself about the room.

'I am not anymore,' she said curtly and carried on fidgeting around with things until I went to her, took the clothes she was folding from her hands and sat her down.

'I am so very sorry to have behaved so appallingly in your presence,' I told her, wiping the tears from her streaming cheeks. She shrunk away from me. 'Good god Annalise, I hope you are not frightened of me!'

'I am not frightened of you, Eleanor, I just.'

'What, what else happened, Annalise? I know you are holding something back from me?'

'There's nothing.'

'Balderdash! I know you, Annalise, and you are not being honest with me.'

'And have you been with me?'

'What?'

'It was what *she* told me, Len, that has made me weep, and whilst I like her no better than you do, she did not deserve—'

'What did she say to you, Annalise?'

'You already know, don't you?'

I swallowed a forming lump in my throat. 'She told you we were once lovers?'

'It is true then.'

'Not precisely, but I own much passed between us.'

'You said I was the first—'

'Oh, Annalise, you are! Nothing tender ever existed betwixt me and that creature! She was cunning and forward, filled my head with many outrageous ideas and introduced so much vulgarity into my mind when I was just an innocent. I own I wished I had seen her character then for what it truly was, but she was a wolf in sheep's clothing. I was foolish, naive... and I went along with it, for a while.'

'Then why keep it from me? I thought there were to be no more secrets between us after—'

I was the one shedding tears now. 'Because I was ashamed. Ashamed of what I let her do to me. What I allowed her to awaken in me, despite the lack of feeling between us. I own she did not precisely force me, but she compelled me greatly to go along with much I did not want to.'

'She said you married her cousin so the two of you could be free together, but she did not love you. It is to her cousin her affections are tied, and now you are bitter with her for abandoning you to him.'

I could hardly believe my ears. 'Annalise, I married her cousin because he was the only one who would take me in my condition, or at least the condition they encouraged me to believe myself to be in. It was her that insisted on the scheme of us being free by it and me that refused it! How ill she has turned this all against me! Oh, what, you believe her words over mine?'

'No. Of course not.'

'Then what?'

'She said I was a poor substitute for you to console yourself with the loss of her.' She broke off into tears again and I embraced her despite her reluctance.

'Oh, Annalise, please tell me she does not know about us?'

She looked up aghast. 'I did not tell her, but she knows alright!'

'Then she will tell him! Oh my, it cannot answer. He will not stop tormenting us if he understands the true nature of our feelings. We must get dressed and try to make another run whilst they are all distracted.

'No. You might be willing to see yourself committed to the asylum, but I am not.'

'But you said yourself, Digby is with Fletcher, Mariella is injured, and Giles, between us, we could manage to overthrow him—'

'And what if he has a pistol too? What then?'

'I don't know.'

'Len, we tried in better circumstances than this and failed. We will not get as far as the end of the street. And if we do, we are known as fugitives now. You have just been seen thumping the lights out of her, and I am wanted for Arson.'

'You are right. I know you are right.'

She kissed me then, so ardently it suspended it all; the panic, the anger, the fear, and I felt instantly a reprieve from it all. The self-disgust at my earlier violation seemed to wane now in the presence of her much-needed comfort. I loved this woman so much it had turned me so soft I could melt at a smile, a touch, a gentle kiss. I would not be separated from her, whatever the price, however dire the consequence, she was worth the paying.

We put a chair across the door and crawled into bed together. She was determined to be intimate, so I yielded to her bidding and pleasured her quickly. Then I made love to her at length, despite my reluctance to give away the taint of him, despite the risk of being discovered at any moment. For I could tell how much she needed my assurance, and I wanted so much for her to understand that those poisonous words spoken to her were not true. That she was, as she had always been: the singular love of my life.

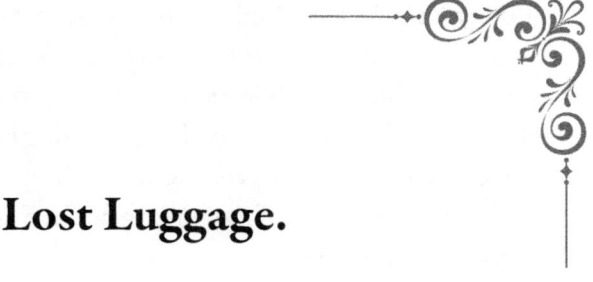

Lost Luggage.

February 1822. - Eleanor.

I awoke to the sun streaming in through the open drapes and blinking against it, turned to see Annalise sleeping next to me in the bed. I searched the room for the clock and sighed.

'Annalise.' I rocked her gently. 'Annalise, we must get up quickly,' I said as she held a hand up to her eyes to shield them from the brightness.

'What time is it?' She asked, rolling over.

'It is a quarter past seven. But you are in my bed, and someone may come in—might have already been in—to check on us and seen you here with me.'

She staggered over to her own bed, sat upon it and sunk her head into her hands.

'I feel the same. It's as though no amount of sleep could adequately prepare me for a day like the one that awaits us.'

She nodded her agreement. 'To be sure.'

'Well, we better make ready. I don't know what time we are to sail, but I'm sure he means to be prompt and avoid any further risk of us trying to escape at the last.

'Len lay back down. Hold me just a moment longer, will you?'

'Alright, five minutes,' I said, reclined back against the pillow, and offered her my outstretched arm to crawl into.

'Have you felt the child move this morning?'

'Yes,' I told her after assuring her several times last night that neither the child nor I had been injured in the scuffle. On that head, Mariella had been the one to come off worst for wear.

'Do you think he will ever bring you home?'

'I don't know,' I answered, disconcerted by her line of questioning and how out of kilter she seemed this morning. I knew it was a hard day ahead, had been a terrible night, but the weight of her misery was difficult to brace myself against. She was the only thing standing between me being ready to commit some desperate act and holding it together enough to board this ship today. But this sense of impending doom was so infectious I had to get up to stop it sinking me.

'Where are you going?' she asked.

'Nowhere, but we are taking unnecessary risks.'

'What does that matter now? He already knows.'

I frowned. 'It matters because the more he dwells on it, the more he will torture us both. Don't you see what a pawn you are in his game now?'

'Oh, to be sure, I do.'

'He has made a puppet of you now, Annalise, to control my strings. We mustn't give him more fuel to the fire.'

She nodded, and I noticed the tear streams on her cheeks and sat back down beside her on the bed and gathered her in. 'Annalise, I hate to see you like this. What can I do?'

'Tell me you will go on loving me, no matter what. No matter how bad it gets.'

'Of course I will. You need not doubt it.'

'I mean it. No matter what?' she said severely, and I pulled back to look at her.

'Listen to me. Nothing could ever alter my feelings for you. Now you need to stop this if we are to get through this day at all. Was it not you who said that I must not give up fighting? That we were together, whatever else? So I am not giving up. I am going to look for every opportunity to get us away from him as soon as I can, alright?'

She nodded, but I could tell my earnest words were not enough to wrest her from such a wicked blue mood. But she wiped her tears and got up, and we went about the motions of our toilette and breakfast before the carriage was there, and we had reached the point of no return.

My only small comfort was to see the horrific state of Mariella as she bid Giles a reluctant farewell so ardent, Digby had to prise her away from him so he could get inside the coach. I made sure to wave and deliver her my best smile as she stood crestfallen, watching us depart. It was a small and fleeting consolation amid all else, and I had the odd sense of the last year flashing through my mind as we journeyed the Falmouth streets, perhaps never to return to them again.

THE JOURNEY TO THE harbour was short, and the ship already loading cargo and passengers when we stepped down from the carriage and were shown to our alighting bridge. It was a scene of chaos; cattle, carriages and crowds swarming along the harbour side with seagulls gliding overhead cawing, as all kinds of portmanteaus and packages were manoeuvred and loaded. I watched our portmanteaus set down from our carriage, get loaded onto a cart, and taken up to a parallel bridge to the one we were waiting our turn to board. It was only then I truly considered the frightful reality of stepping onto it. Not just in terms of my unhappy fate but the vessel itself. I had always supposed that one day I should travel and must face the prospect of crossing the seas, but I'd never had to actually prepare to. The prospect was hardly appealing given that most accounts I had had of sailing were, at best, tales of rackety windswept nausea filled journeys, and, at worst, like those reported in the newspapers of shipwrecks and piracy. Neither instilled much confidence in boarding, and yet, like all else, I was doomed to comply against my better judgement. Then we shuffled up the queue and Digby presented a number of documents to the liveried attendant, who looked us over and nodded us aboard. I glanced at Annalise who was following behind us and walked on slowly beside him, taking care to keep turning about and checking she was still with us. And she was. At every turn and flight of stairs, looking as bewildered at this strange environment as I.

'How long will we be aboard this ship?' I asked Giles, observing the perfunctory and cramped confines of it.

'If the winds are favourable, a couple of weeks. If not, well, as long as it takes. But no need to look so stunned, my dear. She is a good solid ship. I know the Commander well, and to be sure, we are in excellent hands.'

'I don't know why we couldn't have done what most sensible folk do and cross the channel at Kent in a day.'

'We could have, my dear, if you had not kept me running about the country in search of you for months. –You think the Alps are passable at this season?'

I made no answer. I just cast another sliding glance to Annalise before following him on.

'These are your cabins, sir,' said the attendant who had led us through a myriad of corridors, then into a saloon with a long table running down its length and a number of doors coming off its panelled walls. Then he opened one of them, and I was shocked by its impossible size, so small and bare with a cot for a bed on each side of it. I was only glad there were no double beds and gladder still when he announced that Annalise and I would share this one, and Giles and his Valet, the one beside.

We had each gone to our cabins, setting about a rudimentary inspection of them, when another of the ship's attendants appeared at the doorway saying, 'Sorry to disturb you, sir, but we are having trouble locating your luggage. Your log states three large portmanteaus and two bandboxes, but we can only locate two of them.'

'What kind of service are you running here?' Giles barked, unforgiving.

'I saw them come up in the cart myself,' I put in.

'I am very sorry to inconvenience you indeed. Most likely, your tags have been knocked off and they have been mislaid. If you would be as good to send your servants to identify the missing receptacles, I should hope to have the matter settled in no time.'

'Digby, Tulley, you heard the man,' he said to them.

Before I could object to her venturing into some filthy steerage pit to find our things, I was put quite out of countenance by an impromptu introduction of one of the ship's senior officials that had called out to Giles from across the saloon and came bounding up towards us.

'Officer Abery, I hardly recognised you, old fellow. Good to see you. This is my wife, Mrs Eleanor Craythorne.'

'Ah, most happy to meet you, Mrs Craythorne,' he bowed and smiled approving.

'Yes, and you, sir,' I said, distracted, watching Annalise and Digby following the attendant out of the main gallery with an inexplicable sense of apprehension. I paid little attention to the conversation I kept being drawn into, and willed her to hurry up back to me.

'You must join us for a toast!' said the Officer to Giles and I, and before we could refuse him, he had swiftly marched us to the table and poured three glasses for us all, then toasted to a safe and speedy voyage across the seas and a belated one in honour of our marriage. I did not drink of mine but toasted and put the glass back down on the table, which I noticed then, had started to shake a little.

'Good grief,' I said, using it to steady myself as I felt a bump and nearly lost my footing altogether. I sat back down at the table and held on to it.

'Oh, and it looks like we're off !' Said the Officer, draining his glass before it could spill. Then an enormous horn sounded, followed by a gunshot, and I jumped again.

'Off already, are you sure?' I said, concerned.

'My wife has not been to sea before,' said Giles, excusing, and I turned to him, and said, 'Whyever did you let them go off with that attendant when we were so close to leaving? They will be thrown all about the place!'

'Don't be anxious, my dear, they will be back any moment. Besides, the sea is calm now. We are barely moving out of the harbour. If you think this bumpy, you've seen nothing of it yet.'

I did not like the prospect of this. 'I am going to my room,' I told him, reluctantly accepting his help to stagger to my cabin as the floor began to sway. Then I shut the door and climbed instantly into my bed which was so small and confined, I felt like an infant in its crib. But it was preferable to the giddying feeling of the moving ground and trying to hold fast against the sway. I closed my eyes and wished Annalise would hurry up and return to me. She, too, was not used to sailing and would be quite thrown out of countenance by it, I was certain. But another ten minutes or more passed, and still, she did not return.

I was about to insist someone bought her back this instant when I felt the relief of hearing Digby's voice through the thin wall. *They are back!* The relief pour over me and I waited for the door to open. And when it did not, I called out. And when no answer came, I climbed out of bed, held the walls to steady myself, and went back out to the saloon where Giles remained sat in the same place with Digby at his side.

'Digby', I called out. 'Where is Tulley?'

He exchanged a glance with Giles that caused him to put down his glass and come over to me.

'Giles, where is Tulley? That Valet of yours did not leave her alone with the attendant down there, to be sure!'

'No, my dear, he did not.'

'Then wherever is she?'

'Ahh, about that.' He pulled an envelope from his jacket and offered it to me. I didn't know why I should feel so much panic at the sight of it, but I snatched it out of his hands and tore it open.

'I think you might prefer to read this privately, my dear,' he said, leading me back to my room, sitting me in the single chair inside it, and closing the door behind him.

Dearest Eleanor,

Oh, how it pains me to know you will soon be reading this and realising what a cruel departure I have made.

I cannot tell you how sorry I am to deal in this so badly, for you know, this is not my way. Yet I know you would not hear of my telling you I could not go with you now, after learning everything that has come to pass yesterday. But the truth is: I cannot.

I know my refusing to go would likely have led to you being bound for the asylum and not this ship. But so much of yours and the child's future depends upon your going that I could not be responsible for jeopardising it, when so much hangs in the balance.

I am going back home, and your husband will have a carriage arranged by now to convey my passage back to Surrey. I have asked him to make arrangements for a suitable replacement to be made, so you are not left unattended, and he assures me that he will.

I doubt you will want to set eyes on me again after this, but I do hope we will meet again when you are home.

With love and deep apology,

Tulley.

I threw the letter down and thought I might collapse as the words upon it sunk in. *Impossible, she would not, she...* I got up and ran out of the room despite the floor that now seemed to be running away from me, only to try to trip me up every other step.

'Where is she?' I screamed at Giles, and he came towards me with a look that told me he would prefer this to remain a private conversation. The saloon was busy now and I presumed him embarrassed by my manner. But I would not have him steer me back into that cell. I ran past him, screaming, 'Have we left the port?'

'Yes, miss,' a woman said, looking quite put out by my display, but I ran on past her too, straight to the saloon door and pushed through it, having no clear memory of the way we had come, but determined to find it.

I stopped briefly to ask an attendant the way to the deck, and he pointed out the direction, and I ran on faster, noticing Giles and Digby setting quick upon my heels.

'Miss, miss, are you alright?' Asked the gentleman, but his voice was a distant trail. I climbed the stairs he had indicated, two at a time, clinging to the rails as the ship rocked about, threatening to throw me over. But I did not stop. I ran on and on, barely knowing how I found my way or managed to get there without falling. But when I read a sign that directed me to the top deck, I belted up to it, and into such a throng of seaman tying ropes and rushing about, I could barely move through them to see if we had left.

'Excuse me, sir, excuse me please,' I said, pushing my way through them. Their waving hands put terror in me, and I quickened my pace until I burst through to the rail and saw the land shrinking away from view.

'No!' I screamed and fell to my knees. 'No, Annalise. Annalise!'

'Eleanor,' I looked to see Digby at my side and Giles scooped me up in his arms against my attempts to shove him off me.

'You! You knew the whole! You have them let me down at once!'

'Eleanor, the ship has left; there is nothing to be done,' he said flatly.

'Then you will have the crew take me down in one of the row boats and drive me back to shore.'

'That is quite impossible. Now, will you come back to the cabin? You are making such a show of yourself up here. Look at you.'

A crowd of onlookers had formed about us, and some concerned-looking officers had gathered to see what the fuss was about.

'You!' I pointed at one of them. 'You, sir, you must take me off this ship at once. I cannot go.'

'I'm sorry, ma'am; it is too late for that,' he said, bewildered.

'You will put me down in one of those boats, or I warn you, I will jump overboard and swim the distance myself!'

His eyes widened, and he glared at Giles.

'You will forgive me, Officer. My wife is not herself,' he apologised, gathering me up and steering me away.

'Shall I have her put in the brig?' he asked him.

'No, I shall handle this Officer.'

'You will not make me go with you! I screamed and shoved him off of me. Without thinking, I rushed to the nearest rail and began climbing it. I should rather die trying to swim my way back to my Annalise than be dragged off to sea with nothing but him aside me. I heard a terrible shriek from the crowds behind me before I felt someone grab me by the waist and pull me down.

'Get off me! Get off me! How dare you! You will set me down at once!' I demanded, and when I realised Digby had me, I began to kick harder.

'Do not let go of her, Digby.' Giles told him, and the pair of them wrestled me along the slippery deck and back down the stairway with the attendants clearing them a path through the awestruck onlookers.

I fought them both with all my might, and shocked myself with my strength as I planted facer after facer on them, and eventually, freed myself from his grip on the next set of stairs. Not realising, as I released myself from his grasp, that I would freefall my way down the remainder of them, headfirst.

To be continued...

Coming Next...

Cicisbeo. Volume 4.

An unwelcome trip abroad.
An agonising separation.
A new family.

Eleanor finds herself on a ship headed to Venice with the last person in the world she would consent to going with.

It wasn't supposed to be like this. She was supposed to be living out her confinement in the comforting arms of her lover, Annalise.

How will she cope with the sudden changes thrust upon her? Powerless and totally at the mercy of the man she loathes and who is determined to mould her into the dutiful compliant wife she has, so far, failed to be.

Anticipated for release: Winter 2023.

www.ingramcontent.com/pod-product-compliance
Lightning Source LLC
Chambersburg PA
CBHW072339020726
47506CB00004B/936